EAST COAST ROAD

For Poppy, Izzy, Wilf, Johnny and Betty, who,
between them, walked with me all the way from
Scotland to Cambridgeshire.

First published in 2020 by
Bluemoose Books Ltd
25 Sackville Street
Hebden Bridge
West Yorkshire
HX7 7DJ

www.bluemoosebooks.com

British Library Cataloguing-in-Publication data
A catalogue record for this book is available from the British Library

Paperback 978-1-910422-63-2

Printed and bound in the UK by Short Run Press

EAST COAST ROAD

By Anna Chilvers

Bluemoose

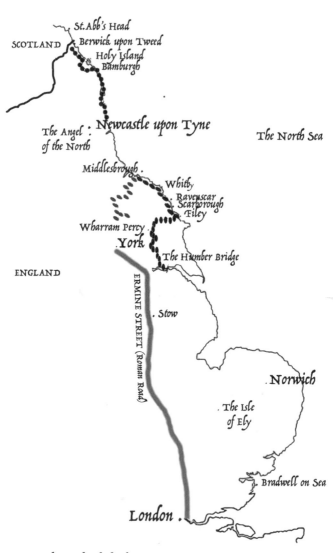

St.Abb's Head

SCOTLAND
Berwick upon Tweed
Holy Island
Bamburgh

The Angel
of the North

Newcastle upon Tyne

The North Sea

Middlesbrough

Whitby
Ravenscar
Scarborough
Filey

Wharram Percy

York

The Humber Bridge

ENGLAND

ERMINE STREET (Roman Road)

Stow

Norwich

The Isle
of Ely

Bradwell on Sea

London

••••• The Northumberland Way
••••• The Cleveland Way
••••••• The Yorkshire Wolds Way

Act One

Chapter One

At first Jen didn't know what it was. It could have been bags of rubbish, or someone's rucksack which had grown too heavy for them. But as she went nearer, limbs separated out from each other and she could see two people. They were lying with their arms spread wide. She and Rebecca had done the same ten minutes ago, except they'd done it standing on their feet.

At the top of the hill the Angel of the North spread his wings. They were brown, not gossamer white like school nativity angels. Their squared shape contrasted with the sculpture's curved body. Jen and Rebecca had taken it in turns to stand at his feet, arms spread out in imitation, while the other snapped a picture. Now Rebecca was taking more photos, up close, for her portfolio. Jen could see her small figure appearing and disappearing around the Angel's feet.

Jen walked closer to the figures on the ground. She didn't want to interfere in what might be some kind of private spiritual moment, but she was curious. They were very still, lying there with their legs together and their arms spread wide like they were pretending to be aeroplanes, their fingertips just touching. They were face down.

How could they could breathe, with their faces pressed close to the earth like that? Jen watched the outline of their bodies to see if there was movement. She couldn't see anything. The breeze ruffled their clothes.

"Are you alright?" Jen called.

She couldn't tell if they were men or women, or one of each. They were both wearing dark blue canvas trousers and green waterproof coats. The nearest one wore a yellow hat, which covered most of their hair, just a few short brown strands stuck out at the bottom. The other had their hood up, covering their head entirely. Even their hands were covered with gloves. Jen couldn't see any skin as their faces were pushed right into the grass.

"Do you need any help?"

A gust of wind rushed up the hillside, filling their jackets so they made a cracking noise. Jen turned and ran up the hill as fast as she could.

Rebecca was crouching behind the Angel with her head close to the floor, taking photos from ground level.

"There are some bodies," Jen gasped, the cold air hurting her throat as it rushed in.

"Hang on," said Rebecca.

"No, really, there are two people lying on the ground and I think they're dead. A suicide pact or something."

Rebecca lowered her camera and looked up at Jen.

"Bodies?"

"Come and look."

Together they ran down the hill. It was still early and there was no one about. Cars were roaring past on the roads which walled the Angel's sanctuary, but none were parked in the carpark. No one was walking across the grass in any direction. When they reached the place where the bodies had been, there was nothing. There wasn't even a place where the grass was flattened.

There was a lane between two hedges and Jen ran over to the entrance, but there was no one walking up the lane. There was no sign of a green waterproof jacket or a yellow hat.

"They must have gone," said Rebecca. "Maybe they were just messing about and they were too embarrassed to get up when you appeared."

Jen shook her head. "I saw them from right over there, they weren't moving at all. And where could they have gone? There's nobody here."

"Someone playing a trick on you? They might be hiding somewhere. In the hedge or something."

The idea that someone was hiding and watching creeped them both out. Rebecca said she had enough photos. They walked quickly back across the mound to the car park.

Before Jen got into the car she looked back to where the Angel stood, its back to them and to the city of Newcastle, arms stretched in welcome to all travelling north. Later there would be people here, visitors taking photos, laughing and dropping litter. There might even be an ice cream van. Right now, there was nobody. Jen could hear traffic on the A1 and the road into Newcastle, early commuters trying to beat the rush. Between those two walls of sound, the silence seemed full, like a balloon, as though each molecule of air had sound bound up inside it. Maybe it wasn't sound. Maybe it was life or memories, or something to do with two people wearing blue trousers and a yellow hat who had vanished into thin air. The air was holding a secret.

Jen slid into the front seat of the mini.

"You sure you're not seeing things again?" said Rebecca.

"What do you mean?"

"Well, that nun you thought you saw on campus..."

"I did see her."

"Jen, did something happen when you went home at Easter?"

Jen closed her eyes for a moment. Breathed in until it felt like her lungs might burst. Then she let the air out slowly through her nose, controlling the flow. She turned to Rebecca.

"Back to York in time for breakfast?"

The sun was up above the horizon and the graininess of the May dawn was disappearing.

Rebecca stared at her for a moment, then shrugged. "OK."

"Coffee and croissants in the union café," said Jen.

She wondered if that boy would be there this morning. The one with the dark floppy hair and the big coat.

Rebecca pulled out of the car park into the stream of commuters on their way into Newcastle. As they drove away, Jen looked back and saw a bird of prey hovering in the sky, just above the Angel's head.

Jen didn't see Rebecca the next day. Now she had her photos of the Angel, she needed to get on with her coursework. She'd left it to the last minute and only had until the end of the weekend.

Jen still had two more weeks of lectures before term ended in the middle of June. She went to the library and the student union. She chatted to the other students on her course. She tried not to think about the bodies, but if she closed her eyes she could see drops of water on green coats. She could see the curl of hair escaping from the yellow hat, tickled by blades of grass. She could smell the wet earth, the dew.

In the café she looked out for the boy with the floppy hair, and on Friday he was there.

He sat on a stool at a corner table with one of those old books he was always reading, dark covers with titles embossed in gold, the pages either Bible thin or thick as blotting paper. His coat was too big for him, and his hair was a fringe of black silk across his eyebrows. She'd not seen him in the first two terms, only recently, since Easter.

Jen was sitting with a couple of girls from her medieval seminar discussing a presentation they had to give together. She glanced over, and he was looking their way. She turned away quickly.

When she got up to leave, he'd gone. Jen had an essay to write on Marjorie Kempe, so she went back to her room to work, but it was difficult to keep her mind on the subject. As soon as she leaned back or closed her eyes for a second, she was back in the shadow of the Angel of the North watching green jackets for signs of breath.

6

Rebecca messaged her. *Come round. Got something to show you.*

Rebecca had both of her computer screens on and each was displaying a photograph of the Angel. They were taken close-up and most of the screens were filled with detail of the sculpture, but in the background there was the slope of green as the hill descended.

"Look," said Rebecca. She pointed at one of the screens. In the left-hand corner was a figure wearing white. "That's you," she said, "but look over here."

On the other side of the screen, indistinct, there was something yellow on the ground. It was impossible to tell what it was. It could have been a plastic bag, some litter.

"I've tried blowing it up, but it doesn't get any clearer," said Rebecca.

Jen peered at the yellow blob. Could it be a hat on a human head, attached to a body? It was possible.

"Now look at this one."

The photo on the other screen was similar, but angled slightly to the left so there was a better view of the place where the bodies had been. It was much clearer than the other photo. Rebecca zoomed in. Jen was crouching, her hand stretched out towards the grass. There was nothing yellow at all. No body, no coat, no blue trousers, no walking boots.

"These were taken ninety seconds apart," said Rebecca. "You came up the hill to talk to me straight after."

Jen stared at the empty space on the grass in the second photo. She remembered crouching, how she had been going to touch the nearest body, shake them a little, ask again if they were OK, but she'd chickened out. She'd been scared they wouldn't answer.

Rebecca shrugged. "It was early, low light levels. Things can look weird at dawn and dusk."

Jen thought about the drops of dew gathering together to form a sudden rivulet in a crease in the green jacket and spilling out onto the grass. She remembered that the curl of hair escaping from the hat was dark brown, that the hat itself was knitted in a thick single rib.

"You think I made them up?"

Rebecca looked at Jen and their gazes locked for a moment, then she looked away.

"Maybe you just have a strong visual imagination," she said. She closed the pictures and turned off the screens. "Fancy a drink?"

Chapter Two

Rebecca's boyfriend, Craig, was in the bar with some of his friends from Psychology, so what was supposed to be a quiet drink was suddenly rowdier. Jen decided she would just have one, then leave them to it. Rebecca wouldn't mind if she was with Craig.

They sat at a corner table and Jen noticed the boy with the fringe sitting alone at a table on the other side of the bar. Jen thought about pointing him out to Rebecca, but she and Craig were kissing. Jen tapped her fingers on the side of her beer bottle. They were always kissing. They'd only been together for two months and they couldn't keep their hands off each other.

Jen crossed the bar and sat down opposite the boy. She pulled at the corner of the beer label.

"Hello, I'm Jen," she said.

He smiled. "Finn."

"What's the book?"

Finn handed it to her. It was bound in dark blue cloth and the pages were roughly cut. She opened it and saw poems, black print in the centre of the creamy page. They were in French.

"Baudelaire – *Les Fleurs du Mal*. The Flowers of Evil. Some of these poems were banned in France until 1949. Sixty-nine years ago, that book would have been contraband."

"If we were in France," said Jen.

"Yes, if we were in France." His eyes were dark brown.

Jen could feel a tic beneath her left eye, but she didn't blink.

"I'm doing a course on Baudelaire," she said. "I've got a lecture tomorrow."

"You're studying French?"

"Literature."

Finn nodded. "That one," he said, pointing at the page, "would definitely have been banned."

"*À celle qui est trop gaie*," Jen read. "What's it about?"

"Beauty, anger, rage, sex."

"Wow, sounds amazing."

"He was an amazing poet, but pretty fucked up as a person – if he really thought the way he wrote."

"Are you doing literature too?"

"I'm a geologist."

"Then why…?"

"My gran gave it to me. She's French. She died earlier this year."

"I'm sorry."

"No reason for you to be sorry."

Back in her room, Jen sat on the bed and closed her eyes. She thought about Finn and how his arm had touched hers as they were talking. She took off her jeans and looked at the scars on her legs. Just silver lines – they had healed completely. She touched them with her fingertips. Flat, not raised, they felt just like the rest of her skin.

She opened her laptop and searched for *À celle qui est trop gaie*. She found several translations; some gave the title 'To she who is too lovely' and some 'To she who is too gay'. They were all the same poem though. The poet, unable to stand the laughter and gaiety of this lovely girl, felt he must destroy her. Like ripping a flower to shreds because it's too perfect to bear. The poet wanted to cut the girl open and inject her with his venom – and his use of words like 'lips' and 'dizzying sweetness' made it pretty obvious what kind of venom.

Jen ran her hand from her thighs to her waist. The poem horrified her and excited her. She thought about the story of the Buddha's conception that Rebecca had told her, his mother impregnated through her side by an elephant.

Jen hadn't cut herself since she'd been at uni. She was done with that.

She closed the computer and lay on the bed. She turned onto her front, lay with her face in the pillow, her arms stretched out to the side in the same way the two people had. It was a narrow bed, next to the wall. One arm draped down to the floor and the other bent upwards from the elbow. She counted. At thirty she had to lift her head and breathe in.

She sat up and googled *yellow woolly hat*. There were quite a few hits, including some on eBay. Most of them were for children or were sports hats with logos, but halfway down the second page there was one that looked like the hat she'd seen. She clicked on the 'Buy It Now' button before she could stop to think about it. Yellow wasn't her colour. She wouldn't wear a hat like that.

She lay down and thought about Finn. It was easy to talk to him. She hoped she would see him again in the bar tomorrow. She'd tell him she'd read the poem and they could talk about it. She might tell him about the Buddha's mother and the elephant. Or even about her cousin.

No one else could see her cousin. Even Jen hadn't seen her in ages. Once, just before her GCSEs, her cousin had come into Jen's room at night and taken the knife out of her hand. She didn't say anything at all, but when Jen tried to make a grab for it, she stepped back and there was nothing to hold on to. She was always like that; slippery, evasive.

In the morning, Jen stopped by Rebecca's room on the way into uni. She was working, with both screens on.

"Can I see those photos again?"

Rebecca flicked back through the images until she came to the one of Jen staring at the empty ground, then the previous one with the yellow blob.

"Can you zoom in?"

"I told you, there's nothing to see," she said, but she clicked until the area filled the screen, swipes of green and brown merging into each other, the yellow solid in the middle, blurring out at the edges into an irregular squashed shape.

"Can you see a shoulder?" Jen pointed at a smear of brownish green next to the yellow. "If you were looking straight down, at the crown of the head, that could be the slope of a shoulder. And they were wearing green jackets. That sort of colour."

Rebecca clicked the mouse and the photo filled the screen again.

"No, Jen, I don't think it's a shoulder. I don't think anyone was there. Look." She pointed at the corner of the photo where the bodies had been. "Apart from the yellow thing, there's nothing that couldn't be just grass and shadows. A trick of the light."

"I know what I saw," Jen said.

"Well you saw something that wasn't there then."

Jen felt tears rising and turned away to blink them back.

"Are you walking over?" she said.

"No, I want to spend some more time on this."

"See you later then."

Rebecca caught Jen's arm as she walked towards the door.

"Are you OK, Jen?"

Jen nodded. "I better get going, I've got a lecture in twenty minutes."

Rebecca let her go. "Let's meet later in the café," she said. "I'll text you."

Jen let her eyes flicker back for a moment to the yellow thing in the corner of the screen, then left the room.

The first time Jen met her cousins was the year Natalie Portman came to Ely. It had been in the newspaper and everyone at school was talking about it. Danny was at high school by then and he was pretending he was too cool to care, but Jen could tell he was just as excited as her. They'd gone to see Star Wars with their mum and dad a couple of years before – an almost unheard-of family outing – and since then Danny had been collecting posters and cards. Jen was collecting stickers for a sticker book, and her favourite was a photo of Natalie Portman as Padmé Amidala. They were filming at the cathedral that weekend and Jen was hoping to catch a glimpse.

Donna, their mum, was nervous, but not because of Natalie Portman. It was because her sister was coming to stay, the sister she hadn't seen or spoken to for fifteen years. She was bringing her daughters, whom Donna hadn't known existed. Jen was excited. Two new cousins and a Hollywood star all in one week!

When they arrived, there was another; a third cousin who never showed her face, who wasn't introduced, who stood next to doors and curtains, slipping out of sight if you looked. No one else seemed to notice her. Donna was doing her bright and breezy hostess performance, and Aunty Barbara was quiet, as though she didn't know how to act. Jen knew how she felt. She always wanted to hide when Mum started organising people. The two flesh and blood cousins with cotton dresses and brown legs did as they were told.

When they were sent out to the garden, Lyddie, the oldest one, said "Let's play May I."

Jen didn't know what that was, but it turned out to be the same as Grandmother's Footsteps.

"Don't you need more people to play that?"

Lyddie tried to get Grace to play, but Grace was too little and just sat on the grass.

"We could skip," said Lyddie. "Have you got a skipping rope?"

Jen thought there was one in the cupboard in the hall, but when she went in, the other girl was there, standing in the dark patch of shadow behind the stairs, and Jen didn't want to walk past. She asked Donna to find the skipping rope, and she bustled through, switching on lights and pulling things off the shelves. When Jen looked at the shadow again there was no one there.

Later she asked Lyddie if she had any other sisters and Lyddie said, "No, there's just me and Grace."

Jen was wearing the yellow dress with the white stripes and the white frilled bib. It was an old dress that her gran had produced from a trunk. Her mum had said, "That was Barbara's, why do you still have that old thing?" – but Jen liked wearing it. After it was washed she had to wear it for at least an hour before it softened, before it stopped letting the draught up into her knickers and hung against her bare legs like curtains, like it knew it was hers.

Lyddie was a year younger than Jen and she was supposed to play with her. Grace was a toddler.

There was spider's web in the hedge with a fat brown spider in the centre moving its legs. Jen thought it might have caught something, a fly maybe. Donna and Barbara were sitting in chairs near the back door, drinking tea. She could hear them. They weren't shouting, but she could tell they weren't friendly.

"You mean Mum's known where you were all this time?" said Donna.

"I made her promise," said Barbara. "I said if she told you, then I'd properly disappear."

The spider's legs were waving as it wrapped the fly up into a tight ball. The smell of washing powder rose from Jen's dress as the sun warmed the cotton.

"You were blackmailing her?"

Jen could tell from the wobble in her mum's voice that she was trying not to cry.

"Not really. She could see it from my point of view. After the abortion, then you and Steve, there was no way we could go back to being a happy family."

There was quiet in the garden. The spider finished wrapping the fly and moved across the web. Further down the road someone was mowing the grass. There was a chink as one of the grown-ups put their mug on the floor.

"And now?" said Donna.

Jen turned and ran across the grass to her cousins. She stopped in front of Lyddie.

"Can you play ring o' ring o' roses?" she said in a loud voice.

Lyddie grinned at her. "OK."

Grace was chewing a daisy stalk. The grown-ups were still talking. Jen took Lyddie's hands they started to skip in a circle. Jen sang loudly. The mower paused then started again.

"We all jump up with a one two THREE," Jen shouted.

Lyddie leaned towards her and whispered, "I like your dress."

The other girl was older than Jen. She gave the impression of someone who was tall, taller even than Danny who was nearly twelve. She had long hair, or maybe something draped over her head; Jen couldn't tell, because she only glimpsed her from the corner of her eye.

Peripheral vision, Danny said it was called. Jen asked him when he was sitting at the dining room table with his homework and Aunty Barbara was giving Lyddie and Grace a bath.

"Danny, do you ever see things to the side of you? Behind almost. Then when you look, they're not there?"

"Peripheral vision," he said.

"What?"

"That's what it's called. Being able to see things that aren't in front of you."

"Are they real things?"

"Of course they're real." He put down his pen and laid his hands on the table, looking straight ahead. "Try it. Walk up behind me, to the side a bit, and I'll tell you when I can see you."

Jen stood in front of the sideboard, then crept forward silently. It was like the game, May I, but Danny never wanted to play games like that. When Jen was still quite far behind him – at least three patterns on the carpet – he said, "Stop. I can see you now."

"No you can't!"

"I can. You try it."

They swapped places and Jen found that she could see even further back than Danny.

"That's good," he told her. "You can get jobs if you have good peripheral vision. Pilot, spy, dog trainer, all sorts."

"But what if the things aren't really there?"

Danny snorted and picked up his pen. "If they're not there then you can't see them," he said.

Jen tried closing her eyes as tight as she could, then opening them suddenly. She stared into the dark corners of the room. There was no one there. No ghosts, no invisible cousins. Danny must be right. She'd probably got overexcited because of Lyddie and Grace coming, because tomorrow they might see Natalie Portman and, if they were lucky, Natalie might see them too. She might even smile at them.

Later that night when she was in bed and Lyddie was snoring on the camp bed on the floor, Jen saw someone standing by the window, clearly silhouetted against the moonlit sky. Jen couldn't remember if she'd closed the curtains earlier, but they were open now. The girl had her back to Jen and she was looking into the garden. She was wrapped in something – a blanket, sheet, a cloak? She stood very still.

Jen lay in her bed, trying to keep her breath silent, not moving even her toes. It seemed like forever, but eventually the girl at the window turned around and Jen saw her face for the first time. She was about fourteen or fifteen and she looked very calm. Jen thought she'd seen her somewhere before. Her face was round, framed by the head covering.

She walked straight past Jen's bed, skirted around Lyddie on the floor, and went through the open door. Jen didn't turn over, didn't look, barely breathed, but she knew where the girl had gone. She'd disappeared into the spare room where Aunty Barbara was sharing the pull-out sofa bed with little Grace. Jen knew that when her cousins went back home to Scotland, this

16

other cousin would go too. She remembered where she'd seen her before – in the cathedral. Her cousin looked exactly like the statue of St Etheldreda.

The yellow hat arrived in the post two days later. Jen ripped the package open and put the hat straight onto her head. She looked in the mirror. It made her face look small, and her hair stuck out the bottom and tickled her neck. She turned one way then the other, then she took it off and put it in her underwear drawer, hidden behind her knickers and underneath the socks. She balled up the packaging and shoved it into her bag. Later, on her way into uni, she put it into a bin outside McDonald's. She didn't mention it to Rebecca.

Chapter Three

Danny didn't read books unless they were full of useful information. He didn't understand Jen's love of novels. She'd tried to enthuse him, told him the beginning of exciting stories so he would have no choice but to read the book to find out what happened next, but it didn't work. Once or twice he'd watched the film version instead.

"Some people are just not fiction readers," her gran, Dorothy, told her.

The Christmas after Dorothy died, Danny gave her a second-hand book for Christmas. Jen knew he wouldn't have read it himself and asked him why he chose it.

"Gran used to go on about him."

Jen looked at the cover – J.D. Salinger.

"There was some other book he wrote, she thought I might like it."

Jen opened the cover and looked to see what Salinger had written.

"That one – *The Catcher in the Rye*," said Danny, pointing.

"Did she say anything about this one?" asked Jen, flicking through the pages of the thin paperback.

"No, but it says on the back that it's about a brother and sister, so it seemed appropriate."

Jen had lost count of how many times since then she'd read *Franny and Zooey*. She bought a new copy before she left home for uni, not wanting to wear out the copy Danny had given her. He'd written in the front, *Happy Christmas Jen, from Danny xx* in red biro.

She'd read *The Catcher in the Rye* since then, and just about everything else by Salinger, but nothing could ever touch *Franny and Zooey*. Sometimes she thought that if she were put under hypnosis, she might be able to recite the whole book.

Jen had got into the habit of going to the café at 10am and sitting with a double espresso and a glass of water until it was time to go to her lecture at eleven. A few days after she first spoke to Finn, he turned up at the café too.

"Mind if I join you?"

Jen blinked. Her mind had been elsewhere, in Paris with Baudelaire taunting a glass seller in the street. Baudelaire had just dropped a vase from his third storey window, and the glass seller's wares were shattered across the pavement. His livelihood. Jen looked up to see Baudelaire grinning with glee. The sun glinted on the shards of glass, and a rainbow hung above them in the air.

The young man cried out, "Oh, my poor children, my poor family! How will I feed them now?"

"Of course." Jen moved her bag from the seat onto the floor to make room for Finn. "Have you got a lecture?"

"I'm on my way to the library." He hesitated, "I saw you in here and thought I'd come and say hello."

She felt a grin spread across her face. He grinned too.

She tried to think of something to say. Last time they had chatted so easily, but suddenly she couldn't think of anything at all.

"What are you doing at the library?" she asked.

"What are you reading?" he asked at exactly the same time. They both laughed. She showed him her book – *Les Fleurs du Mal and Other Writings*.

"I thought I'd better at least read some of it before my lecture."

He looked at the open page, French on one side, English on the other.

"Do you read French?" he asked.

She shook her head. "No, I'm reading the translation. Do you?"

"Not really. My family lived in France for a while and I went to school there for a few terms."

Jen flicked through the book until she found the poem she'd read the night before. She bent the pages back so the right-hand page was hidden behind the spine. "This poem you were reading the other day. How do you say it in French?"

"*Á celle qui est trop gaie*," Finn read.

"And in English?"

"To she who is too... I'm not sure – too happy? Too cheerful?"

"The book says gay."

Finn shrugged. "In the old-fashioned sense."

"Do you translate it into English in your head? Or can you think in French?"

"Simple stuff I can just do – but this is harder. It's not very nice, this poem."

"I know right."

Jen flipped the book round and reread the English translation. She felt a sudden pain in her side and nausea swept up from her stomach. She clasped her hand over her mouth, but Finn didn't seem to notice, and the feeling passed.

"Do you want to come to the lecture?" she asked.

"I have to do some research," said Finn, "on fossil formation. Maybe you could tell me about it later?"

Jen wrapped her hands around her coffee cup. She managed a smile.

She could have done a science subject at uni. Sometimes she wished she had. She liked the idea of cool facts, information that was unequivocal; *this* happened and therefore *this* will happen. She knew that objectivity broke down eventually, even in science; that the top scientists had to make assumptions and leaps in the dark, had to theorize when there were no hard facts to hand. But that all started so much earlier with other subjects. There wasn't a simple answer to what made Baudelaire so angry.

Not in his poetry anyway. Maybe she'd need to be a historian or a psychologist to get to the bottom of it.

When they'd finished their coffee, they walked together across campus. There was a chill breeze and Jen thought about the yellow hat hidden at the bottom of her underwear drawer. What would Finn say if she told him about the bodies she'd seen, that Rebecca said never existed? He'd probably have an explanation. Even Rebecca had an explanation and she was an artist, for God's sake. Jen decided not to try it. She wound her scarf an extra loop around her neck.

They said goodbye at the turning for the library. Jen was walking away when he called after her, "Do you fancy a drink later?"

She turned. His eyes were the colour of the earth in winter. Nausea curdled her stomach again, but she chose to ignore it.

"OK."

"Great," he smiled. "Eight? Nine? Shall we meet in the bar?"

"Eight," she said. "And let's meet down by the lake, then we can walk to the bar together."

"Eight, by the lake. See you there." He grinned, then walked away towards the library.

At the door to the lecture theatre, Jen stopped. The nausea had subsided but she had a pain in her side, like stitch. There was an image in her brain, created by the poem, and she knew if she closed her eyes it would grow and fill the space behind her eyes. She found it difficult to keep her eyes open in lectures, not because she found them boring, but because but the rooms were so brightly lit, so brownly furnished, she didn't want to spend an hour looking at them. Behind her eyelids, she could allow the words of the lecturer to paint patterns, create colours, new paths.

> ... *Oh dizzy sweetness!*
> *Between the new lips of this wound,*

More vivid and more beautiful,
Infuse my spleen into you, my precious!

She could watch the lecture later online. She needed to get off campus for a while. Breathe the air where no one knew who she was.

She walked across the Stray to the allotments. The vegetables here grew in straight lines and some of the gardeners had interspersed them with flowers. There was an atmosphere of industry and calm. Jen could feel tension leaching out of her cells. She put her hand on her belly, crossed the main road and walked down to the river.

A group of Japanese tourists were taking selfies near the water, four women, smiling and holding out a phone on a stick at arm's length. There was no one else down here. Jen sat on a wall, her feet dangling above the cobbles. She watched a pair of geese glide past with a brood of goslings swimming behind in a line.

York was like Ely in so many ways. The Minster, the old town, the river wide and slow. Sometimes she thought she should have gone to university somewhere else, somewhere completely different. London, Edinburgh, or even Paris where her cousin Lyddie was planning to go. But she'd promised Rebecca, and to begin with York's familiarity had seemed like a good thing.

She jumped off the wall and headed into town, walking quickly, weaving amongst the tourists and the shoppers, knowing where she wanted to be.

The entrance was unobtrusive, between two shops, easy to walk past. There were wallflowers in bloom in the small graveyard, forget-me-nots along the base of the wall. The peace was sudden and immediate, even before she reached the doorway to the church.

She'd been here a number of times since Easter, and every time she hoped she would see her other cousin. She wasn't sure why she would be here, in a church in York, but it felt right.

The vicar was greeting a couple at the entrance, telling them the history of the church. Jen avoided his eye as she walked up the aisle to the front. The pews were a higgledy-piggledy collection of boxes, each containing a bench or two, and a small door to get in. The sides were too high to see over. Jen wasn't sure if you were allowed in the boxes. She didn't like the idea of being shut in anyway. She walked across the front of the church where there was an open space with a stone altar, and sat down on a bench. Light fell through the windows onto the stone. It made her think of cliffs and caves, of dark water lapping in and out, day after day, as the moon rose and fell. She loved that the church was so bare. The curves of the arches moved her more than the most intricate carvings or paintings could have.

A bird flew across the window and its shadow moved across the church.

She heard footsteps. She hadn't seen anyone walk in, only the couple with the vicar and herself. It had to be her cousin.

She held her breath, pushed her nails into her palms.

The person who appeared from behind the pulpit was a man. He was wearing a leather jacket and black jeans, and his grey hair was tied back in a ponytail. He had a beard which was long but not full. He was looking about the church as he walked. When he saw Jen sitting on the bench, a stillness fell over him. His eyes stopped darting about. He sat down at the other end of the bench.

Her cousin wasn't here. Just this man. She would sit for a while and then walk back to the university. See if the lecture from this morning was online yet.

She closed her eyes and thought about Franny learning to say the Jesus Prayer.

"Lord Jesus Christ, Son of God, have mercy on me, a sinner."

She said the words quietly under her breath. Then she tried them again with no sound, just mouthing the words.

Lord Jesus Christ, Son of God, have mercy on me, a sinner.

She felt the shape of her lips as they moved. She opened her eyes and glanced towards the man. He was sitting still with his head bent, his lips moving like hers.

Jen liked the idea of saying something over and over so many times that it became part of her being, like breathing, like blinking. But she didn't like the Jesus Prayer. She didn't want to make that part of her; *I am a sinner, I am unworthy, Lord Jesus, male patriarch God, take pity on poor little me.* That's not what she wanted at all.

Julian of Norwich, the medieval anchorite who bricked herself up in a church and gave out advice through a window, she'd said something pithy. It had been on everything in the shop in Norwich when they went on a school trip for A-level history: tea towels and pencils and keyrings. *All will be well* or something. She'd taken a photo. She scrolled through her phone until she found it.

All shall be well, and all shall be well, and all manner of thing shall be well.

She wasn't convinced. All those 'sh' sounds. She'd be walking around hissing like a snake. And would things be well? They hadn't been up to now. Though that was the point, wasn't it? It was the repetition, saying it over and over, that made it true. If she said it constantly, all of her waking hours, then eventually she would believe it, and it would become who she was.

What if she chose something else? How about Baudelaire? If she repeated his lines over and over, would that become who she was?

Oh dizzy sweetness! I want to infuse my spleen into your wound, my precious!

She might have to reword it to make it more like a prayer. And take off the last two words so she didn't sound like Gollum. She could just go with the first part – *Oh dizzy sweetness! Oh dizzy sweetness! Oh dizzy sweetness!* If she said that over and over, she might go mad, her head a hive of bees and sticky honey.

The vicar had stopped talking. In fact, he didn't seem to be in the church anymore, and the couple had vanished too. Maybe he had taken them outside to show them something in the churchyard. There was a patch of red light dancing on the side of the pulpit where the sun was coming through the stained glass. Vertical lines of sunlight beamed through the arches, hit the stone and spread across the walls. She didn't feel sick anymore.

The man in leather got up and walked to the door of the church, his lips still moving. Jen found herself following.

Outside, a bird swooped in front of her, then flew up towards the Minster. Jen had heard there were peregrine falcons nesting in the tower.

The man walked across the churchyard and out of the gate, where he turned right. He was walking fast, with purpose, and Jen had to dodge tourists to keep him in view as he passed the front of the Minster. Just before they reached the main street, he went into another church on the corner. St Wilfrid's was bigger, standing proud at the junction, unmissable.

Jen reached the steps and went in. The foyer had racks of literature, a cabinet of items for sale. Jen picked up a leaflet. It was about Saint Wilfrid, the seventh century bishop, and his visit to Rome. She stuffed it into her bag and went through a door into the body of the church.

This was a very different place to the church they had just come from. It was bigger, with high ceilings. Huge frescoes at the front surrounded an altar spread with ornate cloth and laid with candlesticks and flower arrangements. The body of the church was dark, and although there was much more space in here, there seemed to be less air. No vicar loitered to greet tourists. People were sitting in the pews. Jen counted them – four men and one woman, all sitting separately, quietly, with their heads bowed. None of them were the man with the ponytail. Jen couldn't see him at all.

She walked to the front of the church where steps led up to the altar. A sign read, *Do not pass this point. The apse is alarmed.* She turned right and walked down the side of the church to the chapel where candles could be bought and lit. There were quite a few burning in the intricate branches of the candelabra, and a box of fresh candles was on a small table next to a slot in the wall for money. There was no man with a ponytail and scrappy beard. There was no one at all. Just the smell of hot wax and a red glow in the space behind the candles. There was nowhere else he could have gone.

Jen could feel the nausea rising again. She turned and quickly retraced her steps, along the red carpet of the aisle, through the glass doors and onto the front steps.

How could a man vanish into thin air?

She took some slow deep breaths, allowing the oxygen to pass into the cells of her body, willing her stomach to settle.

Something caught her eye. Further up the main road, the man was walking away from her. There was no way she could catch him up. Just as he reached a corner he glanced back in her direction, looked straight at her, then disappeared from view.

For a moment she thought she would run after him, but her gut cramped. She grasped her stomach and felt a hot rush through her oesophagus. Not here. Not right in the middle of town. She couldn't be sick on the steps of a church.

But she could. It burst through her mouth, across the three steps, spattering her white shoes. She felt immediately better.

She glanced around. No one was nearby or seemed to have noticed. She walked away quickly, down the steps and back across town, stopping off at a newsagent to buy a bottle of water.

Chapter Four

Most of the children from Jen's primary school had gone to the local secondary school, but her mum wanted her to go the school she and her sister had attended when it was the Girls' Grammar – the school Dorothy used to teach at. It wasn't a grammar school anymore, or even a girls' school. Danny went there too.

Jen only knew two other kids when she started, one boy and one girl, neither of whom she was particular friends with. So when she found herself sitting next to Rebecca in form, and Rebecca told her that she had just moved to Ely and didn't know anyone at all, it seemed meant to be. It turned out they both liked reading and hockey and they both hated the cliques and hierarchies that seemed to underpin school life. Rebecca had moved from York to live with her aunt and uncle after her mum and dad had been killed in a motorway accident. She liked Ely, and her aunt and uncle were kind, but she missed York.

One day in history when they were studying the War of the Roses, Rebecca jumped out of her seat and ran out of the classroom. The teacher said Jen could go after her, and she found her in the toilets crying like Jen had never seen anyone cry before, wailing loudly, with intermittent screams, her face red and shiny. Soon a teacher arrived and took Rebecca away to the first aid room. After that she started seeing a therapist. Jen watched her warily, but there were no more outbursts.

Finn was waiting for her on the bench by the lake, which was impressive because Jen was always early. She sat down next to him.

"Did you know all swans belong to the Queen?" he said.

There were three swans swimming in a line near the edge of the water, their wings folded. Jen thought of the swan-shaped soap dish her gran had kept in her bathroom. She imagined placing a bar of soap on these swans, in the middle of their backs between their upturned wings. Bright jewel-coloured soap, or maybe Pears soap, which would look like a piece of amber nestled amongst the white feathers.

"Do they know?" she asked.

The water was still as glass and each swan had a perfect double in the water.

"I guess not. It's ridiculous really. Like saying you own all of a certain type of tree."

"Or the air that we breathe."

"You're not allowed to kill them or eat them. Only the royal family are allowed to eat swan. It's the only offence still punishable with the stocks."

"That's not true!" Jen looked at Finn and saw he was laughing.

"Idiot." She thumped his arm.

The swans swam in an arc out into the lake, keeping in formation one behind the other. Finn pointed to the reeds at the water's edge.

"Look, that one's looking after the nest."

One swan was sitting in the unwieldy pile of straw and broken reeds, watching the others' progress.

"Do they take it in turns?"

Finn shrugged. "I think they mate for life," he said. They stood watching until the swans disappeared behind an island. "Bar?"

"It's such a nice evening, it seems a shame to go inside."

"A walk then? And a drink once it gets dark?"

They walked along the edge of the lake, then headed between the chemistry labs and over to the Stray. New growth on the trees shone in the fading light. There was a patch of late bluebells near a fence – the smear of blue reminded Jen of the light from a computer screen. It was dotted with tiny white flowers which caught all there was of the evening light and shone like stars.

"Stitchwort," said Finn.

Jen wondered if she should take his hand. They were walking side by side, right next to each other, and their arms were only inches apart. It wouldn't take much, she could just reach out with her fingers, nudge into his palm with her thumb. She thought about the evening ahead and how it might end, and what difference it would make if she did take his hand now, how that would set something solid and known between them.

She moved her hand away from him quickly and lay it flat on her belly, increasing the gap between them.

"Are you OK?" he said.

"Just stomach ache," she said.

"Do you want to head back?"

"No, walking is good."

They were nearly at the road. She concentrated on the movement of her legs, the roll of her feet on the compacted mud of the path.

"How was the Baudelaire lecture?"

Jen thought, *I could tell him that I ran away at the last minute and went and sat in churches in the city centre, looking for my dead cousin, or more accurately, my non-existent cousin.* But she'd watched the lecture later, so she knew what it was about. Easier to pretend she'd been there.

"I don't know, I didn't go," she said.

"Why not?"

"I hate him. Baudelaire. I don't want to know anything more about him. He was misogynistic, misanthropic, horrid."

"He was probably just messed up – by religion, and the expectations of the time. He expresses his conflict in his poems, but I don't think you can use them to judge him personally."

"Well his poems are what I have to read. Personally, I hope I never have to meet him."

Rebecca was in the bar with Craig and some friends. When she saw Jen she rushed over and threw her arms around her.

"I handed it in," she said. "I did it."

Jen turned to introduce Finn, but he'd disappeared.

"Do you want to buy me a drink?"

"Rebecca, haven't you had enough?"

"I'm celebating. Cerebrating."

At the bar Jen bought beers for herself, Finn and Rebecca. Rebecca dragged Jen over to the table where all her friends were drunk, though not so drunk as Rebecca.

"We're going to Kuda," said Craig. "You coming?"

Jen looked over at Finn who had just reappeared near the bar.

"Maybe," said Jen.

Rebecca picked up her drink and took a long swig.

"Come on Jen, you've got to catch up."

Jen took a sip. She shuffled along the bench to make room for Finn, but before he came over Rebecca was sick. Most of it went on Jen. Her white jeans were covered with beige slime.

"Oh fuck," said Rebecca.

Jen went to the toilets and tried to wipe the sick off with some paper towels. She got most of it off, but there was a yellow stain. She took a handful of towels back to the bar. Craig had taken Rebecca outside for some air, and the others had moved to the bar, so the table was empty. Finn appeared and helped her wipe down the table and bench.

"Sorry," said Jen.

Finn grinned at her. Craig called from the door that he was going to take Rebecca home.

"I'll take her," said Jen. "I need to go and get changed anyway."

"Are you sure?" Craig stepped inside. "Will you come on to Kuda after?"

"Yeah, I might."

"She's sitting on the wall outside." He lurched forwards on his toes, then went to the bar. The crowd opened a little to let him in.

"I can come and help," said Finn, behind her.

"No, you go on to Kuda too. I might catch up later."

Rebecca leaned against her as they walked across campus. The night air smelled sweet, but Rebecca's breath reeked of alcohol and vomit. Jen tried to turn her head away, to breathe in the scent of white lilac, but she had to concentrate on her friend who was in danger of falling at every step.

Jen took the key card from Rebecca's bag and let them into the halls. Rebecca's room was on the ground floor, so there were no stairs to negotiate. As soon as they got inside, Rebecca fell on the bed asleep. Jen checked she was lying on her side, that she couldn't roll on to her back, that nothing was blocking her airways; then she switched out the light and left the room.

Back in her own room she stripped off her stained jeans, filled the sink with water and put them in to soak. She took the yellow hat out from the drawer where she'd hidden it and pulled it onto her head. She stared at herself in the mirror. It was strange to see herself in a colour that wasn't white. She pulled a face at herself.

She had been going to change her clothes and go to Kuda to meet up with Finn, but she didn't want to anymore.

She had a shower, then, after drying her hair, she put the yellow hat back on and got into bed with *Franny and Zooey*. She turned off her phone. The world was pretty strange, so right now she was going to stick with something familiar.

Chapter Five

The evening before their maths GCSE, Rebecca turned up at Jen's with her revision. Jen was lying on her bed, reading.

Rebecca flopped onto Jen's beanbag. "Want to test each other?" she said, waving her maths book.

"I can't look at another equation. My head will pop."

Rebecca thumbed through pages of maths for a few moments, then looked up at Jen.

"What's the book?"

Jen flipped it upright so Rebecca could see the cover.

"*Franny and Zooey*. That's a weird title."

"Danny gave it to me."

"Oh..."

Jen carried on reading. She'd read the lines so many times she could almost recite them, but she found her gaze running across the words, registering their shape and sound but not the meaning. She was aware of Rebecca in the room. She was waiting to see what she'd say next.

"Are they names? Are they the characters?"

"Yes. They're brother and sister."

"And he reminds you of Danny?"

"Zooey is nothing like Danny. Zooey's cool and clever and he never stops smoking."

"Are you like Franny?"

Jen shrugged. The fact was that Franny was cool and clever too, and both siblings smoked like there was no tomorrow, but there was something about the girl. She felt a connection.

"She's trying to find God by saying this prayer over and over."

"Oh, I didn't think..."

"What?"

"Well, what with your mum..."

"It's not like that. It's not all singing in public and 'look what we've done, aren't we good'. This is a quiet thing."

"Like, connecting to God within."

"Yeah, maybe."

Jen closed the book and lay it on the bedside table. She'd lost the thread; she could pick it up later.

"Franny has a kind of breakdown, like she can't bear all the phoney people around her making out they're important. She wants simplicity."

"She should become a Buddhist."

Rebecca's aunt, Lucy, was a practising Buddhist. A couple of times, when Lucy had been working at the university at the weekend, Jen had gone with Rebecca to meet her at the Buddhist Centre. They'd eaten in the café and had a look around. Jen had liked the peaceful atmosphere, but she didn't feel at home. She felt too big, as though her elbows were too sharp, her hair had too much static. She'd felt like ringing all the bells at once, stamping her feet a little too loudly.

Rebecca went with her aunt all the time. She'd told Jen about the silent meditation, the chanting.

"We did walking meditation once, where you walk really, really slowly round the room, feeling every bone in your feet."

"Didn't you feel like an idiot?"

"No, everyone else was doing the same."

"I don't think I could. I wouldn't be able to move."

"Everyone would look at you then."

Jen swung her legs around and sat up on the bed with her knees bent, her back leaning against the wall.

"Franny's brother has died. Not Zooey, their older brother, Seymour. I think that's what it's all about really. Trying to make sense of that, connect to him somehow. That's why everything seems so phoney to her. She's seen how close death is, only a step away, and it seems like everyone else is merrily dancing on the cliff edge, like that's what's important, and they don't even look at the huge drop, and anyone could go over at any moment."

"How is praying over and over going to help her?"

"I guess it's something to hold on to, a connection to something beyond life, which might just end at any moment. She wants something that will continue to exist."

When Jen looked up, Rebecca was staring at her. Then her friend leaned forward, took hold of Jen's hand and squeezed it. Jen looked away quickly.

She shook her hand free and stood up. "Come on, let's go down to the river, see who's about."

In the morning when she switched on her phone there were four messages. Two were from Finn. One from last night asking if he should wait for her so they could go to the club together, and one from this morning asking if she was OK. There was also one from Rebecca saying, *OMG bring me coffee.* The last one was from her cousin Lyddie asking if she wanted to come up and stay on the island for a while in the summer.

She replied to Finn saying sorry about last night, and asking if he would like to meet later that morning in the cathedral gardens. She rinsed out her jeans and put Franny and Zooey back on the shelf. She might read the rest later. It was rare that she didn't read it all in one sitting, but she'd suddenly been so tired last night.

She put on some leggings and a long white shirt with Indian embroidery, then went to find Rebecca, stopping off en route at the coffee shop.

Rebecca was still in bed. She let Jen into the room and got straight back between the covers. It was a sunny morning, but she had the blinds down.

Jen gave her the cardboard cup of coffee, then sat in the chair.

"Thanks chuck," said Rebecca. "I feel awful."

Jen glanced at the clutter-free desk then back at Rebecca.

"Have you got any lectures today?"

"No, I've only got two more seminars. That assignment was the main thing. Hence the blow out."

They both sipped their coffees.

"Did you go back out?"

"Nah, I went to bed after I got you home. I was tired."

"I think I'm going to be sick again."

Rebecca dashed across the room to the tiny bathroom and slammed the door behind her. There was the sound of retching, then teeth cleaning, and then the shower went on. Jen took her copy of Baudelaire out of her bag and began to read. She had to write an essay on him before the year was finished.

The poet seemed to be having a problem reconciling the different aspects of his nature. On the one hand, he idolised the pure and the innocent, but he also revelled in sensuality, which he believed to be corrupt, which meant he and the women he loved were damned. He was pretty angry about it.

Rebecca emerged from the bathroom. She was a better colour.

"How about I get dressed and we go and get breakfast?" she said.

Jen entered the gardens from the behind the Minster. Finn was sitting on a bench near the Lady Chapel reading a book. She could see the back of his head, bent slightly over the page, the sun glinting off his hair.

There were more benches on this side of the garden and she sat down. It was a sunny afternoon and the laburnums were in blossom. A slight breeze moved the branches and sent dappled shadows waving across the grass. Tourists wandered in twos and threes along the paths, stopping to hold up their phones for photographs of the cathedral. It was looking particularly fine this afternoon, glowing almost white in the sunshine.

Jen noted the slight movement of Finn's elbow as he turned the page. He lifted his head and looked right along the path, then left. Looking for her, she supposed.

She got up and walked back out into the street. She did a circuit past the front of the Minster and entered the gardens to the left of the Lady Chapel, then slowed down to a saunter. She was five minutes late.

Finn looked up from his book and saw her. His face broke into a smile.

Oh my god, what am I doing?

"Hey, Jen."

"What are you reading?" She sat down next to him and looked at cover of the book he'd closed on her approach. It was called *The Floating Egg*.

"It's about geology. Fossils and the Yorkshire coast."

"Cool."

"I'm like a little boy when it comes to dinosaurs and stuff. I've not really grown up."

"Do you have dinosaur posters on your wall?"

"Maybe."

His eyes were lighter when he laughed. Jen looked at the ground and breathed into her belly.

"We could get chips and walk along the river," said Finn. "Are you hungry?"

She was hungry. She'd sat with Rebecca while she ate a huge fry-up in the cafeteria, but she'd only had a croissant herself. Finn shoved his book into his backpack and they left the gardens.

"Did you go to Kuda last night?"

"For a bit. Once I realised you weren't going to turn up, I made a quiet exit. Some of the others were getting a bit messy."

They dodged crowds of tourists at the front of the Minster, then momentarily lost each other as they went either side of a parked van.

"Sorry I didn't go," said Jen, when they were side by side again.

"I expect you were tired."

"Not really. I went back to my room to change and thought, I'll just read a few pages of my favourite book, and suddenly I'd read most of it and it was the middle of the night."

"What is it?"

"*Franny and Zooey* by J.D. Salinger."

"Oh. I haven't read that. I've only read..."

"...*Catcher in the Rye*. Lots of people don't even know he wrote anything else."

"So, tell me about it. Why is it your favourite?"

Jen stopped.

"Oh my god. Look at that."

"What?" Finn looked around, then followed Jen's gaze. They were outside a charity shop and Jen was looking at the window display. "What is it?"

"That jacket."

There were three shop dummies, a male and female in evening dress, and another female in sportswear. It was this third model that Jen was pointing to. It was wearing white tracksuit bottoms and a white sports jacket with silver reflective stripes. The fabric of the jacket was light and thin.

"Do you ever get this thing, where you look at something and you absolutely love it, but you know you shouldn't?"

"Shouldn't?"

"Like it's not cool, or it's not fashionable. But the bit of you that likes it is the same as when you were five and you liked princess dresses and didn't care about being cool."

"Do you feel like that about..."

Jen turned to him and she could feel that her face was shining.

"Just look at the white of the sleeves. It's like something you'd want to lie in, wrapped up, and everything would be OK. It's so light it would barely touch your skin. And it has shiny silver bits..." Finn looked at the dummy in the window. He had a tiny crease at the top of his nose, and Jen felt her body tense. "Do you think I'm an idiot?"

"Of course not." The crease vanished when he smiled. "I've just never felt that way about clothes. I feel like I'm missing out."

Jen hoisted her bag on her shoulder. "The chip shop's just round this corner." She started to walk, but Finn grabbed her arm.

"Don't you want to buy it?"

She looked at his face, then at the jacket in the window. "Well yes, but..."

"Come on. I'll buy it for you as a present."

Finn pushed the door of the shop and went in. Jen hesitated, then followed.

The jacket fitted her perfectly. The white fabric was tissue thin, almost transparent, as light as she had imagined. She looked at herself in the mirror. She would never have been allowed something like this when she was a child. Not practical, her mother would have said, what's the point of it, it's not even going to keep you warm.

"You look amazing," said Finn.

She wouldn't let him pay. "You can buy the chips," she said.

Walking along the river in the white jacket, licking salt from her fingers, Jen said, "So, what are you going to be when you grow up? Are you sticking with the dinosaurs?"

"Maybe." Finn screwed up his chip wrapper and put it in a bin. "I'm going to France this summer. They found loads of new fossils a few years ago, in some quarries at Angeac-Charente. I'm going on a field trip. I'd love to find something new."

"For the whole summer?"

"Yes, eight weeks."

"That's fab." She looked at the chips in her wrapper. She'd only eaten half of them. Maybe there was too much vinegar. She balled them up and shoved them into the bin. "I'm going to stay with my cousins in Scotland. On an island."

"Brilliant. I love Scotland."

Jen nodded. They'd reached a patch of grass where the geese congregated in family groups. Green goslings scurried after their parents. Jen and Finn picked their path around them, careful not to anger the adults.

"We could write to each other," said Finn.

"What, actual letters?"

"That would be really cool."

"Yes, it would."

The sun was shining through the leaves of the trees and flashes of red light strobed Jen's vision as she walked, temporarily blinding her. She felt Finn reach for her hand, and she let him. His hand was warm and dry, big enough to enclose hers. Some ducks squabbled on the river, chasing each other with a swoosh of water. The fabric of her new jacket touched the skin of her arms. Her stomach settled and she smiled.

Rebecca was busy packing. There was a stack of cardboard boxes next to the window and a huge suitcase open on the bed.

"Hey, Jen!"

"You're nearly ready to go."

"Yeah, tomorrow. What about you?"

Rebecca was pulling clothes out of her wardrobe and rolling them up to put in her suitcase.

"I've still got an essay to hand in."

"You could write it at home. Come back with me."

"Hmm, I don't know. I find it difficult to work with Mum around, and Terence."

"Surely he's not there all the time."

"You'd be surprised. And he's always trying to convert me, even though you'd have thought he'd have got the message by now."

Rebecca pulled a long dress out of the cupboard. It was streaked in different shades of green and was covered with intricate embroidery.

"You should come to Glastonbury," she said. "It'll be a laugh. The shifts are only six hours long, so there'll be plenty of time for doing stuff. There's still places."

"I'm going up to Scotland," said Jen. "To visit my cousins."

Rebecca looked up. "Oh, I didn't know."

"It's only just been arranged."

Actually, nothing was arranged. Jen had texted Lyddie back saying she wasn't sure what she was doing yet. She wondered if Aunt Barbara even knew that Lyddie had invited her. She couldn't go home to Ely, that was certain. Since Easter, the campus had seemed like the only place she was safe, but soon she would have to leave. She had to spend the summer somewhere.

She watched as Rebecca took the last items out of the cupboard, then turned to the drawers under the desk. Jen's room was exactly the same layout as Rebecca's. The drawer Rebecca had pulled open was the one Jen kept her underwear in. Rebecca's was full of pens, crayons and paint.

"Rebecca, you know those bodies at the Angel of the North?"

"The ones that you imagined. What about them?"

"Do you think they could have been ghosts?"

"No I don't."

"Why not?"

"Because I don't believe in ghosts. We'd been up all night and you were tired. You imagined it. Forget about it."

"What do you believe in?"

"What?"

"What do you think happens when people die?"

Rebecca shrugged. She pulled over a cardboard box and started filling it with handfuls of stuff from the drawer. "They rot in the ground. They're food for worms."

"I thought you were a Buddhist."

"I am. But that doesn't mean..."

"Don't they believe in reincarnation?"

"I like the Buddhist approach to living. It makes sense to me."

"But not their approach to death?"

"No."

"Can you do that? Can you pick and choose what you want with religion?"

"Of course you can. People do it all the time. I mean, like Christians don't believe the world was actually made in seven days – at least, not the sane ones."

"But isn't that what karma's about? That what you do in one life affects what you get in the next?"

Rebecca pulled the drawer completely out and tipped it upside down over the box so all the contents fell out in a noisy rush. "Look, religion is just stories really, to make sense of the world. I mean, that story about how the Buddha's mother was impregnated through her side by an elephant, then gave birth through her side – I can agree with Buddhist principles without having to believe that."

"So no reincarnation?"

"No."

"And no ghosts?"

"No."

"What about people who say they've seen ghosts? Are they liars?"

Rebecca banged the drawer on the floor to get the dust out of the corners. "Not necessarily. They might believe they saw a ghost."

"But you think they're mistaken?

"Yes, I do." Rebecca slid the empty drawer back onto its runners.

Jen packed the books from the small bookcase into two boxes. "I might stay in Scotland for the whole summer."

"Well if you change your mind..."

"I know. Glastonbury."

Rebecca looked at her. "You never know, you might even enjoy it."

On her way to the library, Jen saw a man walking ahead of her. He had a long grey ponytail and a leather jacket. She walked faster, gaining on him until she was walking next to him. They were approaching the bridge, and she looked at him as they walked in step.

It was the same man. His lips were moving, just like they were when she'd seen him in the church.

"Who are you?" she said.

He turned and looked at her. He said, "Seek and you will find."

"What?"

"She knows you're looking for her."

"Who? Do you teach here?"

"She sends word. She says all will be well."

He turned and walked away. Jen chased after him, but his pace had increased and even when she started to run she couldn't catch him. He disappeared between two trees, then vanished behind a building. When Jen reached the turn, there was no sign of him.

She found she was near the statue of the Buddha, so she walked over and stood looking at the candles and the flowers, the handwritten notes pinned up on the shrine. One of them caught her eye and she moved closer to read it. It was written in old fashioned handwriting and quite difficult to read, but it said, *All will be well. E.*

Jen glanced both ways to make sure no one was watching from the nearby building, then she quickly unpinned the note and slipped it into her pocket.

Chapter Six

There were so many memories, but some were more precious than others. Some Jen relived over and over, taking them out like a polished stone to turn in the light. Every time she discovered something new.

When she was twelve, her mum let her go camping with Danny. They set off on their bikes after school on a Friday. It was May and the evenings were getting longer. Danny had the tent strapped to the back of his bike and she had the frying pan, some tins of beans and sausages, eggs, bread and butter. They both had a sleeping bag and a bottle of water.

They cycled out of the town along Queen Adelaide Way. After a couple of miles they met the Great River Ouse which lay still beside the road, its water dark, broken by squabbling ducks and afternoon sunlight. Jen often cycled to Rebecca's house or across the town to school, but she'd not been this far before. After Prickwillow the lane was long and straight. A ditch ran alongside the road, its water reflecting the bright sky in a line of silver. Every now and then there would be a row of trees, tall and straight, their trunks slicing the light. Danny said they were poplars. Jen's legs ached.

"We'll stop and rest for a bit," said Danny. "We must be about halfway."

They sat at the side of the road and drank some water next to a sign for pick-your-own strawberries.

"I love all the straight lines," said Jen.

Danny looked left and then right. The land stretched away, flat in every direction. "Sometimes I wish we lived somewhere else," he said. "Somewhere with mountains or cliffs."

Jen screwed the top back on her water bottle. She lay on her back and stared up at the sky. She could see tiny bubbles in the air, but she knew they were actually in her eyes.

When her legs were rested, they got on their way again. By the time they reached Isleham, she was starving.

They found a spot and put up the tent. They often had the tent up in the garden, so they knew exactly what to do. But when Jen crawled inside, she knew this was different. At home there was the sound of traffic on the road, people talking in their back gardens or in their kitchens with the windows open, and it didn't seem much removed from the house.

There were other people here on the campsite, but there was no traffic. The air seemed heavier. When she breathed in, she thought of it as clear and green. She crawled forward on her belly so her head was sticking out of the entrance. Danny had gone to collect firewood.

Jen flipped over onto her back so she could look up at the sky. In her peripheral vision she could see trees lining the rim of this upturned bowl of blue. Some crows were arguing nearby, and someone was strumming a guitar. She could feel warmth in her leg muscles. They would ache in the morning.

Danny returned with an armful of wood, and together they built a wigwam shape which they stuffed full of newspaper Danny had brought with him. But when they tried to light it, the wind blew out the match. After a few attempts, they managed to get a flame going in a corner of the paper. It flared orange, then green, then died to a line of black, having only burned a bite out of the paper. Danny sighed.

"Have you got a lighter?" asked Jen.

He shook his head and started rearranging the screwed-up balls of paper. Jen crouched next to him, peering in between the pieces of wood.

"Hiya."

They both looked round. A person with long hair and a guitar slung over their back was smiling at them. Jen couldn't tell if they were a boy or a girl.

"You OK?"

"Yes," said Danny. "Well, no. We can't get this fire going."

"Come and share ours."

"Well..."

"We were going to cook on it," said Jen. "We have sausages."

"Bring them. We've got a barbecue going. I'm Stan, by the way."

Danny looked at Jen. She knew he was thinking that she was only twelve and that their mum trusted him to look after her.

"We've got beer," said Stan, "and music." He patted the side of his guitar.

"Erm... OK," said Danny. "For a bit."

An alley of trees led from where Danny and Jen had erected their tent and opened out at the other end into a field. Jen looked at Stan as they walked. She wasn't sure he actually was a him. He was wearing eye makeup. He had no facial hair and his voice was very light.

His friends had three tents and a camper van in a circle. The fire in the middle was bright, and Jen realised the light was beginning to fade from the sky. There were nine people sitting on chairs and blankets around the fire, and to the right a barbecue was smoking meaty fumes into the evening air.

"Hey, shove up and make room for these guys," said Stan.

Someone took their sausages and put them on the barbecue, handed them burgers dripping with ketchup, butter melting out of the buns. Someone else handed them both a bottle of beer, and Stan started playing his guitar. A few of them sang along softly.

Jen and Danny sat on a blanket and Jen leaned against her brother. The light was fading fast now and the fire crackled. Bits of papery ash floated up on hot currents of air, and the heat made Jen's face glow. These people were all older, even than Danny, grown-ups just about.

She took a sip of the beer. It tasted disgusting, but she was careful not to react. She swallowed and quickly took a bite of her burger to get the taste out of her mouth. Stan was playing a song she knew by Green Day and she found herself humming along under her breath. *I hope you had the time of your life.*

Later, when the sausages had been cooked and shared around, when she'd managed to swallow the last dregs of bitterness from the beer bottle, when the stars began to appear in the sky and Danny had disappeared behind the hedge for a wee, someone took out tobacco and rizlas and something else in a small plastic bag. They rolled a long cigarette, lit it, took a couple of drags, then passed it around the circle.

Jen looked into the darkness behind the tents, but there was no sign of Danny. The person next to her had the cigarette now. She held on to the empty beer bottle, breathed in smoke from the fire, breathed out again. Then the cigarette was in her hand, and she lifted it to her lips and sucked.

She'd never tried smoking... anything. The hot smoke hit the back of her throat and she coughed.

"Breathe it in slow," said the guy who'd handed it to her. "Into your lungs."

She tried again, felt the smoke trickle down the back of her throat and her chest seemed to expand, her eyes grow larger.

When Danny came back a few minutes later, the joint had moved on. Another was being made by the person sitting next to them, and Danny frowned.

"I think we should probably get back to our tent," he said.

"Do we have to?" Jen watched as leaves were sprinkled along the line of tobacco, then then rolled between expert fingers.

"Yes," said Danny. "Come on."

Stan waved across the circle before returning to his strumming. They walked along the alley of trees, and the sounds of the party moved into the distance. The hedge blocked out the firelight and they were in darkness. There was a crescent moon and the stars were bright.

"This isn't like the campsite we went to last year," Jen said.

"No," said Danny.

They'd rented a static near the beach on a site where the caravans were in straight rows into the distance. In the centre of the site were a shop, a café and a nightclub. Dad had put the TV on as soon as they arrived and Mum tutted about the people in the neighbouring caravans. Danny and Jen had escaped to the beach as much as possible, sometimes climbing around the headland at low tide to the next beach that the tourists didn't quite reach.

"Don't tell Mum you had beer."

"OK," said Jen. Her limbs felt loose and heavy and when she turned her head quickly the stars left streaks across her vision. "I like it here," she said. "It's quiet. Can we stay up all night and watch the stars?"

Danny laughed. "You'll be asleep in five minutes."

They snuggled into their sleeping bags but left the tent open so they could lie on their backs looking at the sky.

Danny knew her well; she was a sleeper, always dropping off the moment her head hit the pillow, and tonight was no different. But later she woke up. Danny was on his side, breathing softly through his nose. The party in the next field had fallen silent. Clouds covered the sky so the moon and stars had disappeared. The world was heavy and dark.

Jen wriggled out of her sleeping bag. She needed to wee, but there was no way she was walking to the toilet block on her own. She went to the back of the tent and crouched on the grass. She could barely make out where the canvas was, it was so dark. She didn't remember ever being in such silence.

An owl called out and made her jump, and she realised she wasn't alone. There was someone crouching beside her. She looked. The person was wearing dark clothes, but Jen could just make out her face. It was her cousin.

She stretched out her arm towards Jen and took her hand. The owl called again, and then flew out from the tree behind them, a dark shadow against the black of the sky. Jen could hear Danny's breathing in the tent, a rasping sound that was almost a snore.

Her legs began to ache from crouching. The cousin stood, still holding Jen's hand, pulling her up to standing next to her. Jen felt her nightshirt fall back against her skin, and the touch of the night breeze on the inside of her thighs.

The cousin began to walk. She moved very slowly, and Jen, in her bare feet, shuffled along beside her. They circled the tent, once, twice, three times. Jen remembered a word she'd read in a fairy-tale – widdershins – which meant anticlockwise. In stories, if things went widdershins, then magic might happen. It might or might not be good.

The third time they reached the mouth of the tent, the cousin vanished. One minute she was holding Jen's hand, the next she was simply not there.

"Jen?" Danny's voice in the dark was scratchy with sleep.

"I just went for a wee," said Jen.

She snuggled back into her sleeping bag and lay down. She listened for the owl. It called once, and then she was asleep.

After a morning reading Baudelaire in the library, Jen was walking across the campus past the lake when her phone buzzed. It was Finn.

Would you like to go to Whitby?

When? She typed.

Now?

He told her he was at the station and there was a bus in twenty minutes if she could get there in time.

I'll do my best, she texted.

There wasn't time to go to her room to drop off her books. She raced up the road and reached the stop just as the bus to the town centre was pulling in. Twelve minutes later she jumped off at the station. Finn was leaning against a pillar. He saw her and waved.

"I already bought the tickets," he said.

The bus to the coast was half full of passengers. Finn and Jen made their way to the back. Jen could feel sweat on her top lip and between her breasts. It was a warm day and the dash across town had been unexpected.

"What if I hadn't made it?" she said.

Finn shrugged. "We could have caught the next one. Though we might not have got there until the evening."

"Is there a bus back?"

"I hope so."

"Bloody hell! What if there isn't?"

"Sleep on the beach?"

Jen laughed. She suddenly felt much lighter than she had for ages. The nausea which was almost constant had vanished. Finn offered her a mint and she popped it in her mouth as the bus started to pull away.

It was a long bus ride, calling at numerous villages along the way, and then across the moors where the heather was blazing purple in the sunshine.

"I've not been to Whitby before," she said.

"It's where Lucy Harker met Dracula," said Finn.

"I've not read *Dracula*."

"Oh, lucky you! You've got a treat in store."

The bus crested a hill and there was the Abbey standing on a clifftop. A line of fuzzy blue marked the horizon, darker than the sky.

"The sea," said Finn.

It was mid-afternoon when they got off the bus. They visited the museum, then walked over the bridge to the old part of town and climbed up to the Abbey. The steps started at the end of a row of shops, but quickly lifted them above the buildings. Jen looked across the rooftops, red, orange and black, jostling together. Higher up, they reached a churchyard with graves going back hundreds of years. They walked amongst them, reading the inscriptions.

On the seaward side, the path was separated from the drop by a fence and a few yards of grass. Finn told Jen to sit on a bench.

"Pretend you're a Victorian young lady," he said, "and something has called you out into the night."

Jen looked at the sea. Sunlight was sparkling on it, so it looked as though someone had scattered it with newly minted coins. There were boats far out on the water. The sun was warm on the bare skin of her arms.

Finn approached the bench and sat down beside her.

"Hello Lucy," he said in a fake Eastern European accent. "Your neck looks beautiful in the moonlight."

Jen leaned her head slightly to one side, exposing it.

Finn leaned in and she felt warmth and wetness where his lips met her skin, the slightest graze of his teeth.

She closed her eyes for a moment. She could hear the shouts of children climbing the steps, the calls of seagulls circling above.

Then she turned her head to meet Finn's.

While they were kissing, she thought – *I wonder if he planned this. It's pretty cool for a first kiss.*

And – *I shouldn't be doing this.*

And also – *God, this is so nice; I could stay here kissing in the sunshine for ever.*

After a while, Finn drew away and looked into her face. He tucked a stray bit of hair behind her ear. He said, "Do you want to see the Abbey?"

At the top of the cliff there was nothing to stop the wind. Jen and Finn lay on the grass next to each other in the middle of the ruined Abbey. When it was whole, this would have been the aisle up the middle where the monks walked. Jen imagined them gliding slowly across the grass, straight over her and Finn where they lay. She looked up and all she could see was sky. All she could hear was the wind and the crashing beat of the waves below, the seagulls. There was a sweet smell – grass maybe, or some other plant. For a moment she missed Danny so much that her lungs hurt. She squeezed Finn's hand hard.

They walked back into town after that. When the shops started to close for the day, they bought chips and ate them sitting on a wall near the harbour.

"We could get a B&B," said Finn.

He'd kissed her again at the Abbey when they'd walked out beyond the fishpond, and they'd been holding hands all around the town.

"I think I should get back," she said. "I've got to get this essay finished."

"We could get the first bus in the morning."

She smiled. "It would be lovely. But not this time."

On the bus, Finn put his arm around her and she rested her head on his shoulder. She thought about the evening she'd given up, where they booked into a B&B together, and found themselves suddenly standing side by side in room where a double bed filled up most of the space and all of their thoughts. Where chintz curtains framed a view of the Abbey and the church, where a kettle stood on the bedside table with two cups, teabags, tiny cartons of longlife milk and gingernuts in individually wrapped packets of three. She thought about lying in bed at dawn and listening to the screams of seagulls welcoming the light, of watching Finn's naked back as he slept, his shoulders rising and falling with his breath.

"You OK?" asked Finn.

"Just feeling a bit travel sick."

"Do you want to move to another seat?"

"No, I'll be OK."

When they reached York, Jen rushed to the toilets and threw up. *That'll teach me.* She washed her face in cold water and popped a mint in her mouth. Took five deep breaths.

Walking back out of town to the campus, she made sure there was space between them. When Finn moved his hand as though to take hers, she adjusted her bag on her shoulder and pretended she hadn't noticed. Near the library she said goodbye, kissed him on the cheek and hurried away without looking back. She knew he was wondering what he'd done wrong. She wished she could tell him, *nothing*. She wished right now they could be lying on that double bed, on top of the floral quilt, shyly tugging at each other's clothes.

She flung her bag in the corner of her room, lay on her bed, and cried.

Chapter Seven

Rebecca had too much stuff for her tiny car, so the next morning her aunt drove up from Ely to help. She took both girls for lunch in the city before loading up. They went to a noodle bar and slurped soup with wooden ladles, shovelled noodles and beansprouts into their mouths with chopsticks. If it had been Jen's parents, they'd have got pizza or fish and chips. Through her teens, Jen had got to know Lucy, who refused to be called Aunt, and Rebecca's Uncle Simon. They had introduced her to jambalaya, kimchi, couscous, baklava and lamb tagine, taught her to eat with chopsticks and tolerate levels of chilli previously unimagined.

After lunch they walked back across the Stray.

"Are your mum and dad coming to fetch you?" asked Lucy.

Jen shrugged. "Maybe. I haven't sorted it out yet."

"There's space in Lucy's car," said Rebecca, "why don't you come with us?"

"Thanks, but I think I'll stick around. We don't have to be out of our rooms for another three weeks."

Rebecca stopped walking and looked at her friend.

"Are you sure something didn't happen last time you were in Ely? It sounds like you don't want to go back."

"I still have an essay to hand in," said Jen.

Rebecca didn't look convinced, but she let it go.

Back on campus, Jen helped carry Rebecca's things out to the carpark, then stood and waved as they drove away. When the two cars disappeared at the end of the road, she looked about her. No one was around. She knew that only some students had gone home, but for a moment she felt as though she were the only person left on campus.

She looked at her phone. No messages. Probably best to leave it that way. But when she stepped into her room, the white sports jacket was hanging on the back of her chair, and she found herself texting despite herself.

Hi Finn, what you doing?

Packing came the reply within moments.

Do you want help?

If you like.

It wasn't the most enthusiastic reply, but that was fair enough. She got his room number from him.

I'll bring bread and hummus and olives.

Cool. I have crisps.

His room was a mess, stuff all over the bed, the floor, the desk. Books, maps, compasses, film, waterproof clothing, dried food and stacking pans. A new compact thermal sleeping bag and a one-man tent. A mobile phone which wouldn't work once he reached a certain altitude.

Jen cleared some space on the desk for the food she'd brought. "When are you leaving?"

"Tomorrow. I'm going down to London for a couple of days first. My mum and dad are in England and we're going to hang out."

"Where are they normally?"

"My mum's a wildlife photographer and my dad's an animal behaviourist. They mostly work in other countries."

"That's so cool. Do you get to go with them?"

"Sometimes. But it's not that cool. I had to go to boarding school."

"More exciting than my mum and dad."

"What do they do?"

"My dad fixes boats. He used to be a car mechanic, but now he just does boats."

"And your mum?"

"She works in an office. She's a born-again Christian."

Jen watched Finn's face, but he didn't react.

"Not your dad?"

"God, no!" Jen pulled a face. "God – ha ha! No, he's not interested in that stuff. She has a friend, a bloke who runs their church, called Terence. Mum worships him and his wife."

"Aren't they meant to worship God?"

"You'd think," Jen said. She helped herself to a handful of crisps and shoved some into her mouth so she couldn't speak. She didn't want to think about Terence. Didn't want to think about the Church. She felt the food slide into her stomach. "You've got the wrong calendar on your wall. This one is for last year."

Finn frowned. He shook his head as though there was a bug in his ear. "You could come to London with me. My parents are pretty relaxed, you'd like them."

"I still have an essay to finish. I need to stay."

"You could do it next week. You don't need to be on site."

"I know... but I'd rather stay here, get it finished."

"OK." Finn picked up a guidebook from the floor and shoved it into the side pocket of his rucksack. "Well, we should definitely write to each other."

"Yes, we should."

"It's only a few weeks."

Thirteen weeks. That's how long it was until term started again. Jen didn't want to think that far ahead. It was seven weeks since she'd been home for Easter. Added to thirteen, that made twenty.

"I wonder if you'll find any dinosaurs."

"A fossil or two, if I'm lucky."

"Send me photos?"

"I will. And you tell me all about your island."

"I've been there before. It's tiny and the road only goes around half of it, so all along the other side there are huge beaches you can only get to on foot, with white sand stretching for miles and no one there except highland cattle chomping on the marram grass."

"Sounds like paradise."

"My cousin says it's awful in winter."

"So you get the best of both worlds, being able to visit."

"I guess."

"Do you want to go for a walk? I can finish this later."

"OK."

They walked into town along the river and stopped at a bar for a drink. It was warm and the sun was still bright in the sky.

"Is your essay on Baudelaire?"

Jen nodded.

"Do you still hate him?"

"Sometimes. But I think actually he hated himself. I think that was the problem. He just sometimes took it out on other people."

"Didn't he have a thing about angels?"

"Yeah, he was looking for some sort of ideal. In himself. In women. But he also loved darkness and night and sex. He couldn't reconcile the two."

"A bit like Jekyll and Hyde?"

"Kind of, but I think the evil side was all in his mind. It was to do with religion. He thought sex and pleasure and the night were corrupt, and the fact that he wanted that stuff made him corrupt too. He thought there was some sort of perfection, that he just couldn't reach it."

"I guess that's what made his poetry so powerful."

"Yes. Poor bloke."

The next day she went with Finn to the station. He had all the stuff for his trip in a huge rucksack. It was higher than the top of his head. They walked along the platform looking for his seat reservation.

"I'll miss you, Jen," he said.

She smiled. Hoped she looked cheerful. "I'll miss you too."

He looked at the ticket in his hand. "This is me."

Jen glanced at the ticket, but then Finn leaned forward and dropped a kiss on her forehead. It would have been easy to lift her chin so her lips met his. To have leaned into his thin body in its black t-shirt and blue denim.

"You sure you're going to be OK on your own?"

"I won't be on my own. Once this essay is done, I'm off to Scotland."

He stepped towards the open door of the train.

"Have a good summer, Jen."

"You too."

The guard blew a whistle. She darted forward and kissed him on the lips, then stepped back quickly before he registered what had happened.

"I'm really glad I met you, Finn."

He smiled.

"You need to get on now if you're travelling," called the guard.

Finn stepped up onto the train. As he pulled the door shut behind him, he said, "I'm glad I met you too, Jen."

The train started to move. She saw him walking along the carriage, looking at seat numbers. Then he was gone.

She'd only glimpsed Finn's train ticket, but she thought it had last year's date on it. Should she have said something? The station seemed to loom up around her. She looked up and saw a bird of prey sitting high in the roof. It had a speckled breast and seemed to be watching her.

Chapter Eight

She spent the evening alternately staring at her computer screen and the pages of Baudelaire. Twice she thought she was going to be sick, but when she went to the bathroom there was nothing. After a while she took the yellow hat out of the drawer and put it on her head. She wished Rebecca was still there. There were things they never talked about. For example, even after all these years she didn't know what Rebecca's parents were called, or how they died. She didn't know anything about Rebecca's childhood in York. But still, they were friends, and sometimes it was enough to be with someone. Sometimes you didn't need to talk.

It was true, she didn't need to be at college to write the essay. She could go home to Ely. She could write her essay at the kitchen table or at the library in town. Her dad had sent a message three weeks ago to say that Lee had left. There was no one staying in her room.

She stared at herself in the mirror. There was a razor on the desk that she had brought with her from the bathroom. It would be easy to break the blade out of its plastic casing.

For nineteen years, home had been a safe place. Maybe it would be fine. Her books were in there in her room, her cuddly toys from when she was a kid, the diaries she'd kept from age twelve to fifteen. Her dad would be in the house. Maybe she could even talk to her mum about Easter.

She swiped at the desk and knocked the razor to the floor. Then she looked back in the mirror and stuck her tongue out. She took the yellow hat off and put it back in the drawer.

The next morning she sat on the train south, watching the hills outside the window flatten into broad plains. Leeds, Wakefield, Peterborough, square block landscapes giving way to fields which stretched as far as the eye could see. Black birds hovering way up, loose 'm's scrawled on the sky. The nearer the train got to home, the less Jen noticed what was outside. The flatness sank comfortably into her consciousness.

After Manea Station the wash had flooded into the fields, and it seemed as though the train passed across a lake, a still mirror which held the reversed top branches of submerged trees, huge motionless clouds, and the undersides of swooping birds hoping to catch dragonflies. She could see the cathedral now, the huge stone ship, docked and beached, pinning the city of Ely into the flatness of the drained fens.

The train passed through wet green meadows, lower than the tracks, dotted with butter-coloured cows. Everything was so normal here, so unchanged. Here she was still a child. She would get home and Donna would scold her for being away. Danny would be out in the garden kicking a football.

She walked from the station down to the river. She hadn't told her mum and dad she was coming. Now she didn't feel ready to face their surprise and hugs of welcome. What she wanted was to slip unnoticed through the back door and up to her room, wait there lying on her bed until she was called down to tea. Later, when her dad was watching telly, she would help her mum with the washing up. They might talk. They probably wouldn't.

She could slip into the city, even if she couldn't slip into the house. She wove through the tourists who were milling down by the river with their brightly dressed children, clutching bags of breadcrusts for the ducks. Some boys from the King's School were getting boats out of the boatsheds. One had his hair dyed in blonde and black stripes and Jen looked twice to check it was hair and not a tightly pulled cap. He caught her gaze and threw her a cheeky wink, a grin. One of the other boys whistled and Jen smiled.

She shoved her hands into her jacket pockets and walked on, aware of the boys watching. Further up, a new white-board fence marked off an area of wasteland adjacent to the river. Jen stopped to read the notice attached to it – an archaeological dig, looking for signs of habitation from the recent past. She wondered if they'd find anything of hers. Lost lipsticks or hairclips, experimental cigarettes, puffed and thrown away with a dark red gloss ring round the filter. Mementos of summer nights sitting on the walls with Rebecca, watching the light fade over the water, gossiping, giggling, smoking. Something of Danny's, maybe.

It was gone six when she eventually walked up the drive to her parent's front door. The house was semi-detached, pink-bricked, built in the sixties, the door painted custard yellow. The roses which outlined the square front garden were blooming red and pink, their fleshy petals inking her with perfume as she brushed by.

Jen rang the bell. She had a front door key in her bag, but she didn't want to just walk in when they weren't expecting her. A dark shape loomed behind the frosted glass and the door opened. On the mat, a pair of large male feet in navy blue socks and brown sandals. A smell wafted over her, musty like brown leather and old books. She looked up and her hands were grasped in two much larger ones.

"Jennifer, how wonderful." She was pulled across the threshold. "So lovely you could come. Your mother will be delighted."

Terence. Oh God!

He was wearing olive green cords, rubbed bare at the knee, and a dark red sweater, machine knitted in an elaborate cable pattern with clusters of what looked like grapes. His dark hair was smoothed from a side parting, streaked with grey, and wisps of his beard tickled Jen's cheeks as he threw an arm round her.

"Donna," he called loudly. "Donna, Jennifer's here. Isn't that lovely! I hadn't realised you'd invited her."

Jen tried to say, 'Invited me to what?' but her voice got stuck, and by the time she'd cleared her throat her mother was there, tea towel in hand, pulling her out of Terence's arms and into her own.

"Jennie, love. How lovely. You've just missed tea, I'm afraid. We had to eat early, because it's our big night. We've got everyone coming to us this evening, and we've got to get down to the church to get things ready. Did I tell you about the week of prayer, love?"

Jen shook her head.

"Well, they've included us, properly, for the first time this year – the council of churches, you know. We've always gone along of course, and been welcomed, but this is the first year we've actually been on the list. Would you like to come? We'd love to have you. It doesn't start 'til seven so you'd have time to grab a sandwich."

"Of course Jennifer will come." Terence's arm landed on the back of her neck again. "Everyone will be so pleased to see her."

"Sorry Mum, I'm pretty tired. I think I'll give it a miss this time. Is Dad in?"

"He's watching the telly." Donna nodded her head in the direction of the living room and turned back into the kitchen, pulling the tea towel from her shoulder. Jen glanced towards the living room door, the flicker of multicoloured light from the TV showing through the open gap, then she followed her mum into the kitchen. She'd talk to Steve when the others were out. She wondered if Lee had left town, or just their house.

Terence sat down at the kitchen table and wrapped his large fingers around a mug of tea. Long black hairs clustered on the back of his hands, between the first and second joint of each finger. He looked enormous in their ordinary semi-detached kitchen. He was six foot two, and broad as well as hairy. Jen leaned against the sink.

It was four years since Donna had been born again. Terence didn't even have a church building then, he preached in the market square and held study groups in his home. One Saturday when they were shopping in town, Donna had stopped to listen. Jen got bored and moved on, said she'd wait for her in Wilko's. She waited a long time before going back to the market square. Her mum was still there, deep in conversation with Terence and his wife, Stella. She was animated and her face shone with tears. Later she told Jen it had been a miracle. She had heard Jesus knocking on the door of her heart, and suddenly she just knew. It was the easiest thing in the world to open that door and let him in. She was flooded with warmth and love, and also sorrow for Him that she had ignored Him for so long, that so many millions still refused to let Him in.

They were called the Friends of Jesus, and four years on there was a congregation of forty-three and an old scout hut which they'd clubbed together to buy as their own. Jen had never opened the door of her heart, despite being dragged along to many meetings. Her refusal to sing songs with the rest of them to Stella's guitar in the marketplace had been the cause of many arguments.

When Donna and Terence went out to their prayer meeting, Jen sidled into the living room and snuggled up next to her dad on the sofa.

'Hi, chicken,' said Steve, putting his arm round her. 'How's tricks?'

They watched a crime drama together, then at nine-thirty Steve went to the pub. Jen, left alone in the house, went up to her bedroom. She picked up her teddy from the chest of drawers and held it to her chest. She couldn't lie on the bed. She pulled the duvet onto the floor and lay there, knees pulled up to her chest, squeezing the teddy hard enough to crush the life from it.

When she got up the next day, there was no one in the house. She walked into town, all the time scanning the streets. She'd not asked her dad if Lee was still in town; she hadn't wanted to mention him.

The sun was shining in yellow pools on the pavements between the shadows of trees. It was the twenty-first of June – Midsummer's Day. The grass by the cathedral was emerald bright. Jen could feel her shoulders starting to burn. She walked into the massive porch of the cathedral and through the little wooden door carved out of the big door. She searched in her pockets for coins for the entrance fee. She didn't have quite enough, but she recognised the lady behind the desk – it was Mrs Shepherd from St Peter's. Jen promised to bring the rest of the money later. Mrs Shepherd shrugged and nodded her through.

As always, she was awed by the vast space above and around her. Here, she felt she should be able to fly. It seemed like some awful mistake that she couldn't leave the ground behind and skim right up to the gargoyles and painted kings, touch noses with Christ in His lanterned majesty, dance high over the organ pipes. She was so ordinary here on the ground.

Just beyond Mrs Shepherd's till was a flat mirror at waist height for people who wanted to look at the ceiling without craning their necks. Jen stood right up against it so that her hip bones jutted against the mirror's support. She closed her eyes and stretched out her back as though she were going to take a dive. Then she looked into the mirror. She nearly fell, but steadied herself with a hand on the frame. The cathedral yawned below her like an enormous u-shaped valley, a sculpted gorge of which she stood on the brink. Strata of pillars and upturned arches marked the cliff face, and religious paintings divided the valley bottom into a patchwork of distant fields. The light in the valley was crystal bright. She closed her eyes again and stepped backwards. She thought of Finn, wondered if he'd like it here.

The cathedral's chill kissed her skin. Sweat from her walk trickled down her armpits and cleavage. She ran a finger inside the front of her t-shirt to remove the moisture, then looked round quickly in case anyone had seen.

Jen walked the length of the nave, quickly, through the Octagon and along the south choir aisle to the far end of the cathedral. St Etheldreda was here. The honey-coloured lady standing serene, surrounded by a small scaffold of candelabra. Few candles were lit, so Jen took one from the box and fitted it into the holder nearest Etheldreda's face. She lit it and watched as the yellow glow gave colour to the saint's cheeks, painted shadows into her eye sockets and behind her ears.

She looked over her shoulder. There was no one else at this end. She edged softly behind the statue. It stood on a raised platform, two feet from the stone wall. Jen leaned back and the stone was like cold metal on her bare skin. She shuddered, then looked at the back of Etheldreda.

She wasn't finished. Or rather, she was only half a statue. The back of Etheldreda was rounded, uncarved stone, not meant to be seen.

Jen slid her back down the stone wall until her bottom touched her upturned heels. She heard a sound like someone choking, which she realised she'd made herself. She put her palms open on the walls at her sides and let the tears fall, running in lines down her face and dripping onto her chest, dampening her t-shirt. She stared at the back of the statue of Etheldreda, and each time the white raw stone swam into focus through the tears, Jen felt the choke claw its way back up her throat.

She might have been there for ten minutes when the brown leather sandals of Mrs Shepherd appeared on the other side of the statue.

"Are you alright?"

Jen wiped her eyes on her arms.

"Um, yes."

Mrs Shepherd didn't move. Her feet were solidly planted on the right side of Etheldreda. She had varicose veins running from her ankles into her feet. Jen slid out.

Mrs Shepherd said again, "Are you alright?"

Jen nodded and smiled at her. The tears had stopped, although her face was still wet.

"Can I call someone for you, Jennifer? It is Jennifer isn't it? Your mother, perhaps."

The best thing Jen could do for this woman was to get out of her morning as quickly as possible. Let her and her cathedral to return to normality.

"Thank you, Mrs Shepherd," she said. "I'll be fine. I'm going home now."

They walked back together the length of the cathedral, and despite the kindly slope of Mrs Shepherd's peach cotton shoulders, Jen couldn't help feeling that she was being escorted out.

Mrs Shepherd said goodbye at the desk. Jen gave a cheery smile and said, "Bye, Mrs Shepherd," as if she were leaving Sunday School. Mrs Shepherd smiled nervously back at her.

The sun was cooking the grass. Jen walked back home. She could work on her essay.

There was still no one in. In the kitchen she found bread in the bread bin, butter and strawberry jam in the fridge. She piled up a plateful and sat at the table. The sun slanted in through the ivy on the outside wall, making sharp pictures of pointed leaves on the table by her plate. The ivy leaf shadows were dark grey, while the table shone bright gold. There was no breeze to speak of. The outlines could have been drawn with a pencil. Jen stood up abruptly. The contrast of light and shade was putting her off her food.

In the hallway was a door which led to the back garden when Jen was very small. Now it led to Dorothy's room which had been built onto the back of the house after she'd had a stroke and couldn't live on her own anymore. Jen was seven when her gran came to live with them. At first she had been angry because some of the garden had been eaten up by this new part of the house, but she'd soon realised that Dorothy more than made up for it. Jen would sneak in to see her after school, and Dorothy would tell her stories and jokes and they would giggle like schoolgirls. She gave Jen old-fashioned sweets like humbugs and barley sugar and told her the names of plants which grew in the garden. Now she was dead. Her room was empty except for her things. The curtains were half drawn and there was a softer light.

Jen sat on the edge of her gran's bed with the plate of bread and jam on her lap. Although this room was newer than the rest of the house, it felt older because the furniture was old and dark. The bed was high. Her toes only just reached the floor. She bent them so they curled under, stretching the tops of her feet. This hurt her ankles a little, so she flexed them the other way. She remembered trying to walk round this room on the point of her toes, telling Dorothy that was how ballet dancers walked. Dorothy said ballet dancers must have different shaped toes than the rest of us then, or else different shoes. Jen imagined having a baby one day when she was grown up, and when the doctor handed it to her after it was born, noticing that it had square toes, like the end of a wood block. She would smile and say to the doctor, "this one's going to be a ballet dancer." After that, she gave up trying to walk on en pointe, but she still walked on tiptoe a lot. She liked the feeling of balance.

As far as she knew, Lee had never been in this room.

She put the plate on the bedcover and stood on tiptoe. There wasn't much space to walk. On the far side of the bed was an armchair with wooden arms and side wings, upholstered in dark green shiny material. In some places, the threads had come loose. Behind this, right next to the bed was a little cupboard where Dorothy kept library books, sweets and biscuits and her teeth at night in a glass of water. At the end of the room beyond the bed was a wardrobe with blank mahogany doors and a bookcase filled with school textbooks. Dorothy used to be a teacher at the girls' grammar school, but that was long ago. Between the window and the door was a tallboy in dark wood. When Jen was little, she couldn't see the top of this even when she stood on tiptoe. Now she could look down on the embroidered linen cloth and the glass bottle that stood on top.

Inside the bottle was a tiny model of the Cutty Sark. Jen knew the story behind this ship-in-a-bottle, although she couldn't remember anyone ever telling it to her. It was bought by her grandad, Fred, on an outing to the Greenwich Maritime Museum in London on the day he first met Dorothy. She was taking a party of schoolgirls to the museum as part of a history project. He was on a work outing.

Fred worked at the sugar factory. Every year in the summer, the factory owners paid for the workers to go on an outing. Before, it had always been boat trips up the river followed by a hotdog party down on the quay. That particular year, 1969, the factory had a new boss and he thought it would be a good idea to make the annual outing a bit more educational. He thought if his workforce had a broader outlook on life then they would be more contented and work better. He booked coaches and took the factory workers to the museum at Greenwich, wanting to carry on the boat theme of previous years.

It was the first and the last time Fred ever went to London. The size of the city unsettled him. He didn't like to think of so many people living in the world that his mind could not encompass them. He liked to be able to walk the streets of Ely in his head as he lay in bed at night and always know where he was going, be sure what he would find around the next corner. Here, in this metropolis, a person could walk for days and days and never see the same street twice.

What made it worse, the thing that made him vow never to set foot on London tarmac again, was that he became separated from his party at the museum. He got lost. If he'd been on home soil, he'd have just hitched a lift or walked to the nearest bus route, but here he was as helpless as a child. He had to swallow his pride and ask one of the museum staff to help him. By the time they had located his party it was too late; the coaches had left for home and he was stranded.

Which was where Dorothy came in. She was shepherding her girls out of the museum when she overheard Fred talking to the museum staff about the best way of getting back to Ely, and she offered him a lift. Fred was so grateful that he gave her the Cutty Sark ship-in-a-bottle that he'd bought for his mother. Three weeks later, after they had met twice to go to the pictures and once for a walk in the park, he asked her to marry him and she agreed. He was forty-six and she was thirty-eight.

Jen picked up the bottle and turned it in her hands. The little ship inside was perfect. She held the bottle between her palms and revolved it slowly so the Cutty Sark capsized then righted itself, capsized, righted itself. She was still standing on tiptoe.

Then the door to Dorothy's room crashed open and Jen dropped the bottle. It hit one of the drawer knobs on the tallboy and shattered, spraying glass across the carpet and Jen's feet. The ship landed sideways on the floor halfway between the tallboy and the bed.

Jen looked at the ship and at the glass on the carpet. She looked at her feet, flat on the floor now, with shards of glass shining near her toes. Then she looked at the doorway where Donna was standing. Their eyes locked. The stare lasted for ten seconds, by which time Jen had contracted inwards away from her skin. She felt sick at breaking Dorothy's bottle. She wanted to hold her gran's liver-spotted hand and beg her forgiveness. She thought about Finn leaving on the train.

"What are you doing in here?" Donna's voice was thin as a wire.

"Nothing. Just looking – thinking –"

Donna looked down at a piece of glass just under the edge of the bed.

"Do you know where that came from?"

Jen nodded.

"It had sentimental value. It was the only thing I had of my father's."

Jen bit her lip. She wanted to say that the bottle didn't belong to Donna but to Dorothy, and that it had never been Fred's as it had been intended as a gift from the moment he bought it.

"Have you nothing to say?"

"I'm sorry. It was an accident."

"Speak up. You're mumbling. What did you say?"

Jen lifted her head. "You startled me," she said loudly.

"Oh, so it's my fault, is it? You come in here poking around, dropping crumbs all over the floor – and guess who'll be the one who has to clear them up? – God knows what you were looking for. And when I find you here, you're so edgy that you drop a family heirloom and destroy it. It can't replaced, you know."

Jen hung her head. "Could the ship be put in another bottle?"

"How? Do you have any idea how they get those things through the neck of the bottle? Because I don't. It's probably done by a machine these days. I doubt anyone knows how to do it. And anyway, it wouldn't be quite the same, would it, the Cutty Sark in a milk bottle, or a Chardonnay empty. The bottle was part of it. I can't believe you were so careless. I thought you respected your grandma's things."

"I do. And I said I'm sorry."

Jen pushed past her mother through to the kitchen. Donna followed and watched Jen get the dustpan and brush from the cupboard.

"I hope you're not going to do that with bare feet. I don't have time to rush you to hospital. I've got to be down at the chapel by one to help with the cleaning."

Angrily, Jen thrust her feet into the first pair of footwear she saw, Steve's wellies standing by the back door. She stared at Donna with tears in her eyes and stamped back through to the extension. Donna looked as though she was about to say something else, but thought better of it.

Jen brushed the glass into the dustpan. She picked up the tiny model ship and placed it back on top of the tallboy. Out of its bottle it looked small and insignificant, like a cheap toy.

The dustpan shone with the light held in the pieces of glass. Jen closed her eyes hard so she saw blackness, then opened them again. She carried the dustpan back to the kitchen.

Donna had found some newspaper and spread it out on the table. Jen emptied the glass into the middle of the paper and together they wrapped it up.

Donna said, "I'm sorry. I overreacted. I know you didn't mean to do it."

"I'll get the hoover," said Jen. "In case there's any splinters."

"Are you OK, Jennie?"

Their eyes locked again.

"I'm fine."

"Look love, I'm going to be out most of the day. I've got the cleaning, and then I've got to catch up on the shopping and visit Mrs McCreadie. But later on, this evening, we can have a nice chat after tea."

"OK."

Jen vacuumed the carpet in Dorothy's room. She did the bed cover too in case there were any breadcrumbs. She carried the empty plate out to the kitchen. Donna had thrown the newspaper parcel in the dustbin outside and gathered her cleaning things. She kissed Jen on the cheek.

"Have a nice afternoon, Jen."

"Mmm. You too."

At the front door Donna stopped, one hand on the door and one on the jamb.

"I just remembered: Terence, Stella and Lee are coming round after supper this evening to chat about the programme for the next quarter. But that's OK, isn't it? We can still have our little chat. They're just like family, after all."

She beamed at Jen and then stepped out, pulling the door closed behind her.

Jen stared at her mother's shape through the patterned glass. Donna adjusted her handbag strap and walked away. Jen threw the plate she was holding onto the kitchen floor and watched the pieces bounce back up from the tiles. They landed in an irregular circular pattern. This time a piece hit Jen's bare calf and cut her skin. The pain was sudden and hot and Jen lifted her leg onto a chair to watch the blood flow up in a feathered line. She washed it with a piece of kitchen roll dampened under the tap and found a plaster in the cupboard. The plaster went red straight away, so she took it off again. She dampened another sheet of kitchen roll, folded it into a small square and fastened it with a long bit of plaster. She put the rest of the plasters into her pocket.

Two minutes of watching and no blood showed through, even when she put weight on the leg. She went upstairs and packed her things back into her overnight bag.

Before she left, she looked into Dorothy's room. There was no sign of glass or crumbs, but the room still looked wrong, empty. The bottle had provided a point of focus, had been a piece of Dorothy. The ship without the bottle looked pathetically small and dull. On impulse Jen reached out, grabbed the Cutty Sark and pushed it into the front pocket of her bag. Then she walked out of the house and headed back towards the station.

Chapter Nine

She was travelling backwards and had the same view that she saw from the train yesterday when she arrived, but this time the flat familiarity of East Anglia was receding. She'd wanted to bury her face in Dad's blue jumper that smelled of smoke and beer from the pub and hear him say, "s'okay pet." She'd wanted Mum to give her a plate of cheese and tomato ketchup sandwiches cut into tiny pieces as a special treat and let her eat them in front of the telly.

Across the fields was a windmill with no sails, seagulls flying around its broken top. Jen felt she was looking down the wrong end of a telescope. Her body scooped up towards the ceiling of the train and her head swam with air as she looked down the tunnel of the carriage, at people munching food, slurping from polystyrene cups and calling crossly to their children. They were solid in their seats and far away. She wanted to draw her knees up to her chest, but the table top blocked her. It loomed up at her. There were tea rings marking the surface and her eyes followed the circles. She unscrewed the blue lid from her bottle of water and sipped. She watched her hand twisting, her arm moving, felt the cold swill of water in her throat. Nothing was connected. She looked back out of the window at the unrolling landscape.

Something was flickering at the edge of her vision. She turned her head quickly. Nothing. When she turned back it was there again. White and pointed, moving just out of her sight, frantic. She couldn't tell if it was inside the train or outside.

She closed her eyes. Behind her eyelids sheets of orange light flashed across red. Then it was there again. The white thing. It was a lotus flower, and the points were the edge of the petals. It was rotating fast, as though it were caught in a whirlpool. The orange light got darker and deeper and red started to seep into the petals.

She opened her eyes abruptly. Two children across the aisle were fighting over a video game, both of them holding on to it and pulling. The smaller child, a girl, started to cry.

"Give it to me," said their mother.

Reluctantly the girl let go, but the boy held fast.

"Now!" said the mother.

He relinquished his hold, hung his head in a sulk.

"You can take it in turns. Aleisha can go first."

The boy shot his mother an angry glance.

Jen thought they probably had a similar age gap to her and Danny. When she was five, he was eight, and they played together in the garden. When he was twelve, he taught her the rules of cricket, but only let her play when his friends had gone home for tea.

Her favourite thing was watching films with him on Friday evenings. They would curl up on the sofa with plates of pizza slices and take it in turns to choose. He liked superheroes, and she liked Japanese anime. They watched the same films so many times they sometimes joined in with the dialogue, and then the lines slipped out into their everyday conversations and became their secret language.

She didn't remember fighting like Aleisha and her brother. She saw him kick his sister under the table, and the little girl wailed loudly. Jen thought about moving seats, but they were nearly at Peterborough. She'd be changing trains soon.

They passed a field of dark brown cows grazing in a meadow. She remembered a conversation she'd had with Danny just before he went off on his walking holiday.

"I want to go somewhere with a bit of drama," he said, "cliffs, mountains, sea."

"They're too obvious." She knew it would wind him up. "Here the beauty is more subtle."

"Hmmph!"

He'd done his Duke of Edinburgh in the Lakes the year before and had seen what a landscape could be. He'd been restless ever since.

The train pulled into the station. As she was standing up, the lotus flower flashed back into Jen's vision, backed by vivid red, dripping from its petals. She stumbled and felt a hot rush of bile in her throat.

"Are you OK?"

The children's mother.

Jen leaned on the table for a second, regained her balance. She nodded at the woman.

"I think I stood up too quickly."

The woman smiled. "That happens to me sometimes. Low blood sugar. Here – take this." She pulled a bar of chocolate out of her bag and handed it to Jen.

Jen was about to refuse when the boy said, "Is that mine?"

"Will we have to share?" wailed Aleisha.

"Thank you," said Jen. She took the chocolate and made her way down the aisle. She could hear Aleisha crying and the boy's voice grumbling. She and Danny were never that bad. There must have been times when they had fallen out, but she couldn't remember them.

On the train to York she found a seat in a nearly empty carriage. She ate the chocolate and it made her stomach hurt. She remembered a time they'd gone to visit an old schoolfriend of their mum's, and there was an orchard. She and Danny had been about the same age as the children on the other train. While Donna chatted to her friend, Danny and Jen had found the trees laden with fruit and helped themselves. The apples were hard and so sharp they dried your mouth, but there were loads of them, and they were just there, so they ate as many as they could.

In the car on the way home, Jen cried because her stomach hurt. Danny said he felt fine, but he didn't look fine. His skin was the same colour as the flesh of the unripe apples, and he kept swallowing.

"That'll teach you not to ask," Donna said.

At York station a nun stood under the departures board, watching the passengers come down the stairs from the bridge. Jen slid her hand into her jacket pocket. The note was still there, folded up and softening. *All will be well.*

She'd seen a nun on campus a few times, but Rebecca said she was imagining it. Rebecca thought Jen should go and see someone, a doctor. Rebecca was in Ely right now, and Jen could have gone to find her instead of running away. Instead she was back here in York, seeing nuns again.

Taxis and buses were coming and going, and people waited with luggage piled next to them. One man had long grey hair tied back in a ponytail. He was muttering to himself and watching passengers leaving the station, as though looking for someone in particular.

Jen put her head down and walked quickly from the station towards the city centre. On the bridge, she looked back. The man was walking the same way, and now the nun was with him. She sped up, wove through the tourists, increased the space between her and them.

The pain was back. It was like someone had put a huge hand inside her and was twisting and squeezing. The sun on her head was hot and she felt lightheaded.

At St Wilfrid's she was tempted by the dark interior, the high ceilings. But she remembered that when she'd been there before, the man with the ponytail had done his vanishing trick. The smell of incense that wafted out when someone opened the door made a vein throb in her temple.

She looked back. They were still coming her way. They were quite a way behind, and they weren't hurrying. It looked like they might be chatting.

Jen walked past the front of the cathedral, past the bench where she'd met Finn. She didn't want to think about him. He would be in London now with his parents. She could have been there too.

She turned into Goodramgate. A busker was playing a guitar on the corner, singing in a reedy voice, not quite in tune. She was nearly there. She would sit in the church and rest for a while. It was possible the man and the nun would find her there – that was the first place she'd seen the man, after all – but she didn't really care anymore. The heat of the afternoon, the people milling about, the busker, the flies buzzing in the heat, the cathedral bells, her headache, the cut on her leg from the broken plate, the pain in her guts, the spinning lotus flower – her senses were screaming.

The verger was talking to some tourists at the back of the church. Jen slipped in quietly and made her way to the seat by the stone altar. The cool air immediately soothed her. She sat down on the bench and let her limbs relax. She thought about the statue of Etheldreda in Ely who was carved only on one side, and Mrs Shepherd who carried her worry in her shoulders. That had only been this morning. She felt in her bag and pulled out the tiny ship.

Once she had found a baby bird in the garden and tried to feed it. Danny said it needed grubs, and you could get them from the fishing shop, but it was evening and the shops were closed. Jen found an earthworm in the garden, but it was too big and wriggly and the bird didn't even try to eat it. By the morning it had died. Her mum shook her head and said, 'you should have left it where it was. There's no good comes from interfering with nature.' Dorothy helped her find a box to bury it in – a big cook's matchbox. After they had dug a hole under the hedge at the far end of the garden, put the match box in and covered it over, Dorothy had given Jen a hug and not complained when her blouse got wet with tears.

Someone was standing in front of Jen. It was the verger, smiling apologetically.

"I'm really sorry, but we close up at four."

Jen looked down. A dark patch of red was spreading across the top of her legs, staining her white shorts. The verger saw it too.

The vice in her guts clamped and twisted and she cried out with pain.

"Oh," he said. "Sit still, I'll phone for an ambulance."

Jen tried to protest, but the blood was slicing out of her shorts and sliding down the skin of her legs like thick tar. She felt the snap of the ship in her fist, then the pain took fire and enveloped her body.

Act Two

I can't see. My eyes are open but there's only mist. I can't hear anything. There is nothing. My lips won't move, my mouth won't open, I can't speak. Breath goes in and goes out. There is weight on my chest, I am pressed flat. Gravity holds me down. I open my eyes as wide as I can. Nothing.

I want to sit up. I want to turn around. I want to shout out. There is no one. Nothing. Breath comes in through my nostrils, but it's grey, it fills my body with grey. My skin is disintegrating. The only thing that separates the inside from the outside is my skin, and the layer is becoming thinner. It is a tissue that trembles.

I breathe in grey mist, I am becoming grey mist. There is nothing inside me. The cells of my skin stretch apart, separate. They are floating away, one cell after another. I can see myself becoming dust. I am breathing the dust that is my own self. I am dissolving, I am disappearing. Soon I will be gone.

Chapter Ten

Her cousin was sitting by her bed on one of those hard plastic chairs, reading a magazine. Jen lay still and watched her. She was dressed as a nun, but only on the top half – the wimple and a pale blue cotton top that no one would ever wear unless they had to for religious reasons. On her bottom half she was wearing jeans.

She must have felt Jen's gaze because she looked up from *Hello!* magazine and smiled.

"You've woken up," she said.

Jen had never heard her speak before. She smiled back.

"You've had quite a time of it, you poor thing."

Her voice reminded Jen of weeping willows and slow flowing rivers, cathedrals filled with air. She tried breathing deeply, but the breaths turned into sobs.

Her cousin reached out and took her hand. Her palm was cool, her fingers light against the back of Jen's hand. The sobs subsided into a series of sniffs.

"They want to discharge you," said her cousin. "I think they need the bed. But they're concerned that you've given them no details."

"I didn't want them to phone Mum."

"Why don't you phone Barbara? You could stay with her for a while."

"Is Aunt Barbara your mother?"

"She'd love to have you. The island would be a good place to recuperate."

"Did she have you first, before Grace and Lyddie? Did you die?"

"Shhh. The nurse is coming."

The cousin let go of Jen's hand. She got up and walked quickly away down the ward, where she sat in a chair by the bed of a sleeping patient and carried on reading her magazine.

The nurse appeared by Jen's bed.

"Well young lady, how are you feeling after your long sleep?"

"Hungry."

"Hungry is good. We'll get you some food brought up. You have a bit more colour in your cheeks."

The lotus flower. She couldn't feel it anymore. There was nothing jabbing into her side. No bloodstained petals. No nausea.

"Did I lose it?"

"I'm afraid so, love."

"I'd like to phone my aunt."

"Your aunt. Good, good. Do you have a mobile?"

"It's out of battery."

"I'll get a phone brought to you. Now, you need to swallow these."

The nurse handed her a glass of water and four pills, two white and two that looked like rabbit pellets. Jen took them. She could feel them in her oesophagus, following a line from her mouth to her stomach, a hard lump that wasn't quite pain. She lay back against the pillows.

"I'm still tired," she said to the nurse.

"I'm not surprised, you lost a lot of blood. You'll need to rest for a while."

When the nurse came back ten minutes later with a phone and a cheese salad sandwich, the cousin slipped under the bed. The nurse stood by while Jen phoned her aunt. Except that she didn't really phone her aunt; she phoned Finn and spoke to his turned-off phone.

"Hello Aunt Barbara, it's Jen."

"I'm fine. Well no, actually I'm not. I'm in hospital."

"Nothing serious. I'm about to leave."

"Well, mum doesn't know I'm here. She's really busy with this convention coming up. I wondered if I could come and stay with you for a while."

"I'll get the train. I'll be fine."

"Thank you. That's really good of you."

"I know. Can I phone her when I get to yours?"

The nurse watched her for the whole conversation. Jen had never been good at acting, but she thought she'd pulled it off. The nurse was smiling approvingly. Jen could hear breathing from under the bed.

I can smell heather. I can smell the sea. I can smell clay. I can smell cowshit. I can see nothing. Not darkness, not mist. I don't know if I have a body. I can feel nothing.

I can smell nettles. I can smell oatcakes. I can smell salt. I can smell heather.

What is a person with no sense but smell? Am I a person?

I try to hear. I try to listen. Even if my cells have dispersed, they must still exist. All matter continues to exist. My cells must be oscillating, ringing the airwaves with sound. I must be able to hear something.

How can I try to hear when I have no body, no ears?

But I can smell.

I can smell heather. I can smell fish. I can smell gorse. I can smell green tea, chamomile tea, white tea, black tea, oolong tea, jasmine tea.

"Otter spraints."

I want to call back. What? What? Otter spraints? What does that mean?

I have no voice. I can smell jasmine tea, white petals, green leaves floating.

"Otter spraints. That's what otter poo is called. It smells of jasmine tea."

I remember seeing. Colour. Light. Water. Rocks. A footpath through heather. A person ahead of me with bare feet, walking.

I remember, I want to say. But I have no voice.

I can see nothing. The voice doesn't speak again.

I can smell jasmine tea. I can smell otter spraints. I can smell heather. I can smell skin. I can smell sea. I remember the island.

When Jen left the hospital, her cousin was waiting in the carpark.

"You didn't phone Barbara, did you?" was the first thing she said.

"How...?"

"I know Barbara. She'd have asked a lot more questions. She'd have said, why don't you phone your dad."

"I don't want a fuss."

"Your dad wouldn't make a fuss. He'd just drive up here and get you."

"Yes, and take me back home, and Mum and Terence would be there, and Mum would go on about how inconvenient it was and how selfish I am, and Dad would slope off to the pub."

"You know that's not true."

"Look, I just don't want to, OK? I'm an adult. I can do this on my own."

"Well, all I can say is it's a good thing I'm here to look after you."

"Thank you. It was nice to meet you and talk to you at last."

They stood facing each other, neither of them moving. The cousin had an obstinate look on her face that was strangely familiar.

"I'm going now. Thank you for visiting me."

"You're not going anywhere without me."

"I may not have really phoned, but I'm really going. I'm getting the train to Scotland."

"I'm coming too."

Jen thought about the journey; the train from York to Edinburgh, the shuttle to Glasgow, then the long winding journey up to the highlands and the ferry to the island. It was a long way, and whatever she'd told the nurse, she was feeling a bit shaky. It might be nice to have some company.

"Well, if you're coming with me you may as well tell me your name," she said.

The cousin smiled. Her brown eyes glowed and she was as beautiful as a film star. She held out her hand to Jen.

"My name is Ethie. Pleased to make your acquaintance."

Jen took her hand and they shook solemnly, then burst into peals of laughter. For the first time in weeks, Jen thought the summer might be alright.

Jen had only been to visit her aunt once before. She was sixteen and coming up to her GCSEs. She'd stopped eating and her mother didn't know what to do with her. Aunt Barbara had phoned one evening when Donna was at the end of her tether. Her dad had done his usual and gone to the pub to get out of the way. After he'd gone, Jen had found a paper bag in her room with a vanilla slice in it. They'd always been her favourite cakes. She smiled; that was Dad all over. You thought he hadn't noticed, then he did something like that. She sat on her bed and listened to her mother's voice in the hallway.

"She sits at the table and looks at the food – won't even pick up her knife and fork. I said, if you get hungry enough you'll eat it, you're not going to just starve yourself to death. I know you're not that stupid. But it seems as though she is. I don't think she's eaten anything for a week now. Only water."

That wasn't true. Jen had eaten something. She'd got up in the middle of the night and grabbed a handful of cereal from the box. It had been so dry it made her gag.

The paper bag had stuck to the icing. She slid her finger along the cream layer, looked at it, then put it into her mouth. Sweetness flooded over her tongue.

Downstairs, her mum was saying, "I wouldn't have time to drive her. There's a big weekend at the Church coming up. She'd have to go by train."

The following day she had travelled by herself to Scotland.

She remembered the shock of the Northumberland coastline, the beauty of Berwick-upon-Tweed, of southern Scotland. She'd seen pictures of the Highlands and the islands; she had expected the scenery to be breathtaking when she got that far north. But nobody had told her about this barren, windswept land.

"Ethie," she said in the station foyer, "how about we stop off on the way?" She wondered what colour her cousin's hair was under the wimple.

"Jen, you've just come out of hospital. You need looking after."

"I'm fine," Jen said.

Ethie frowned.

"Nothing mad. Just a little break. A night or two."

"That's long enough for things to go wrong."

"I have my phone. There's always 999. And I won't need it because I'm fine."

Jen thought she wouldn't mention the dead battery in her phone, or that it felt like someone was scraping the inside of her thighs with blunt fingernails and wringing out her guts.

"Where were you thinking of?" Ethie said.

"Berwick-upon-Tweed."

Ethie looked up sharply.

"It's so beautiful. I saw it from the train last time, and I wanted to get off and stay there but I couldn't because Aunt Barbara was expecting me."

Ethie didn't say anything.

"My brother went walking on the northeast coast. He started in Berwick. We might find him."

Ethie looked up at the departures board.

"It's good to explore new places. Be impulsive."

"It's not new to me," Ethie said quietly. "I've been to Berwick before."

She turned and walked to the ticket office where she bought two tickets to Oban.

"Would it be OK if we broke the journey?" she asked the girl behind the glass screen.

The girl looked at the nun in jeans and smiled.

"No worries. As long as you complete the journey within the calendar month."

Ethie handed the tickets to Jen, who put them in her pocket.

"Thanks, Ethie," she said.

Jen sat uncomfortably in her train seat. She shifted from one buttock to another, and each time there was a gush of blood. She'd put on her only pair of blue jeans; all her other trousers were white.

After Durham she got up to go to the toilet, but she was overcome with dizziness and sat down again.

"You OK?" said Ethie.

"Tired."

She dozed for a while. Newcastle passed in a haze of lights. The noise of people getting on and off, the train whistle. Through the thin skin of her eyelids she was dimly aware of Ethie sitting upright on the other side of the table. Her hands were in her lap, her gaze fixed on the view through the window, her nun's veil framing her face, bare of makeup and shining with health. Jen was pleased she was there and let herself drift off.

She was woken by a sharp pain. She sat up and opened her eyes. Ethie smiled at her.

"Trains go so fast, don't they? Look, we're nearly at Berwick already."

Jen put her hands on her belly. A line puckered Ethie's forehead but she smoothed it away.

"You're looking a bit pale," she said. "Maybe you do need the sea air."

The train pulled into Berwick station. As they stood up to disembark, Jen's legs bucked and Ethie had to hold her arm as they walked down the aisle.

On the platform, Jen said, "I need to find the toilets," but before Ethie could reply, the world went black.

When she came to, Jen was sitting on a bench and a woman she'd never seen before had her arm round her shoulders.

"Hello love," the woman said.

There were a few people on the platform, waiting for trains, some of them casting curious glances in their direction.

"You fainted, pet," said the woman. "Your friend's gone to get you some hot tea and a taxi."

Jen nodded and relaxed. For a moment she'd thought Ethie had abandoned her, gone back to whatever realm she'd come from. She didn't bother wondering where they were getting a taxi to. She leaned against the woman and closed her eyes. The pain had subsided, but she felt as though her limbs were made of lead.

"Jen, try to drink some of this."

Ethie held a paper cup to Jen's lips. Jen didn't take it from her; she let her cousin tip the cup, felt the hot sweet liquid run over her tongue, managed a swallow.

"Thank you." Her voice came out in a breathy whisper.

The woman stood up.

"Are you two going to be OK? Are you sure you don't want me to call a doctor?"

"She's just come out of hospital."

"Oh pet, someone should have collected youse in a car. You shouldn't be travelling around on trains."

"There was a flower," Jen said.

"What, pet?"

"A white flower. Inside me. It was beautiful but the petals came apart, and it bled."

The woman frowned. "Are you sure she's..."

89

"It's OK," Ethie interrupted. "I've got us a taxi. I'll look after her."

The woman looked hard at Ethie, at her wimple, her young bare face, her jeans and trainers, and said, "Get her into bed as soon as you can, and don't do any more travelling for a while."

Chapter Eleven

Jamie had met her off the train in Oban. He was Aunt Barbara's husband, but he'd never been to visit Ely and Jen had never met him before. She saw his strong forearms, scrubbed nails and green eyes and couldn't imagine calling him Uncle.

He said, "You look like your aunt did as a girl."

As the days passed, Jen learned the sound of his footsteps on the path, the time he set his alarm in the morning. In the kitchen at breakfast, he wore his dressing gown, walked about in bare feet. Jen wondered if they might accidentally touch on the way to the sink or the toaster. She was on alert, her senses ready. She started eating.

She'd gone into the studio one day, out in the barn, and seen the painting he was making. A girl dancing in an orange dress who looked a lot like Aunt Barbara, but had flaming hair like her own.

When Barbara and the girls went to the beach for the day, she pretended she felt ill. Jamie was spending the day in the studio. She waited until the sun was high in the sky, put on her bikini and went to sunbathe on the grass in front of his window.

After twenty minutes or so, Jen was uncomfortable and bored. The pages of her book glared white and hurt her eyes. She grabbed her towel and wandered into the studio.

Jamie wasn't there. There was an empty mug on the floor and the room smelled of fresh oil paint, but he must have sloped off without her noticing. He'd changed the colour of the girl's hair, and the painting didn't look like her at all.

Back in the house, she put on her jeans and a baggy t-shirt and went through to the kitchen. Jamie was opening a can of tomato soup.

"I've boiled some eggs," he said, "and made soldiers. That's what my kids always like when they're poorly."

That day was the third time she'd seen Ethie. After lunch, Jen had gone straight to her room. She didn't come out until she heard the others come home from the beach. Jamie had called up the stairs, but she hadn't answered. She pulled the duvet over her head and shoved her fingers in her ears.

She was sharing a room with Lyddie though and couldn't stay there indefinitely. When Lyddie came up to get changed, Jen acted as though she'd just woken from a nap. She went to the bathroom and splashed her face, then joined the family in the kitchen.

Ethie was standing in the corner near the door to the pantry, in a place that never got light from the window. She was wearing a dark robe that covered her from head to foot. Just her mouth, nose and eyes shone white from the dark corner.

Jen looked at the others. They were all busy doing things. Jamie was putting a salad together at the table, Lyddie was getting cutlery from the drawer and Grace was checking something in the oven. Barbara wasn't in the room.

The figure wasn't moving, just standing still, her hands held together in the region of her lap, her head slightly bowed.

Barbara walked in from the garden carrying a handful of herbs, and Jen knew straight away that she saw her too. She didn't look into the corner where the girl stood, but straight at Jen. Her face had gone white.

Nobody else noticed. They carried on with their meal preparation, and after a moment Barbara seemed to come to herself.

"Mint for the salad," she said, handing the leaves to Jamie. She never once looked into the corner.

The girl stayed where she was while they ate their food, but when Grace went to the freezer to get ice cream, she moved, her feet taking tiny footsteps which made her seem to glide. She kept moving round the table until she was standing behind Jen, and put her hand on Jen's shoulder.

Jen tried not to gasp. Ethie's hand was warm and light through the fabric of her t-shirt. Aunt Barbara was sitting directly opposite. She scraped her chair back and stood up suddenly making everyone jump.

"Coffee, anyone?" she said loudly. When no one answered immediately she said, "What the hell, I'll have a whisky. Anyone else want whisky?"

The girl stayed with Jen all evening. She sat beside her on the sofa and followed her when she snuck outside to smoke one of Barbara's cigarettes. Jen ignored her, but Barbara was clearly agitated. The line on the whisky bottle went down. Jamie threw puzzled glances at them both.

At bedtime Jen said, "I think I'll go home tomorrow."

Everyone looked at her, but it was only her cousins, the two flesh and blood cousins, who protested. Both her aunt and uncle looked relieved.

It was after she got back from Scotland that she started to cut herself.

She drifted off, letting Ethie talk to the taxi driver. Behind her eyes she saw drifts of brown and red, bursts of stars which might have been streetlights they were passing.

They seemed to be in the taxi for quite a while. She hadn't thought Berwick was that big. Eventually it stopped and Jen opened her eyes. It was dark outside, but over to the right it was even darker, a huge spread of blackness, spotted by some lights far out. *Boats*, she thought. *The sea.*

The driver was saying, "Are you sure this is where you want dropping?" and "Is your friend alright?"

Ethie opened the car door and cold air rushed in, making Jen widen her eyes. Ethie helped her out and the taxi drove away. They were on a hilltop.

"Where are we?"

"Coldingham," Ethie said. "Come with me."

Behind them was a huge building. Ethie knocked on the front door loudly. After a few minutes, it was opened by a nun wearing the same coloured veil as Ethie. The details blurred for Jen after that. She was walked down some corridors, leaning on Ethie as her legs didn't have the strength to move on their own. It was quiet. Ethie and the nun spoke in hushed voices, but Jen paid no attention to what they were saying.

There was a small room with stone walls, and a narrow bed with white sheets. She was undressed and washed. By Ethie? By the other nun? She couldn't remember. She lay down on the narrow bed and fell into a deep sleep which seemed to last for days, although she didn't dream and there were no colours, only blackness and clear white light. She was somehow aware of the passing of time, and how things were changing. Her body was knitting itself back together in tiny stitches, one by one. She lay as still as a rock.

Bare feet walking, long skirt, cheesecloth, bells on a string, incense, hair swishing.

"We tell ourselves stories."

It's the same voice. Low, warm. A woman's voice. An island voice.

"Sometimes things are too difficult to remember, so we make up stories."

We're walking in grass, through fields, in the middle of the island. I can't see the grass. I can't see the fields or the bells, the skirt, the hair. I know them.

Today the smell is shampoo, chamomile, incense, sweat dried on skin. Today the voice stops speaking and sings songs to me. Here am I little Jumping Joan when nobody's with me I'm all alone Jack be nimble Jack be quick Jack jump over the candlestick Mabel Mabel strong and able take your elbows off the table

"Stories keep you safe. Here are some stories. Wrap yourself up in them, tie them tight. I will sing to you."

Little Miss Muffet sat on a tuffet Peter Peter pumpkin eater Mary had a little lamb a lamb a lamb a lamb a lamb

I can smell nothing hear nothing see nothing. I am wrapped tight. I cannot move. Nothing can hurt me.

Chapter Twelve

It was daylight and Jen was alone. There was a narrow window and a shaft of light shone into the room. She lay still on the bed and moved her toes, then her fingers, then her head from side to side. She was wearing some sort of nightdress made of white cotton. Tentatively, she slid her hand down her body and between her legs. She was wrapped tightly in bandages. Jen laughed out loud. *I'm wearing a nappy*, she thought. *They've put me in a nappy.*

The tightness was comforting. Her legs were bare beneath the cotton. She saw there was a cross on the wall, and that the window had no glass. Then she fell back to sleep and dreamed of Finn.

She'd tried not to think about Finn. This whole time, in Ely then York, at the hospital, on the train, the night-time taxi ride, the long dark sleep, she'd kept him out of her mind. But now he came to her in her dream. He was smiling and said, "Jen, Jen, you've got to come outside and see this. It's amazing. It's the best place I've ever been." She found it was easy to climb off the bed and hold his hand and follow him through the door. They ran down a stone corridor, then another. There was an archway at the end, and beyond that a great hall filled with nuns. They were chanting. The roof of the hall was gone, open to the sky and there were seagulls circling. The sky was blue.

"Look," Finn shouted to be heard above the nuns' singing. "Look at the sea."

She looked through the broken arches at the side of the great hall, and there it was, the sea, sparkling and reaching forever. Finn leapt onto the base of a broken pillar, and Jen sprang up after him. He enfolded her in his arms as they stood listening to the nuns' choir, the seagulls' cries and the hush of the sea on the shore.

The air was morning cool and touched her bare legs beneath the nightdress. She wrapped her arms around Finn's back.

"I'm sorry," she said.

He stroked her hair.

Ethie sat on the edge of her bed.

"I've brought you some soup." She wasn't wearing jeans anymore, but the full nun's outfit. She had something hanging on a chain from her neck that looked like a huge gold coin, but the folds of her robes partly covered it. It was thick and heavy. *That much gold would cost a fortune*, thought Jen.

"Do you think you could eat a little?"

Jen found she could sit up in the bed, and although her limbs were a bit stiff, there was no pain. She was excited about the soup. She was ravenous.

Jen slept for most of the next two days. Ethie visited regularly, bringing bowls of vegetable soup, hot crusty rolls and mugs of a steaming potion which tasted disgusting, but that Ethie told her would build up her strength. She remembered the days when she wasn't eating and how her periods had stopped. She wondered about refusing the soup, but it smelled so good and she was hungry.

On the third day, she woke up early and listened to the seagulls circling over the sea. When Ethie arrived, Jen told her she wanted to go outside.

"I'm not sure..."

"I just want to get some air."

They both looked at the window, which let in all the air you could want. Jen knew what the view was from the window because she'd got out of bed when she was alone. You couldn't see the sea, although you could smell it.

"I'll ask," said Ethie.

"Are there any books here? I'm a bit bored, I could do with something to read."

Ethie shook her head.

"Magazines? Anything?"

"No. Only the... There's nothing."

"Only the what?"

"I could bring you your bag. They'd let you have that."

"Who would let me?"

Ethie said nothing.

"OK. I won't ask any more questions. Yes please, I'd like my bag."

She knew the only books in there were the copy of *Dracula* that Finn had bought her in Whitby, and Baudelaire. She wasn't convinced that *Dracula* would be her thing and she didn't feel like tackling Baudelaire, but it was better than nothing.

Ethie came back later with the bag and a bowl of cherries.

"Did you ask about me going out?" Jen asked.

"Tomorrow," Ethie replied.

Jen leafed through Baudelaire but couldn't fix her attention on any of the poems. Her mind wandered to Finn, and she wondered where he was now. She'd lost count of the days, but it was more than a week since he'd gone to London. She tried to imagine sight-seeing with her own parents, but she couldn't picture either of them in the big city. Donna could never be away from the Church for long, wouldn't believe that they would cope without her. Steve's life was work, telly, pub – sometimes a game of Sunday morning footie with his mates. He never left his habitat. She could imagine Aunt Barbara and Jamie meeting up with Lyddie and Grace in London, Paris, New York. She put herself into that picture with them but could only think of herself as a hanger-on.

Finn would be in France by now. Jen thought about high mountain passes and eagles soaring overhead. That reminded her of the peregrine falcons in York Minster. She thought about walking in thin mountain air, of moving from one place to another, looking for openings in the cliff faces, hoping today would be the day they found something exciting.

She picked up *Dracula* and opened it at the beginning. Half a page later, she put it down again. There was enough strange stuff in her world. She didn't need this.

She went to the window. There was a view of a field, of fat cows grazing in the sunshine. In Ely, she'd got through her GCSEs on a diet of cream cakes supplied by her dad, crisps and breakfast cereal. She found it hard to eat in front of her mum.

The cows walked a few steps to a new patch of grass.

Jen left the window and tried the door handle. The door wasn't locked. Ethie must be out there somewhere with other nuns doing their daily stuff, whatever that was. Jen's knowledge of nuns came almost entirely from *The Sound of Music*. She went back to her bed and lay down, closed her eyes and tried to sleep.

When she got back from Scotland she'd phoned Rebecca, and they met down in the marina in the early evening. Rebecca was seeing one of the boys from the King's School and she talked non-stop, giving Jen all the details.

"Do you miss your mum and dad?" Jen asked, when Rebecca stopped for breath.

Rebecca's face closed up. It reminded Jen of when you twisted the pole of a venetian blind and the slats turned, closing off the world outside. Or inside.

Neither of them spoke for a minute or two. They watched the boats and the ducks on the water. Jen shuffled her feet against the wall. She'd never talked to Rebecca about food, and she didn't talk to her now about cutting. Some subjects were best avoided.

"You got any tobacco?" Rebecca asked.

Jen shook her head.

"Come on, let's go and find the others. Someone will have some."

The next morning Ethie arrived at Jen's room early. She'd brought porridge with raspberries and a spoon made of wood.

"They have strange crockery here," Jen said. "It looks really old. From a museum or something."

Ethie said, "We can go outside if you still want to."

Jen nodded, spooning the porridge into her mouth. "Has this got honey in it?"

"Yes, they have their own hives."

It was delicious. Donna used to make porridge sometimes, but it was always grey and solid, covered with gritty sugar. On the island they'd eaten porridge with salt. Jen would remember this breakfast.

When she'd eaten, she slipped on her trainers and Ethie opened the door. Jen hesitated before stepping into the corridor, but there was no one about. She remembered the dream where she'd run hand in hand with Finn. It had been like this, but older-looking, dirtier. The walls here glowed red-gold and the floor was clean, strewn with dried herbs. Ethie walked ahead, her robes sweeping the ground as she went.

They turned a corner and ahead there was the arch, just like in her dream. *I must have seen it when I arrived, stored it in my memory*, thought Jen.

But the great hall beyond the arch wasn't like her dream. It had a roof painted with scenes from the bible, framed by carved, white stone. The pillar she'd stood on with Finn wasn't broken and the walls were intact. Stained glass windows kept out the sight of the sea, although it could still be heard. There were no nuns. The hall was empty.

They crossed to a door at the back of the hall, which Ethie opened, and they were outside.

"The abbess suggested we go to the gardens to collect strawberries," Ethie said.

She picked up a basket from the step and set off around the sides of the church. *Or was it an abbey?* thought Jen. *A priory?*

The days fell into a pattern. Ethie would come to her soon after dawn with breakfast, and then they would go to the vegetable gardens where they would pick peas or beans or raspberries. Sometimes they went for a walk across the cow field to the woods, but Jen got tired quickly, so they never went as far as the beach.

Standing in the field, she watched the waves rolling in and realised they had become the background rhythm of her days. The sound of her breath, her heartbeat, crashing in, and in.

There were no other buildings near the priory – just a few cottages down the hill, a couple of miles away. It was remote and wild and some nights the wind howled around the walls, pushing cold fingers through Jen's glassless window, making her snuggle into the blankets. The coast was jagged and toothed, bitten into bays, washed by the sea. Some days the water was as blue as the flowers that grew around the priory walls, that Ethie told her were called alkanet. The nearest beach had a stretch of sand, then rocky outcrops spreading like tooth decay.

In the afternoons Jen slept, tried to read, daydreamed about Finn. Sometimes she thought about Danny walking the coast. He'd not been up this far, but she felt close to him here. She never saw anyone except Ethie.

"How long are we going to stay here?" she said one morning.

"Until you're well enough."

"I am well. Look at me. Rosy cheeks and everything."

"You need time to recover."

"Ethie, I'm bored out of my skull. This is a lovely place and all that, but I never see anyone except you. Most of the time I'm on my own, and there's only so many times you can read *Dracula*."

That afternoon when she woke from a nap, there was a copy of *Hello!* magazine on the end of her bed. She recognised the cover from that afternoon in the hospital in York. She laughed. Who'd have thought it? Her nun-cousin, a thief.

It was that night that she was woken from her sleep by the sound of loud knocking and a male voice raised in anger. The knocking went on and on. Then there were footsteps running in the corridor. Her door burst open and Ethie appeared, backlit by the lamps in the corridor walls. She was wearing her nun's habit and carrying a basket, full to the top, covered with a cloth.

"Jen, get your things, we have to go," she said.

Chapter Thirteen

They hid in the mouth of a cave on the beach until light began to creep into the sky. It smelled of seaweed and wet stone. Jen looked out across the flat sand.

Her cousin was crouching near the water's edge. Her head was bare and her hair was cropped short and uneven. From this distance she could have been a boy, except for the habit. She was holding her hand out, and Jen saw there was a bird on the sand a few feet from her cousin. It was smaller than a seagull, and a different shape – its beak pointed downwards. It had the distinctive profile of a bird of prey.

Ethie was still as a statue. The bird hopped closer, until it was next to her outstretched fingers. Still Ethie didn't move. The bird opened its wings and flapped them, but Ethie's hand stayed where it was. Then it flew up into the air and circled above her head. Ethie looked up at it. The bird circled again, then flew high into the sky. Jen could make out the straps dangling from its feet. Not a wild bird then. It flew higher and higher, then swooped down one more time, just feet above Ethie's head, before flying away inland.

Jen followed its flight until it disappeared from view, then turned her head back to look at Ethie. She was coming back up the beach towards the cave. Jen lay her head on her arms and pretended to be asleep.

"I can't come to Scotland with you."

Ethie had replaced the wimple and was standing in front of Jen with her hands on her hips.

Scotland. The island. Lyddie had invited her, but after that one text there had been nothing. She'd probably forgotten. Jen wasn't expected.

"Where are you going?" she asked Ethie.

"South. I have a friend in Norwich. I need her advice."

"What sort of advice?"

"I'm being followed. Jules will know what to do."

"Followed?"

"The man at the priory, last night.... He..."

"Who is he?"

Ethie shook her head and touched the gold coin which hung from her neck. "He... he's my..." She looked as though she might cry. She'd never looked anything but serene before. "I don't want to talk about it."

Jen stared at her cousin's face, then looked away at the sea, at the line where it met the sky.

"Will you get the train?"

"No, I'm sticking to the coast."

There was a boat, far out, catching the morning sun and glinting. It was hard to tell if it was moving. Jen looked back at Ethie.

"I'll come with you."

"I need to keep moving."

"I don't want to be on my own."

Ethie paused, then nodded. "No, that wouldn't be a good idea."

Half an hour later they were walking. They crossed the beach, climbed over the rocky headland and continued into the next bay. The beaches were pitted with rockpools where anemones blossomed and seaweed floated green and brown in the clear water.

The path headed inland through crops on the clifftops. The sun was above the horizon now. Jen sat down on a boulder at the side of the path.

"I need a rest," she said.

Impatience flashed across Ethie's face.

"I'm sorry. I've been lying about in bed for weeks, I'm not used to this."

Ethie softened. She'd kept the wimple on, and Jen felt more comfortable with her like that. Without it, she had seemed vulnerable, more human. Right now Jen needed someone she could depend upon.

"Of course. Sorry. It's just that he'll be coming after us as soon as he realises we're gone. The abbess won't be able to keep him out for long."

"You're not going to tell me who we're running from?"

Ethie shook her head, walked a few steps along the path, then back. "How long do you think you need to rest?"

"I'll be fine in a minute. Why are we walking? We could get a bus."

"It's safer," Ethie said.

Getting information from her cousin when she didn't want to give it was like the whole blood from stones thing. And most of the time Ethie didn't want to give it.

"Are we walking all the way to Norwich?"

Ethie shrugged.

"Have you got anything to eat or drink in that basket?"

Ethie pulled back the cloth and removed a stone bottle. She offered it to Jen.

"Small beer," she said.

"What?"

"Just drink it."

Jen took a swig and it reminded her of the alcohol-free beer Terence drank on social occasions. She didn't want to think about Terence. She handed the bottle back to Ethie.

"Are you ready?"

Jen could have done with sitting for longer or something to eat, but her cousin was already walking towards the stile at the end of the field.

The sun rose in the sky as they walked. Sometimes the path hugged the coastline, sometimes it took a detour around a bay, or crossed through fields on the clifftops. They didn't see anyone. They passed through a fishing village, but no one was about.

At one point the path went steeply downhill to a wide bay. As they descended Jen saw two people sitting on a wall near some Portaloos. The man was passing a flask to the woman who wore a yellow hat.

"Look," she said to Ethie.

"What?"

"Those people."

"Where?"

The sun flashed on the sea, making Jen squint. When she looked again, the couple had gone. The wall had people on it, but they were made of stone; tiny figures of women reaching out to the sea with their arms.

"There was a fishing disaster," said Ethie. "Those are the wives of the fishermen that died."

"No, not them…" Jen remembered the way Rebecca had looked at her at the Angel of the North, the photographs with no bodies in them. "Never mind," she said. "I probably imagined it."

The bay stretched in both directions, backed by the high cliff. The road and the beach were clearly visible, but there was no one about. No walkers, no one drinking tea from a flask.

"I think we've got a good start," said Ethie. "If he didn't see us leave last night, he'll still be watching the priory."

Jen looked at her cousin, the word *Who?* on her lips, but this time she didn't say it out loud. Ethie set off at a pace past the still-sleeping houses alongside the beach.

The path wound back uphill. Jen's legs ached, and she could feel a tugging in the tops of her thighs. She wanted to rest.

For half a mile Ethie had been looking behind, sometimes into the sky. Jen looked up too. The sky was periwinkle blue.

High above them a bird of prey was hovering, silvered by sunlight, like an aeroplane arrested in flight.

"We need to get out of sight," said Ethie. "Come on."

To their left was a small cove and a headland scarred with caves. At the furthest point was an arch, a scatter of rocks and stacks. A tiny path, probably made by sheep or rabbits, led down to the beach. Ethie scurried down, and Jen followed as best she could.

Jen's feet slipped on the sand and she grabbed at the vegetation, spiking her hands on gorse. Ethie was already at the bottom. She looked up at Jen, then at the bird in the sky.

"Come on," she said. "We need to hide."

Jen thought, *I could just sit down and refuse to move. I could cry. I could shout at her.*

She wiped her hands on her jeans, took a deep gulp of sea air, then carried on down the path, feeling carefully with each footstep, going as fast as she dared.

They hurried past caves and rockpools, out to the end of the beach where the rocks broke into boulders. Ethie held her hand out to Jen as they jumped from one to another. Between them the sea was lapping gently.

"Is the tide going in or out?" asked Jen.

Ethie looked up to where the bird was hovering. "This way," she said.

Jumping over ever widening strips of water, they passed under the stone arch and onto a rocky platform on the far side. It was studded with limpets whose points pressed into the soft soles of Jen's shoes. Ethie looked back.

"He won't be able to see us here," she said.

"I think the tide's coming in," said Jen. It did seem to be rising. As each wave crashed, less bare rock was visible. "Are we safe here?"

"He won't be able to reach us. Even if he does spot us, he won't be able to get across the water. Look, it's already cutting us off."

"Ethie, I'm not sure being cut off is a good plan. What if we end up underwater? Can you swim?"

"Look, these rocks up here have pockets of dry sand. The sea doesn't come up this far. We'll be fine."

"Maybe. If you're right. But how long will we have to stay here?"

Ethie pulled back the cloth from her basket and produced a punnet of strawberries. "Here, eat," she said. "You'll feel better."

Jen realised she was ravenous and shoved strawberry after strawberry into her mouth, until she saw Ethie wasn't having any. She pushed them back to her cousin.

The sun was high in the sky now. It was hot out on the rocks with no shelter. The water was getting closer and the rocks they sat on had become an island.

"Have we got any water?" Jen asked.

"Just this."

Ethie handed Jen the stone bottle of small beer. It was nearly empty.

"This isn't enough. We could be here for hours."

"I'll be fine," said Ethie. "You have it."

Jen took a tiny sip and handed it back. "We better make it last," she said.

There were seagulls circling above. Jen searched amongst them for the falcon, but the sky was too bright for her to focus. She was hot in her jeans, but glad of her white sports jacket. Thin and reflective, it kept the sun off her arms and shoulders. She pulled the collar up to protect her neck. If she needed to, she could unzip the hood from its pocket and cover her head as well.

Ethie's robes were made of thick, black cloth.

"Get down!" Ethie pulled Jen down behind the rocks. "There's someone up there."

Jen lay flat on her belly against the hot rock. As best she could, she peeped over at the shore. There were two people on the clifftops. One of them wore a yellow hat.

"It's the people I saw before," she said. "They're walkers. They're not after us."

"Over there." Ethie pointed to where the stone arch framed the portion of the beach where they'd come down. Someone was standing on the sand. The bright sun made it impossible to see them properly, but Jen thought it was a man. He seemed to have a bird on his arm.

"Who...?"

Ethie shook her head and put her fingers to her lips which were moving, possibly in prayer.

The man on the beach walked back and forth, looking out to sea, then back inland. After a while he sat down. The bird hopped onto his shoulder. The sun rose higher. The waves rushed in, near to Jen and Ethie's feet, as the area of dry rock got smaller and smaller. Jen could taste the strawberries in her stomach.

I'm so thirsty. She wanted to say it out loud. Surely he was too far away to hear. There were other sounds – waves, gulls, even the distant bleating of sheep in the fields. She lay still and didn't move. She said nothing.

It must have been nearly midday. The falcon was flying in arcs above the water. The tide hadn't turned, but the man on the beach got to his feet. He looked all around, then whistled. The bird came straight to him and landed on his shoulder. The man walked back up the cliff path, turning only once to have another look.

Jen glanced sideways at Ethie and saw her eyes were full of tears.

"Ethie..."

"Wait."

They watched until the man and the falcon had completely vanished from sight, then Ethie sat up. Jen ached from lying still for so long. She moved slowly to a sitting position, but her stomach cramped, bending her double.

"You need water," said Ethie.

They were surrounded by sea water, and they'd been lying on wet rocks. Their clothes were hot and dry on their backs, soggy at the front, sticking to their skin. Jen had never been so uncomfortable and despite herself she could feel saltwater leaking from her eyes as well.

Ethie pulled out the stone bottle, but it was practically empty. All they could do with the remaining beer was wet their lips.

Jen wished Rebecca were there to tell her there had never been any walkers wearing woolly hats in the sunshine and that she'd imagined the man and the falcon, to hand her a bottle of water from her bag – because Rebecca would never set off on an expedition like this without adequate water. But there was no Rebecca. Only Ethie.

Jen lay on her back on a dry bit of rock and pulled her jacket over her head to cover her face and keep her from getting burned. It wasn't a soft bed, but she was so tired it did the trick. Her wet belly up, she would dry off. She could sleep until the tide turned and they could get off these rocks. Her eyes half closed, she saw Ethie in silhouette through the thin fabric of the sports jacket. She was kneeling, facing inland, her hands clasped in her lap, her lips still moving.

Jen closed her eyes completely and sank into the red glow behind her eyelids.

Next thing she knew Ethie was shaking her arm.

"Jen, Jen, look!"

Jen sat up. Ethie was pointing to the wet place where they had been lying, where water was still running down the rocks in a thin sheen.

"What?" said Jen.

"The water. Look, it's still running down."

"And?"

"It wouldn't do that if it was sea water. The waves just go over, or they retreat. This is coming out of the rocks."

She was right; the water was coming from a small gap between two rocks. The stone beneath was dark and slimy and didn't look as though it ever dried out.

"So…"

"It's not the sea, it's freshwater. We can drink it."

Jen looked at the dark shine on the rocks, the streaks of algae, the seaweed and limpets which surrounded them.

Ethie was holding the stone bottle out to her.

"Here, have a drink."

It was heavy.

"Did you…?" If you held the bottle at just the right angle, you'd probably manage to redirect a bit of the flow where the water emerged from the rock. Maybe.

"I've tried it. It's fine to drink."

Jen didn't feel like she was in a position to argue. She lifted the bottle to her lips and the water was sweet and clear. She drank a few sips then offered it to Ethie.

"Have as much as you want," said her cousin. "We can refill it."

Jen drank, letting the water flow down her throat to sit heavy in her belly. She was immediately cooler.

She didn't quite drain the bottle before she handed it back to Ethie. The tide had turned while she was sleeping and it wouldn't be long until they could return to the beach. A patch of sand had been exposed and was marked by footprints. Jen looked at Ethie's feet, which were bare and sandy. The footprints appeared from behind the arch, formed a circle on the sand, then continued across the rock near Jen and Ethie. Jen blinked. It seemed as though the footprints carried on across the platform, indentations in the dark rock. The bright sun must have affected her vision.

Ethie was refilling the bottle.

"We'll be able to go soon," she said. "Half an hour, tops."

"Can we stop and rest now that guy's gone?"

"A friend of mine is on Holy Island. Another day and we should get there. Can you make it?"

"As long as I can sleep somewhere."

"We'll find a cave or something." Ethie looked up at the sky, and Jen followed her gaze. It was blue and clear. There were no seagulls flying, no birds of any kind. The only noise was waves rushing the beach. The sun beat on through the afternoon.

Chapter Fourteen

E thie's Holy Island friend wasn't what Jen expected. For a start, she hadn't expected to recognise him.

"This is Wolf," said Ethie.

"I've seen you," Jen said. "In York."

Wolf inclined his head. "I often have business in York."

They met on the far side of the island, away from the crumbling priory, beyond the castle, the bagpipes, the garden by Gertrude Jekyll, the tourists with their ice creams and selfie sticks.

Ethie and Jen had scrambled over a crumbling headland to find Wolf sitting on a rock halfway along the beach. He was wearing black leathers and biker boots, and his grey hair was tied back in a ponytail. He had long legs, long arms and a long nose. His wispy beard was darker than his hair and he was balding at the front. His lips were moving silently as he stared out to sea.

Ethie knelt beside him on the sand and put her palms together. Their lips moved in unison and their eyes were closed. Jen couldn't make out what they were saying but whatever it was, they both knew it by heart. She knelt down next to them and watched the waves crashing onto the beach. She hoped their prayers wouldn't go on too long. Picturesque as this place was, they'd be stuck on the island if they hadn't left before the tide came in, and Jen didn't want to get cut off again.

She hadn't felt any pain since she woke up. A few days before they left the priory, she'd stopped using the bandages. She'd felt held by them, but she was OK now, even though she was tired.

Her legs and her shoulders ached, and she wanted to lie down and sleep in the sun. Two days of non-stop walking had taken it out of her. But she was OK.

"Jennifer." Wolf's deep voice jolted her out of her reverie.

"Oh, everyone calls me Jen." Except her gran, and sometimes her mum.

"Jen." Her name sounded oddly truncated in his mouth. "We need to go."

As if it was me keeping them waiting, she thought, but she stood up, grabbed her bag from where it lay on the sand and followed Ethie and Wolf across the beach and through the dunes.

The tide was on the turn. Jen would have preferred to walk along the hard surface of the road, but Wolf set out across the sand.

"Is it safe?"

"If you follow the sticks, yes. Monks have been walking this way for centuries."

Jen fell in behind Ethie in her nun's dress and Wolf in his bike leathers. There was sinking sand if you strayed from the route. Her blue jeans felt hot on her legs, but her white jacket was cool. There weren't any cars on the causeway. She couldn't see any other walkers.

"No one else is crossing," she called out.

Ethie turned and smiled encouragingly. Wolf walked on ahead.

At the halfway point the water began to pool at the edges of the path. It seeped through the fabric of Jen's shoes; but they reached the mainland safely. A woman was standing on the beach. She was wearing a brown tunic over jeans. Her hair was cropped short, unevenly as though it had been hacked off with a knife.

"Oh God!" said Wolf. "The local saints!"

Ethie was trying not to grin.

The woman started waving as she walked in their direction.

Wolf looked at the path leading away from the beach, but the woman was almost upon them. There was no escape.

"Nadia," Wolf said, nodding.

"You're leaving already?"

"Egfrith and his men are out. We have to get some distance behind us."

"We can keep you safe on the island. There are hiding places. Berta is currently in seclusion at sea, but I will help you."

"The young ladies want to return to the south."

Jen looked at Ethie, but her lashes were lowered and her mouth clamped shut.

The woman frowned. Jen could smell her. The tunic was stained and stiffened. Her bare toes curled in the sand, brown from dirt or tan.

"There is much still to discuss between us," she said to Wolf.

"It will have to wait until another time."

"I am not convinced, as yet, that you are a suitable escort for these ladies. Is your heart pure?"

"My heart is beating in my chest, my back and my legs are strong, and if we can get hold of a bike, we can get some real speed. That is of more use to the ladies than fasting and prayers."

The woman bent her head. "She is still attached to the things of this earth. See the medallion about her neck."

"It is the medallion that has kept her safe thus far."

"It is God that watches over her."

"And as God's servant, I am going to get her away from these parts as quickly as I can."

Ethie had stopped smiling. She put her hand to her neck. The medallion was hidden beneath her shawl, but a glint of the gold chain showed.

Nadia nodded. "Perhaps distance will bring perspective."

"It will give us time to reflect."

"I can give you a ride to Bamburgh."

Behind the dunes was a battered red Toyota Hilux. They climbed in, and Nadia reversed the vehicle out onto the road, working the pedals with her bare feet.

"Hold on."

They needed to. Nadia swung the truck around the bends and put her foot down on the straight. Luckily there wasn't much traffic about, although a car beeped its horn as they sped out from a junction, and Jen's heart was in her mouth when they overtook a tractor coming up to a bend.

Then there was the huge dark shape of the castle, the village nestling in front and the sky wide open behind.

"You should be able to cover some distance from here, if you stick to the coast," said Nadia, as they jumped out onto the tarmac, shaking on their land legs.

The brakes screeched as she turned the truck around, then she drove off in a cloud of dust. They walked down the road, past the squatting castle, onto sand that stretched out flat and pale to the sea.

A week before Easter, Jen had arrived home from university. She let herself in and walked through to the kitchen at the back of the house.

"Steve?" her mum called from the living room.

"No, it's me."

Her mum appeared in the kitchen a few moments later. She had a needle and thread in one hand and a piece of blue felt in the other.

"Jen, what's the matter?"

"The matter?"

"Has something happened at college?"

"It's the Easter holidays."

Donna frowned. "Oh. Yes, I suppose it is." She looked back over her shoulder then down at the fabric in her hand. "Are you here for the whole week then?"

"Two weeks. Mum, what's up?"

"Nothing. It's lovely to have you. It's just…"

"I don't have to stay the whole time."

"No, Jen, of course stay as long as you like. It's your room, after all."

"My room?"

"Jennifer!" Terence appeared at Donna's side. "Have you come to help with the banner? Come, come, meet the team."

Jen found herself bustled through to the living room. Stella was sitting at one end of the sofa and a man was sitting at the other end. A huge banner was draped across their legs, and both of them were sewing pieces of felt on to the part where they sat. The man was young, blonde, good looking. The banner had the text *Jesus is King* marked out in pen, and they were filling it in with pieces of felt.

"This is Lee," said Terence. "I expect your mum's told you all about him."

Jen looked at Donna, who had the grace to flush.

"Lee's staying with us," her mum told her, "Just temporarily, until he can find somewhere else."

There were three bedrooms in the house: Jen's, Danny's and her mum and Dad's. Then there was Dorothy's room in the extension. There wasn't a spare room.

"I didn't know you were coming home," said Donna.

Lee said, "Oh, I can move out while you're here. I can sleep on the sofa, there's plenty of room."

He had a small beard and his teeth flashed white when he smiled. Jen wanted to hate him.

"Lee has just joined us," said Terence.

"Everyone's been so welcoming," said Lee. "I only arrived in Ely a few days ago, and I've never had so many friends."

"Lee has opened his heart," said her mother, "and welcomed Jesus into his life."

That was Jen's crime of course, that however many opportunities she'd been given, the door to her heart hadn't budged.

Lee's crimes had been petty and numerous and had landed him with a spell in jail, and it was there that he'd heard the knock at the door. A comment from one of the guards when he was leaving had sent him in the direction of Ely, searching for Terence whose name he had been given as a possible guide and mentor, which of course made him irresistible to Terence.

While Donna made tea, Lee went upstairs to move his belongings out of Jen's bedroom.

"Is it necessary?" asked Terence. "If Jennifer is only here temporarily, I'm sure there's no need to disrupt your guest."

"I thought you said Lee was only here temporarily," said Jen.

"Oh, I should think it would be a few weeks, maybe months. It's not always easy to find accommodation."

Jen went into the kitchen and watched her mother putting teabags into mugs, pouring boiling water from the kettle.

"Sorry love," said Donna. "You don't mind, do you?"

Jen opened the window of her room wide. She pulled the sheets off the bed and threw them out onto the landing. She found a joss stick in one of her drawers and lit it. She found a sock that wasn't hers under the bed and threw it out of the window.

She was remaking the bed with fresh sheets when there was a tap at the door.

She said nothing, but the door opened and Lee took a step into the room. Jen glanced at him, then looked away. His arms were heavily tattooed – snakes and dragons in red, black and green wound up and down his arms. He was wearing a brown t-shirt and jeans and his feet were bare.

"I just wanted to say I'm sorry," he said. "About the room."

She tucked in the edges of the sheet, then shook out the duvet cover.

"Do you want a hand?" asked Lee. "I always tie myself in knots with those."

"It's fine." She didn't want to show him gratitude. She wanted to scream at him to leave her alone. She wanted him never to have been there.

"They're all so kind," said Lee. "I've never had anyone be kind like this to me before."

His feet were brown and shapely, with golden hairs shining on his toes.

"They never told me you were so pretty," he said.

She pushed the door and he had to step back quickly so it didn't hit him in the face. She leaned her back against it, then her knees bent and she was sitting on the floor.

I wish Danny was here, she thought. *Everything would be different if Danny was here.*

Jen watched Wolf's legs scissoring across the sand with seemingly no effort. A triangle of sea appeared between the leather of his trouser legs, flash, flash, flash. Behind him, Ethie took smaller steps and seemed to glide across the sand in her robes, as though her feet were an inch above the ground.

"I don't know if I can go much farther."

Ethie and Wolf both turned around. The sea behind them swayed, the horizon lurching like water in a bath.

Wolf frowned. "We need to cover as much ground as possible before nightfall."

Jen looked at her cousin.

"Ethie, I can't..."

"Is there a place we can rest? Just for half an hour, so Jen can find some strength."

Wolf shook his head. "It's not safe here in the open. Egfrith will have his men out. We need to keep moving."

Jen nodded, and stepped forward. She was too tired to even ask him what he meant. Her feet were hot irons and her bones molten lead.

They'd walked from beach to beach, from Bamburgh to Seahouses, over hard sand and soft sand, crossing streams that cut channels down to the sea. Across a headland, then another headland into Beadnell Bay. Sun shone on the sea and shone on the sand. Jen's eyes hurt. She closed them and she could see bright red, flashed across with black. She remembered Rebecca getting migraines when they were younger. She opened her eyes again.

They took a path that led away from the beach through swathes of marram grass. The heat of the sand burned through Jen's soles. The grass tickled her ankles. Her hair was hot. Everything looked red and her eyes narrowed to slits. The ground tipped and she fell.

"She's not used to this," Jen heard her cousin's voice. "She's not been well."

Ethie and Wolf were leaning over her.

"Jen, have a drink."

Jen took the stone bottle and put it to her lips.

"You go on," she said. "They're not looking for me. I'll be OK. I'll find a village."

"No," said Ethie. "I'm not leaving you. It's my fault you're here."

"I'll carry you," said Wolf.

Jen laughed.

"I mean it," he said.

"I'm not a child," said Jen.

When they were children, Danny used to run around the garden as fast as he could with her screaming on his back until Donna came out to tell them to be quiet.

Wolf crouched down in front of her, presenting his leather clad back. "Climb on," he said.

Jen giggled.

Wolf was tall, and although he was thin, his shoulders were broad. She handed the bottle back to Ethie and got to her feet. She leaned into Wolf, wrapped her arms round his neck, and let him grab her legs as he stood up. She felt as though she were eight years old. She remembered walks along the river with Dad and Danny, getting tired on the way home. She looked over Wolf's shoulder at the path and watched his boots appear in her vision. Right left right left. The black leather was hot through her clothes. She could smell the herbal tang of Wolf's hair, and felt something she hadn't felt for a long time. Something that smelled of buttered toast, of gorse bushes, of lavender from the garden, dried and sewn into bags. Something that had been lost.

She felt safe.

Later, she wondered if she'd slept. Wolf's stride rocked her from side to side and she gradually let her weight sink against his broad back. Her skin stuck to his leather jacket, then peeled away a bit with each step making a rhythmic, tearing sound. Her legs hurt, pinned to his bony hips, but she ignored it; any bruising would be worth it. He and Ethie walked in silence, keeping to the coast, racking up the miles.

High Newton-by-the-Sea, Low Newton-by-the-Sea, Embleton Bay, Dunstanburgh Castle, Craster, Cullernose, on and on. Iron Mount, Sugar Sands, Howdiemont, Longhoughton Steel, Boulmer. Jen clung to Wolf's back, eyes closed, and she thought she could hear Danny's voice reciting the names.

Eventually, Wolf lowered her onto the beach and rubbed his shoulders. She thought about the dead weight of someone sleeping, and how dedicated to Ethie he must be to do this for her.

"We can stay here for the night," he said.

Jen looked around. Sand, rocks, the sea still quite far out.

"The sea doesn't come right up, only when there's a spring tide."

He led them up the beach and a gap appeared in the rocks, hiding a lean-to shelter. Inside were four beds made from mounds of dried grass and blankets. There was a small burned area at the front where someone had made a fire. Jen sank down onto one of the beds, and although the hay stuck through the blankets and pricked her skin, she didn't care.

A small river fed into the sea and Wolf and Ethie went to see if they could catch some fish. When they returned the sun was low in the sky, out of sight behind the cliff. They built a small fire. Jen lay on her prickly bed watching them, the nun and the biker cooking tea on the beach, the evening light casting a glow around them.

I know this can't be real, she thought. *I'm dreaming. I'm hallucinating. But I like these two, I'm safe with them.*

They called her when the food was ready. The oil of the fish soaked into the heavy bread which Ethie produced from her basket. Jen felt the blood moving in the muscles of her legs, the warmth of her skin after a day in sea air and sunshine. She felt heavy and clean. The sun sent out its last display of red and orange on the water, and then the sea went dark and they were bathed only in the glow of the fire.

Wolf went into the back of the shelter and found three small stone carved cups and a bottle of Jack Daniels. He produced a pack of playing cards.

"Poker?" he said.

"You bet," said Ethie.

They both looked at Jen.

"OK," she said, "but you'll have to teach me."

Jen had never been good at games, and she discovered she didn't have the face for poker. They played for pebbles, and as Jen's pile dwindled, Wolf's and Ethie's grew. They took less and less interest in showing her the ropes. As the bottle emptied, they became competitive.

Eventually, Jen dropped out of the game. She drained her whiskey and went back to her bed. The last she saw before falling asleep was Ethie's face, lit with the red glow from the fire, studying her cards with a focus that reminded her of her Aunt Barbara. She remembered one morning at dawn on the island, going down to the barn and seeing her aunt at work, thinking no one was up, shaping a piece of stone with her chisel, seeing nothing, not Jen, not the cat bathing in a patch of sunlight, nor the bird which flew in through the open door and flapped at the windows looking for a way out. Jen shooed at it with her jacket until it found the open doorway and flew into the sky. Barbara didn't look up once. When she saw Jen later at breakfast, she showed no indication that she'd seen her, but asked her if she'd slept well, and picked at the stone dust trapped under her nails.

Ethie must be Barbara's daughter, Jen thought. *She looks like her.* And she fell asleep with the sound of the waves in her ears.

Chapter Fifteen

Jen found herself liking Lee despite herself. He went out of his way to show her he knew he was the intruder, to apologise for taking her room. When her mum wasn't around, he made little jokes about Terence and Stella and the Church. He may have opened the door of his heart, but it hadn't shut off his sense of humour the way it had for some of them.

He talked to her about music, which he knew a lot about, and books, of which he knew very little, but was full of questions. He listened to her answers.

"What's your favourite book?" he asked.

"It's by Salinger," she said. "He wrote *The Catcher in the Rye*." She waited, but he said nothing. "It's called *Franny and Zooey*."

"Is it a romance?"

She laughed. "No. It's about a brother and sister, and about death and God and existential angst."

"What happens? Do they go on an adventure?"

"No. Nothing really. She – Franny, the sister – has a breakdown, and Zooey talks to her. She's much better at the end."

"You're not selling it to me." Lee laughed and looked at the books on the hallway shelf. "Choose a book for me to read. Something exciting."

He had been doing gardening work for some of the parishioners and his skin had caught the spring sunshine, tanned a shade darker than his hair. Jen wondered if tattoos darkened or faded in the sun.

In the mornings, Lee cooked breakfast – scrambled eggs or porridge or bacon butties, for himself and anyone else who was around. For years, the most Jen had eaten first thing was a bowl of cereal. Nobody had cooked breakfast for her since Dorothy had died.

She remembered the camping trip with Danny, the breakfast of fried eggs and bread eaten in a field wet with dew. How the next field had been quiet when the two of them packed up and left. On the way to the toilet block, she'd looked at the squatting, bright-coloured tents, imagined she could see the breath of the sleepers sucking in the canvas walls, pushing them out with the exhalation.

When the weekend arrived, Lee asked her if she wanted to go to the pub and she agreed. She wore white jeans and a white shirt with silver pumps. She put some lipstick on. When they left, Donna winked at her and Jen scowled back.

They sat in the beer garden so Lee could smoke. There were picnic tables and views across the river, and on a summer evening it would be packed, but it was April and there was still a chill in the air. There were a few smokers, but most of the noise came funnelled through the doors of the pub where people were eating.

Lee brought vodka chasers with their second pints.

Jen shook her head. "Not for me thanks."

"Suit yourself." He knocked them both back, followed by a long swig from his pint. "Do you reckon Tez and Stella are a bit kinky?" he asked. He took a rizla from the packet and made a line of tobacco along the centre.

"I've not thought about it."

"I reckon they dress up, like, as Jesus and stuff."

"Eugh! Don't!"

"And like, he blesses her while she sucks his dick."

"Stop it!"

He laughed out loud, then lifted the cigarette to his lips and licked the gum along its edge. "Maybe she ties him up with his arms out in a cross."

"Can we talk about something else?"

He flicked his lighter and the end of the cigarette flared, sending an orange glow across his face. As it died back again, he inhaled and the ends of the tobacco crackled and burned.

"Sorry."

By the time he'd finished his pint, she was less than halfway through hers.

"It's my round," she said.

"You bought the first one," he said.

"And you bought the second, so now it's my turn."

Lee frowned and stood up. "I'll get them." He disappeared into the pub before she could argue.

This time he only brought one vodka, but it looked like a double. He knocked it back in one. "What about Donna?" he said. "Do you think Terence is doin' her as well?"

"Donna's my mum," said Jen.

"Maybe they have threesomes."

"Lee..."

"Maybe they'll let me join in. She has a nice arse, your mum. I wouldn't say no."

Jen stood up. "I'm going home."

"You haven't finished your beer."

"You have it."

She walked across the beer garden. She knew he was watching her, but she didn't look round. She was near to tears and felt furious for letting him get to her. She walked quickly across the town, breathing in gulps of the fresh night air.

At home she let herself in quietly, so as not to be heard over the television, and went straight up to her room.

Despite the whiskey, Wolf was awake first in the morning. When Jen woke, he was crouching next to the fire, warming baked beans in a pan. Ethie was still asleep.

Jen sat up and circled her shoulders to get the blood moving.

"Good morning," Wolf said.

"I'm starving."

"Butter that bread, then we can eat."

Ethie lifted her head, groaned, and lay it down again.

"We should get going in half an hour," said Wolf.

"What time is it?" Ethie spoke into her elbow which she'd wrapped around her head.

"It's light."

"Water!" She extended her arm and stretched out her hand.

Wolf and Jen exchanged a glance. Jen picked up the water bottle and put it in Ethie's hand. Her cousin shuffled up onto her elbows and took a long swig.

"Are those the beans with little sausages in?" she asked, wiping her mouth with the back of her hand.

Wolf nodded.

"Good. And is there any fruit?"

Wolf reached into his backpack and pulled out a plastic pot of fruit salad. It was an individual-sized pot, the size of a yoghurt pot, with a cellophane lid.

Ethie grinned and held it up to look at the fruit inside.

"Melon," she said. "Strawberries, grapes, cherries."

"Have you been to a shop?" asked Jen.

"It's too early for shops," Wolf said.

"Then how...?"

"Scavenging."

Wolf spooned beans and sausages out onto three plates. Jen added a thick slice of bread to each one and handed them out. Ethie was stuffing fruit into her mouth.

"I shouldn't drink whiskey," she said around a large strawberry.

Soon they were on their way, having covered the fire with sand and scuffed over the marks of their feet.

"Are you OK to walk?" Wolf asked Jen.

"I think so," she replied.

"I'm not," Ethie grumbled. "Can you carry me today?"

"You need to get your blood moving," replied Wolf.

Jen enjoyed walking in the cool of the early morning.

They circled the town of Alnmouth, and then walked through the dunes at the edge of the beach. The sun was rising behind a bank of thin clouds which every now and then broke apart, letting the sunlight pool onto the sea. There were hundreds of birds on the beach, pecking at the sand, staring seawards, sometimes running at each other and squawking, flapping their wings.

"Godwits," Wolf told her. "Lapwings, redshanks, sandpipers, black-headed gulls."

The rest and food had done Jen good and her legs felt strong. She walked beside Wolf with her head up, breathing in the smell of seaweed and salt, warm sand, cool air. Ethie walked a few steps behind, saying nothing.

They walked through the town of Warkworth, past the castle and along the river to Amble, with its quiet boats and preening cormorants. They walked through the morning and into the noonday sun as they headed south down Druridge Bay. They saw an island with a lighthouse, which retreated into the distance as they walked across dunes and salt marsh, over wide expanses of sand. They walked at the edge of the sea, hopping away from the waves. They forded a river, and walked a broad path through a nature reserve and back out onto a stretch of white sand which stretched as far as the eyes could see in both directions. Ethie gradually perked up, but by late afternoon they were all tired.

"There's a cottage just near here where we can stay," said Wolf. "It's quite hidden."

It was in a hollow in the dunes with a path down to the seashore. It belonged to a friend of Wolf's and was practically empty – just an old wooden chair, a camp bed, a microscope. Wolf brought in armfuls of dried grass and a sweet-smelling plant that Ethie said was meadowsweet and covered them with blankets from the camp bed.

"I'll go and find food," he said, and left.

Ethie adjusted her head dress, removing the outer part and tying the underlayer around her head like a scarf. "I'm going to swim," she said. "Are you coming?"

Jen shook her head. Ethie untied the fastening of her habit and let it drop to the floor. Her underwear was white and reminded Jen of things she'd worn as a child. The knickers had a small oval flower design at the front and her matching bra was really a crop top. Her breasts were small.

Across her back, shoulders and thighs, were scars. Not like the scars Jen had on her legs and stomach, thin pink lines that shone silver if they caught the sun; these scars were much more recent, raw and red. In some places the skin was still broken, patched with dark scabs. Yellow bruises bloomed across the tops of her legs.

"Ethie!"

Ethie gave a quick grin, then ran out of the cottage and down the path to the sands. It was a huge beach, miles long, but they'd hardly seen a soul all day, only a couple of dog walkers. Jen looked out of the window and watched her cousin run into the waves until she was submerged, and just her head bobbed above the water, like a seal in a headscarf.

It was after midnight when she heard a tap on her bedroom door.

"Who is it?"

The door was pushed open, making a sharp right angle of light and Lee stepped into her room.

"I'm asleep," she said.

He pressed the light switch and she covered her eyes, blinded by the yellow glare.

"You're the only one worth talking to in this town." She could smell the alcohol, overlaid with the sweet smell of skunk.

"Please will you leave my room."

He walked over and sat on the bed.

"I've seen you looking at me tats."

"Lee, I was sleeping. I'll talk to you tomorrow."

"I've got more you know."

"I'm sure..."

"You wanna know where?" He flipped open the button at the top of his fly and shuffled on the bed.

"No, I don't."

He tugged his jeans down from his hips. "I didn't mean it you know. I don't really want to do your mum."

"If you don't leave right now, I'm going to scream really loudly."

"Oh, you don't wanna do that." He lurched towards her, trying to find her face with his. She pushed and he fell off the bed, his trousers hanging off his arse, a green dragon sliding out of his black pants and down his inner thigh.

Jen leapt out of bed and opened the bedroom door wide. "Get out."

He got to his feet and shuffled out of the room holding his his fly closed with one hand. "You sure?" he said, turning back. She slammed the door in his face.

The next day, she found Steve in the kitchen eating a bowl of cornflakes before going to football.

"Dad, can you put a lock on my bedroom door?"

Donna appeared from behind the cupboard door. Jen hadn't realised she was in the room.

"Why on earth would you want that?" she said.

Steve wiped the back of his hand across his mouth. "What, like a bolt?"

"Yes, a bolt would be fine."

"Why do you want to lock yourself in?" Donna stared at her.

"I'll see if I can pick one up in town later."

"No, you won't. Why would she want to lock herself in? What does she want to do in there?"

"I'd just feel more comfortable, Mum."

"Well, I don't want it. You're not even here most of the time, and I don't want any locked doors in this house. That's final."

Steve tipped the bowl towards himself and spooned the last of the milk into his mouth. He stood up and took his bowl to the sink. "I'm off then. See you later."

"Don't bother going to the hardware shop," said Donna. "You'll be wasting your money. I'm not having any locks in this house."

Steve ruffled Jen's hair and left the room. She knew what would happen. He'd buy a bolt, Donna wouldn't let him fit it, and it would end up out in the garage.

I could just go back to York, she thought. But it was Easter, and the university would be deserted. *Or I could push something across the door.*

Chapter Sixteen

Jen wasn't at all sure that she wanted to return to East Anglia, but she told herself she didn't need to go all the way with Ethie and Wolf. This way she could look for Danny. For the moment she was happy to go along.

But she hadn't expected to find herself in a nightclub in Newcastle upon Tyne. She'd assumed they would skirt the cities or cross them quickly in the pre-dawn hours after the last revellers had gone to bed, before day began – Ethie never did what Jen expected.

"We're going into town," she said. "Do you want to come?"

"You can stay here if you like, we'll be back before dawn," said Wolf.

She could sleep of course, but the idea of a night alone in the cottage didn't fill her with joy.

"What are you going to do?"

"There's a club we know," said Ethie.

Her cousin had taken off the robes and put her jeans back on. She'd found a white blouse from somewhere – long sleeved, soft cotton with demure pearl buttons. Jen had only seen her bareheaded once before – that unguarded moment on the beach when Ethie didn't know Jen had seen her. Her hair was brown, cut short around her ears like a small boy's. Jen guessed she'd cut it herself. She looked incredibly young.

But when they got into the city it was Ethie who took control, choosing a bar, then another, trying different cocktails, choosing songs on the jukebox. Wolf followed her and watched, keeping an eye on her.

"How come you know Newcastle so well?" Jen asked when the last bar closed its doors and threw them out into the street.

"I've spent a lot of time in Newcastle," Ethie said, putting the stress on the middle syllable, hiccupping afterwards. "The next place is the best."

The next place was a black door between two warehouses in a street of industrial buildings. Wolf knocked, and Jen wondered if it was a special knock; it sounded as though it had a pattern to it. The door opened and someone said, "State your business."

"Revelry, gambling and fornication," Wolf replied.

"God's blessings be upon you."

"And on this house."

The doorman was dressed as a monk. The three of them stepped inside, and the door closed behind them. The monk led them down a short corridor and through another heavy door, and they were in a nightclub. There was a small stage where a woman in a gold dress was singing "Cry Me a River". There were tables scattered about, most of them full, and a small dancefloor where a couple were smooching to the music. There was a bar at the other end of the room, and waiters moved between the tables. The air was cloudy, and at first Jen thought it was dry ice, before her nostrils caught the scent and she noticed people were smoking. Each table had an ashtray on it and some of them were full to overflowing.

"What is this place?" she asked.

"It's called Dissolution," said Ethie.

"Dissolution?"

"It's been here for years, but you have to know about it."

"What was all that stuff at the door about fornication?"

"It's a password. Don't worry, you don't have to fornicate – not unless you want to." Ethie let out a peal of laughter, then tugged at Wolf's arm. "The music's a bit slow. Will you ask them to speed it up?"

Wolf led them over to a table where there were a couple of spare seats. A waiter appeared and asked if they'd like a drink.

"I'd like a Harvey Wallbanger," Ethie said loudly, and burst into laughter again.

"And Madam?"

Jen hadn't been putting it back like the other two, but she'd had a few beers and she wasn't much of a drinker at the best of times.

"Oh, just a Coke please."

"Coke! Don't mind if I do!" Ethie laughed again.

Jen stared at her cousin. She was jittery, energetic, brittle, but Jen was sure she hadn't taken any drugs. It must just be the drink, the excitement, nervousness about Egfrith, whoever he was.

Jen looked around the table. A couple wearing evening dress were on one side kissing passionately; they had no eyes or ears for anyone else. Two bikers on the other side, both wearing leather with long beards and ponytails, were watching the singer and didn't seem to notice the new arrivals at their table.

"Where's Wolf gone?" Jen had to speak loudly in Ethie's ear to be heard above the music, and Ethie giggled.

"He's gone to fornicate," she said even more loudly. There was a pause in the music just at that moment. The bikers looked their way and smiled. The couple carried on kissing. Ethie put her hand over her mouth and hiccupped.

"Whoops!"

"But I thought..." Jen had thought the drinking and the poker were aberrations. Her mother never drank. Terence preached temperance at the Church of the Friends of Jesus, but she knew other denominations were not so strict. Catholics, for example, Anglicans, liked to tipple now and again. This was something else.

"Is this a brothel?" she asked, making sure she spoke when the singer was in full voice.

"No, ha ha, no. You can't really fornicate here, not unless you do it in the toilets."

"Then..."

"Wolf has a loverrr! He owns this place. They'll have gone to his office."

The waiter appeared with the drinks and Ethie was delighted with her cocktail. It was garnished with wooden sticks laden with slices of orange, cherries and mint leaves. She took one of the sticks out and examined the fruit carefully, touching the rind of the orange, the sticky surface of the cherries.

Jen sipped her Coke and looked around the room. A few more people were dancing now, but mostly they sat in small groups at their tables, chatting, smoking, listening to the music. Some, like the couple at their table, were entwined, their hands moving over each other's bodies, seemingly oblivious to the rest of the room. A lot of them were in evening dress: long dresses with plunging necklines, in fabrics which glowed and glittered in the lights from the stage and bar; the men in suits, dress shirts, bow ties. There were also quite a few bikers, and some people like her and Ethie in ordinary clothes.

She noticed someone come onto the stage and speak to the singer. The woman nodded to the band, and they started up again with a fast dance tune. Jen didn't know what sort of music it was, but it seemed to go with the clothes and the smoke and she wondered what era she'd found herself in.

Ethie cheered. She'd eaten all her fruit and now she drank half of her drink in one swallow and leapt to her feet. "Come on, Jen, let's dance."

Lots of people had the same idea, and in moments the dancefloor was crowded with people jumping and spinning, swinging their partners and jumping in the air. Ethie was leaping up and down in some sort of frenetic pogo. Jen shuffled to the edge of the dancefloor. She couldn't do this sort of thing. She'd seen YouTube clips of northern soul dancers' acrobatics, and what these people were doing was every bit as amazing, though the music was older. Ethie had found a partner now, and he was spinning her round and round until she fell back dizzy into his arms and slid down to the ground in a graceful arc between his open legs, then she was back on her feet shimmying and shaking. Jen thought, *this must have always happened. Why would it be new, why would people only want to dance like this in the past seventy years? It must have happened since time immemorial.*

She stayed at the edge of the dancefloor, watching as the band moved from song to song and the dancers developed a slick of sweat. Jen noticed that the floor was covered with white powder.

She saw Wolf standing near the stage watching the dancers, and next to him was a man in a brown leather jacket and jeans with neatly coiffed hair and a gold chain at his throat. They were standing close so that their upper arms were touching. Ethie might have been wrong, of course. They might have just been chatting. Still, Jen felt herself colouring and looked away.

Then someone grabbed her hand. She was pulled into the melee, she was spinning and falling, but before she reached the floor she was up again, and she found that her feet were moving despite herself and she felt her face split into a grin. She'd never been much of a dancer. She and Rebecca went to clubs occasionally, and sometimes she was persuaded onto the dancefloor, but she hadn't enjoyed the heaving bodies all around her and the smell of sweat. Finn had laughed at her when she told him, told her he'd take her out sometime and they could let their hair down. "You need to learn to lose control," he'd said, but they hadn't had the chance.

This was different though. In the clubs she'd been to, everyone was zoned into their own experience, jostling, bumping up against people who had nothing to do with them, cheek by jowl with strangers. Here, everyone seemed to work together as a whole. Jen didn't know what she was doing but it didn't matter because everyone else did, and she knew that if she fell, someone would catch her and the dance would go on.

Even so, she tired quickly. After a few songs she excused herself and made her way back to the table. Ethie seemed like she could go on forever, moving from one partner to another, her short hair standing up on end now, spiked with sweat. Wolf and his friend had disappeared again. The snogging couple from the table were on the dance floor and the bikers had moved into a clinch. Jen closed her eyes. There was so much to take in, and she was tired. The music continued, but she welcomed the blackness of not seeing.

"We tell ourselves stories so we can be safe."
I can smell the shampoo that you use. It smells of chamomile. You make it yourself from plants that grow on the island.
How do I know what is a story and what is real?
Is Ethie my story?
I can smell strawberries, I can smell sweat, I can smell skin, I can smell whisky.

Wolf nudged her and she opened her eyes. The club was emptier, the singer had left the stage and the band were playing quietly while couples smooched on the dance floor.

Ethie stood next to Wolf. Her blouse was drenched with sweat and Jen noticed that her nipples showed through the fabric. She'd smoothed her hair back so it looked gelled into some sort of teddy boy style.

"I can't believe you went to sleep." She grinned at Jen, and her voice sounded more like the one Jen knew.

"Come on," Wolf said.

Jen followed them across the club. The bikers were on the dance floor with their arms around each other, heads on each other's shoulders, swaying slowly, and the woman and her man were kissing again.

If Rebecca were here, she'd say, *God, get a room can't you?*

Wolf opened a wooden door next to the bar that Jen hadn't even noticed. Then the darkness of the club was gone and she was in another place. This room was bare; stone walls with no decoration, the only window a small vent high up on the left wall. The floor was concrete. There was a long wooden table with benches down each side, where three men and two women were sitting. The table was littered with glasses, bottles, ashtrays and playing cards.

"Poker?" she whispered to Ethie.

"Yes," Ethie said, her eyes sparkling.

An hour and a half later, Jen was pretty bored. She'd joined in the game, but the rest of them were serious players and she was out of her depth. They were playing for small white chips, of which there were piles on a table at the side of the room. They'd all started off with ten for free, but if they wanted more they had to pay for them. One of the women was keeping a tally. Once Jen had lost all ten of her chips, which didn't take long, she dropped out.

Ethie had changed. The drunkenness had gone and she was intense; her face was unreadable and her hands holding the cards were still as stone. A bottle of Jack Daniels passed around the table and everybody drank except Jen. Gradually other people dropped out of the game. Wolf threw his hands up in the air.

"I'm out."

There were just three of them left now: Ethie, Wolf's partner, Jerry, and another man called Beau, who had greeted Ethie and Wolf by name. Ethie was on a bad streak, down to her last few chips. Beau pushed three piles into the middle of the table. He poured another round of whiskey.

He was a strange-looking man with a huge floppy bow tie, a waistcoat and a jacket with a high collar. His eyes were very dark and seemed to be watching everyone at once, without moving. His hair swept back from a high forehead.

Jerry and Ethie looked at their cards. Jerry shook his head slowly, then laid his flat on the table. Ethie knocked back her whiskey in one.

"I'll raise you," she said.

Beau smiled. "You seem to be out of funds."

"I'll take three more piles of chips."

"You are very sure of yourself." There was a hint of an accent in his voice. German? French? Jen couldn't quite place it.

Ethie smiled at him, a full smile which made her eyes sparkle.

"Ethie," said Wolf, in a worried tone.

"I'm sure," she said.

The woman keeping tally brought the new chips over to Ethie, who pushed them into the middle of the table. There was a silence in the room. The two card players focussed on each other. It seemed to Jen that there was a kind of hunger in Beau's face. Ethie seemed carefree and confident, but when Jen glanced at Wolf, she saw him grab Jerry's hand.

Beau turned his cards over. He had a royal flush.

Ethie deflated before their eyes. Slowly, she turned her cards over. Full house: two kings, three queens.

Beau leaned forward and made a show of examining her cards. After a few moments he looked up at her.

"It seems that you owe me quite a lot of money," he said.

Ethie was staring at the cards as if willing them to be different.

"I don't have it now. I'll get it for you."

"I'll take that gold medallion you always wear around your neck."

Ethie lifted her gaze to meet his. "I don't know what you're talking about."

"Oh yes you do. It has a cross on one side and a lamb on the other."

"Oh, that. I used to own that, but I haven't got it now, so I can't give it to you."

"I don't believe you. I have it on good authority that you wear it at all times."

Ethie pulled at the neck of her blouse, exposing first one shoulder, then the other. "Look, it's not here."

Beau closed his eyes. When he opened them, he looked across the room, away from Ethie. "It will be about your person somewhere."

"What are you going to do, strip me and search me? Even you aren't that low, surely."

Beau stood up and walked across the room, his boots clacking on the concrete. When he spoke, his back was turned. "There are better things I can do. I know someone who's looking for you and I heard he's in Scarborough at the moment, not far from here. I have his mobile number right here and I can just give him a call. Is that what you want me to do?"

He spun round and held out his phone so that Ethie could see the screen. She went white. His thumb was hanging over the call button.

"No," she said. "Don't." She looked around the room, at Wolf and Jerry, at Jen, at the others sitting still as statues waiting to see which way this would go. "I'll get you the money – I promise."

He pressed the call button, put on the speakerphone so they could all hear it ringing.

"Please don't," whispered Ethie.

Then someone answered. A voice said, "Beau, Beau, is that you?"

Ethie pulled the medallion from her jeans pocket and flung it onto the table.

"*Bonsoir*, Egfrith, pardon me, I believe I sat on my phone." Beau ended the call, picked up the medallion and put it in his jacket pocket. The game was over.

Ethie was crying. Beau opened a new bottle of whiskey and walked around the room filling people's glasses. Wolf put his hand over the top of his. "We're leaving," he said.

"Oh, such a shame, we were having such fun. There are still some hours of darkness to enjoy before the daylight comes."

Outside, Wolf and Jerry hugged, then Jerry turned to Ethie and hugged her as well. She was snuffling like a child.

"Don't worry," said Jerry. "Something will be done. The medallion will be returned to you."

Ethie sniffed. "Thanks, Jerry."

The three of them walked away. Jen put her hand into her pocket. "I have this," she said. On her palm, the medallion glittered in the streetlight. Wolf and Ethie looked at her in astonishment.

"How...?"

"When...?"

"I took it from his pocket when he was pouring whiskey."

Ethie hiccupped, then laughed.

"Bloody hell," said Wolf. "Good thing I know how to hotwire a bike."

Chapter Seventeen

Danny had been offered a place at university and come September he'd be moving to Cambridge. It wasn't that far from Ely, but Jen felt like he was going to the other side of the world.

Before he left home, he was going to walk the Cleveland Way as part of his gold Duke of Edinburgh Award. The night before he left, they went for a walk down by the river. It had been a nice day and there were still tourists about, stopping on the bridge to look at the boatyard, sauntering past weeping willows where a grassy patch of park met the riverbank. Behind them were the cathedral gardens and the building itself, turning the rest of the town to Lego. Danny and Jen sat on the steps in front of a waterfront bar. A couple walked in front of them. The man had his wallet in the back pocket of his jeans.

"I could steal that," said Danny.

"He'd notice."

"I bet he wouldn't."

"What will you bet?"

"My leather jacket."

Jen had tried Danny's jacket on before, posed in front of the bedroom mirror. It was a biker jacket, way too big for her, and black, a colour she never wore. But when she'd looked at herself, hidden inside the leather like a child dressing up in adult's clothes, she hugged herself, breathed in deeply. The jacket smelled of patchouli and of Danny. He'd bought it second hand in a shop in Cambridge when he went for his interview.

"So, if he notices you'll give me your jacket."

"Scout's honour."

"What if he calls the police?"

"He won't."

"How do you know?"

"Because he won't notice me take it." The couple stopped to watch some ducks on the river. "Come on."

They went down the steps, veering left behind the couple. Jen found she was holding her breath, but nothing happened. There was no sudden shout, and Danny was swinging his arms by his sides. When they reached the bridge, Jen breathed out and laughed. "Chicken," she said.

Danny held out his palm and on it was the man's wallet, fat and brown and stuffed with cash.

"How the hell did you do that?"

"Told you," said Danny.

"I don't believe it."

The couple had started walking again and were nearly abreast of Jen and Danny. The woman was talking and the man was smiling. They didn't seem to notice the two of them leaning against the wall as they walked past.

"Danny!" Jen said under her breath.

"Excuse me." The couple turned as Danny caught up with them. "I think you dropped this."

The man took the wallet with a look of astonishment. "Oh, thank you."

"I told you," said the woman. "It's not safe in your pocket."

The man was looking at the wallet. "I don't know what to say. You've saved me a lot of trouble. Can I give you a reward?"

Danny shook his head.

"You must," said the woman. "It would have ruined our trip."

"No, I just saw it fall. I didn't do anything."

The man had taken out a twenty-pound note and tried to put it into Danny's hand, but he wouldn't take it.

"Please. It would make me feel better. Take your girlfriend for a drink with it."

Jen was trying not to laugh. The words, "He's my brother!" burst out of her.

"Well, take this and make sure he gets something nice with it," said the man, and he shoved the note into Jen's palm. "Young men like you," he said to Danny, "restore my faith in humanity. Thank you."

"You have a wonderful brother," said the woman. They turned and walked away. The woman took the wallet from the man and zipped it inside her shoulder bag. Danny looked appalled.

"We can't keep it," he said.

"My brother the thief," Jen grinned.

Danny snatched the money from her and chased after the couple. They turned and Jen saw him gesticulating, then them reluctantly accepting the money. They walked on out of sight and Danny returned.

"What did you say?" asked Jen.

"I asked them to give it to charity."

"Cool."

"I get to keep my jacket though."

"You could have a career doing that," Jen said. "Will you teach me?"

Wolf stopped the bike outside the cottage. "Get what you need and be quick."

The girls ran inside. Jen grabbed her books from her bed, stuffed them into her backpack along with some clothes that were lying about. Her dead mobile was already in the bag with her wallet. She didn't have anything else.

Ethie had rolled up her nun's clothes and was trying to fit them into her basket.

"How are you going to carry that on a bike?"

Ethie frowned. Ever since she lost the medallion she'd seemed confused and scared, and for the first time Jen felt like she was in charge.

"Put them in here," she said, holding out her backpack. "If we stuff everything down, we'll get it in." Then they were back on the bike, roaring off into the night, Jen at the back clinging to Ethie for dear life.

They stuck to country lanes, zigzagging this way and that, and Jen had the feeling they were going south, but she couldn't be sure. It seemed like they were travelling through the night forever, but when they stopped it was still dark. They were next to a bus stop in a village.

"We'll leave the bike here," Wolf said. "I'll let Jerry know, he'll get it back to the owner."

"What are we going to do?" asked Jen.

"The first bus will be along soon," said Wolf.

Light was coming into the sky. Ethie sat on a doorstep with her head on her knees. Anxiety or a hangover kicking in. Most probably both.

Wolf sat on the bus stop bench, his hands in his lap, his lips moving. Jen sat next to him and watched a pair of cats stalking their night-time territories.

"What are you saying?" she said after a while.

Wolf let his voice become audible. "Lord Jesus Christ, have mercy on me, a sinner. Lord Jesus Christ, have mercy on me, a sinner."

"That's the Jesus Prayer," Jen said. "That's the thing they say in *Franny and Zooey*."

He smiled and nodded and kept saying the prayer, silently without ceasing.

By the time the bus came there were quite a few other people waiting, men and women in dark coats and overalls, heads down, still with the smell of sleep about them. They nodded to each other as they arrived and cast curious glances at the three strangers. Nobody spoke.

The bus was full. Jen, Ethie and Wolf went to the back and sat crammed on the seat either side of two surly men and a woman who had nodded back to sleep.

Although it had begun to get light, the yellow glow inside the bus threw the outside world back into darkness. Jen couldn't see anything except when they passed through a village. More people got on and, by the time they reached the outskirts of a town, the aisle was crowded with people standing, holding onto the backs of seats and the overhead bar to keep themselves from stumbling as the bus turned sharp corners, raced round a roundabout.

Jen couldn't see Wolf and Ethie on the other side of the passengers. Surrounded by strangers, hurtling through the failing dark, coats and hats reflected in bus windows, she felt the world falling away from her. *I could be anyone*, she thought *None of these people know me.*

The bus stopped outside a huge factory and all the other passengers got off, leaving the three of them alone at the back of the bus. *I could follow them into their lives. No one would ever find me.* Ethie had fallen asleep, her head dropped onto Wolf's shoulder. His head was bowed but his eyes were open, and his lips were still moving. The bus rattled its way into town through the empty streets.

The bus turned sharp left and Jen saw a sign for Middlesbrough Bus Station. They pulled in beside a long glass and concrete shelter and the three of them got off, stumbling with tiredness.

Wolf steered them to a small café with Formica tables and ordered strong coffee and egg butties all round.

"We've got a head start," he said, "but we need to keep moving. The moment Beau notices the medallion isn't in his pocket, he'll be after us. If we're lucky he won't notice for a while, but he could have spotted it straight away, so no rest I'm afraid."

"Could I have a banana?" said Ethie.

Wolf glanced round. A bowl of oranges and bananas and apples was sitting on the counter. He gave Ethie some coins and she went up to the counter.

"Are you going to be OK?" Wolf asked Jen. "No more taking it easy."

"I'm sorry."

"Sorry?"

"Sorry I took the medallion. I don't know what came over me, I was just angry at the way he'd been with Ethie and did it without even thinking, and now I've got us into all this trouble."

"Jen, you have no idea. We, Ethie and I, especially Ethie, are completely in your debt. OK, we're running, but it would be a lot worse if Ethie had lost the medallion."

"Why?"

"It's a long story, but let's just say there's someone who would like to hurt Ethie, cause her harm, and that medallion is her protection."

"Is it magic or something?"

"In a way. It's symbolic. Its power is in what it represents."

"Is it Egfrith?"

"Yes, that is his name."

"And this Egfrith believes in the medallion, does he?"

"Oh yes. If she lost it and he got to hear about it, she'd be in a lot of trouble."

Ethie sat back down with her banana. She held it in both hands then laid it down on the table and ran her finger along its length. She looked up at the other two and grinned.

"Bananas are amazing. I can never get over bananas."

"Why do you say the Jesus Prayer?" asked Jen.

Ethie was peeling the fruit, looking at it, lifting it to her mouth, in a way which would have seemed suggestive in another person. She looked like a child with a treat. Jen remembered the night before in the club, the cocktail with the cherries and oranges.

"Remember Nadia? Who gave us a lift?" said Wolf. Jen nodded. "She and her sister, Berta, they live on islands, shut themselves away from the world in the hope that that way they will find God."

Ethie pulled the last piece of the banana out of the skin and put it in her mouth. "Ascetics," she said with her mouth full.

"They believe that if they control their surroundings, eat simple food, have few clothes or possessions, then they will be closer to the divine."

"You don't agree?"

"I believe we carry God within us. That we can live in the world and still have that connection."

"And the Jesus Prayer?"

"Is a way of strengthening that connection. I hope. Like breathing brings oxygen to the body, praying without ceasing can make you one with God."

"How long have you been saying it?"

"Not long enough." He looked at Ethie who had finished her banana, then out at the bus station which was bathed in daylight. "We need to get going," he said.

They caught another bus out of the city. Ethie was still wearing the jeans and white shirt from the night before, and in the morning light, with her short hair standing on end, she looked younger than ever. Jen sat next to her, and Wolf on the seat in front. Ethie was looking out of the window, pointing every now and then to things that caught her attention – a horse, a bad-tempered looking sheep, a pointed hill that Wolf said was named Roseberry Topping.

Jen thought about the marks she'd seen on her cousin's thighs and stomach, about Egfrith whom they were running from, and Beau whom they'd cheated at poker, and she wanted to put her arm around Ethie. She'd never had a younger sibling. Lyddie and Grace were both younger than her, but they were different. They didn't need her. Lyddie was blonde and confident, as good looking as her father, and Grace was a sculptor. She was sixteen and didn't care what she looked like. She tramped around the island in wellies and an old fisherman's jumper and produced work that had art colleges fighting over her. Jen was a bit scared of her. Ethie wasn't like them.

Jen stretched out her arm and took Ethie's hand. Her cousin turned and looked at her. After a while she looked back out of the window, but she didn't remove her hand.

They got off the bus just before it reached Saltburn and walked into the edge of the town underneath a huge redbrick viaduct.

"Where are we going?" Jen asked.

"We'll keep moving south," said Wolf. "Stay out of towns. Walk in the mornings and the evenings. Beau and Eg, they'll both be looking for us."

"We can find sanctuary in Whitby," said Ethie.

Jen had arrived back at university on Easter Monday. She hadn't told anyone at home what had happened, or that she was leaving. She walked across campus and didn't see a single person, only ducks, geese, swans.

She let herself into her room and lay down on the bed. She listened. Normally there was a constant hum of traffic from the main road, but this was a bank holiday. A crow called from the tree outside, and there was a flurry of quacking and splashes from an altercation at the lake. The sky was grey with low hanging clouds. Jen pressed into the mattress. She lay still, listening, until it got dark, and then she fell asleep.

When she woke, she was in the same position on the bed and the dark was fading. She hadn't eaten since she left home yesterday morning. Her stomach hurt. In the communal kitchen she looked in the cupboards, the fridge. There wasn't much food. She found hash browns in the freezer and put them under the grill. There were frozen peas and half a tub of Haagen Dazs, spaghetti, three tins of baked beans, some cream crackers, half a box of Coco Pops. She ate the hash browns with her fingers, sitting on the floor in front of the fridge.

Later, when it was dark, she went outside in her pyjamas and bare feet. She tiptoed across the bridge and between the buildings, past the handkerchief tree, and round the corner to where the Buddha sat. She sat down, facing him, her legs crossed.

They left Saltburn along a red sandy path which climbed up the edge of the cliff. The sea was shining in the morning sun. The path had a sign engraved with an acorn.

"What's that for?" asked Ethie.

"It's the sign for the national trails," said Wolf. "This is the Cleveland Way. It goes right down the coast."

"My brother went to walk the Cleveland Way," said Jen.

"We know," said Ethie.

"That's why we're going this way," said Wolf.

Act Three

"*G*et up, move, you can't stay still."

I don't want to hear the voice. I know the voice. It's my aunt. Her name is Barbara, and she lives on an island.

"Stand up, move your feet, walk."

She is the mother of my friend Ethie. She's my aunt. My friend Ethie is my cousin.

"You're making up stories. Ethie is not my story, she's your story."

You lost a baby.

"I never lost a baby. It was never a baby."

But she's my cousin. She's your daughter. She's helping me to find my brother.

"She's not mine, she's yours. Ask her to take you to the bridge. You must keep moving."

I want to find my brother. I want to see Danny.

"Go to the bridge. Get up. Move."

I can't smell you anymore.

I don't want to hear you.

I want to lie still.

Chapter Eighteen

The path stuck to the cliffs, tracing the shape of the country where it met the sea. All day it was there, blue and calm, a vast expanse on their left, simultaneously calming and terrifying, beautiful and completely other. The drop down to it was often dramatic, but fences to their right kept them out of the farmers' fields and firmly on the last strip of earth between land and sea. Jen thought about the land, stretching inland for miles, across mountains and valleys, towns and cities, supporting the lives of millions of people, and none of it accessible to her or Ethie and Wolf as they walked this path between barbed wire and certain death.

How would it feel to jump? If she chose the right spot, where there were no rocks beneath, where the cliff fell straight and true into a depth of water, would she survive the impact? Would she be able to dive and swim? She'd never been a strong swimmer. Not like Danny.

They passed through Skinningrove where the boats had all gone out to sea and ponies were left to graze the fields. There were makeshift huts of wood and corrugated iron, but not a person to be seen. Jen shivered even though the sun was strong.

They followed the headland round the high cliff of Boulby, and passed though Staithes, a small town falling over itself getting down to the water, its houses stepping on each other's heels, its pub kissing the water on a narrow beach.

At Runswick Bay, the beach stretched out wide and flat and the sea sparkled like a day in childhood. They walked across the sands, making sure not to step on the small clear jellyfish that pocked the sand.

The path took them up to the clifftops again. They walked in single file and rarely spoke. Jen's body was learning the rhythm of walking and her old trainers covered the miles smoothly. The steps ate up the hours of the day, and it was late afternoon when they reached another high point and she saw Whitby Abbey below them, its ruined arches framing pieces of the sky.

"This is Kettleness." said Wolf. "We'll wait down in the quarries along from here until night falls, then go into the town under the cover of darkness."

There was a steep descent through woodland. Jen caught hold of tree branches to steady herself, felt the slide of her soles on the rough ground.

Then they were in the abandoned quarries. The path drew a line between two distinct landscapes. On their left, the old spoils heaps stretching into the sea, bleached white and grey, devoid of life. Jen stood still looking at the shape of the land, backed by the blue of sea and sky. It reminded her of one of the vases on the shelf in her mum's kitchen, banded with mineral colours.

"Look, meadowsweet," said Ethie. Jen turned around. On the other side of the path, a huge bowl of greenery, an abundance of wildflowers, birdsong. Ethie snapped off a head of white frothy flowers and handed it to her. Jen put it to her nose and sniffed. It was hay and summer and childhood, and also the bed which she'd slept in at the cottage.

"What's this?" she asked, moving her hand through a stand of green plants that looked like wire brushes gone soft with life. They were everywhere, tall and pricked with black seedpods.

"Horsetails," said Wolf.

"They don't look like horses' tails."

"They're older than horses. They've been around since the dinosaurs were. They've seen everything there is to see."

"There's a spot over here where we can rest," said Ethie. "Come on."

On the day they'd visited Whitby, Finn had taken her to the museum. He wanted to look at the fossils.

"They blasted the whole coast," he told her, "looking for alum."

"Alum?"

"It's a mineral. Really important for – well, just about everything. For industry. And this was one of the only places you could find it. So there are loads of old quarries all along the coastline."

"Don't they use it anymore?"

"They can make it now. In a lab."

"How come I've not heard of it, if it's so important?"

"Some things are like that. Some of the most essential things are unspectacular; we don't even notice they're there."

"Some people, too."

"Maybe. But the thing is, while they were blasting the cliffs to bits, they kept finding fossils of huge creatures that hadn't been seen before. It changed our whole understanding of the history of the world."

"And they're in this museum?"

They were in a park on a hill topped by a low-slung building with views across the town. "They're embedded in the walls."

Inside they walked through an art gallery to a crowded room at the back of the building and paid their entrance fees to a woman who gave them a laminated diagram of the museum. The fossils were in the left-hand corner, some of them, as Finn had said, integrated into the building.

They didn't hold her interest in the way they did Finn's, and soon she wandered off to look around the rest of the museum. She read about St Wilfrid's connections with Rome, and Saint Hilda who had supposedly turned the snakes of Whitby to stone when she founded the abbey here. The stone snakes were ammonites. She walked quickly past the glass cases of stuffed animals, pinned butterflies and birds' eggs, and the grotesque Victorian puppets dangling from their strings.

Finn found her staring at the mummified hand of a hanged criminal, the Hand of Glory, said to bring bad luck to all who owned it. "It's like something from Edgar Allen Poe," said Finn.

"Can we leave please? It's really creepy in here."

"I guess it is. Come on, we'll go to the Abbey."

With Finn she'd entered the Abbey through the visitors' centre, but Wolf went to a wooden door built into the wall. It had a large metal knocker and he rapped it hard three times. After a few minutes, it was opened by a monk. He led them into a hall that Jen didn't remember. She could hear the sea, but the roof and walls were keeping the sky out. Wolf talked to the monk in hushed tones and Ethie paced back and forth. Jen heard the names Egfrith and Beau and saw the worried look on the monk's face.

"Someone else will have to be found to accompany them," he said quietly. "It is imperative that you leave for Rome immediately. The synod needs you to represent them; no one else has your experience."

Jen thought about lying on the grass in the middle of the ruined abbey with Finn. The night in the bed and breakfast that never happened.

"Could I charge my phone?" she said.

"Pardon?" said the monk.

"I want to phone someone. Have you got a plug point where I can charge my phone?" The monk looked at Wolf who nodded, and the monk rang a little handbell. Another monk appeared out of the shadows and the first monk spoke to him softly.

"Please come this way, lady," the new monk said to Jen. She looked at Wolf and Ethie.

"It's OK, you'll be safe," said Wolf.

Jen hoped that Ethie would come with her, but she was paying close attention to the conversation and she didn't seem to notice as Jen followed the monk down the length of the hall, out through a small wooden door into the night air. Jen looked about her. This was more familiar. Mown grass rolling over hillocks, the stumps of pillars, huge arches open to the sky, the call of seagulls above the shush of the sea.

The monk had a huge bunch of keys which looked like something from a gothic novel. They were on a big iron ring and each key was longer than a finger, ornate and heavy. The monk used one of the keys to open a door which took them through a storeroom filled with cardboard boxes and till rolls and into the gift shop. Jen expected there to be an alarm he'd need to turn off, but nothing happened. No bleeps or flashing lights. Moonlight coming through the windows cast the shelves and tables into relief, strange rectangular mounds on the backs of four legged beasts, all motionless.

"I believe this is what you're looking for." The monk was pointing to a plug socket behind the till.

"Thank you." She stopped staring around her and unzipped her bag, groped about to find her phone and charger, which were right at the bottom.

"It will probably take a while to charge," she told him.

"I can wait."

He folded into himself, seemed to turn himself off almost. He was wearing a monk's robe with a hood, and his face disappeared inside the hood until it wasn't visible. His hands were held together inside the folds of his robe. He was still and silent, a shadow. He seemed like part of the shop, the silent merchandise waiting through the hours of darkness for the arrival of light and people and the chink of coins.

Jen plugged her phone in and sat down on the floor. It was completely out of battery and it would be a while until there was enough to even turn it on. She closed her eyes and fell asleep.

When she woke she was disorientated. Her phone was flashing and the monk was still standing in exactly the same position, but the quality of the darkness had changed. The piles of books on the sale tables had more weight to them, gave a sense of substance to the surrounding air.

Jen turned on her phone. She had thirty missed calls, twenty-three texts and seven voice messages. She blinked at the screen. It was hard to look at its bright glow in the darkness; maybe she was imagining it. She never got any calls or texts. Not many, anyway.

She scrolled down the list of numbers and saw her mum, her dad, Finn, Rebecca and some other numbers she didn't recognise. She thought about reading the texts, listening to the messages, but she just wanted to talk to Finn. The longing that had come to her last night intensified when she saw his name on the screen of her phone. He wouldn't answer. It was the middle of the night in France as well, and he probably had no signal anyway. But she would hear his voice on the answerphone message, and she could talk to him even if he couldn't reply.

She dialled the number. He answered on the second ring.

"Jen."

"Finn."

"Jen, is that really you?"

"Where are you, Finn? Are you in France?"

"Thank God! Jen, are you OK?"

"Why are you awake?"

"Jen, where are you? Everybody's looking for you. Including the police."

"The police?"

"You're officially a missing person. Jen, I'm so glad you're OK. Tell me where you are."

"I'm in Whitby right now, but I think we'll be moving on soon."

"We? Who are you with?"

"Oh, some people I met. I'm fine. Why am I a missing person?"

"You've been gone for weeks. No trace of you since the hospital."

Jen was quiet. Finn knew about the hospital. Had they told him why she was there? Did her mum know? The police?

"Jen, Jen, are you there? I'm coming to get you."

She imagined it, the homecoming, her mum tearful and angry, desperate to get back to her church duties, her dad throwing an arm round her shoulders and giving her a squeeze before sloping off.

"No," she said.

"Jen, everyone..."

"You can come. But I don't want to go home. You can tell them I'm OK, but not where I am."

"Jen, you don't understand. Your mum is frantic. Your Aunt Barbara has come down from Scotland."

"Are you with my family?"

"I felt bad for leaving you alone in York. I kept thinking about your face when the train pulled out of the station, I kept thinking I should have tried harder to get you to come with me. I haven't stopped thinking about you, to be honest."

The table in front of her was mostly different editions of *Dracula*. Paperbacks, hardbacks, some gothic in design, some with film stills on the covers. When they'd visited together, Finn had asked her to choose which one she wanted, and she'd gone for a plain black paperback, slim, with pages of tiny print. It was in the bag by her feet, scuffed and bent from many readings.

"I'm not coming home."

"Danny is here."

"What?"

"Danny, your brother, he's here in the room with me now. I'm sharing his room. He can hear this conversation."

"You're sleeping in Danny's room? Does Mum know?"

"I'm sleeping on a camp bed on the floor."

"I can't believe you're there. That you're with Danny."

"Everyone's waiting to hear from you."

"Is Lee there?"

"Who?"

"From Mum's church. A blonde guy with tattoos."

"I haven't seen anyone like that. I saw Terence and Stella though. I knew them straight away from your descriptions."

"Finn, I miss you."

"God Jen, I –"

"I want to see you. But if you bring all those people with you, you won't find me."

"OK. Just me and Danny."

"I might not be in Whitby. We're going south."

"Keep your phone on. We'll set off straight away."

"OK."

"Are you alright, Jen?"

"Tell Danny I've been looking for him." Jen ended the call and turned the phone off. The gift shop was grey now, the glimmerings of day creeping in through the windows. She'd been there all night.

She stood up and turned to the monk, still motionless by the wall.

"I'm done," she said.

The monk lifted his head. Jen could see the beginnings of a beard growing on his chin, wispy and thin. His eyes were shadowed by his hood. He walked to the door and unlocked it with one of the huge iron keys and held it open for her. She walked through and it slammed shut behind her.

She turned quickly. She was alone in the ruins of Whitby Abbey and apart from the light, it was just the same as it had been that time with Finn. Seagulls were circling and she could hear the sea far below. The ruins of the old abbey stood black against the sky. There was no sign of Ethie or Wolf. A new day was beginning and it was very different from the one she'd been in yesterday.

She was trespassing. She couldn't be here when the staff came to open up. She had to get moving. She walked quickly across the grass, past the old monk's grave and the high arches, alongside the fishpond and down to the wall which bound the west of the Abbey grounds. She found a foothold and managed to hoist herself up. It wasn't graceful, and the wall cut painfully into her belly, but she was over. She was on the road and before long the sun would be coming up over the horizon. She hoisted her backpack over her shoulders and started walking.

She had no food. She dug into her pockets to see if she had any money. Her fingers touched something metal and she gasped. She still had the medallion.

She could have given up, phoned Finn or her mum and dad, caught a train, gone home. But she was worried about Ethie. Where was she? And was Ely even a home to Jen anymore? She decided to keep heading south. She'd stay hidden, not draw attention to herself, look out for signs.

Chapter Nineteen

A mile down the coast, the path went through the middle of a caravan park. Jen put her head down as she walked. It was way too early even for dog walkers or morning runners, but she felt exposed walking past the mobile homes. The sun filled their windows with red fire. It was easy to imagine someone behind them looking out.

The path broadened to a road which passed between a shop, café and shower block. She heard a vehicle approaching and ducked quickly behind a parked car. Reflected in its mirror she saw a milk van come to a stop outside the shop. A man got out and picked up a pile of three crates which he took round to the back. As well as milk, the van carried sliced white bread, butter and eggs. Jen dashed out and helped herself. She left two pound coins on top of the bread crate. She didn't know if it was enough, but she wasn't going to hang around.

There was a carrier bag on the ground which someone must have dropped. It was a bit wet, but seemed clean enough, so Jen gave it a shake and put her items into it. She had to keep moving. She could get some miles behind her before the rest of the world woke up.

The path passed in front of a white flat-roofed building with huge foghorns on the roof.

Stop singing Jen, you sound like a foghorn.

Shut up Danny! What's a foghorn, anyway?

Something that makes such a godawful noise it scares even fog away.

Gran says I have a nice voice.
Gran has a hearing aid.

These things were massive, bigger than the biggest of the organ pipes in the cathedral at home. They were painted matt black, and so were the chimneys. They contrasted with the white painted house and looked like litter dropped by a giant. The path took Jen behind the neighbouring lighthouse and past a cliff where hundreds of seagulls were making more noise than a school playground. She was glad to get away from the buildings, even though she suspected they were empty.

A host of sparrows flew up from the path as she approached. They settled in the grass to one side of her, then flew back and landed on the path ahead. As she reached them, they did it again.

"Don't worry about me, sparrows."

They flew out to the side, then back onto the path in front of her. It felt like they were leading her somewhere, and after a few minutes they settled on some stones at the side of the path. This time they didn't immediately fly up when she approached. At first glance, the stones seemed to be randomly scattered amongst the grass, but as Jen watched the sparrows twittering and hopping about, she realised the stones had been placed in a pattern. She stepped closer and the sparrows got louder.

The stones were laid in a spiral on the ground. She could walk into it, follow it around until she reached the centre. Jen looked about her. Why here?

The path ahead disappeared amongst trees and dropped down into a ravine carved by a stream. Jen peered through the gap. Stone steps had been carved out of the hillside and dappled sunshine fell through the leaves. Below, the stream sparkled over stones.

She turned back to the stone spiral. As she stepped into the opening, the sparrows flew up in a cloud into the trees of the ravine.

Shall I walk in?

If she did, she'd reach the middle and the only thing would be to turn around and go back the way she'd come. She didn't want to retrace her steps.

She followed the path down the steps to the stream. Here she sat on the floor and drank milk from the carton in her bag. The place was a suntrap, and even this early the stones were warm. She thought about the statue of Etheldreda at the back of the cathedral, its warm honey stone, the light from the candles.

She preferred it here.

I can smell homebaked bread. I can smell heather. I can smell turpentine. I can smell clay. I can smell smoked fish. I can smell chamomile.

Why you?

"You need to find the way back."

There wasn't a way back. The stones led into the middle, but there was no way out.

"If you don't find the way back, you will be stuck."

It's not my fault. If I walk into the stone spiral, I will be stuck in the middle. Why is it you?

"There will be more stones. Look for the stones. Sometimes when it seems you are the farthest away, you'll turn the corner and the way is before you. Sometimes you can see it, smell it, and you think you are close, but the way is long and winding."

I can smell grass. I can smell sea. I can smell stone warmed by the sun. I can smell sweat. I can smell skin.

"You're right, a spiral won't do. But keep going, you will find a way."

Why is it you? Aren't you needed on the island? Lyddie, Grace, they need you. Are you looking for Ethie? Is she your daughter?

"We tell ourselves stories to protect ourselves from the truth."

Is she your truth or mine? Where is she? I've lost her. I'm alone. I can see nothing. I can smell gorse. I can smell cliffs. I can smell sea. I can't hear you.

Seagulls cry as the wind carries them. They cry as the sea lifts them up. They cry my name, my name, my name, and it bends in the air, it twists and turns, it comes straight at me and I curl myself into a ball.

Jen felt stronger. The sea was on her left, fields to the right, seagulls and ravens calling as she passed, cows munching the grass, some lifting their heavy heads to watch her.

Looking at the morning light on the water, she felt something ease inside her. This was her. She was on her own, enjoying the strength of her own body. The cows, the crows, the gulls didn't care what stories she told herself. This was just the cells of her body, the movement of her limbs, the air in her lungs and a morning world with no one in it other than herself.

She rounded a corner and two people were sitting on a stile. She stopped. A man and a woman, eating cereal bars. They were wearing walking clothes and boots covered in mud. The woman was wearing a yellow hat and a green jacket.

Jen let the breath back in. The strangers nodded at her.

"Beautiful morning," the man said.

"Yes," said Jen, following their gaze out to sea.

"You come far?" said the woman.

"Not really," Jen gave a vague wave back up the path. "You?"

"We've done the Coast to Coast. Nearly there now." The woman beamed. "Can't believe it's going to end."

"I don't think we're going to know how to stop walking." The man laughed. "Maybe we'll just carry on and walk home."

"Where –?"

"York," the man said, guessing her question, incorrectly as it happened. "Bit of a journey back; bus from Robin Hood's Bay, train from Scarborough."

"So much sitting. I don't know how we'll do it. Do you live in Robin Hood's Bay?" the woman asked her.

They were looking at her now, not the view – at her shoes which were not walking shoes, her white sports jacket, the backpack with badges and graffiti, her lack of Gore-Tex. She thought about what Finn had said about the police and she wondered if she'd been in the newspapers, even on the telly. These two might have seen her, they might right now be matching up the police description with the suntanned girl they saw before them.

"Yes, yes I do," she said. "I stayed over with a friend last night. Have to get back, my mum will be wondering where I am." She mustered a smile and the couple smiled back.

"Have a nice day," said the woman.

"You too," she said, and she walked on, leaving them pouring tea from a flask.

"Is he here?"

Jen looked around the coffee bar. There was a group in one corner in animated discussion, and a girl on her own with a huge latte. No sign of Finn.

"That's strange. He's been here every morning recently."

"What does he look like?"

"He wears a long black coat sometimes. He carries a duffel bag. He has floppy hair which falls over his eyes."

"And he's always on his own?"

"I've never seen him with anyone else."

"I've never seen him full stop."

Rebecca was giving her that look, the one she gave when Jen was being too gullible, too naïve. When she fell for the April Fool's news item on the radio or got pulled into the banter of the boys down at the boatyard. Jen felt like squirming. But she wasn't a schoolgirl anymore.

"It's not the first time, Jen. There was the nun, and the so-called bodies at the Angel of the North." Jen did squirm, but she kept it inside, she didn't let it out onto her face. She turned away and looked at the coffee menu.

"You think I've made him up?"

"I think you're having a hard time, Jen. Maybe you could do with some help."

Jen could feel saliva pooling beneath her tongue. When she blinked, a white flower flashed before her eyes. The lotus flower. She opened her eyes wide.

"What do you want?" she said. "I'm buying."

The path bent away from the headland, and the couple were out of sight. Jen could see the sweep of the town in the bay ahead. It was properly morning now. She needed to get out of sight. The path moved closer to the outlying houses until it was running alongside the back gardens. One house was set back from the others, surrounded by a huge garden, with a shed near the hedge. She walked quickly, glancing about her as she neared the house to make sure no one else was on the path. She crawled under the fence, squeezed through the hedge and slipped quickly through the door of the shed which she closed behind her.

Her eyes adjusted to the dimness. A small dirty window let in some light. The shed was tidy, with a wooden slatted shelf covered with plant pots, a set of shelves above with labelled boxes, seeds, string, slug pellets. A keen gardener. She hoped they weren't planning to do any early morning gardening today.

She sat on the floor and considered her options. She could skirt Robin Hood's Bay, keeping to fields and hedgerows, and get more distance behind her, all the time looking out for people. It was summer and as the day grew into itself there would be tourists. She might spend most of the day hiding in ditches and crammed between hawthorn and brambles. She could walk boldly through the town, hoping no one would look at her or recognise her. That would probably be the best course of action if she could pull it off. But she was on edge; she would probably look like a cat walking through a dog sanctuary. She could catch a bus, but that way she was more likely to be noticed. There would be the interaction with the bus driver, then she'd be sitting there on a bus, giving all the other passengers a chance to get a good look at her. The last option was to stay where she was until dark, but it wasn't even breakfast time yet.

She realised she was starving. She would think more clearly if she had some food. She looked at her provisions: a pint of milk, a loaf of bread, six eggs. She took a swig of milk and contemplated dry white bread. Then she noticed, on the slatted bench, an electric kettle half-filled. She smiled.

How many eggs could a girl eat? She put two of them in the kettle, plugged it in and switched it on. It took about three minutes to come to the boil. She switched it on again. It clicked off in about ten seconds, so she left it for a minute and did it again. What did her mum say? Four minutes for soft boiled. But her mum's eggs were always too runny, the white only just white, sliding off the spoon. She brought it to the boil one more time, then fished the eggs out with a teaspoon that was standing in a mug next to the kettle.

The shed was full of steam now, the window clouded over. It was facing the sea rather than the house. No one would notice. She hoped.

She cracked the eggs open and placed each one on a piece of bread. They were perfect, the white firm and the yolks still soft. She imagined telling her mum, the best way to cook an egg is actually in a kettle, and her mum's harumph, "Don't be silly, Jen."

After she'd eaten her egg sandwiches, she opened her backpack to get her phone. Maybe she should look at one or two of the messages, even if she couldn't handle all of them. The phone had slipped down to the bottom and as she furtled about, some of the clothes spilled out, and she was looking at the nun's habit. Of course! She had offered to carry it for Ethie, but now Ethie had disappeared, leaving Jen with her clothes and the medallion. Jen touched the fabric. It was quite soft, which surprised her. She'd thought nuns' clothes would be uncomfortable, that that was the point of them. That and modesty of course, keeping God's property under wraps from prying eyes.

No one would be looking for a nun.

She adjusted that thought. No one who was looking for her, Jen, would be looking for a nun. The police, her family. Anyone who'd seen her picture in the paper would not look at a nun walking by and wonder if she was the missing girl. On the other hand, anyone looking for Ethie might well be looking for a nun. As far as she knew, that included two people – Beau from the poker game and the mysterious Egfrith. Was it worth the risk? Ethie hadn't been wearing the habit at the nightclub, but Beau obviously knew something about her and Eg, so he might know about her nun persona. If Eg caught up with her, he would see straight away that she wasn't Ethie. She could deny all knowledge and he'd have to let her go. And anyway, Ethie and Wolf had disappeared. She had to fend for herself.

She shoved the eggshells into a plant pot and packed her provisions back into the carrier bag. She thought about putting the habit on over her ordinary clothes, but it was already getting hot outside and was going to get hotter. The fabric of these robes was pretty heavy, and if she walked the cliff path there would be no shade. She removed her jeans, t-shirt and the white jacket and climbed into the robes. She felt like a child dressing up, but when she fastened the wimple over her hair, it was as though she'd stepped behind a screen. Her face was showing – she touched it with her fingertips – but no hair was visible, her pierced ears hidden behind folds of fabric. She couldn't see herself – the window was too grimy for reflections, but she knew that she no longer looked like Jen. She was a generic nun. She could do this.

She stuffed her own clothes back into the backpack, which was now considerably lighter, and she was ready to leave.

It would be strange to be standing at your window and see a nun break out of your shed, or walking the cliff path and see a woman of the cloth pole-vaulting a hedge. But unless she wanted to stay here all day, Jen had no choice. She took a deep breath and opened the shed door. No one was in the garden. She didn't look towards the house. Keeping close to the shed wall, she scurried round to the place where the garden met the cliff path. There were two women approaching from the town, so she kept down low behind the hedge and waited for them to pass. They had a dog, and although the people didn't see her, the dog knew she was there. He barked once and started snuffling at the hedge on the other side.

"Come on, Moby," called one of the women.

"Probably a rabbit," said the other.

The dog had a final woof, then ran after his owners. It was quite a way before the path turned a bend. Jen could have waited until the women were out of sight, but by then someone else might be coming. They had their backs to her. Now or never.

She stood up, pulled her robes up above her knees and in thirty seconds she was back on the cliff path. The hem of her robe caught on a twig and she looked most immodest for a nun. She disentangled herself then walked sedately towards the town.

Chapter Twenty

Tourists were arriving in droves and the car park was already over half full. She walked down the winding lane to the harbour. A lot of people looked at her, but she didn't feel on show. They were looking at her clothes, at who they thought she was, not at her. There was a small crowd gathered outside the pub by the jetty, and she recognised the couple from the clifftop earlier that morning, sitting with pints of beer and huge grins, taking selfies on their phones with the pub sign behind them. She didn't linger. She followed the path along the edge of the beach and away from the town. People might think it strange to see a nun out walking, but they wouldn't associate her with a missing girl.

On the clifftops she could see crenellated buildings. Ravenscar. It didn't look far, but distance could be deceptive. Maybe a mile, maybe two.

The robes were not as hot as she'd thought. They were loose and airy so she felt almost as though she were walking in only her underwear. She could feel the touch of her own skin where her legs met.

Keep your phone on, Finn had said, but she'd turned it off. She did want to see him, but if he was bringing Danny with him, they would find her without the phone.

She kept walking. She passed a youth hostel and was tempted by the thought of a bed where she could lie down and rest. She'd already walked quite a few miles. She imagined cotton sheets against her skin, her face sinking into a soft pillow. But this wasn't the place.

The path wound back up the cliffs, across fields, climbing all the time. She began to sweat beneath the robes. Ravenscar was getting closer. She passed the ruins of some old buildings and suddenly she was on the road, walking into the village.

The visitor's centre was closed, but the toilets were open. Quiet lay across the village like a blanket, a muffler, so even if something did make a noise – a car, a motorbike, a speeding van – it wouldn't cut through. The grass was mown under the trees. No one was about. Jen sat on the grass in the shade and wondered if all the living had departed. If they'd all gone to Scarborough, or York, or London, or if there had been a worldwide disaster and nobody had told her.

There were flies under the tree. Although she was mostly covered by the habit, they managed to find the only exposed flesh and buzzed around her face. She flapped at them, but they didn't go away. In fact, the swarm grew larger. They seemed to be coming down from the canopy of the tree. Jen looked up at it. She should know what it was. She could imagine Dorothy shaking her head. Was it a chestnut? A sycamore?

She got to her feet and moved away. Some of the flies followed her. She shook her head, and it felt strange inside the fabric of the wimple, her hair restrained. She had a sudden desire to tear off the habit, to run, to shout – but there might be people behind some of those windows across the road, and a stripping, screaming nun would be a spectacle by anyone's standards. The whole point was not draw attention – at least, not that sort of attention.

She walked quickly along the road. A notice board showed a map of the village. There was more of it across the headland, maybe she would find signs of life on the other side. The flies stayed near the tree, and soon she was walking along the cliff edge. From up here, the sea looked like a pool she could dive into, a huge pool that could swallow her up and might choose to spit her back out, or might keep her in its briny depths. She could become a sea creature. Like a selkie but the other way round. Selkies took off their sealskins to become human on land; she could take off her habit and become a sea creature in the water. What would she be? Starfish? Seahorse? Lobster?

She could smell the salt. If she jumped from here she probably wouldn't land in the water, but on the rocks at the foot of the cliff. It would be messy. What's black and white and red all over? A nun who jumped off a cliff.

She wasn't here to smash herself to bits on the rocks.

The path veered away from the cliff edge across some mown grass and onto a village green. There was a shop and a café, and the café was open. Food. This was where Danny would come to.

There were no other customers. The proprietor looked up casually, then snapped to attention. She supposed this was how it must be if you were a policeman – people saw the uniform, made judgements, adjustments, behaved in a certain way.

"Hello... er... Sister, should I call you Sister?" Jen smiled, she hoped beatifically. "Can I help you? I mean... is there anything I can get for you?"

Jen cleared her throat. She was sure this man was about to be disappointed, but she couldn't think of anything clever or saintly. "Please could I have strawberries and cream in a cone?"

"An ice cream?"

She nodded. "Strawberries and cream."

The man got to his feet. "Yes, yes, of course. Absolutely. Strawberries and cream."

He pushed back the sliding glass top of the freezer, took the scoop from its bath of milky water and with his other hand a cone from the stack at the end of the counter.

"Are you visiting?" he said.

She said, "I'm walking the coast path."

He looked down at her trainers, then at her habit. "Walking. I didn't know... well, I suppose... are you on your own?"

Jen nodded. "I'm meeting some friends here."

He handed her the ice cream. "That's one pound and eighty pence."

Jen put her bag on one of the café tables and unzipped the top, using one hand only as the other held the ice cream. She rummaged inside the top pocket hoping there would be enough coins.

"Actually, don't worry. It's on the house."

"Really?"

"Yes. I mean, we don't have many... you know... people like you, not often... It would be my pleasure."

"Thank you," said Jen. The ice cream was starting to melt and a drip ran across her hand. She licked it, then saw the man was staring at her, fascinated. "You're very kind," she said. Did all nuns have to put up with this? The free food was OK, but really...

She walked away from the café, across the grass to where some benches were hidden between trees. She sat down and ate her ice cream. There was no one about, no cars on the road, just the faint buzz of flies and the hum of the sea, out of sight. She almost wondered if she'd imagined the man in the café.

Then she heard something. It was faint to begin with, and far away. The sound mixed with the heat at the back of her brain. It definitely wasn't a fly, or even a wasp or bee. It was a vehicle. She heard it change gear, and the noise got a bit louder.

Jen looked up at the sky. It was clear and blue. So different from the sea. It was a canvas to paint on, and she wished something would cross it, a plane high in the air, a flock of birds, even a single bird. Anything other than this expanse of hot shining air, the sound of the vehicle getting closer and closer.

When it appeared, the engine sounded like a roar in her head. It was a small green car, quite old. It drove past the café and parked at the edge of the grass near where she sat. Two people got out of the car. The passenger was Finn. She watched him walk over to the cliff path, saw him dashing his hand at the flies buzzing about his head.

The driver was Danny. He walked into the café. He came out a few minutes later with two cans of Coke. He handed one to Finn.

"The guy says there's been no one in all afternoon, except a nun," he said.

Finn had had his hair cut, so although it still flopped in his face, it wasn't in his eyes. He was brown, really brown. He had cut short his trip for her. He'd been to Ely and found her brother and brought him here. Jen found it hard to believe.

Danny looked the same as always.

Although she was there in plain view they didn't see her, because of course, they weren't looking for a nun. She could choose to do nothing. She could just sit here and watch them. She'd wanted to see Finn and now she could see him. She'd wanted to see Danny, and there he was.

Then she noticed something else. Beneath Finn's tan was another colour, grey or white. There were creases marking his forehead and his eyes were darker than normal, pooled with anxiety.

She heard Danny say, "Is there a pub? A shop? There must be something."

Finn had his phone to his ear, and she guessed that if hers was switched on it would be ringing. Danny walked past her, Finn following behind, speaking into his phone. "Jen, we're here. We're in Ravenscar. Where are you?"

"I'm here," she said.

Finn stopped in his tracks and looked at the screen of his phone. He looked up, but still not at her. Behind her, beyond her. Slowly his eyes stopped moving and came back to the centre of his vision, and eventually he saw her eyes and knew who she was.

"Someone must have seen her," Danny called from across the road. "I'll walk on..."

Then he stopped too.

Finn and her brother. The two men she loved most in all the world.

"Fuck," said Danny. "Have you become a nun?"

Finn hadn't spoken. He'd been staring at Jen and she at him. At Danny's words, a familiar light came into his eyes, and suddenly they were both laughing.

"What?" said Danny. "What's funny?"

Jen realised she hadn't laughed for weeks. She'd forgotten how good it felt. She couldn't stop and tears started from her eyes. Finn sat down next to her on the bench and took her hand.

"Jen, why…" he began, then started again.

Danny was grinning at the two of them. "Well, I suppose you do look pretty weird."

"You looked right at me…" Jen managed.

"Well, we weren't looking for a nun," said Danny.

"*The hills are alive…*" sang Finn.

"Don't," said Jen, the laughter taking her over again.

After a few minutes they calmed down and were quiet. Finn and Jen sat on the bench holding hands, Danny stood next to them.

"What now?" Finn said after a few minutes.

"I'm not going home," said Jen.

"You should let your mum know that you're alright."

Jen stiffened. "Did you tell her?"

Finn said nothing and Danny shifted from foot to foot.

"You did tell her."

"No," Danny said quickly. "We didn't. But Aunt Barbara was up before we left…"

"She's staying with Mum?"

"Yes. She's been there for three weeks now. We told her you'd phoned."

"They've all been worried sick," said Finn, and added quietly, "so have I."

"Why are you even here? Why aren't you in France?"

"I checked my phone and heard the message you'd left, pretending to speak to your aunt, saying you were in hospital."

Jen looked down. Finn's eyes were difficult. They could pin you like a butterfly. Mostly she didn't want to get away.

"I'm sorry, I shouldn't have done that."

"I'm glad you did. I came straight back, but you'd left the hospital by then." He squeezed her hand. "Why didn't you tell me, Jen?"

"You wouldn't have gone."

"Of course I wouldn't have gone."

"But you were looking forward to it. You'd been planning for ages."

"Jen, the fossils aren't going anywhere. I can do it another time."

"I'm going to the café to get something to eat," said Danny. "Do either of you want anything?"

They both shook their heads.

"Have you walked all the way from Whitby?" asked Danny, returning with a sandwich and a bag of crisps.

Jen nodded.

"Bloody hell!"

"It's not that far is it? Ten miles? Fifteen?"

"This is the girl who used to complain if she had to walk a mile and a half to school."

"Danny! That was years ago. Anyway, I've been walking a lot. We walked most of the way from Berwick-upon-Tweed to Newcastle. And to Whitby."

"We?" asked Finn.

"I. I mean I walked all that way."

"You said 'we' on the phone."

"Well, there have been other people on the path. You know, fellow travellers."

"I bet they all want to talk to the travelling nun," said Danny. "Where did you get that costume, Jen?"

Jen said nothing. She was suddenly more tired than she'd ever been. She didn't know if she'd be able to stand up from the bench. All of her limbs ached, her back, her shoulders. Both of the boys were staring at her.

"We need to get you somewhere you can have a bath and a rest," said Finn. She wasn't up to arguing, or even speaking. "Come on, let's get you in the car."

Finn stood up and held his hand out to her. She let him pull her to standing. She couldn't put one foot in front of the other. "I'm really tired," she whispered.

Danny took her other arm and she let them walk her to the car and bundle her into the back. Finn got in next to her and Danny into the driver's seat.

"Where to?" he said.

"We need a B&B or a hotel," said Finn.

"Filey's not far. I stayed at Filey on a geography field trip," said Danny.

"Go for it," said Finn.

Jen let her body sink into the car seat, leaned towards Finn until her head was resting on his shoulder. He put his arm around her. She thought how much nicer it would be if she wasn't wearing the wimple, if her hair was tickling his face and she could feel the warmth of his shoulder against her cheek. She realised he was wearing the same t-shirt he'd been wearing the day they went to Whitby, and then she fell asleep.

Something was in the room with me. I kept my eyes closed. The only sound was the clicking of the bedside clock, a distant car across the town. It was deep into the night, when the minutes crowd close together and the air can barely squeeze between them. When you never know what will be crouching in wait after the next breath. When the best thing is electric light, a book, a film, a mother. I didn't move, didn't want the intruder to know that I was awake. I could smell them – an unwashed, animal smell. I thought they were down in the corner, near the bookshelf.

Sometimes things come into my room and stay in the shadows until dawn lifts the edges of the night.

But shadows didn't smell like this.

I tried to filter the air coming through my nostrils, but it was no good, the smell got inside my head, and I found myself swallowing. My stomach clenched. I hadn't eaten anything. Mum had made a pasta bake because Lee said it was his favourite, but the idea of chewing pasta, the clammy lumps between my teeth, the slide of the oil against my gums... No thank you. I would have eaten some salad, but it was easier just to leave the table. Mum going on, saying, but Jen you used to love pasta, *Dad saying nothing. Lee at the table, keeping quiet, watching. It was better to go up to my room and shut the door.*

The smell was in my blood now, pumping around my body, into my calves, my wrists, my toes. I wanted to gag.

A sound. They had moved. Although my eyes were closed, I could tell that the darkness on one side was denser, that something was looming over me.

Sudden coolness against my skin. The duvet lifting off. The smell was all around. It filled my nose, my mouth, my ears, the pores of my skin. I couldn't move.

Something touched my side. A finger? A claw? It was hard, sharp like a nail. It was in the gap where my t-shirt didn't quite meet my pyjama bottoms. I tried to open my mouth to scream but my lips were stuck together. My breath was stuck in my body.

It jabbed hard, breaking through the skin and the flesh beneath, pushing deep into my side. I could feel it inside me. Something bigger than a finger, something hard and unyielding, something that had no business being inside my body.

I opened my eyes and saw him. The huge head, the trunk, the look of ecstasy where the streetlight glinted in his eyes. His head was thrown back and I could see the white of his throat gleaming in the darkness.

The pain in my side was intense, sharper than anything I'd ever managed myself. I wondered if there would be any sign in the morning, if there would be a scar, if I would need to go to hospital again for stitches. This time they couldn't blame me. He was moving back and forth, in and out. The pain spread in waves. I closed my eyes, heard him grunt, grunt, push, push, shout.

Then he was quiet. After a moment he withdrew. Something floated through the air and landed softly on my belly. I lay still, barely breathing as he left the room, closing the door gently behind him.

The air readjusted itself, back into its normal folds of light and dark, warm near the ceiling, but cool around my body. It flowed in through my nostrils, and out again.

There was a new smell in the room, something fresh and sweet. I touched the skin above my hip, moved my fingers slowly upwards and found the gaping wound was closing upon itself, stitching itself back together. In the morning there would be nothing to see.

But there was something else. The smell touched all the molecules in the air, setting them to vibrate. I could feel them, my skin rose in goosebumps. I touched my belly.

There was a flower on my body. It was the source of the smell. I propped myself on my elbows and looked. The light from the street was enough for me to see. It was a white lotus flower, fresh and glistening with drops of water. As I watched, it was absorbed into my belly, leaving a wet patch on my smooth skin.

I pulled the duvet back over myself. Cocooned in its warmth, I lay still and waited for daylight.

Chapter Twenty-One

The car stopped in a residential street of tall houses, most of which had signs in the front gardens advertising rooms, minibars, full English breakfasts.

"I'll go in and ask," said Danny.

He disappeared up the steps to the nearest B&B whose sign said *We Have Vacancies*.

Jen looked out of half-opened eyes, her head still on Finn's shoulder. His arm around her back and his hand on her waist felt like the most comforting thing she'd ever known. She should have phoned him weeks ago. She should have trusted him.

Trees were planted at regular intervals down the road, and Jen squinted at them until their leaves blurred into each other and the slight movement caused by the breeze became the breathing of monsters. She shook her head and sat up.

Danny opened the driver's door.

"They've a single and a double," he said.

"Perfect," said Finn.

The proprietor didn't seem so sure when they walked in. A middle-aged woman with dyed blonde hair and dark pink lipstick, her eyes widened into circles of blue outlined with navy eyeliner.

"Oh," she said, looking at Jen. "I didn't realise. You said a girl..."

"Oh yes, the clothes, I forgot," said Danny. "It's only fancy..."

"Danny and I will share," said Finn. "It's fine."

She frowned. "It's a double, not a twin."

"That's OK," said Finn, smiling.

The landlady looked at him, and for a moment it seemed she was about to protest, but she said nothing. She produced keys from behind the counter, her lips slightly pursed.

"Just one night is it?"

"I don't know," Danny looked at the other two.

"We have guests arriving for the weekend. You'll have to find somewhere else if you want to stay longer."

She showed them to the rooms. The double room was en suite with an actual bath.

"This is for you boys," the lady said stiffly, "and you, my dear, are across the corridor."

The single room was obviously intended for children. The wallpaper had elves and fairies leaping across it, and the curtains were blue with clouds and rainbows.

"Breakfast is at 8.30," she said. "I'll leave you to it."

They waited until she had disappeared round the curve in the stairs before collapsing onto the bed in giggles.

"Oh my God!" said Danny. "She didn't know which was worse, two men sleeping together or one of us sleeping with a nun."

"You should have told her you were my brother," Jen said, the tears coursing down her face for the second time that day. "She might not have minded us sharing then."

"No, that would be worse," Danny gasped. "An incestuous nun!"

"We should have pretended we were having a threesome," said Finn. They rolled about on the double bed hooting with laughter.

Later Danny went out to get food, and Finn helped Jen take off her clothes. He'd run a bath using the lavender bubble bath supplied by the B&B. She stood in only her underwear while he folded the nun's robes as best he could, then he turned to her and touched her hair that had tumbled free as soon as the wimple was removed.

"You can tell me anything," Finn said. "You know that, don't you?"

"I didn't know what to say," Jen said.

"It doesn't matter." He ran a finger down her nose, over her lips and chin. "Go and get in the bath. It will make you feel better."

In the bathroom she removed her bra and knickers and stepped into the hot water. It did make her feel better. She could feel the warmth soaking into her muscles and, for the first time in ages, she relaxed.

Finn called through from the room, "Are you OK? Shall I wash your hair for you?"

"Yes please."

The bubbles came up to the top of the bath, covering her body. Only her head was showing above the water.

Finn ran the shower over her hair.

"Is that too hot?"

She shook her head. The heat ran down her head, across her forehead and eyes, in rivulets down her nose and onto her lips. She tasted it. It felt as if her scalp were melting like sugar, as though along with the dirt, her hair and her skin and her bone were washing into the water, and there was only lightness at the top of her spine.

Finn put shampoo on his palms and massaged her scalp, rubbed her hair into a lather. She almost believed things were OK, that she could lie back now and let Finn take care of everything. His fingers were hard against her head and her body sank deeper into the water.

She'd checked earlier when the boys weren't looking – the medallion was still in her backpack. It was half a centimetre thick, as big as the lid of a jam jar. She was pretty certain it was gold.

When her hair was washed and conditioned and rinsed clean, Finn left her to it and she got out of the bath, wrapped herself in all of the towels provided by the B&B. She went back into the room and Finn was lying on the bed looking at a magazine.

"I found it in the bedside cupboard," he said, waving it at her.

"I'll just get dry."

"Oh, yes, I'll go and see if Danny's back."

He left the room, and she dried her body, then dressed in t-shirt and jeans. She was rubbing her hair with the damp towels when the boys tapped on the door.

Danny had found takeaway pizzas and beer. They sat cross-legged on the bed, eating slices from the cardboard boxes.

"What next?" asked Danny.

They were both looking at her.

"I don't know. I need to sleep," she said.

Finn chewed a mouthful of olive and pepperoni and swallowed.

"We all had an early start," he said. "Things might seem clearer in the morning."

Danny drained his bottle of beer. "I'll leave you two lovebirds," he said. "Don't do anything to upset Mrs Landlady."

Finn grinned.

"At least, do it quietly," Danny said. He ruffled the top of Jen's head.

"Danny," Jen called after him.

"Yes?" He stopped in the doorway and looked back at her. In the glow from the hallway light his brown hair shone golden.

"I've missed you. It's good to see you."

He grinned. "I've missed you too, sis."

Then he was gone.

Jen and Finn cleared away the debris and sat on the bed.

Jen was pretty sure she was recovered. She didn't even have the same aching in her legs. Any aches and pains she had now were from exercise, and that felt different. Like it was doing her some good rather than draining her energy away.

"Do you want me to sleep on the floor?" Finn asked.

She shook her head. Finn put his arm round her and she snuggled against his shoulder. He kissed the top of her head, and after a few moments she lifted her head so their lips met.

"You said you wanted to go to a B&B," she said.

"Are you OK? I don't want to—"

Jen kissed him, pushing his lips open with her own. She slid her hands under his t-shirt and felt the warm skin of his back against her palms.

"Jen, I really—"

"Let's go to bed."

She pulled his t-shirt over his head, then took her own off too. She hadn't put any underwear back on after the bath. She slipped out of her jeans.

"You too," she said.

They lay naked on top of the covers, facing each other, the orange light from the streetlights bathing their bodies. Finn drew a line with his finger from her shoulder, across her breast and stomach.

"You're beautiful," he said.

Jen pushed up against him and they kissed. She put her leg over his and pulled him close, so she couldn't tell where her body ended and his began.

Finn was asleep on his back, one arm flopped out to the side and the other on her thigh. The waxing moon was shining through the window, making everything stand out in shades of grey and black. Jen gently removed Finn's hand and slid out from under the covers. She crept across the room to the bathroom. She didn't flush the toilet so as not to disturb him, and when she came back into the room he hadn't moved. She went to the window and looked at the street below. A cat was walking down the middle of the road but nothing else was stirring. She could just make out the sound of the waves. They couldn't be far from the beach.

Silently she pulled on her jeans and t-shirt. She stuffed the medallion into her back pocket, then she slipped the nun's robes over the top, keeping an eye on Finn as she did so. He was still sleeping.

The door opened with a soft click. She stepped out into the corridor and closed the door behind her, stood still for a moment just in case, then headed off down the stairs and into the street.

It was easy to follow the sound of the sea. She turned into another street, just like this one, except the houses had balconies and some of them turrets. She could smell it now. She walked faster, and then there it was, ink black in the moonlight, the waves quietly rushing the beach. She took a deep breath and crossed the promenade, started down the stone steps to the sand.

She would bury the robes. She would fling the medallion out to sea. She would return to the B&B in her own clothes, get back into bed with Finn, and in the morning they would wake and begin the rest of their lives. Danny would drive them back to Ely and she would talk to her mum.

Her foot had just reached the sand when everything went black. At first she thought she'd fallen, but then she felt arms around her waist, pinning her own to her side. She was lifted off the ground and she kicked out, making contact with someone's shins. It made no difference. She tried to shout, but the fabric that covered her was stuffed into her mouth and she choked. Something sharp jabbed into her arm.

She thought she heard someone calling her name. She thought she heard a loud crack. She heard doors being opened, and she was shoved headfirst into a space. The arms no longer held her and she flailed wildly, trying to remove the covering. Something else was thrown in beside her, then the door was closed again. She pulled the fabric off her head. She was in pitch blackness. An engine started, and the space was moving. The back of a van. She felt with her fingertips, feeling the metal walls, the empty air to the other side. She dropped her hand. There was someone else. A person lying on the floor of the van. They were breathing.

She ran her fingers up their chest, found a chin, a nose. She'd felt this face before. The eyes were closed. She felt heavy, so sleepy. She touched the top of the head and felt the silky hair she'd kissed earlier, then something else, something sticky and wet, and suddenly her nostrils were filled with the metallic smell of blood.

"Oh Finn," she whispered. "Finn, what have they done to you?"

She groped for his hand, but she couldn't stay awake. Her eyes closed in the darkness and she fell back into a deep sleep as the van drove into the night.

Chapter Twenty-Two

It was daylight. She was lying flat on her back in a small room with high ceilings. A stone roof, damp in places, stone walls. Light was coming in from behind her, but from the way it fell she could tell the window was pretty high up. She could feel cool air on her face and hands. The window must be open, unless it was another one with no glass.

She tried to sit up, but her body wasn't having any of it. It may as well have been made of stone like the walls. She said his name out loud.

"Finn."

There was rustling, a movement. Someone moved across the room until they were standing in her field of vision.

"You're awake."

"Sort of."

Ethie was wearing the same clothes she'd been in at the nightclub, though the white shirt was now streaked and stained. She had a bruise on her left cheek, and her hair was thick with grime.

"Where's Finn?" Jen whispered.

"Finn?"

"They got him when they got me. They hurt him."

Ethie shook her head. "I've been in here the whole time. They caught me in Whitby, just after Wolf had left. I went down to the boat to say goodbye to him, and after it had put to sea, I turned to go back up to the Abbey and they were there."

"Wolf has gone?"

"He was called to Rome. There was a senate meeting, and he had to go."

"You haven't seen Finn?"

"They brought you here in the middle of the night. You were out cold. There wasn't anyone else."

Jen pressed her fingers against the stone bench she was lying on, trying to will strength into her arms and legs. She managed to raise her head an inch.

"It will come back. I was like that to begin with, but look." Ethie circled her hands in front of her, shimmied her hips. "It only takes an hour or so."

"I have to find Finn."

"Well, there's only one way out of here and it's locked with a huge key which the jailer keeps on his belt. Also, you can't move."

Jen could feel hot tears welling and she blinked. Her eyelids and her tear ducts worked. She raised her fingers one after the other.

"They'll probably come by with some food soon. Whatever they're going to do to us, they're not starving us," said Ethie. "We could ask about your Finn then."

Jen lifted one hand, touched the edge of the robe she was still wearing.

Ethie laughed. "Look at you, wearing my robes. Nobody would guess, if they didn't know, which of us was which."

"Did they take the medallion?"

Ethie stopped laughing. "You have the medallion?"

"I did. Unless they took it when I was unconscious. It was in my back pocket."

With Jen trying to push with her feet and hands, and Ethie shoving her from the side, they managed to roll her over so she was facing the wall. More of the same grey stone. Ethie yanked the robes up above Jen's waist and pulled the medallion from her pocket.

"Voila!"

"Why didn't they take it?" said Jen. "Surely that's what they're looking for?"

"They're a superstitious lot. They wouldn't want to start looking underneath a nun's habit. They might invoke the wrath of God."

"They know I'm not a nun."

"They wouldn't take any chances. Not until the boss arrives."

"The boss...?"

There was the sound of a key being placed in the lock. Ethie quickly slipped the medallion over her head, letting it fall underneath her shirt out of sight.

The door swung open and a man came in. He had long hair tied back in a ponytail. Like Wolf, he was tall, slim, all in leathers, with biker boots and insignia plastered across his shoulders, but he was much slighter than Wolf – much younger too. He was wearing eyeliner and blue eyeshadow, and possibly lip gloss.

"Stan!"

He looked at Jen, frowning. He was holding a tray with two plates, each piled high with a full English breakfast. There was also a plate of toast, a cafetière of coffee, butter and marmalade.

"We met once, years ago. I was only twelve." Stan didn't seem to have aged a day. "Me and my brother were camping and you had a guitar."

He nodded and grinned. "I still play. You want me to bring it, and sing you a song?"

Ethie had moved out of Jen's line of sight.

Jen said, "Where's Finn?"

"I've just got to finish my rounds, then I'll come back with the guitar."

"My friend, Finn. He was brought here at the same time as me. Where is he?"

Stan shrugged his shoulders.

"I've brought you breakfast," he said. There was a stone ledge to the right of the door and he turned to lay the tray down.

Jen slowly pushed herself up into a sitting position. Her feeling was returning. She felt as though she had pins and needles in her spine, which was a really weird sensation.

Ethie stood near the door looking down at the breakfast tray.

"What have we got?" she asked.

Stan turned to her, smiling.

"Freshly laid eggs, home-cured bacon and chef's sausages, all from pigs reared here in the castle grounds. A special recipe known only to the castle chef. Which is me, by the way. Swedish potato cakes, homemade bread from my own fair hand, preserves made from fruit from the castle gardens."

"And coffee."

"The coffee is brought in, but it is of the best quality. Can I pour you a cup?"

Ethie nodded.

Stan picked up the cafetière.

"And you?" he was saying to Jen, when Ethie snaked out her hands, found the pressure points on either side of his neck and pressed as hard as she could. He crumpled to the ground.

"Bloody hell!" said Jen. "Is he dead?"

"I hope not. I've never tried that before." She righted the cafetière which was spilling its contents onto the stone floor.

Stan had fallen on his side and the keys were attached to his belt underneath him, but when Ethie pushed him he flopped onto his back. His arms fell out to the side, and Jen saw that his wrists were crossed with scars. Ethie detached the keys. Before she stood up, she held her hand beneath his nose for a second.

"His chest is moving," said Jen. "It's OK."

She swung her legs around so that her feet were on the floor and pushed herself up to standing. Ethie stood next to her.

"Put your arm round my shoulders and lean into me."

With Ethie supporting her upper body, Jen found she could shuffle her feet, one then the other, in a semblance of walking. As they left the room, Ethie grabbed two slices of toast and gave one to Jen. "He can eat the rest when he comes round," she said.

They closed the heavy wooden door behind them and tried the keys until one fitted. It made a heavy clunk as they turned it, but there was no one about to hear it.

"What is this place?" said Jen.

"Scarborough Castle," said Ethie.

"I thought that was in ruins."

Ethie shrugged. "Sometimes it is," she said.

Jen stared at her, then she shrugged too. This wasn't the moment. They had to find Finn.

The corridor was bare, narrow and gloomy, lit only by a flare at the far end. There were other doors leading off it, but none of them were locked, and all led into empty rooms like the one the girls had been in. At the end was another passageway.

"This way," said Ethie. "I bet he's in the tower."

Jen could feel the blood moving through the veins in her legs. She remembered days at school when they'd sat on the floor for assembly – sometimes she'd knelt for the whole hour, and when she stood it felt like this, as though her blood were full of tiny blades and her joints were cased with rust. But she could walk now; she didn't need to lean on Ethie anymore, even if she couldn't straighten her legs.

Halfway down the passage on the left was a small arch leading to a flight of stone steps going upwards. Ethie grabbed Jen's hand and pulled her that way. The steps were narrow and spiralled up. Jen's legs ached.

Then they heard the sound of footsteps coming down.

The spirals of the stairs alternated between light and dark. Every other turn there was a narrow slit window, but in between, the windows were bricked up. Ethie and Jen climbed onto the ledge of one of the bricked windows and pressed themselves back into the shadows, holding hands. The sound of feet came nearer, then a man came into view. *Well*, thought Jen, *almost a man. Boy, really.*

In the gloom it was hard to see him, but he was light of build, though tall, with short blonde hair and a bounce in his step as he ran down the stairs. Ethie tightened her grip on Jen's hand so hard it was difficult not to cry out. But the boy-man didn't look their way; he kept running down the stairs and was soon out of view. They waited, not moving or speaking until all echoes of heel on stone had stopped ringing through the stairwell. Ethie's grip gradually loosened.

They stepped down from the ledge.

"Who was that?" asked Jen.

"Eg," said Ethie. "Come on, quick."

Jen followed, frowning. Eg was the man Ethie was afraid of. She'd imagined someone thuggish, some sort of ogre, not this good-looking boy, who was surely quite a bit younger than Ethie, younger than herself too. If she'd had to hazard a guess from the brief glimpse, she'd have said he was maybe seventeen, eighteen.

She followed Ethie's feet, up and up, round and round, until they came to a small door at the top of the tower. It was locked.

"The keys," said Ethie, and Jen passed them over. Most of them were far too big, but there was one smaller key which slid into the lock and turned. Ethie opened the door and Jen followed her in, hoping they weren't walking into the lion's den.

Like the room they'd been locked in, this one was lit from high above by a tiny slit of a window, so the lower half of the room was cast in shadows. The first thing Jen saw was a breakfast tray like the one in their own room. Untouched. Then she saw the figure lying motionless on a stone shelf. *They wouldn't bring him food if he was dead*, she thought.

She went to him. The wound in his head was nasty and nothing had been done to clean it up, but he was breathing regularly, and he was warm. Jen smoothed her hand over his hair on the unwounded side of his head. She lifted his hand and held it in hers.

"Finn," she said, and she thought his eyelids flickered. "He's unconscious," she said to Ethie. Ethie felt for Finn's pulse, lifted his eyelids and looked at his eyes one at a time.

"He's drugged. Like you were."

"So he should come round soon?"

"Depending on how much they gave him, yes. They've brought him breakfast, so they must be expecting him to wake up at some point."

Jen wanted to sit next to Finn, but Ethie wouldn't let her. "If someone comes, we should be behind the door so we can surprise them, not sitting there like a bloody present."

"We'd hear their footsteps," said Jen, but Ethie was having none of that. They sat next to each other, their backs against the stone wall, and Jen watched Finn's chest rise and fall.

The light in the room got brighter as the sun rose in the sky outside. Finn slept on. Jen's legs were tingling, and she rubbed them with her hands.

"You OK?" whispered Ethie.

Jen nodded.

"Did you find your brother?"

Jen nodded again. She wondered what Danny was doing. He had never been an early riser, but she was sure it must be mid-morning by now, and he wouldn't have wanted to miss his breakfast. When Jen and Finn didn't turn up, he would probably have eaten his share before going to look for them. Sooner or later, he must have discovered they were gone.

She'd only just found him.

She felt Ethie take hold of her hand.

"As soon as Finn wakes up and we get out of here, you can go back to your brother. They won't stop you. It's me they want, and I have the medallion now."

"Is it Beau?"

"I don't think so. I think this is Eg's doing."

"Why is he after you?"

"Because he loves me."

Jen opened her mouth to speak but Ethie put her finger to her lips.

There were footsteps coming up the stairs.

Chapter Twenty-Three

The sound of boots on stone, getting nearer. Jen looked across at Finn and saw that he'd opened his eyes. He was looking at them. Ethie put one hand over Jen's mouth, her other finger to her lips and she opened her eyes wide in warning. Finn blinked in acknowledgement. The steps were close now. Light steps, moving quickly – someone young and fit, someone running.

The door opened and Eg walked into the room. He stopped just inside the door. He glanced at the untouched breakfast tray, then at Finn lying with his eyes open. His back was to the girls.

Eg said, "They're not interested in us, you know. There was no point in you following her. They don't want you or me."

Finn said nothing.

"They're only interested in one thing. You've seen the robes your girl is wearing. What do you think they mean? You've lost her. She's gone, given herself to Jesus. Lucky bastard."

Finn blinked, but still said nothing.

"Have you seen her muttering something? Words with no sound, her lips moving like she's got something really important going on?"

Finn shook his head. His eyes were watching Eg's face. He didn't send even a flicker of a glance towards Jen and Ethie.

"Well, she will. Just you wait. First the robes, then the muttering, then she'll start locking herself away and won't have anything to do with you."

Finn's lips parted and he appeared to be trying to push himself up with his arms.

"It's called the Jesus Prayer. Once she starts with that, it's curtains for you, mate."

Finn licked his lips and stretched his neck a little.

"So, I have to decide what to do with you."

"Sa da skies," said Finn.

"What? I can't tell what you're saying."

Finn stretched again and swallowed.

"I could kill you. If I were my father, I'd kill you."

Finn shook his head.

"I'm not my father. I'll probably just let you go, but that does seem a bit boring."

"Skies," said Finn. "Not Jesus."

"Skies? What are you on about? I might have to kill you just for being so weird. Spit it out."

"Jen. She's in de skies. Not a nun."

Eg frowned, then suddenly laughed out loud. "Disguise. I thought you were off your head or something. Disguise. Is that what she told you?"

"Let her go."

Eg walked across the room and sat down beside Finn's legs. The girls could see him properly now, and if he turned his head he would see them too. At the moment he was looking at Finn.

He was wearing leather trousers and a loose tunic. His hair was cut carefully to look dishevelled and his ears were pierced with small gold hoops. Jen could see that he had shaved – there was a small cut below his ear – but his skin was very smooth and she didn't imagine he had to do it often.

"I could let her go. I mean, I don't need her, not really. But she has something of mine."

His head turned slightly in their direction. Finn coughed, shuffled onto his elbows, and Eg looked back at him.

"The drug is wearing off, I see. Sorry about that. A bit cowardly I know, but I've never been one for knocking people out by brute force. In fact, sorry about your head too."

Finn lifted the fingers of one hand to his face. There was dried blood on his forehead and his hair looked wet and sticky.

"It's probably not as bad as it looks," said Eg. "Heads bleed a lot."

Just then three things happened at once. Finn sat up, as though he'd suddenly regained the use of his limbs, a bird landed on the windowsill, and Eg turned his head towards it, catching sight of Jen and Ethie.

There was silence.

The bird called out, flew into the room and landed on Eg's shoulder. It was a falcon and Jen thought it could be the same one she'd seen on the beach further north.

"Jennet," Ethie said, under her breath.

Eg walked across the room and pulled Ethie up by her hand, so she was close to his chest. The bird cried out again and Ethie glanced at it briefly, then back at Eg. For a moment it seemed as though they were going to kiss, but Ethie pulled back.

Eg ran his finger along the neckline of her blouse, bent his head and kissed her throat.

Jen slid up the wall into a standing position.

"Eth," said Eg. His voice was husky. His hands held her upper arms. Ethie could have easily broken out of his grasp.

Jen edged around the room towards Finn, who was on his feet now.

"Eth, these clothes..."

Jen expected Ethie to knee him in the groin, slap him hard, but she didn't. Her eyes were full of tears and she lifted her hand to Eg's face, stroked his cheek.

"Nothing's changed," she said softly. "The clothes don't mean anything."

Eg made a choking noise. He pulled her tight against him again, lowered his head and kissed her hard. Ethie was trapped.

Jen had reached the stone shelf and held out her hand to Finn. He took it and pulled her gently towards him.

At first Ethie was wooden, but gradually she responded and Eg's grip on her loosened. They pressed together in a mutual embrace.

Finn and Jen shuffled across the room, trying to make no noise, no sudden movement. The bird watched them with its golden eyes. Neither Ethie nor Eg paid them any attention. Then Ethie pulled away. She put her hands on Eg's shoulders and pushed him to arm's length.

"No," she said.

"But you love me. You know you love me."

"I'm not free to love you. I belong to another."

"Eth..."

She put her hand inside her blouse and brought out the medallion, held it in front of Eg's face.

"I still wear this."

Eg turned away, walked across the room to the bed then back again. He didn't seem to notice it was now empty.

"Why? Why can't you put all that behind you and stay with me?"

The bird spread its wings and flew onto Ethie's shoulder.

She was crying. Eg came back to her and traced her tears with his fingers. She stood still, the medallion in her hand at chain's length, looking into his face.

"See, Jennet wants you to stay too."

She shook her head.

"Eth, I love you."

She choked. "I love..." she said. He reached for her, but she stepped back from his grasp. "I love God."

She suddenly darted forward and grabbed at Eg's back pocket. She was holding a syringe.

"Your turn," she said to Eg.

"You don't have to," he said. "I'll let you go."

"You've never let me go," she said.

"That's because I can't give up hope."

"Well, give it up now. We're going. And you are going to have a nice sleep. Hold him."

Jennet flew up in the air, flapping her wings. Jen and Finn stepped forward from the door and grabbed hold of Eg's arms, one each. He didn't put up a fight. Ethie pushed back his sleeve and injected the contents of the syringe into his arm. Almost immediately, his body slumped. He fell towards Ethie, who caught him and softened his fall. The syringe clattered on the stone floor. Jennet flew out of the window and up into the sky.

"Will he be alright?" said Jen.

"Presuming it was the same stuff he gave us, then yes, in a few hours," said Finn.

Jen looked at him in surprise. "You can talk."

"I was bluffing," he said.

Ethie was kneeling on the floor next to Eg. She touched his hair, which had fallen across his eyes.

"Ethie, we need to get going."

"He's seven years younger than me, you know."

"Ethie!"

She let her fingers trail down his face and stood up. "My first husband was an old man," she said.

Jen and Finn were outside the door. Ethie gave one last look at the unconscious figure on the floor and followed them.

"Are you going to lock him in?" Jen asked. Ethie shook her head.

They crept back down the stone stairs, listening all the time for footsteps, but there were none. They could hear gulls, the ever-present noise of the sea, and children's voices, playing.

Jen didn't remember the stone steps being so worn when they came up. In some places they'd crumbled away to almost nothing and they had to step down two at once. They came to the window ledge where she and Ethie had hidden earlier and it was open. The view through the slit was of a broad sweep of grass, and there were children running through the castle ruins, their parents walking behind them.

At the bottom there was a rope across the entrance to the stairwell, and instead of coming out into a stone passage, there was grass, broken stone, sunshine and daylight.

Ethie hopped over the rope, but Finn and Jen stood holding hands and staring.

"Come on," said Ethie, "before anyone sees."

Jen stepped over the rope and Finn followed. Ethie was already walking across the grass towards the castle entrance. There was a gift shop, a ticket office, people milling about. Ethie walked straight through the exit and onto the small road which led to the castle. On the right were some gothic-looking houses. On the left, past a graveyard, houses tumbled down the narrow streets to the sea front. They could hear the noise of the beach travelling up through the town, children's shouts and laughter, and the low rumble of traffic moving along the coast road.

In the graveyard Jen removed the nun's habit and offered it to Ethie, who shook her head. "I think it's easier without it," she said. "Leave it here, someone will get rid of it."

Jen frowned. Surely, apart from being litter, there was something sacrilegious about just dumping it. She rolled it into a ball and placed it behind a gravestone.

"Anne," said Ethie. "I like her. She's more fun than the other two."

Jen looked at the inscription on the stone. Anne Brontë. She looked quizzically at Ethie, but didn't ask.

Finn was leaning against the wall. He looked terrible, with dried blood all over his face and clothes.

"Come on, let's find a bus," said Ethie.

"We don't have any money."

"I do." Finn pulled a couple of ten-pound notes from his pocket.

"Excellent. This way then."

Ethie seemed to know where she was going, so Jen took Finn's arm and followed in her wake. Before long they reached a crossroads. The train station was on the other side.

"Actually, we could get a train to Filey," said Ethie. "The bus driver might not let you on." This was directed at Finn, who was leaning against Jen. He looked as though he'd been in a drunken fight, and it not long past breakfast. Ethie was looking pretty dishevelled too, so Jen bought the tickets and they found some seats on the platform.

"Your brother will be wondering where you are."

"Oh fuck! Danny!" Finn checked his phone and found a bunch of messages.

"Tell him to meet us at Filey Station with the car," said Ethie. Finn peered at the screen, but seemed to be having difficulty getting his fingers to press in the right place.

"Give me the phone," said Jen. "I'll call him."

Danny was frantic. "What the fuck!" he said. "Can you stop with the disappearing acts?"

Jen gave him the instructions. "And Danny, can you go to Boots and get some first aid stuff? Finn's hurt."

"What do you mean?"

"Antiseptic wipes, bandages, painkillers. Oh, and a clean t-shirt would be good."

"What's happened to him? Where have you been?"

"Don't forget, Danny. We'll be at Filey in about an hour. Oh, and we've got a friend with us who needs to get to Norwich."

"Norwich?"

"Can you drive us there?"

There was a pause. "Fuck, Jen, whatever!"

She ended the call and turned to Finn. His eyes were closed now, but he had colour in his cheeks. The wound wasn't bleeding.

"It will be the drugs making him woozy," said Ethie.

"What about us?" asked Jen.

Ethie shrugged. "Maybe they gave him more."

Danny was waiting when they pulled into Filey Station.

"Bloody hell," he said, looking at Finn.

"Did you bring the stuff?" Ethie asked.

"Who are you?"

"Let's get going," said Jen.

Jen got in the back with Finn. Danny drove and Ethie directed. Jen used the wipes to clean Finn's face and dabbed at the edges of the wound. He smiled at her.

"Does it hurt?"

"Not much."

The t-shirt Danny had bought had a picture of the Buddha on it. Jen slipped Finn's bloodstained t-shirt over his head, being careful not to let it touch the wound, and threw it into the back of the car. She touched his chest with her fingers, and their lips touched.

"Hey, you two, how about you stop that and tell me what's going on? I paid the woman at the B&B but she was very suspicious. I brought your stuff."

"Will Eg come after us?" Jen asked Ethie.

"Hang on a minute, are we being chased?"

"I don't think so," said Ethie. "He doesn't usually."

"Usually?"

"But there's also Beau. He won't give up easily."

"Do I need to break the speed limit?"

"Probably best not to get stopped," Finn said.

Jen dabbed at the blood on Finn's neck, then slipped the Buddha shirt over his head.

"What's that noise?" said Ethie. "Is it meant to do that?"

A loud squeal was coming from the bonnet, followed by a cloud of black smoke.

"Fuck!" said Danny. He pulled over to the side of the road. There was a bang followed by more smoke.

"Is this your car?"

"No, I borrowed it."

"Well, whoever you borrowed it from isn't going to be too pleased."

"Actually, it had failed its MOT and was on its way to the scrap heap. They didn't want it back."

"Good thing," said Finn, as there was another loud bang and the engine died.

They all scrambled out and stood on the verge looking at the car, which seemed to have shrunk. They were on the edge of town on a residential street with bungalows, detached and semi-detached houses with gardens and hedges sealing them off from the traffic.

"What now?" said Danny.

"We'll have to walk," replied Ethie.

"Walk? To Norwich? Are you mad?"

"I've walked further," she replied.

"What about the car?"

"Someone will get rid of it."

Jen looked at Ethie. Did she know what she was talking about? A habit in a graveyard was one thing, but surely they couldn't just abandon the car here on the street.

Danny opened the boot and retrieved Jen's backpack and jacket, and a pack each for him and Finn. "At least we've broken down by a footpath," he said.

Across the road, a track led between the houses. There was a signpost next to it with an acorn on it.

"Are we back on the Cleveland Way?" asked Jen.

"No, the Yorkshire Wolds Way. Look – the Humber Bridge, seventy-nine miles."

"Oh good," said Ethie. "That's the right way."

"Seventy-nine miles! That's going to take forever."

"Three days if we get a move on." Ethie crossed the road and started walking up the track. There was tree branch lying across the path. She bent and picked it up, stripped off the few leaves, then walked on with her new walking stick. "This is great," she called over her shoulder, "you should all get one."

Danny swung his pack onto his shoulders. Finn frowned as he put his on. He was still looking pale, and as they crossed the road his legs shook.

"You going to be OK?" Jen asked, taking his hand.

He nodded. Ethie was way up the path, swinging her stick and her hips as she walked.

"What's in Norwich anyway?" asked Danny. "And who the hell is that annoying girl?"

Chapter Twenty-Four

My name is Etheldreda. My first husband was an old man; an acquaintance of my father's who needed a wife for official functions, someone to stand by his side. My father assured me that was all he wanted, and he was right. Tonberg let me live quietly in my apartments, only calling on my services for state functions, banquets, parades of arms. On those occasions he apologised for disturbing my reveries and taking me from my devotions. He never once tried to touch me as a husband touches a wife. Considering I had no choice in the matter of marriage, I could have done much worse. Did do much worse, the second time around.

I was sixteen when I married Tonberg, and he was sixty-seven. I had already dedicated my life to my true love, my Lord and Saviour, and nothing could deter me from my life's path. When my husband died peacefully in his bed three years later, I thought my duty done. I returned to my father's palace and asked that I might now be allowed to live out my days in the abbey at Dunwich, in the company of my sisters in Christ, worshipping at the throne of the Lord Jesus.

At first all seemed well. My father allowed my remove to the abbey. I spent two sweet years with my Lord, who gave permission for me to fast for Him, and in return gave me wondrous visions of His passion where I was granted the great boon of washing his wounds, combing His ragged hair, and on one unforgettable occasion, kissing His sacred lips.

I had great hopes of an afterlife, of an eternity in the Lord's kingdom, but the life I lived for those two years was as perfect as this human frame can imagine, and I often experienced such rapture as must be a foretaste of Heaven.

Then came the evil day when my father, the King, sent his men to fetch me and carry me back to his worldly palace, where he informed me I was to be married again.

It was politically expedient for my father to provide a wife for the new young king of Northumberland. My two eldest sisters had taken the vow, and my sister Sexburga was already married. His name was Egfrith, and he was fourteen years old, two years younger than I had been on my first wedding day. This time I was the older woman. Again my father assured me that I was to be wife in name only, that the boy had no interest in marital relations, that I would have my own quarters and for the most part, be left alone.

All had been arranged by letters and messengers over a period of months while I had been sweetly oblivious. I had no choice. English girls of this day and age would find it difficult to understand that a girl, a woman, had so little say in what happened to her in her life, but it was thus. My father was very approachable, and I was able to let him know my feelings and wishes. When he could, he would accommodate me, as for the past two years, but now I had become something of greater value to him, a means of binding his kingdom with another. As much as he loved his daughter, he loved his kingdom more.

I set off for Northumberland with a heavy heart. I had no fear of my new husband, as the gentle Tonberg had led me to believe that husbands could be benign and benevolent. I was sorrowful at leaving my life at the abbey. Even though I would be able to spend most of my life in prayer and devotion, I would not be able to give myself exclusively to Jesus, and that time spent with His dear soul in my cell was most precious, all the more so now that I was losing it.

Also, the journey was very long. The abbey at Dunwich was set within beautiful countryside and we novitiates were not forbidden to take exercise. Many of my fellow inmates took themselves for regular rambles across the heath and the marshes. Some said they felt closer to God beneath the huge skies with His creation all about them. I preferred the presence of the Lord Jesus with me in the confines of my cell with none to witness. I ate very little, sometimes nothing for days or weeks, and my body was weak, unprepared for an arduous journey.

At times I thought I wouldn't make it, that Jesus was going to take me to Him, make me His bride before I could be given to another. I prayed that it would be so. But my troublesome human flesh refused to break, and after many weeks we arrived at the castle which was to be my home.

The ladies of the castle were shocked at my appearance, and I wasn't allowed to meet my prospective husband for over a month. During that time I was bathed many times, my hair was combed more than it had been combed in the previous twenty years. I was dressed in silken garments and made to eat honey, eggs and butter. Eventually, they brought me a looking glass and I didn't recognise the woman who stood before me. Her skin was white and soft and her flesh was plump on the bones. Her hair fell in waves over her shoulders. She was beautiful, and I cried hot tears to think that I had never looked so beautiful for my true husband. Would it have brought solace to my sweet Jesus to have seen this vision before Him during His darkest hours? I fell to my knees and prayed for Him to take me now, before I was given to another.

It was not to be. I was led through passage after passage until we reached a great hall laid out for a banquet. Already the company was gathered, and musicians began to play to herald my arrival. At the head of the table stood a sallow youth, my new husband, Egfrith, waiting to meet me for the first time.

My first thought was that he seemed scared of me. I was led to the seat at his side, and he greeted me with all the expected formalities. He was barely more than a child. I had little experience of the world, but I felt I had nothing to fear from this boy, that he could easily be moulded into the type of husband I wanted him to be. He would have no interest in me, an old woman, already a widow. Indeed, during the course of the banquet he barely spoke a word.

We were married the following day in the castle chapel. The wedding ceremony was officiated over by a tall monk with a serious face, whom the others referred to as Brother Wilfrid.

The usual wedding ceremony was preceded by another exchange of vows.

Brother Wilfrid said, "Etheldreda, Princess of Anglia and soon to be Queen of Northumberland, has given her life to the Lord Jesus Christ. She has agreed to this marriage to Egfrith, son of Oswy, on the condition that it is a marriage in name only. Do you, Egfrith Bernicia, King of Northumberland, agree to these conditions?" Egfrith, the child king, nodded. "Do you agree that Etheldreda be allowed to live a life of quiet devotion with her Lord and Saviour, and that her duties as queen will be purely functional and political?"

"I do," mumbled Egfrith.

"Do you accept that this marriage will never be consummated?"

"I do." His voice sounded petulant, impatient, as though he longed for this to be over, to get back outside with his hawks and horses.

"Please repeat these words after me," said Brother Wilfrid.

He handed Egfrith a large gold medallion on a chain.

"I give you this medallion as a sign of my promise."

"I give you this medallion as a sign of my promise," said the boy in a soft voice.

"As long as you wear this medallion,"

"As long as you wear this medallion,"

"I will respect your promise to be a bride only,"

"I will respect your promise to be a bride only,"

"to the Lord Jesus Christ Our Saviour."

"to the Lord Jesus Christ Our Saviour."

As he said "Jesus Christ" his voice cracked and deepened, from the high tone of a boy into the bass of a man, but on

"Our Saviour" it was high again. I had no brothers and was not familiar with this breaking of a voice, the first sign of a child becoming a man. I wondered if he was making fun of me, but as he turned to hang the medallion around my neck he was trembling. He was hating every minute of this. I remembered a messenger who once came to my father's palace whose voice did the same thing, and how my father had patted him on the back and laughed and given him a pint of beer as a reward.

The marriage ceremony followed, and when the vows were over we knelt to pray. I closed my eyes and spoke fervently to my Lord and Master, begging His forgiveness for this betrayal, for the rich food I had been eating, for the luxury all about me, and beseeching Him not to abandon me, to still come to me in the darkness of my room, which I promised to keep spartan in His honour. I did not speak these words aloud, but my lips may have been moving, because when I eventually raised my head I found the whole room waiting for me to be finished. Brother Wilfrid was smiling.

My husband did not look at me. We did not hold hands, touch or kiss each other. When the ceremony was over, I was led away to my chambers, and my husband went I know not where.

It was thus for the next three years. I kept my promise to my True Husband, insisting that my bedchamber contained only a simple wooden bed, a cross on the wall, and a portrait of my Beloved Saviour in the throes of His passion. I wore a simple dress of woven hessian and its roughness against my skin, the sore patches where it rubbed, were a joy to me, as they reminded me of the pain He had suffered. I longed to ask for a hair shirt, for a strap with which to scourge myself, but dared not ask. The ladies of the court tutted, telling me that I was a queen and as such should have sumptuous hangings, jewels and gorgeous clothes.

Food was a trial to me. I was rarely called upon to perform my queenly duties, but when I was it took the form of a banquet or stately dinner. The food was rich and in vast quantities, and as queen I was required to partake. The first occasion took place when I had been living at the castle for a few months. I had been refusing the rich food they brought me, had even managed a week or two of fasting. As a result I felt closer to my Lord, and had come close to that heightened state in which my beloved felt He could come to me. Then I was called to a banquet and was required to eat such a large quantity of rich food that I was ill for many days with diarrhoea and vomiting. At the end of this period I was weak and thin, and gloriously empty.

The ladies said I must accustom myself to the food so that the next time my body could cope, but I had seen another solution. I knew from childhood experimentation that if I put two fingers right to the back of my throat, as far as they would go, I could make myself vomit. Rather than wait for my body to empty itself, I could void myself immediately after eating. This way I could also avoid the censure of the ladies on a daily basis, as I could eat the food they brought me, then rid myself of it straight away in the privacy of the privy.

They seemed surprised that I remained thin when I ate all of the food they brought, but I smiled to myself. They could not guess my secret, as none of them had known the rapture of the Lord as I had. They could not know the joy I experienced at the touch of my Saviour in the darkness of my bedchamber.

Sadly, I was able to reach this ecstasy less and less often. Sometimes He came. One night I lay on the rough wooden bed in a state somewhere between sleep and wakefulness, my skin hot and sore beneath the hessian which I would not remove even at night. I opened my eyes and saw Him standing there, wearing the loin cloth of His crucifixion, His dear skin torn by the barbs and points of the guards who prodded Him, a gaping wound in His side.

He held out His hand to me and I sat up. He guided my hand to his side, held it to the wound and I gasped. I could feel the warmth and wetness of His blood, the tatters of His flesh. Gently he pushed my hand until it moved through the lips of flesh and inside His body, and I was truly one with my Lord. I began to tremble and shake and a feeling like no other swept through my body. I felt I must void all fluids, lose my own self completely in this glorious union with my Saviour.

Despite the pain He must have felt, a smile hovered on His lips. He did not speak to me, but I knew He was grateful for all I did for Him, that He knew that my body was His alone, and that my vows were unshakeable. I moved my fingers inside him and knew that He was flesh. He leaned over me, still holding my wrist so that the whole of my hand was inside Him, and kissed me with His blessed lips. At that I swooned, and when I woke, He had gone. The only trace of Him was a slight moisture and a smell of something like blood on my fingers, although they were not stained red.

After that I redoubled my efforts to keep my body pure for Him, refusing all food. I managed to purloin one of the scrubbing brushes which were used on the stone floors, and concealed it beneath my robes where its hard bristles could scrape the soft skin of my thighs. Locked in my room before sleep, I removed the hessian robes and used the brush to scrape the skin of my breasts and stomach until I drew blood. I beat myself with its wooden back, and even pierced myself with its handle in imitation of the way my Lord had pierced his flesh with my hand. This last brought on the ecstasy I had known with my Lord, and once more I swooned. In my sleep, Jesus came to me and touched my body with His lips, licked away the blood and gave me sweet relief. He removed the wooden handle and replaced it with His body, and we were of the same flesh.

The ladies broke down my door the next day and found me naked and unconscious on the wooden bed, my body bruised and sore, the Lord's seed upon me. I was taken from my room to the sanitorium where they kept me for many weeks. Mostly I lay quietly with my eyes closed even when I was awake, reliving those joyous moments with my Lord and Saviour. I quietly took the potions and broths that they fed me, as I did not want the effort of refusal, did not want to break this most holy reverie.

It was broken eventually by a demand from my husband that I attend a state function. I had been excused on a couple of occasions due to my ill health, but this visit from a neighbouring king was of great importance. As in the time before my wedding I was bathed and combed and dressed in the softest, richest clothing, covered with jewels and taken to my husband, who was awaiting me in his antechamber from whence we would make an entrance to the banqueting hall.

We had been husband and wife for three years by that time, but we hadn't set eyes on each other for the best part of a year. He had changed almost beyond recognition. No longer a boy, he had grown a foot taller, and had the makings of a beard. He was broader across the shoulders, though still narrow in the hips, and his face had grown into itself, so that his straight nose, blue eyes and broad mouth no longer jostled for position in his face but worked together as a harmonious whole. He was more beautiful than any man I had seen, and I forced myself to lower my eyes.

"Etheldreda," he said softly, and I looked up again. Something in his eyes and voice brought familiar feelings to my body, particularly between my legs and at the point of my breasts. "Etheldreda, my queen, you look lovely," he said, and I felt guilty at my betrayal.

I dropped my eyes again, but I think Egfrith must have seen, in that moment, something of the turmoil that was inside of me, because as we stood side by side, waiting for the doors to be opened and the herald to trumpet our arrival, he did something he had never done before. He reached out for my hand and placed it on his arm, covered it with his own hand, and thus we walked into the banqueting hall, man and wife, a king and his queen.

Chapter Twenty-Five

E gfrith began to visit me in my quarters. At first I refused to see him, as was my prerogative in our marriage contract. But sometimes lying in my cell at night, I saw his face as it was on that last occasion, and I became curious to know the sort of man he was becoming, who it was that I was married to, and eventually I agreed to see him.

Since the spell in the sanitorium I had been eating some of the food brought to me by the ladies. There was more flesh on my bones. Although I sometimes hated myself for it, I couldn't bring myself to turn away the food, and I had no desire to vomit or to scourge myself. I felt, during those days, a gentle well-being throughout my body, and I began to move about more, to walk the rooms and corridors of my quarters, and even on occasion to venture out into the garden. There were moments in the night when I would be filled with a furious anger against myself. There had been no visions, no visits from my Lord and Saviour. But the next day, when breakfast was brought to me, it was hard to bring that anger into focus, and when I tried to visualise my Dear Lord's face, it became superimposed with that of the young Egfrith.

So it was partly with curiosity that I went to meet my husband, but also with a hope that seeing him in the flesh would rid me of these visions, that somehow I would be able to bring back my previous dedication to Jesus.

The first time, we didn't know what to say to each other. We had only ever met on formal occasions, when there was a set of rules and all our words and actions were scripted in advance. We were not alone. Egfrith was escorted by a manservant, and two of the ladies of the court, Sewenna and Sewara, accompanied me. These people stood at the back of the room while Egfrith and I sat in chairs. We looked at each other. Neither of us spoke.

After some time, we both began.

"How are you finding...?"

"What is it like...?"

We laughed, both having spoken at the same time, then fell silent again.

"Would you like to see my falcon?" he said, and I nodded, unable to think of anything else.

We walked outside, through my own gardens and into the castle courtyard where Egfrith kept Jennet, his pride and joy. We were followed at a short distance by Sewenna and Sewara, tutting about being made to walk through long grass, and the manservant who held his chin up and walked ahead of them, not liking to be seen in such lowly company.

Jennet was sitting on a perch high up in the rafters of a barn. She was not tethered or trapped. Egfrith whistled and she turned her head. Even from that distance I could see her bright eye. He whistled again and she took off, pushing with her powerful legs and soaring first upwards, then circling down through the narrowing spaces of the courtyard until she landed on Egfrith's arm. He looked at her, then at me, and his eyes were shining too, his face animated in a way I'd never seen it, and I felt something bubbling up through me that I hardly recognised. I laughed.

"You are made for each other," I blurted out.

Immediately I felt foolish for saying such a thing, but Egfrith was smiling.

"Isn't she the most beautiful thing you've ever seen?" he said.

The bird was gripping his arm with her claws, and I saw that his sleeve, made of sturdy leather, was scuffed and scratched. She put her head on one side and looked at me and her feathers seemed to flow like water. Her orange gaze was fierce and intelligent, and I was glad I wasn't on the wrong side of her.

"Jennet," Egfrith said softly, and she turned her head to look at him.

He fished his free hand into his pocket and brought forth some meat scraps. He held them out to her and she took them gently in her sharp beak, swallowed them back in a gulp.

"Do you want to feed her?" he said, holding out a lump of fat.

I was scared to feed her, but I didn't want to appear pathetic, so I took it from his fingers. It was greasy and cold, covered with fluff and lint from his pocket. Jennet watched the exchange from hand to hand, and when I held the fat out, tentatively, she jerked forward and took it. I felt the sharp end of her beak graze my flesh.

"There, you've made a friend now," said Egfrith. "Would you like to hold her?"

I didn't want to hold her, but I hesitated, and he summoned a servant, asked him to bring a glove for the lady. A huge leather gauntlet was brought and fitted onto my right arm. Egfrith made some strange whistling noises, and Jennet hopped from his arm onto mine.

She was lighter than I expected. I could barely feel her claws through the thick leather. She regarded me with one orange eye, turned her head so she could look at me with the other. Egfrith slipped me a scrap of congealed meat, and this time I held it nearer to her. She took it gently from my fingers.

I gasped.

"Enough?" asked Egfrith.

"Yes," I said, my voice rushing out in a breath.

He whistled, and she returned to him. Then he gave another protracted whistle which undulated, and she flew up into the sky, circled above us, riding on the air, her wings spread.

"She's amazing," I said, as Jennet returned to her perch.

"Isn't she," said Egfrith.

We stopped looking up at the bird and looked at each other. I remembered when I was a small girl and ran free in the grounds of my father's palace, how it felt to run full pelt along woodland paths and out into the open grassland, and how sometimes when my father was there and in a good mood I would run straight into his arms and he would lift me up in a smooth movement and swing me round and round, and I laughed out loud and my chest was light and free and I was happy.

"Shall I walk you back to your quarters?" asked Egfrith.

I nodded. This time he offered his arm and I took it, my fingers lightly touching the scratches made by Jennet the falcon, and we talked.

He came most afternoons after that. Sometimes we went to visit Jennet, sometimes we walked in the gardens and looked at the flowers, but mostly we talked. He told me about his life here, growing up in the castle, how his mother had died in childbirth so he'd never known her, other than a portrait in his father's chambers. How his father was often away, sometimes travelling to visit neighbouring lords and kings, a few times in battle, and how in awe of him the young Egfrith had been, how he wanted to love him, but could never get close enough, could never let go of the fact that his father was the King. He was kind enough, but distant, and when he died Egfrith was sad, but mostly terrified that now he must wear his father's mantle, being a boy of just thirteen.

Much of this he told me out of earshot of the courtiers who always trailed behind us.

"It's so good to be able to say these things," he told me. "I'm King, and am not allowed to admit to any weaknesses, but in fact I am riddled with them."

I told him of my family home in Anglia, my beloved sisters, and how I decided at the age of eight that I too would wed myself to Christ. I told him about the flat lands, about the estuaries and mudflats and the wading birds that came to feed there in the winter. I didn't tell him about my ecstasies in the dark cell with my Beloved. I had no more of those visions, and they seemed to be fading into a past to which I had less and less desire to return. Once I woke in the night from a dream in which it was Egfrith who came to my cell wearing the loincloth of our Lord, but his body was not wounded, it was smooth and perfect and he touched me in the same way that Jesus had touched me, and I woke with the same ecstatic buzzing in my veins. I thought this dream was probably a sign from my Lord that my actions were displeasing to Him, that I should stop these daily sojourns with my husband. But in daylight it was hard to heed the warnings. I was as happy as I had been as a child.

Sometimes, mid-conversation, our eyes would meet and there would be that familiar stone weight in my pelvis, the rising of sap, and I would lower my eyes. Other than to hold Egfrith's arm as we walked, or the occasional brush of our fingers as we handled Jennet, I never touched him, and he never attempted to make any untoward move towards me.

This had probably been going on for about three months when I received a visit from Brother Wilfrid. I had come down from a lunch of partridge and sorrel to my drawing room where Egfrith habitually waited for me. We were planning to take Jennet out to the field to hunt, and I was skipping on the stairs, a song on my lips. But it was not Egfrith waiting for me; it was the monk with his grey beard and piercing eyes, which this time reminded me of Jennet's, although they were much darker.

"Good afternoon, Sister in Christ," he greeted me.

I stood still. I felt like a child caught running when they should be walking.

"Good afternoon, Brother Wilfrid."

"I hope I find you in good health."

I had never been in better health. I rarely looked in the glass, but when I did I saw a rosy-cheeked, full-faced girl-woman with shining eyes. I no longer wore hessian robes, but a simple white dress tied at the waist with a sash.

"Thank you, yes."

"I see the north coast and sea air are agreeing with you."

I felt that Brother Wilfrid was saying something other than the words he spoke.

"We have been lucky recently, with a spell of good weather."

He smiled and nodded, accepting my evasion.

"And in other ways, Sister? How are you faring?"

During this exchange my eyes had been darting between Brother Wilfrid and the open doorway where I expected Egfrith at any moment.

"I am well."

"That is good. I expect—"

"Where is Egfrith?"

My husband's non-appearance and the presence of the monk must be connected.

"Ah..." Wilfrid coughed once, covered his mouth with the back of his hand then dropped his arm again. "Egfrith has gone away."

"What do you mean?"

"He has been called away on a matter of state importance. He must travel far into the land of the Scots and will be gone for some time."

"He's already gone?"

"He left this morning at dawn."

"Why didn't he tell me? Why didn't he say goodbye?"

"It was quite a sudden departure," said Wilfrid.

I felt as though I were drained of blood, or that my blood was turned to water as some of it began to leak from my eyes, and my legs were too weak to hold me. I stumbled and Brother Wilfrid stepped forward to catch me before I fell. He guided me to a seat at the side of the room, where I sat with my head in my hands. Egfrith wasn't coming today, or tomorrow, or any day for the foreseeable future. The sunshine coming through the windows seemed thin and drained of joy. I could see it through my fingers, then all swam out of focus again.

"You have become very close to your husband," said Brother Wilfrid.

"Has he taken Jennet?"

"I don't..."

"Jennet, his falcon, is she gone too?"

Brother Wilfrid cast a glance back to the manservant standing near the door. He was one of the castle servants, though not Egfrith's own personal servant who always accompanied him. The servant gave a small nod.

"Yes," said Brother Wilfrid. "The falcon has gone with him."

He wouldn't want to be without her. She would be useful in hunting, as well as a companion for him on his travels. But now I felt even more bereft. We had been a threesome, Egfrith, Jennet and I. Now the two of them were together and I was alone. I felt my shoulders shaking and found I was crying like a child.

Brother Wilfrid stood up.

"This has come as a shock to you."

My sobs got louder. Brother Wilfrid coughed again.

"I will take a turn about the garden while you compose yourself," he said, but still he hesitated. "Can I call someone, one of the women?" he asked.

I waved my arm to the back of the room where, as always, two or three of the women were waiting in the shadows. He nodded, reassured, then left me alone.

Sewenna came and sat beside me. She put her arm around my shoulders and I turned into her embrace, burying my face in her bosom. I had never known my own, but I imagined this would be how it felt to be comforted by a mother. Gradually I calmed down.

I stood and smoothed down my dress, dried my face with my sleeves, and breathed in deeply.

"I will go out to Brother Wilfrid," I told Sewenna, and she nodded, tucked a strand of hair behind my ear and beckoned the other women to follow.

He was looking at the white roses at the end of the garden. I walked on silent feet and stood beside him.

"Has Egfrith been sent away? Is it because of me?" I asked, my voice steady.

"Not exactly. This visit has long been necessary, in order to seal good relations between neighbouring kings."

"But he's been sent now because of me."

He turned to look at me.

"Sister Etheldreda, do you still wear the medallion which Egfrith gave you on your wedding day?"

Truth be told, I had never worn it. It was heavy and uncomfortable and seemed unnecessary. It was in a box in my room with a couple of other items I didn't want to lose. I shook my head, looked down.

"I have heard reports of the growing friendliness between you and your husband."

Who? Who had been reporting on us? The dour manservant? One of the women? Which one of them was the spy?

"Sister," he took my hand and tried to look into my face, but I kept my eyes cast down. "You have not taken the vow as yet. You have expressed a desire to dedicate yourself to the Lord, but there are many ways of doing that. It is possible to be a devoted servant of the Lord Jesus Christ and also a wife to a man."

I knew that of course. I was a wife for the second time.

"If you want to become a wife to Egfrith in more than name," he continued, and I looked up at him wildly before looking back at the grass, "that is a possibility."

He paused but I said nothing. I could hear the blood pounding in my ears.

"I want you to have time to think about this," he said. "Spend the next few weeks in prayer and contemplation. Speak to the Lord and ask Him what He wants from you. It may be that His wish is that you serve Him by being a wife to Egfrith and the mother of kings."

Still I said nothing, and he continued.

"Egfrith will be back when the leaves begin to turn on the trees. Perhaps by then you will know what the Lord wants for you."

"What about Egfrith? Have you spoken to him? What does he want?"

Brother Wilfrid lifted the hand he was holding and covered it with his other, so my small white hand was enclosed between his.

"Egfrith will await your decision," he said.

He left me soon after. He had told me he was staying at the castle for the time being, and if I should need him I could send one of the women.

I can see you. You are wearing a black vest and jeans and sitting on a chair. The chair is in grey space, there is nothing else. But I can see you. You are smiling at me and your lips are moving. If I can see you I must have eyes. If I have eyes, perhaps I have ears too.

"Would you like me to read you a story? I've got Dorothy's book of Anglo-Saxon tales here."

Dorothy, my gran, is dead. She read stories to me from a red book. Stories about saints and kings.

"I know you loved it too. She told me."

You are leaning forward, holding the book. You smell of heather. You smell of chamomile. You smell of skin and salt and clay. I have found Danny, but I can't tell you. I have no voice.

You open the book and begin to read. The words leave your mouth and sit in the grey space. They become confused: a stream of words wrapping around each other, a tangle, a knot, I don't know what you are saying, I don't know how to stop you. The words are filling up the space and I can barely see you. I can't breathe.

I can't breathe, I can't listen, I can't look at you anymore.

Act Four

Chapter Twenty-Six

The path followed field edges for the first few miles, right angle after right angle.

"Can't we just walk across the middle?" asked Ethie, swiping at the crops with her stick.

The fields were full of wheat or barley, ripe and swaying in the warm breeze. Sometimes the farmer had left a good strip along the border. Sometimes they had ploughed right up to the hedge, and the path was churned mud, rucked up under the soles of their feet.

Then they entered another landscape, where the ground sloped down at a vicious angle. The right edge of the path was higher up the slope, and their ankles pulled constantly to the left.

After a couple of miles they sat down for a rest. The sides of the valley were planted with wide sweeps of crops which looked like they'd been painted on with a giant brush.

"I hate this," said Ethie.

"It was easier walking on the clifftops," Jen agreed.

"It's amazing," said Finn. "Look at the colours, and those lines where the tractor has driven through."

Ethie glared at him. "I don't think the drugs have worn off yet," she said.

Actually, Finn was getting stronger as they walked. To begin with he'd been at the back, limping along, but how he was striding next to Danny and it was Ethie who trailed behind.

Danny handed out cereal bars from his backpack and passed round a bottle of water. "We'll feel better if we keep moving," he said.

Three miles on, they reached a road and Ethie sat down on the verge.

"Enough," she said.

"We're in the middle of nowhere," said Finn.

"Bus."

"No buses. Look, it's a country road."

"I want fruit."

"No shops, no fruit. We have to keep walking."

"Actually, there is. Look." Danny pointed over the hedge. The path had come out onto the road next to a house with a large garden. At the top it was planted with flowers, but at this end it was a vegetable garden, bordered with fruit bushes – raspberries, gooseberries, redcurrants, strawberries.

"That's someone's garden. We can't just help ourselves." Finn seemed to have lost in patience what he had gained in energy.

Ethie was on her feet. "I'm not planning to steal them," she said. "I'm not a thief."

A large wooden gate was open on its hinges. She marched up the drive, past a white van, and knocked on the door.

The others watched from the verge. The door was opened by a woman. She and Ethie spoke for a few moments, then Ethie disappeared inside.

"What's she doing?" asked Finn.

Ethie and the woman reappeared from the back of the house. Ethie was holding an empty ice cream container.

"There's far too much for just me," they heard the woman say. "My daughter's not really interested. Prefers to get her food delivered in a van. Thinks plastic packaging means it's safer. I always give her something from the garden, but my guess is it goes straight in the bin."

Ethie waved to the others and the woman beckoned.

"Come on round and help yourselves."

They filled the tub and ate berries straight from the bush. Ethie was particularly delighted with the blackcurrants. Her fingers and mouth were stained purple and she had a dark streak down her once-white blouse. She looked more and more like a street urchin.

"Where are you going?" asked the woman.

"I've been looking at the map," said Danny, "and I hoped we'd make it to Wharram Percy tonight. But we're making slow progress."

"I could ask my window man. He's going that way."

She was having a new window fitted in her downstairs room and the fitter was about finished. He agreed to give them a lift.

"A couple of you will have to sit in the back," he said.

The lady made them all a cup of tea and brought out a tin of flapjacks.

"It's nice to have some company," she said, as they all sat around on her lawn munching.

When it was time to move on, Ethie and Danny got into the back of the van. The sheets of double glazing were held in place by a timber frame. There was a small space between them and the double back doors.

"You'll be fine," said the driver. "The roads are pretty straight, and I won't go too fast."

"My stick!" said Ethie. She leapt back out of the van and found the stick where she'd left it on the front step. She climbed back in, lay the stick on the floor beside her and hugged her knees to her chest.

"What's that for, catching rabbits?" said the driver.

Ethie glared at him and he chuckled and closed the doors.

Jen and Finn got into the front seat.

"Wharram Percy?" asked the driver.

"That's what Danny said," Jen replied.

"You know there's nothing there except an old ruin?"

Jen shrugged. "I'm sure Danny knows what he's doing," she said.

Finn and Jen sat squashed together thigh to thigh, holding hands. Finn was nearest the driver and Jen was by the door. The seats had high headrests. Finn leaned back against his and closed his eyes.

As they drove through the village, an ambulance came the other way. The road wasn't very wide, and the van driver pulled over to the side to let it past. Two pedestrians stood at the side of the road waiting to cross. They were wearing walking clothes – waterproofs and boots. They looked overdressed for the weather. The woman was wearing a yellow hat.

As the van pulled away, the woman saw Jen through the window of the van and she started forward, waved her arm at her. She spoke to the man and waved again. Jen looked back as the van drove away, but there was a bend in the road and they quickly vanished from sight.

"Were they waving at us?"

"Who?" said the driver.

"That couple, walkers."

He shrugged. "Didn't see anyone."

Jen had a sudden pang of longing for Rebecca. That day at the Angel of the North, Rebecca insisted the people didn't exist. Now Jen was in a van with Finn and a strange window fitter, and in the back were her brother Danny, and Ethie who was probably a ghost, or maybe a figment of Jen's imagination. Rebecca would say, *get a grip, Jen.* She'd suggest going for a pint or shopping for shoes. She'd wave her arms and the phantoms would disappear.

Jen looked at Finn. He was pale and the wound looked as though it might have been bleeding again. His eyelids were blue tinged and slightly swollen. His lashes lay dark and soft on his cheeks. They must have walked more than twenty miles, him with a head wound and the drug still in his system. She'd never seen him irritable before. She gave his hand a squeeze and his jaw relaxed into the echo of a smile, although his eyes stayed closed.

After a couple of miles, his muscles softened and he was asleep.

"You walking the Yorkshire Wolds Way?" the driver asked.

"I guess. Kind of by mistake though."

"Long way to go by mistake."

"Tell me about it."

"Is he OK?"

"He's fine. He hurt his head."

"Looks nasty. I'd get it looked at if I was you."

They were approaching a town. The fields had stopped and the road was lined with houses.

"Where's this?" asked Jen.

"Malton. We just need to pick up the Beverley road. That's where I'm headed."

At a roundabout a jeep roared up behind them and the driver swore.

"Watch it mate!"

But the jeep stuck close. As they travelled along the B road it stayed on their tail revving and roaring.

"What the fuck?"

Jen held tighter onto Finn's hand and leaned against him. He didn't wake. The road ahead was empty. The van driver put his foot down. The jeep behind kept up. Jen glanced in the driver's mirror and saw the jeep had French number plates.

The van driver slowed.

"I'll let him get past me," he said.

But the jeep didn't pass him. It beeped its horn and pulled in even closer behind.

"What's he doing? He's going to bump me if he's not careful."

There was a jolt as the jeep knocked into the van from behind.

"Fuck!"

And again.

"He's doing it on purpose."

He put his foot down again, but this time the jeep pulled out to the side and drove up against the side of the van, scraping against the paintwork. The van driver tried to pull away, but the jeep kept pushing and forced him off the road into a tree. Jen felt herself jolt forwards and the seatbelt cut into her shoulder. Her face was buried in the air bag which had shot out on impact, accompanied by the crack and tinkle of breaking glass in the back of the van.

Finn was suddenly awake.

The van driver opened his door and leapt out to confront the driver of the jeep who was also out of his vehicle.

"What the fuck…?" began the van driver.

"*Où est-elle?*"

"What are you talking about?"

"I know you have her. Open the van."

"You've broken all my glass."

"Fuck your glass."

Jen felt the door open. Someone grabbed her arm and pulled her out of the van.

It was Beau. He pushed her forward so she was standing in front of the van driver.

"This one was with her. Where is her friend?"

Finn jumped out of the van and pushed Beau. "Leave her alone!"

Beau pushed him back and Finn tumbled into the nettles at the side of the road.

"Is she behind?"

Beau went to the back of the van and pulled the doors open. Jen and the driver ran after him, followed by Finn, back on his feet.

Inside was a mess. The glass had all broken. Some of it was in large pieces, and some in shards on the floor. It caught the sunlight and shone so the back of the van appeared to be filled with light. Danny was standing right by the door, pressed against the wall of the van, his hands spread flat. There was no sign of Ethie.

Beau turned to the rest of them.

"Where is she?"

"I don't know what you're talking about," said the driver. "I was giving these people a lift. I'd like your insurance details."

Beau looked back into the van. The light seemed to be even brighter, as though the glass were burning. Ethie's stick rolled out onto the road.

"Where is she?" he yelled at Jen.

Finn stepped in front of her. "I don't know who you are, but I'm calling the police." He pulled his phone out of his pocket.

"*Merde!*" Beau peered one last time into the back of the van and then leapt into his jeep and tore off down the road.

They watched until he was out of sight.

"I got his registration," said Finn.

"Where's Ethie? Danny!" Jen was frantic.

Danny jumped down onto the road. "She's in there."

Ethie appeared first as a silhouette in the light of the broken glass, then she was her real self, covered in blackcurrant stains with dirty hair and the medallion still glinting at her neck.

"I'm calling the police," said the van driver. "I'm going to report that maniac. The footpath to Wharram Percy is half a mile up the road."

Chapter Twenty-Seven

I spent the first three days in anger and frustration. My limbs had grown used to activity, and the quiet stillness of my cell was no substitute for lively conversation and shared laughter. I was angry with Egfrith for going away without saying goodbye, I was angry with the castle spies, I was angry with Brother Wilfrid for interfering, when nothing had passed between Egfrith and myself which could not pass between brother and sister. These thoughts raced through my head one after the other, stoking my fury, but I knew there was falsehood held within them. After a day of angry pacing, I sat down on the edge of my hard bed and wept. My feelings for Egfrith were not those of a sister for a brother.

Recently my dreams of him had become more frequent and more shameful. Shameful because I was the bride of Christ and should keep myself only for Him. In the dark of my room, visions came to me of nakedness and of union, but this was not the Holy Union with Christ, it was something altogether more human, more animal. I should be shamed by these dreams. But when I saw Egfrith after dreaming of him, I didn't want to turn away in shame, rather the opposite. I wanted to run to him and wrap my arms about him, lift my face for him to kiss.

Egfrith was just a boy. I could see his desire in his face. There had been times when we had held each other's gaze for longer than was normal, and my breath had caught, and I had wondered what would happen next. But of course, we were always accompanied, always chaperoned, and now it seemed that even those private moments between us had been witnessed and reported on.

I refused to speak to any of the women, not knowing who I could trust. Even Sewenna could be the snake in the grass. I stayed in my cell and ate nothing but a little bread and water.

After three days my anger subsided and I was much weakened. I locked the door to my room and lay on my bed, running my tongue across my lips.

God must give me a sign, and give it to me soon. Was I to wait here at the castle for the return of my husband, so that we could be united in true matrimony and bliss? I trembled at this thought. It seemed a sin to even think of it as a possibility. Like wishing for treasure chests of gold and jewels, it seemed childish and greedy to wish for something that I felt would bring me such pure pleasure.

If this was not God's wish, I wanted to know it straight away, that I might put all thoughts of Egfrith from me. This was the dilemma which had been placed before me. We could not continue with the pleasant dalliance we had been enjoying. It was time to take Egfrith wholly unto myself or to reject him.

I wasn't sure how long it took a person to die of thirst, but however long it was, that was the time I gave to God to make His wishes known to me.

The first day in the locked room I spent on my knees in prayer. Only for a few brief minutes did I walk about the cell. My mouth felt dry and when I closed my eyes I could see a tumbling brook, the waves on the seashore. But the day passed into night without too much distress, and it was easy to ignore the taps and calls which came through the door in the evening. They lasted only a brief half hour and were not insistent.

The following morning I awoke from a dream of Egfrith. He was holding my hands and looking into my face, but he was crying as he looked at the medallion I was wearing about my neck.

I crossed the room and took the medallion from its wooden box. It was less heavy than I remembered, its weight could be enclosed in my palm, I could hide it from view by curling my fingers around it. I could easily fling it from my narrow window, where it would fly through the air to land in the brambles on the far side of the wall.

Instead I hung it on my neck. The chain was cold and the weight of the coin nestled between my breasts. It felt like a brand. But brands were not removable. If I had been branded by God, if I had been marked as His, chosen by my Lord Jesus Christ to be His bride, who was I to take this brand and throw it into the brambles at the first sight of a pretty boy, the promise of afternoons with hawks and horses in the sunshine, of nights in the King's own chambers exploring each other's bodies? The thought made my body flush hot, and I longed for Egfrith.

But surely I belonged first and foremost to the Lord.

I knelt at the open window and prayed to God to show me the truth. Was my desire for Egfrith based on lust and human weakness? Was it sinful? Or was it His wish for me?

"My sweet and beloved Jesus, please give me a sign," I said, over and over again.

Darkness fell on the second day and still I knelt at the window, the medallion about my neck. I didn't sleep that night, or if I did it was for seconds only and I woke immediately as my body caught itself in collapse, jerked me back to the kneeling position. There were more taps on the door, the voices out in the corridor more urgent now, but I continued to pray and blocked the sounds, as well as the food smells they brought with them.

Daylight came. I tried to stand, but my legs were too painful from being bent beneath me all night. My chest and head hurt, and my mouth was dry. I stumbled and fell against the wall, and my hand touched something rough. It was the scrubbing brush I had used on myself all those months ago, the time they had taken me off to the sanatorium. It must have fallen when they moved me, skidded across the floor where it had been overlooked until now.

Was this God's sign?

I picked it up and looked at it, ran my fingers across its bristles. They were hard and sharp. I pulled up my gown and ran the brush lightly down the inside of my left thigh, past my knee and to my ankle. It was almost a pleasurable feeling. If God had left this tool for me to find, pleasure was not His intention.

I breathed in deeply. My skin had forgotten pain, once its common companion. I ran the brush down my leg again, but this time with all the force I could bring to it.

The soft skin of my inner thigh rose immediately in welts and it one or two places a bead of blood arose to the surface. The pain was excruciating. I dropped the brush and wept.

All that day it lay on the floor where I had dropped it. I crawled to my bed, lay down on my front and prayed to the Lord Jesus Christ in His own words. Let this cup be taken from me. I wanted to be Egfrith's wife. That much was clear to me. In my weakened state, with the pain of dehydration entering my muscles and bones, my human weakness devoured me and I entreated Him. Let me go, free me that I may go to my husband in love and become his in body and in soul. I bargained with God, promising that if I bore a daughter I should give her in my place, promising to be devout and virtuous, to hold my human lust within the bounds set by God and His church, if only I could have Egfrith I would give anything the Lord wanted in return.

But there were no other signs. The brush lay where it had fallen and if I turned my head I could see it. Waves of pain washed through my body. I could hear knocking and calling outside my door, but these noises seemed far away. At some point I fell into an uneasy slumber.

That night, the third with no water, my Lord and Saviour came to me in my cell. He had not come to me for many months and I knew I should be overjoyed to see Him. He sat on the edge of my bed and He was wearing the robes of the desert, His hair and body covered with the white and blue cotton of paintings, their fabric designed to protect Him from the fierce heat of the sun. Only His face and hands were bare. He smiled at me, and put His hand on my thigh where the welts from the brush were subsiding.

"My child and my bride," He said sadly, "have you forgotten me?"

I closed my eyes and shook my head, and each movement was accompanied by a fresh onslaught of pain.

"Have you forgotten that I am a jealous God?" He said, and His voice was a caress.

He kissed my lips and left. I fell back unconscious, not stirring until daylight once more poked its fingers through the window.

I rolled off the bed. My strength had departed as the water left my body.

I crawled across the stone floor to where the brush still lay, grasped it with my hands and held it against my body for a few moments. The bristles were sharp, but the back was made of hard wood, and this was the side I brought against myself as I beat myself about the head, arms, chest and shoulders. I cried out loud as I did it, but I know not what words came from my lips as I was too far into delirium to understand.

I believe this is where they found me when they broke the door down. The women had become so concerned they had applied to Brother Wilfrid and he had given the orders. I was lying unconscious on the floor, the brush in my hand, limbs akimbo, my nightdress torn and my body bruised.

Brother Wilfrid told me I stirred only once as they carried me from that cold room, and that the words which fell from my lips were, "Sweet Jesus, sweet Jesus."

I never went back. Sewenna and Sewara, under Brother Wilfrid's instruction, brought me to full health with their care. As I had recently been strong in body, this took only a matter of a few days. Brother Wilfrid came to see me.

"Good morning Sister. I am glad to see you have recovered."

I was sitting in a chair and I wore the nun's habit I had worn on my arrival at the castle three years earlier. My hands were held in my lap and my eyes cast down to the floor.

"I am ready," I said.

"Sorry?" He leaned forward to catch my words.

"I am ready to give myself fully to God. I wish to take the vow."

Brother Wilfrid said nothing. He regarded me quietly, but I did not look to meet his gaze. I could feel the cold weight of the medallion under my clothes, next to my skin.

Eventually he said, "Very well, my child."

I looked up then, into his face which was as calm as a father's.

"But I can't stay here," I said urgently, "I cannot be Egfrith's wife. I never wish to see him again."

Again, Brother Wilfrid said nothing for some time. His eyes were dark and unreadable, his mouth held a smile of compassion. I wished I could throw myself at him in the way I used to with my father when I was a child, feel his strong arms about me, his breath in my hair, and that the world would rock back onto its axis and everything would be right again.

But he was not my earthly father and I was no longer a girl.

"Poor child," he said eventually, tuning in to my thoughts, "I am sorry you have had this burden to bear."

It was arranged that I should be taken to a local abbey further up the coast, at a place named St Abbs. There I would be received by the nuns and preparations would be made for me to take my vows. Perhaps at some point I would be able to travel south and once again take up residence in the abbey which had been the sweet home of my youth.

Wilfrid travelled north with me, but did not come further than the outer grounds of the Abbey. We parted at the gate. He was to return to the castle where he would await Egfrith's return, inform him of my decision and begin proceedings to have our marriage annulled. Egfrith was very young, very handsome and would have no problems finding another wife. If this thought caused me pain, then I accepted it willingly as part of the gift I gave to my true Lord. I wondered aloud if my father would be angry at my decision, but Wilfrid didn't think so.

"This is not a political matter," he said. "You have done your duty well these past three years. Your father would be proud of you and happy for you."

I wondered if I would ever see my father again. Since my eldest sister took the vow she had been in deep seclusion. Maybe this was to be my life. I felt a wave of coldness pass through my body, but then I remembered I would not be alone, I would be with my beloved Saviour, and if I fasted enough, if I managed to get hold of a scourge, then surely He would visit me every night as is appropriate for a husband with His new bride. I remembered the night He came to me and placed my hand inside His wound, the feel of His hot wet entrails, the slippery blood, the heat of his rod and staff as it pushed against the cloth of his loins. I felt the familiar rush of heat, of a sliding wetness between my legs and I smiled. There was no reason for me to be lonely.

Brother Wilfrid rode back the way we had come and I was taken in by the nuns. On reading the letter I brought from Brother Wilfrid, they were very kind and solicitous. I was given a dry cell with a slit of a window through which I could hear the susurrations of the sea. I had been surprised and a little alarmed at the exposed location of the abbey, out there on the clifftop with only seabirds as neighbours, and nothing to stop the fierce winds that blew in from the North. But as I stood in my cell and the draught blew cold through the window, biting straight through my robes and making goosebumps of my skin, I realised this was something else I could bear for the glory of Jesus, my Saviour.

Brother Wilfrid was to tell Egfrith of my decision, but not of my whereabouts. We guessed he would assume I had travelled south, but even if he knew I was here, he would not gain entrance to the abbey, so I knew I would never see him again. Sometimes my chest tightened at this thought and tears rose to my eyes, but I forced them back, determined that from now on all my tears would be for the suffering of my Lord and not for the insignificant comings and goings of man or woman.

Chapter Twenty-Eight

They spent the night in the grounds of the church at Wharram Percy. It was far from the road, and the sound of the police siren was faint when it came. Danny had a small tent in his backpack – not big enough for four – and it was decided Finn and Jen would sleep in it. They put it up next to the stream. Finn had begun to shake and although it was a warm evening, he was complaining of cold.

"You need to get well again, for Jen," said Danny. "She won't thank you if you bail on her, and neither will I."

Finn was asleep in minutes. Jen watched his face in the blue glow of the tent as daylight leached from the sky. The only sounds were their breathing and the occasional lowing of cows in the nearby fields. No traffic. For a short while she heard Ethie and Danny talking, then she too fell asleep.

They all woke early. The birds were loud, and cows had gathered at one end of the field ready for milking, calling out impatiently. Jen crawled from the tent onto the dewy grass. Danny was lighting a small fire.

"I found these in your backpack." It was the remaining half a loaf and four eggs that she had taken from the milk van in Saltwick Bay.

"What will you cook them on? We don't have a pan."

"I found this." He brandished a hubcap at her. "I've cleaned it in the stream and with water from my water bottle. And here's the handle." In his other hand he had a forked stick. "I can heat half an inch of water in it, the eggs will be half boiled, half poached."

Ethie appeared from the ruins of the church, where she had spent the night. She looked as though she'd been crying. She had black smudges round her eyes.

"Did you sleep?" asked Jen.

"It was not my intention to sleep."

"We've still got a long way to go," said Danny. "Sleep would have been a good idea."

Ethie glared at him. When the eggs were cooked, he shelled one, put it between two slices of bread and passed it to her. She shook her head.

He kept his arm extended. "Eat," he said.

"I'm not hungry."

Danny continued to hold the sandwich out to her.

Finn appeared from the tent and Ethie turned to look at him, ignoring Danny.

"Fine," said Danny. "More for everyone else." He gave the egg sandwich to Finn, who had more colour than yesterday. "But don't complain to me when you're hungry later."

Soon they moved on. The path took them into a landscape populated by sheep, where hill folded against hill and the path wound between them like a snake through flour sacks. Sometimes it took them up to the top, only to drop back down on the other side into another long winding valley. They didn't see any other people.

At the end of one valley they found a circular labyrinth made of earth.

"Stop, I want to walk into it," said Jen.

Danny wanted to keep going on, and Ethie turned her back, but Jen was insistent.

"I just need to walk through it."

"I'll come with you," said Finn.

They followed the spiral to its centre, hand in hand. But there was no way out. In the middle the mound curved around in front of them, blocking their way.

"Isn't it meant to lead you out as well as in?" said Jen, disappointed.

"We can get out, over here."

"Not without climbing over though. I thought it would lead you out again, but it leaves you stranded."

"Only if you choose that. You can go back the way you've come. Or you can jump. Here, take my hand."

They scrambled over the mound into the next channel and walked out of the maze back to the others.

"I don't know what you're so bothered about," said Ethie. "It's just some lumps in the ground."

A few miles later a lane led them between mown verges planted with cherry trees, into the village of Huggate.

Ethie was lagging behind, walking with one hand inside the neck of her shirt, the other gripping her stick. She looked up regularly at the sky, but there was nothing to see, other than the high clouds.

Outside the village pub, two men were talking.

"I'm off to Hull today," said one of them, "but I can go via Brough if you need me to."

"That would be brilliant. Save me a trip."

The two men disappeared together into the pub. An open back truck was parked on the road near where they'd been standing.

"Brough's on our way," said Danny.

When the two men came back out, the driver swung into the cab and the other man put a box on the front seat.

"Cheers mate," he called out, as his friend drove away.

In the back of the pick-up, the four friends lay flat so as not to be seen.

After about half an hour the truck stopped and the driver got out. He took the box from the front seat and they heard his footsteps walking away.

Quick as they could, they clambered over the sides. The man was knocking on the door of a café, which was opened by a woman. He handed the box to her and they spoke.

Danny, Jen, Ethie and Finn walked down the street, hands in pockets. They headed downhill. There was a strong smell of salt and the air was full of the calls of seabirds.

"The River Humber," whispered Ethie.

**

The days passed quietly and I fitted into the rhythm of abbey life. During that time I did not starve or beat myself, as I knew a time would come when I must take the long journey south, and that I must be strong enough. In consequence, my nights passed in quiet sleep, disturbed only by particularly strong gusts of wind. There were no visits from my Lord, no visions or ecstasies. Sometimes I woke with the feeling I had dreamed of Egfrith, but I did not dwell on those dreams, rather let them slip away from me with the vestiges of sleep. Soon the days became shorter and the winds colder. I rarely stepped out of my hut, but from my window I could see a tree that had grown bent in the fierce winds, half doubled over, and I noticed its trembling leaves turn from green to yellow, then orange and brown.

Egfrith would have returned by now. Wilfrid would have passed on my news. I prayed more devoutly than ever, spending all my waking hours on my knees, concentrating on the face of my Lord which hung on the wall of my cell, so I would not see that of Egfrith. As I slipped into sleep in my cell at night, my unruly mind sometimes fell to wondering what Egfrith's reaction had been, if he was angry or sad at my loss. At these moments I spoke the name of my Lord out loud, wishing more than ever that I had a scourge to focus my attention.

The winter was cruel. The wind from the sea carried ice in its breath, and much of my time was spent pacing my hut, rubbing my limbs to keep the blood flowing. I went more often to mass where I could be in the presence of other bodies and the warmth they gave off. I knew that everything that came to me here was a gift from my Lord, and that I should bear the cold with fortitude, but the pull of candlelight and the company of others was too much for me. I prayed to Jesus to forgive my weakness.

Soon after the year turned, when the days began to lengthen and the cold reached its worst, I woke with ice in my hair and on my breath. My robes were frozen stiff and there was a feverish heat in my body. I stumbled out of my hut at the call of the matin bells and collapsed at the door of the church.

I was in a fever for some weeks. I remember very little of this time. I know that I dreamed of Jesus and also of Egfrith. I called out in my sleep, and sometimes I felt that I was Jennet, soaring through the skies, riding the currents, returning to land on the arm of the one I loved the most. Of the nuns who tended me, I remember nothing.

The leaves were back on the trees when I was able to leave my bed. The nuns told me they had feared for my life, but God had saved me, so He must have a great purpose for me. They walked me around the hut, then on one warm morning, into the abbey garden.

They told me that Brother Wilfrid was nearby and that he wished to speak with me. When I was strong enough, they would take me to meet him. I improved quickly after that. I wondered if Wilfrid had news of Egfrith. Although I tried to keep him out, my husband crept often into my thoughts.

The day came when, supported by a nun on each side, I walked the length of the lane to the gatehouse where Brother Wilfrid was waiting for me.

"Dear Sister," he greeted me. "You have been face to face with death. I am glad that you have returned from the encounter."

I bowed my head.

"I come to bring news."

"Yes."

"Preparations have been made for your journey south. You are to return to Anglia, where you will be received back into the abbey at Dunwich. There you will continue to prepare for your initiation."

"Brother, I am ready now."

He shook his head slowly. "No child, I think not."

"I have prayed every day. I have been most devout. I have borne all the gifts of my Lord, cold and sickness and hunger."

"Sister Etheldreda, your intentions are exemplary, but there is a part of you which still clings to the world... no, wait," as I was about to interrupt. "The nuns have told me that you spoke freely in your sleep, that you often mentioned your husband. Even now, I see a spark light in your eye at the mention of him. You long for news of him, my child."

I dropped my eyes again. I could not deny it.

"When you are back home, with many miles between you, and where the climate is more gentle, you will learn slowly to keep your focus on the Lord. Then, you may be ready to take the vow."

Three weeks later we set off. Brother Wilfrid planned to accompany me all the way, as he had recently visited with my Aunt Hilda at Whitby, and she currently had no need of him. After I was settled in my new quarters, he would return there to join the synod and prepare for his next visit to Rome.

The weather was clement, the sun shone and the views out to sea were so spectacular they took my breath away. We travelled at a gentle pace and on the second day, I saw the castle of the King of Northumberland glowing in the late afternoon sunshine. We didn't stop, and Brother Wilfrid said nothing. We were both travelling incognito, in plain brown robes, that no one would pass on news of us.

Wilfrid had told me nothing of Egfrith, of how he had received the news of my decision, or what he was doing. But this need for disguise created a knot of excitement in my chest which I was unable to disperse. I kept my eyes on the road ahead. I had spent three years of my life at the castle. In human terms, those last three months had been the happiest I had ever spent. It was a great temptation. I prayed as we rode past, beseeching God to give the strength to keep me true.

That night we took lodgings at an inn. Brother Wilfrid was particularly solicitous of me as we partook of a simple meal before retiring, and exhorted me to prayer when we parted to our rooms.

I could not sleep. I tossed and turned in the flea-ridden bed, listening to the sounds of things scuttling in the corners of the room. At one point I thought I heard footsteps outside. Probably the village men, returning from their revelries.

It was in the darkest hour that I sat bolt upright in my bed. Someone was tapping at my door. I lay back down, but it continued. Not hard, just a light tapping. I thought I heard someone whisper my name. I got up and paced back and forth. I knelt beside my bed and tried to pray, but the words would not form on my lips. I went to the door and opened it. There was a figure cloaked in black, his dear finger to his lips.

He held out his hand to me and I took it. We crept silently down the stairs and into the night, across the village green to where his horse was waiting beneath some trees.

I stopped, pulling my hand from his.

"I cannot come with you."

"Etheldreda, I can't let you go."

"I have made my decision. It was made before we ever met, when I was but a child."

"We could be happy."

"Egfrith, I belong to the Lord. This you knew when we married. It cannot be changed at the whims of man."

"Whims?" he grabbed my hand and pulled me to him so our bodies were touching and our faces close together. "Eth, I want you to be my queen, my companion, my playmate, the mother of my children and the co-ruler of my kingdom. These are not whims, this is the deepest, truest thing I have ever felt, that I will ever feel."

He kissed me then. I felt his lips on mine, soft and warm, the moisture of his mouth, the skin of his face rubbing against the tenderness of my own, and I wanted to give in. I wanted to melt against him, let him throw me onto his horse, then to ride, my arms about his waist, back to the castle where we would live the life he spoke of. My arms reached for him, my body pressed itself against him. I felt the hard jab of the medallion as the pressure of our bodies forced it against my breasts.

I pushed against him as hard as I could and freed myself.

"No," I gasped. "It cannot be."

He took a step towards me and I stepped back. I pulled the medallion out from beneath my robe and held it before me like a talisman.

"I still wear this."

"Eth, I love you," he said.

I swallowed. I wished I had not opened the door to him. I wished my flesh were not so weak.

"Egfrith, I am not free to love you in the way you wish. Soon I take my vows. We must part now and never see each other again."

"No!" he reached for me again, but I evaded his grasp.

"Goodbye, Egfrith."

I turned and ran, and he didn't follow. I ran up the stairs and threw myself on my bed and sobbed until I thought my chest might burst and my body break in two.

Brother Wilfrid said nothing the next morning, although he could not fail to notice my swollen face, and had probably heard me in the night. He ate breakfast, although I couldn't manage anything more than a cup of ale, and then we continued with our journey.

For the next few days I wondered if we were being followed, if there was a man on horseback who sometimes appeared on the horizon only to disappear again, a bird that flew high in the sky above us. I said nothing of this. A week later we crossed the great river and the land of the North was behind me for ever.

Chapter Twenty-Nine

Danny did a project at school on suspension bridges. He showed Jen pictures of them on the internet.

"The Humber Bridge used to be the longest in the world," he told her. "It's nearly a mile long."

Jen wasn't keen on bridges. When they went over them in the family car, she closed her eyes. Sometimes she closed her eyes when she was walking over a bridge, but mostly she just held her breath and walked fast.

"There's a footpath," Danny told her. "People walk over it, and run. There's a race every year that goes both ways."

Jen shuddered. "You wouldn't catch me doing that," she said.

"It's perfectly safe," said Danny.

"It's perfectly safe," said Finn.

They were standing on the path leading up to the bridge. Ethie was sitting on a wall, swinging her legs.

"Look, all those cars going over," said Danny, "lorries too, the bridge takes their weight. It's not going to break when you walk over."

"I know."

"I'll hold your hand," said Finn.

"I'll hold the other one."

"No."

"Just cross the bridge," said Ethie. "She'll follow."

"But..."

"Leave her alone."

Finn and Danny looked uncertain. Ethie slid off the wall and started walking. Her steps were slow, and Jen wondered if she was in pain, but neither of the boys offered to hold her hand. They looked at Jen.

"Are you sure?"

"Just do what she said. Go."

They set out across the bridge. Danny had the longest legs, and although Finn was getting stronger, he couldn't keep up. Soon the three of them were stretched out in a row, Danny in front, then Finn twenty feet behind and Ethie falling further into the rear. Finn looked round a couple of times, but Jen waved him on.

She didn't start walking until Ethie had passed the midpoint. By then Danny was almost out of sight, a stick person moving behind the railings. Jen couldn't see Finn because a family was coming the other way and blocked her vision.

Ethie was moving slower and slower.

Jen couldn't hold her breath for a mile. She wrapped her arms around herself, smoothing the shiny fabric of the sports jacket between her fingers. She breathed in, breathed out and set off.

Every few yards there was a little hole, and if you looked down you could see the water way below. Jen kept her eyes fixed firmly on the ground in front of her feet.

After a while she felt her muscles relax. This was OK, this was walking, it was safe, she could do it. She didn't look left or right. She didn't look ahead. She'd catch up with the others when she did.

The cars passed, each with a whooshing noise. Jen started to count them.

Her legs were moving one in front of the other. She was nearly halfway.

A juggernaut went past. It didn't whoosh so much as roar, and Jen felt the shockwaves rock the ground beneath her feet. *Oh God*, she thought, *I'm right in the middle.*

But she kept on walking. She could see the brown river water in her peripheral vision, but pretended she couldn't. Ahead was dry land. Ahead were her brother and her boyfriend. Was Finn her boyfriend? How could you tell such things? They'd not discussed it, she couldn't imagine discussing it. But that night in the B&B in Filey, it had felt right.

She was nearly there. There were trees below the level of the bridge. Soon she would be above land, not water.

A group of people were blocking the path, standing in a small circle. One of them was speaking into a phone. Something was on the floor in the middle of them.

Jen pushed forward and looked. Ethie was lying on her side, her stick on the ground beside her. A woman was putting her into the recovery position.

"She just collapsed," the man was saying into his phone. "She was walking along and fell. Probably fainted."

"She's my friend," said Jen. "She's my cousin."

She knelt down beside Ethie and put her hand on her shoulder.

"Eth."

Ethie's eyelids fluttered a bit, then her eyes opened.

"She seems to be waking up. There's someone with her now, her cousin I think. I can't see any injuries."

The man listened for a moment then ended the phone call. "You OK?"

"They're not coming, unless we call back. They said to give her water and sugar."

"Fruit," whispered Ethie.

"Fruit?" said the man. "Yes, I guess fruit will do."

"Is everything OK?"

Jen looked up. Danny and Finn had come back and were standing in the circle.

"We'll take care of her," said Danny. "She's with us."

"Here," said a woman. She thrust a banana into Jen's hand. "Give her this."

Then the crowd melted away.

Ethie ate the banana and drank some water from Danny's bottle.

"Come on, you daft ha'peth. Let's find somewhere to camp up for the night," Danny helped her to her feet.

"Are you OK?" Finn asked Jen.

She grinned at him. "Yes. I made it."

They found a spot to pitch the tent behind a hedge at the edge of a field. If the farmer came along he'd probably tell them to clear off, but the light was fading, and they'd pack up early in the morning. Leave no trace, Danny was insistent on that.

As soon as the tent was up, Ethie planted her stick in the ground and crawled inside. The walk from the end of the bridge had been slow and painful, along the riverbank, through a nature reserve, Danny and Finn both supporting her. When they stopped and let go of her arms, she nearly fell again.

"I'll see how she is," said Jen.

The boys nodded, and Jen squirmed feet first through the tent's opening, so she was lying next to Ethie, both of them on their tummies, supported on their elbows.

"You have to leave me," said Ethie.

"Don't be silly."

"I'm slowing you down. I can't keep up."

"We're not leaving you."

"It's me they're after."

"Not only you. I'm a missing person. And I didn't notice you leaving me behind when I was ill."

"You needed me then."

"And you need me now. We'll find a way. If it's important to get to Norwich, then we'll get there. Have you heard from Wolf?"

Ethie frowned and shook her head. "He can't help us anymore."

Jen moved her forearm so her hand covered Ethie's and squeezed.

"If I don't make it, you should find Jules. And you should go to the cathedral."

"We'll go together."

"You'll find what you're looking for at the cathedral."

"Ethie, we're not leaving you. Have you eaten anything else?"

Ethie shook her head.

"I'll get you something."

Danny and Finn were leaning against the gate, looking across the darkening fields to the river. The brown water flowed slow as mud, dotted with white and orange detritus, which on closer inspection was a group of swans and the reflections of lights on the far bank.

They didn't hear Jen approach.

Danny was saying, "We have to get her back."

"It's up to her."

"She's been ill. She needs looking after."

"We can look after her."

"You know that won't do. She needs her family – the rest of her family."

"But you've heard her, she doesn't want to go to her family. She's dead against it. We can't force her."

"We could call Barbara."

Finn was quiet for a moment. Their open bags were on the ground halfway to the tent, the tub of fruit in the top of one. Jen slid it out quietly.

"I'm not calling Barbara," said Finn, "unless she agrees to it."

"She won't agree to it. Don't you see? She thinks she's OK here, that everything will be fine. I don't think she even knows where she is. We have to decide for her."

"I'll talk to her."

"If you won't call Barbara, then I will."

Jen coughed. Both of them turned.

Their faces were in shadow, but she could tell they were both wondering what she'd overheard.

"The river is beautiful," she said. They turned back to look at it. It was so quiet. They could hear the plash of the water on the river beach, the squawks of water birds.

"Is Ethie OK?" asked Finn.

Jen shrugged.

Back at the tent, Ethie took the box of berries eagerly. She thrust in her hand, shoved currants, gooseberries and raspberries into her mouth. Juice ran between her knuckles and from the corner of her mouth. Jen watched, fascinated.

Once, Rebecca had a dog for the summer. His name was Homer and his owners had gone travelling. Rebecca had been nagging her aunt and uncle for a pet of her own, and when their colleague asked if they knew anyone who'd take Homer, they thought it would be a good way to test the waters. It turned out that dogs and Rebecca didn't work well together – she wanted a creature to be her soulmate and devoted companion when she needed it, but wasn't really prepared for the time and effort she'd need to put in herself. Homer ended up spending quite a bit of the summer at Jen's house. Jen, Danny and Dorothy were all really sorry when he returned to Cambridge at the end of the summer.

Jen remembered how excited he was by food. How his eyes shone as he drooled and hopped about. How when you put his bowl in front of him, he almost dived in headfirst.

Ethie shovelled in more fruit, and more, until the box was empty and her hands were purple. She pushed the box and the lid away from her and wiped her hands on the grass.

"Better?"

Ethie nodded. She folded her arms and lay her head on them as a pillow.

"Good idea," said Jen. "Get some sleep."

I crossed the bridge.

"You haven't crossed the bridge."

I walked it. I walked across the Humber Bridge. You told me to go to the bridge.

"That's not the bridge. If you'd crossed the bridge you'd be home. Are you home?"

What do you mean? What home? Your home is an island in the sea, but you were born in the fens like me. Water runs in our veins. We are like fish. Why would I want to be in Ely?

"When you reach the bridge, I will be there to help you."

I already crossed the bridge. Do you think that was nothing? Do you know how hard it was?

"Let the stories carry you. You'll get there. When you get to the middle, that isn't the end. Keep walking and come out again."

I feel eyelids. I feel them close. I don't want to look at you sitting in that chair. I don't want to know about the bridge. I already crossed it.

At Easter, Rebecca went abroad with her aunt and uncle. She wasn't in Ely. If she'd been in Ely, Jen might have gone to her. Rebecca would have known what to do. She'd have told her aunt, and Lucy would have taken charge, taken Jen under her wing. Rebecca had never felt at home in Ely, even though she'd lived there for seven years. She said it was like a really long holiday, that she was a Yorkshire girl at heart. She missed the rain.

Jen was pressed right up against the canvas. She moved her head and took in a deep breath. With her head tipped back she could see stars. The front of the tent was open.

She turned onto her belly, corkscrewing herself so as not to roll backwards and squash Ethie. She leaned on her elbows and looked out. It was dark, but the stars cast a bit of light and a quarter moon was hanging above the water casting a silver cone of light across the surface of the river.

She looked to see if Ethie was awake, but her cousin wasn't there. The other half of the tent was empty space.

"Ethie?" she called quietly. There was no reply.

She'd probably gone outside for a wee. It must have been her movement that had woken Jen. She leaned her chin on her hands and closed her eyes, opened them again to starlight.

Somewhere nearby, her brother was sleeping. Danny, her big brother who'd been at the hospital the night she was born and demanded to hold her even before they cleaned her up. He was three years old, and when their parents decided it was time to go to hospital, they had dropped him off with Dorothy. It was nine in the evening, and she'd tried to put him to bed, but he had screamed and yelled and cried and demanded to be taken to hospital to see his new sister. By one in the morning Dorothy had had enough. She bundled her grandson into the car and they arrived at the maternity hospital just as Jen was making her entrance into the world. Twenty minutes later, Danny was gazing into her blinking eyes.

Dorothy loved telling that story. How Danny had taken his favourite train with him to the hospital – Percy the Green Engine. He'd pulled it out of his pocket to show to his new sister, but it caught on a thread. He tugged and the thread broke and he bashed baby Jennifer in the face with Percy's wheels.

"But you didn't cry," said Dorothy. "You just kept staring at him and blinking."

The nurses had taken the baby away from him and given her to their father. Eventually Danny was persuaded to go home with his dad and gran, but only after they'd promised to bring him back first thing in the morning.

When Danny was eleven and Jen was eight, he was embarrassed by this story. When she was thirteen and he was sixteen, Jen was embarrassed by it.

Now she was nineteen, and Danny was out there in the darkness with Finn, who might be her boyfriend. She might be in love.

She heard a noise near the gate. There were pools of darkness behind the hedge on either side, but she thought she saw movement. Something pale, perhaps a white shirt. Then the noise again – a sob or an intake of breath.

"Ethie?" she called, a bit louder than before.

There was no response. Jen got out of the tent as quickly as she could. She ran to the gate.

"Ethie!"

Her cousin was squatting on her heels. One hand was held out in front of her, as though in supplication, palm up, fingers down, wrist exposed. In the other hand she held a piece of glass. She was using the broken edge to cut a line from her inner elbow.

"No! Ethie, no!"

Her cousin looked up and the moonlight lit up her face, the tear-shine of her eyes, the berry juice, the streaks of clean skin where the juice and dirt had been washed away.

Jen shook her head. "Don't," she whispered. "It won't help. It doesn't make anything better."

There was a line of blood beading up along the edge of the glass, but Ethie released the pressure. Then the others appeared out of the darkness. Danny crouched beside her, and took the glass from her. She fell against him, sobbing.

"Give me your t-shirt," said Danny. Finn stepped forward, pulling his shirt over his head.

Their mum thought he was going to be a doctor. That story, the night-time visit to the hospital, she thought it was an early interest in matters medical. But she was wrong. He'd done well in all of the sciences at school, but he wanted to build bridges. He'd been offered a place at Cambridge to study civil engineering.

"Tie it round her arm, above the cut, as tight as you can."

Finn did as instructed. Ethie was shaking now.

"We need to get moving," said Danny. "We'll set off at first light."

"But how…?" began Jen.

"We'll hitch," said Danny.

Chapter Thirty

Their mum never knew about the hitching. It started when Danny needed to get to London to sort out a visa for a school trip to Japan. He was going to visit the Akashi Kaikyo Bridge, the longest suspension bridge in the world.

This was in the days before Terence, before Donna was born again, but she was doing something that day which took her out early. She'd gone before Jen left for school or Danny went to the train station. She dropped a kiss onto each of their foreheads and left.

Jen looked at her brother munching toast and jam at the kitchen counter. Their dad always left for the boatyard before seven. It was only three weeks since Dorothy had died, one week since the funeral. There was no one else in the house.

"Can I come with you?"

Danny had been gazing out of the window, but now he turned his attention to his sister. She smiled at him.

"I won't be annoying."

"You can't help being annoying. It's part of the job."

"What job?"

"Little sister. Brat."

Jen grabbed a spoon from the work surface and threw it at his head. He ducked and the spoon flew across the room. There was a loud crack.

"Fuck!" said Jen.

It had hit a jug on a shelf. It wasn't a jug that was ever used. Donna had gone through a phase of collecting pottery and two kitchen shelves were filled with ceramic vases, jugs, bowls, all for decoration only.

Danny took the jug down. It was turquoise with splashes of pink and violet, and a ridged pattern circling it from top to bottom. There was a small chip in the rim, and a crack from there down to the bottom of the handle.

"Is that new?" asked Jen.

"I think so. Look, it's really clean here where the chip has come away."

"Mum will kill me."

"She won't notice. Not for ages anyway. She won't know it was you."

He took a few crumbs of dirt from a plant pot on the windowsill and rubbed them into the broken surface.

"There, it's not fresh anymore. Don't worry."

He put the jug back on the shelf.

"Thank you," said Jen. She picked up the spoon from the floor where it had fallen.

"I'm not going on the train," said Danny.

"What?"

"To London. I'm saving the money. I'm going to hitch."

"Oh!"

"I'm leaving in ten minutes, so be ready."

They got a lift from a van driver who was going to Epping, and then caught the tube the rest of the way. Danny got his visa sorted and they got a lift back to Cambridge with some students, where they caught the train for the last stretch home. They were back before either of their parents.

"Do you remember all those trips we went on?" Jen asked Danny. "That last summer you were at home?"

Danny's exams were over and once he was back from Japan, he had weeks with nothing to do. Inspired by the trip to London, he and Jen went on a series of daytrips, him impersonating their Dad to explain her absences at school – *glandular fever,* *she might be away quite often I'm afraid.* They had a day at the seaside in Great Yarmouth, a couple of days sightseeing in London, and other days when they just took whatever lifts came along, pot luck as to where they'd end up.

"Yes, and I remember Mum going ballistic when she found out."

Danny was standing at the edge of a roundabout with his thumb out, while Ethie, Jen and Finn sat on the grass verge. One of Donna's friends had spotted the two of them and told her, and that was the end of it. That was just before Danny set off to walk the Cleveland Way.

A car pulled up.

"Norwich?" asked the driver, looking at Danny's cardboard sign.

"Yes, or that direction."

"You're in luck. That's where I'm headed."

Jen sat in the back seat next to Finn. They held hands. Ethie sat on the other side of him, her forehead pressed against the window. Danny chatted to the driver. He'd always been good with strangers, with small talk. The rest of them were silent.

The landscape was huge, golden fields of wheat, followed by grazing cows, then more wheat. Sometimes a power station or brick works loomed on the horizon. The sky was blue, with white clouds scudding across.

It can't have always been like this, thought Jen. *This is all* *man-made: the roads, the fields, the factories.*

She looked at Ethie, whose lips were moving. She'd started up with the Jesus Prayer in the night when Danny took the glass away from her, and she hadn't stopped. She hadn't said anything, just the Prayer, and sometimes you could catch the words, "Lord Jesus Christ, have mercy on me, a sinner."

Jen had tried to talk to her, but Ethie wouldn't meet her eyes. She just stared at the floor and kept on with the Prayer.

Jen looked at Finn. There was new blood seeping from his wound. Surely it should be scabbing over and beginning to heal? He smiled and put his arm around her. She tried to relax, feeling the warmth of his body down her side, watching the miles pass by the car window.

***

Brother Wilfrid didn't allow me much rest. Once we left the great river behind, we walked until our legs would carry us no more, lay down to sleep wherever we were, rose at daybreak and continued. Sometimes we found an inn as night fell, but the landscape was wild and forbidding, habitations few and far between.

We encountered the kindness of strangers, farmers who gave us rides on the back of their carts, or parcels of food. But mostly we saw no one.

I kept an eye on the sky, but the only birds were kites, larks, lapwings. Never a peregrine falcon named Jennet.

I tried to focus on the life ahead of me, a life spent with my dear Lord, and I called upon Him to sustain me during this long and arduous journey.

We came to a hamlet by the name of Stow, where they gave us bread, cheese and ale, and allowed us to sleep in the village shelter with the cattle. Brother Wilfrid lay across the doorway, which was open. I slept further in, on bales of sweet-smelling hay.

"I should stay awake," said Wilfrid at sundown. He had been happy sleeping out in the wilds beneath hedgerows, but now that we were in the midst of civilisation, he felt the need to protect me. I knew I was safe. My Lord wouldn't have brought me thus far only to allow defilement by a stranger, and if I was to die by an unknown hand, then I would be all the sooner with Him, so I had no fear.

"Here," I said, planting my staff in the ground outside the door. "This staff is blessed by God and will protect us."

"Thy rod and thy staff…"

"… they comfort me. Blessed words. Brother Wilfrid, you may sleep tonight."

I don't know if he did sleep, but in the morning we continued our journey. I felt refreshed from the relative comfort of our accommodation, and Wilfrid showed no unwonted signs of fatigue. We were some miles on, past the Roman town of Lincoln, before I realised I had left my staff behind in the ground.

***

Your face looms in close and I can see pores in the crease where your nose meets your upper lip, I can see your eyelids, they are the colour of beech leaves in autumn. Your nostrils dilate as you breathe in, flatten on the outbreath.

Can you answer my questions?

"I will try."

Why has Ethie become so weak? She was strong before. She cared for me.

"You are stronger now."

When I am strong she is weak? Have I stolen her strength? Am I killing her?

"Stories are your protection."

Is my blood her blood? My breath her breath? Do we live inside the same skin?

"You are getting close to the bridge."

Will she die? What will happen to me if she dies? How can I live without her?

***

When they reached Norwich, Ethie directed them along narrow roads, then along a track which had grass growing in the middle. At the end was small church.

"Here," she said.

"I've never seen this place before," said the driver. They climbed out of the car; he did a tight three-point turn and went back the way he'd come.

"I'll go in first," said Ethie. "She's not used to visitors, it might be a bit much if we all go in together."

Jen found some tissues in her bag and handed them to Ethie. "You might want to clean some of that juice off your face first, so you don't frighten her."

Ethie's hair was matted, and dirt was ingrained below her ears as well as at the edges of her forearms. Her left arm was bandaged with a strip which Danny had cut from the bottom of his t-shirt. Finn was wearing the Buddha t-shirt – the only one he had – that they'd used as a tourniquet in the early hours. They had tried to rinse out Ethie's blood in a stream, but it was still stained and damp.

Ethie dabbed at her face with a tissue.

"Here," said Jen. She took the tissue out of Ethie's hand and licked it, then used the spit to dab at the juice stains. "My mum used to do this to me," she said.

"I don't remember my mum," said Ethie.

Jen pulled her into a hug. They both smelled of grass and rain and earth. Then Ethie went into the church.

Danny sat down and leaned his back against a gravestone. Finn and Jen sat on a bench and leaned against each other.

They waited, but Ethie didn't return. Danny seemed to be asleep. Half an hour passed.

"Do you want me to go and see?" Finn said.

"Give her a bit longer," said Jen.

But another half hour passed and still no one emerged from the church. Danny was on his feet now, pacing up and down.

"I'm going in," he said.

"I'll go," said Jen. "I know her better."

"What if there's trouble?"

"We'll all go," said Finn.

The church door opened easily and the three of them walked in. It was small, empty and cold, despite the sunshine outside. There was no sign of Ethie. Finn and Danny both took one of Jen's hands as they walked up the aisle, looking into all the pews, listening for any sound. Ethie wasn't in the church.

"There must be another door," said Danny. His voice sounded loud in the stillness.

"Shhh," said Jen. She thought she heard a sound, a footfall.

"What...?"

It came again, behind them. Jen spun round, letting go of the boys' hands. There was a figure silhouetted in the doorway, a tall man with a falcon on his shoulder and a bundle under his arm.

"Eg!"

"Who?" said Danny.

Eg walked down the aisle towards them and held out the bundle. It was the nun's habit they'd left in the graveyard.

"How did you find us?" asked Jen.

"Eth always comes here when she's troubled."

"She said you never follow her this far."

"I follow her everywhere. I'm skilled at keeping hidden."

"Who the fuck are you?"

"But she's not here," said Finn.

"Come with me," said Eg.

The three of them glanced at each other. Finn lifted his hand to his head and touched the edge of his wound.

"I'm sorry about that, my friend. My men sometimes get carried away. I didn't mean for them to hurt you."

"What about Ethie? What are you going to do to her?" asked Jen.

"I wish her no harm. Nor any to you."

Eg held out his hand. The daylight shone through the high windows illuminating his face. He was astonishingly handsome, his blue eyes shining with sincerity, his full lips bending almost to a smile. His hair was pushed back from his face at the moment, but the slightest action would drop it back across his brow. None of them took his hand.

"Where is she?" asked Jen.

He dropped his arm to his side.

"Come," he said.

They followed him. There was a small door, hidden by shadows, to the right of the altar. It opened easily, and the four of them passed into a small corridor, lit by a flaming torch high in the wall. At the end, a wall blocked the way, with just a small hole at chest height. There was a chair next to the wall and a candle on the ground, flickering in a jar.

"Eth?" said Eg. "Eth?" He spun round. "She should be here. Eth, where are you?" He ran up to the wall and put his face to the hole. "Where is she?" he shouted.

A voice answered him. "There is no one here but myself."

"But Eth came to see you. We saw her come this way. Where is she?"

"I have not seen Etheldreda for many years. I would be glad to see her. Is she with you?"

"She was with you."

"I have seen no one for many days."

"Well, where is she then?" Eg shouted, then he turned and sank to the floor, his back to the wall, and put his head in his hands. "Where is she?" he sobbed.

Danny went up to the hole and looked in.

"Fuck, there's a woman in there," he said.

"Please do not use profanities in the House of the Lord," said the voice.

Finn and Jen took turns to look through the hole. There was a room with a small high window, a bed, a table, a pitcher of water, and a wooden chair on which sat a woman wearing white robes. The room had no door, three walls being made of the same stone as the church and the fourth, the bricked-up end of the corridor.

"We're looking for my friend Ethie," said Jen. "Are you Jules?"

The woman nodded.

"She came into the church to see you. About an hour ago. More maybe."

The woman hung her head.

"Perhaps she has been taken," she said in a soft voice.

"Taken by who?" asked Finn, trying to fit his face at the gap next to Jen's.

"A gentleman comes often. He tries to tempt me from my vigil. His lures are the temptations of the devil, but he is charming, persuasive. When he visits, I must cover my head and pray out loud to the Lord."

"Has he been here? This morning?"

"I have not seen him, but I thought I smelled something. A perfume he wears."

"Would he take Ethie?"

"He would try anything, I think, to make me break my vow."

"What is your vow?" asked Finn.

"To stay here in this cell, living out my days in devotion with my Lord and Saviour."

"How long have you been here?"

"Thirteen years. Or perhaps many hundreds. It is difficult to count the days."

"Where might this man have taken Ethie? There is only one entrance."

"You must dismantle the wall."

"What?"

"This wall, that blocks me in. It seems that my vigil has come to an end; he has succeeded. I wish to help you find my friend. You must let me out of here."

The wall was not as strong as it appeared. Danny looked around outside and came back with two pieces of wood he'd found at the back of the church. He and Eg started slamming at the edges of the hole.

"Keep back," Jen called into the hole.

The first bricks soon came away, and the rest were even quicker. The plaster was very old and crumbled easily.

"You could have probably broken out of here with your bare hands," Danny called through to Jules.

"It was never my intention to break out," she replied.

After half an hour they had a hole big enough for a person to climb through, and assisted by Jen and Finn, Jules climbed through into the passage. She was very small. Her hair was covered with a white scarf, and her face was unblemished, ageless.

"Let's go," she said, leading the way.

As they rushed through the church, Jen felt something was different. The light was clearer. The church seemed less spartan. There were prayer cushions and hymn books. The pews looked to be made of a paler wood. But there was no time to stop and look.

Eg tripped on something and they found Ethie's stick lying on the floor at the end of the pew nearest the door.

"She was here," he said.

Jules and Danny were first through the door.

"Whoa!" said Danny, as the others all tumbled out after him.

They had emerged into a modern street. Cars were parked neatly at the side of the road at the end of double yellow lines. A bus rushed past.

Eg was already striding down the road with Jules in pursuit.

"Come on," said Finn. "Let's not lose them."

The road joined a much busier one after a few hundred yards. Here there were people and shops. Jules took hold of Eg's arm and pulled.

"Stop!"

"I want to find Eth. Where is she?"

"You won't find her by just marching off. We need to think. We need to get into his mind."

"Who is he?" Eg shook her hand off angrily. "Why has he taken Eth?"

"Because of me," Jules said quietly. "He searches for purity, but when he finds it, he is compelled to defile it. He wants me, and he thinks if he takes Eth I will offer myself in her place."

"Why would you do that?" asked Danny.

"Because I am her friend."

"He probably wants the medallion too," said Jen.

Eg turned violently towards her. "What do you know of the medallion? What man is this that wants to take it from her?"

Jen shrank back against Finn who put his arms around her.

"If it's the same man, then you know him. He's called Beau." Jules flinched, and Jen knew she was on the right track. "She lost the medallion to him in a poker game, but I stole it and we ran away. He's been after us ever since."

"A poker game? She lost?"

"She was frightened of him. But I got the medallion back for her."

"And still she wears it?"

"Yes. You saw it in the castle."

"What are you lot on about?" said Danny.

"People are staring at us," said Jules.

It was true. The five of them were taking up a large part of the pavement. Jules was dressed in white robes and Eg in high boots and a leather jerkin with a falcon on his shoulder. Finn's bleeding head and bloody shirt didn't help.

"I need different clothes," said Jules, "so I can blend in." She turned to Jen. "You will take me shopping."

"Will I?"

"And him too," Jules said, pointing at Eg.

Eg refused point blank to go clothes shopping. "There is nothing wrong with my clothes. They were made by the best tailors in my land."

"He could get by," said Finn. "He just looks eccentric. But I agree, you probably do need to change those robes."

They decided that the three boys would go and find a coffee shop and wait whilst Jen and Jules went clothes shopping.

"What about money?" asked Jen. "I haven't got any."

Both Finn and Danny reached for their wallets, but before they could pull them out, Eg handed Jen a wodge of cash. She flicked through it. All twenties.

"There must be hundreds here," she said.

"I have no need of it," said Eg. "Come, let us discuss our battleplan."

Chapter Thirty-One

Some weekends, Jen and Rebecca went shopping in Cambridge. At first they went with Rebecca's aunt, Lucy, but as they got older they got the train on their own. They'd wander around the shops, trying on outfits they couldn't afford, spraying themselves with perfume and using the testers in the makeup section. When they were sixteen, Rebecca got a part-time job after school, so she had a little bit of money to spend.

"What do you think of this?"

"Ha! You'd look like your aunt."

"No, I wouldn't." Rebecca put the shirt back on the sales rack, riffled through and found a yellow embroidered dress. "This would suit you."

Jen looked at the dress. It was pretty, and the shape was great too, it would fall from her hips with a bit of sway, not too much. "Have they got it in white?"

"Jen, you can't only wear white. This would go really well with your hair and your eyes. It would make me look ill. You're lucky."

Jen didn't answer. She used to wear all sorts of colours, but lately, given a choice she wore white. She felt less self-conscious. Any other colour she tried seemed brash and garish, ostentatious. She found the same dress in ivory and held it against herself.

Rebecca squinted, her head on one side. "Yes, it's better than the yellow. But I think you should have the yellow on principle."

"I haven't got any money," said Jen.

"I will buy it for you as a present. No, don't even argue, it's not up for discussion."

"Not the yellow one though. I wouldn't wear it."

Rebecca held the two dresses out, one in each hand, and looked from one to the other.

"Well, I hate to encourage you, but the white one is nicer. You'll look amazing in it."

They took the dress to the changing room, and while Rebecca was trying on an armful of shirts and tops and trousers, Jen slid the dress over her head. It had a silky underslip which slid against her skin, and when she turned, first this way, then that, the sway was exactly as she'd hoped.

At the till Rebecca said, "What does your mum think about you only wearing white clothes? Does she mind the washing?"

Jen shrugged. "Mum's always been good at washing," she said. "She likes it."

"God, I should tell my aunt, she'd send ours round."

"Anyway, it means all my stuff can go in together, and doesn't get mixed up with anyone else's. I hate the thought of that."

Rebecca handed her purchases to the till assistant to be scanned, folded, bagged. "Jen, you're a bit weird these days. Does it even matter?"

"I just don't like the thought of my clothes in the machine with my mum's black knickers."

"Black's meant to make you look thin."

"I don't want clothes to make me look thin," said Jen. "I am thin."

"That's because you don't eat properly."

"Says you. When did you last eat a square meal?"

"Last time my aunt cooked one. Which does actually happen more than you think." The shop assistant handed Rebecca the bag of clothes and they left the shop. "You do look great in white though, Jen, like an angel or a saint or something. Is that the look you're going for?"

"I'm not going for a look. It just makes me feel better."

Shopping with Jules was not what Jen had expected. She tried to steer her to the high street, but Jules had her own ideas. Before long they had spent a good number of Eg's twenties and Jules looked like a different person.

"Shall we go and find the others now?" asked Jen.

But Jules had stopped again. She was looking at a poster in a shop window.

"Her face," she said, pointing at the model. "How does she have this face?"

"Makeup," Jen said. "It's a beauty salon, that's what they do."

"If I go in there, they will make me look like this?"

Jen shrugged, thinking the boys had probably had time for three coffees already, but Jules was already through the door.

When they turned up at the café three quarters of an hour later, Finn and Eg did a double take. Danny spluttered into his coffee.

Jules was wearing tight black leather from head to toe. She had stiletto boots and tight leather trousers, a leather jacket and a black satin vest. Her hair, loosed from the scarf, was red and curly, and her lips were painted scarlet, her eyelashes heavy with mascara.

"I thought you wanted to blend in," said Finn.

"You look amazing!" said Danny.

"Have you come up with a plan?" asked Jen. "How are we going to find Ethie?"

"Do you like my makeup?" said Jules. "It's the biker girl look."

"I can't believe it. You look completely different," said Danny, staring.

"I wouldn't go there if I were you," said Eg.

"What?"

"Religious girls. Just don't," said Eg.

Jen burst into tears. Finn took her hand. "Come with me," he said.

They walked across the road and put he his arms around her. His shoulder was warm against the skin of her cheek.

"Jen, it's OK."

"But Ethie might be in danger. They're all just drinking coffee and chatting, and that man has got her."

"Running around like headless chickens won't help her. Look at Jules and Eg. They both know her, and this Beau character, and they're not panicking."

Jen thought about Ethie, her face when she played poker, giving nothing away, the way she hid her fear in her chest along with the medallion, the way she'd stood up to Beau until he mentioned Eg. She'd thought then that it was Eg that Ethie feared the most. But Eg loved her. It was Ethie's own feelings that terrified her.

"OK," she said. Finn kissed her. "But we need to make a plan. We have to find her."

They walked back to the others.

"I will send Jennet," Eg was saying. "She can spot a field mouse in corn. Beau cannot hide from her."

"He had a jeep when we saw him," said Danny. "I'm sure your bird is good, but she can't fly as fast as a car. They could be miles away already."

"Ethie told me to go to the cathedral," said Jen. "She said I'd find what I needed there."

"What do you need?"

"I don't know. But I think we should go and look. There might be a clue."

"OK," said Danny. "As good a plan as any I guess."

They drained their coffees. Jules slid her leather clad legs out from under the table, and Danny offered his arm. Even with the stilettos she only came up to his shoulder.

"How can she walk in them?" Jen said to Finn. "She's never worn them before, she told me. And look at her."

She was laughing at something Danny had said, looking up into his face.

"I think it's love," said Finn.

The cathedral was a short walk across the city centre. Eg strode ahead, Jennet on his shoulder. Danny and Jules walked together, talking nonstop, her hand still on his arm. Finn and Jen walked hand in hand.

"How's your head today?"

"I've had a massive headache all day," he said, "though I'm less woozy. It seems to be one or the other."

"I wish the wound would heal," said Jen.

"I've been seeing strange lights. Like fluorescent strips. They flash on and off, then they go."

"It's probably concussion. You could have done with a rest, not charging about the country like this."

"It's not just lights. There's a room. And there are people in it. My mum and dad, and my sister."

"I didn't know you had a sister."

"She lives in Australia. She's married with a baby. I haven't seen her for four years."

"You're an uncle!"

"Yes," Finn grinned. "A boy called Joe. I've seen pictures. He's two months old."

"I bet you can't wait to meet him."

"I was going to go at Christmas."

"Was?"

Finn frowned and shook his head. "Look, we're here."

The entrance to the cathedral was through a shop to the side of the main door. Eg was having an issue with one of the assistants who wasn't sure about him going in with Jennet.

"She'll just stay on my arm. She won't shit on the floor or anything."

The woman flinched. "That's not the problem."

"Then what is? Doesn't your God like birds?"

"Yes. Yes, He does. We have our own, here at the cathedral."

"Your own birds?"

"Our own peregrine falcons. They nest in the steeple. They may be territorial."

"Do you hear that Jennet? Friends. Go on, fly."

He lifted his arm and Jennet flew out of the door and up towards the roof of the cathedral.

"She'll have a grand old time visiting," Eg said to the woman. "I'll give her a whistle when it's time to go."

Danny and Jules were inside, but it seemed that all they were seeing was each other.

Jen turned to Finn. "Ethie said I'd find what I was looking for. What can it be?"

"Not her, presumably. She hadn't been kidnapped then."

They walked up the left transept, past small chapels and art exhibitions, across the front of the cathedral and down the other side. Danny and Jules stood at the top of the central aisle, deep in conversation.

"Do you think she's for real?" asked Jen. "She doesn't look like a religious recluse."

"Neither does Ethie," said Finn, "and Eg doesn't look like a Northumbrian king."

Eg was just up ahead of them, watching a screen near the entrance to the shop. He was rocking back and forth on his feet. As they approached, he looked their way. His eyes were shining.

"I don't know. I think he looks exactly like a Northumbrian king. Look at him. He's just like Ethie."

"No, he's not. She's moody and cross. Angry."

"Not always. You should see her when she's excited about something. Like pineapple or mango, or poker."

"Come and look!" said Eg.

They joined him in front of the screen. The cathedral spire was fitted with a webcam. Three falcons were standing on a small wooden platform, two close together and one slightly apart. The bird on its own wore leather jesses.

"Is that Jennet?"

"I love this age. I can watch her and she doesn't know. I can see her in the wild."

"Well, not really wild," said Finn. "It's the middle of a city, and she's not really wild at all. I mean, she's kind of a captive bird, isn't she?"

Eg turned and looked at him. He was five inches taller than Finn, his shoulders were squared, and his face shone with the reflection from the screen.

"Jennet may fly away whenever she wants," he said to Finn. "She catches her own food. She stays with me because she wants to."

Finn held his gaze. On the screen one of the two resident falcons flew up into the air. Jennet turned her head away from the remaining bird and began to preen her chest feathers.

"And what about Ethie? She chooses not to be with you, and yet you pursue her."

"No, you are wrong. Ethie has not learned to listen to her heart. One day she will, and I will be there waiting for her."

"She runs from you."

"She was running from Beau."

"She's running from herself," said Jen.

They both turned to look at her.

"I'm going out to the cloisters," she said.

Outside the sun was shining. The cloisters formed four sides of a square. In the middle the grass was bright green and Jen was momentarily dazzled. Neither Finn nor Eg had followed her. Small steps led into the central space and Jen walked into the sunshine.

A woman was on the grass, pushing a pushchair. She was walking towards Jen, then she turned and walked away again. After twenty steps, she turned again. Her child was asleep in the pushchair. The woman was looking at the ground. She walked in an arc across the grass, then turned again. Each time she turned, she was nearer the middle of the green.

Jen stepped closer. There was a pattern marked out on the grass with pieces of stone. The woman was pushing her child through a labyrinth.

There was no one else in the cloisters. Jen walked around the outside of the labyrinth until she found the entrance. Then she walked away from it, towards the stone walkways, and waited until the woman with the pushchair had finished. The woman reached the middle, then walked out in a straight line, right over the top of the stone, ignoring the boundaries. Jen closed her eyes.

When she opened them a few minutes later, she was alone.

She stepped into the labyrinth. The path took her straight into the pattern, then guided her back out to the outer edge. One moment she thought she was reaching the centre, then she was walking right around to the other side. She thought of pictures she'd seen of the human brain, the two hemispheres, the ridges and grooves.

She wanted to close her eyes, but she needed to see the path. She tried speaking. "All will be well and all will be well." She shook her head and tried again. "Lord Jesus Christ, have mercy on me, a sinner."

She managed to get it out once, but her lips felt dry. She licked them and parted them again. "All will be well and all will be well."

Danny had had girlfriends. He'd brought some of them home, and others she'd heard about, from him or other friends. She'd seen him kissing a girl in the cathedral gardens once, and he had his hand inside her blouse. They were lying on the grass in the sunshine and the girl was pressed right up against him. Jen had turned back and walked home the long way. She'd never seen him look at anyone the way he was looking at Jules inside the cathedral.

Jen turned, then turned again, and she was in the centre of the labyrinth.

There was a circle of stone on the floor. Jen looked down at it, then up into the sky. Three peregrines flew across the clear blue square above her. She thought she heard someone call her name. A woman's voice, familiar. She shook her head and looked down again.

She walked around the circular stone, and then she was back in the labyrinth, going back the way she had come. This was what Ethie meant her to find. The earth sculpture in the Wolds, the stone spiral on the clifftops, they had taken her into the middle and left her there.

Here she didn't even have to turn. She just kept on walking, and she was on her way back out.

She heard the voice again.

"Jennifer!"

Nobody called her Jennifer. Only one person had ever called her Jennifer. She was on the outer edge of the labyrinth now, but there was no one else out here. There was no sound, except the soft fall of her feet on the grass, one after the other. She kept her gaze fixed downwards.

Jen turned and the path took her through the heart of the labyrinth to the exit.

"Jennifer."

She had done it. She'd walked in and she'd walked out again. She looked up.

"Gran!"

Dorothy was waiting for her on the grass, her arms open. Jen ran into them, and let her gran envelop her.

Chapter Thirty-Two

"Where are the others?"

Most of the tables in the cathedral café were full, but Jen couldn't see Finn, Eg or Danny and Jules. Near the window a couple sat with a plate of scones and jam. They were wearing walking clothes. The woman wore a yellow hat.

"They've made themselves scarce so I can have a chat with you."

A waitress arrived at their table with a pot of tea and two enormous chocolate chip cookies.

Jen grinned. "You remembered."

When she came to live with them, Dorothy had kept biscuits in the cupboard by her bed. Chocolate chip cookies were Jen's favourites.

Dorothy put her hand over Jen's where it lay on the table.

"I've missed you," she said.

"I've missed you too, Gran. It's just sad at home. Your room, it's still just like you left it. Danny's too."

"I understand that it was looking for Danny that brought you here."

Jen picked up a cookie and broke a bit off. She shifted in her seat.

"Well, partly."

"What else?"

"I couldn't stay at home."

"Your mother..."

"... she doesn't care. Ever since you and Danny went. She's been born again, and she's a different person now. She's been

279

born as someone else. She only wants to know about Terence and the Church."

"It's been hard for you all."

"At Easter when I went home, she'd got a lodger using my room. She doesn't want me there."

"Do you know where your mum has spent the last three months?"

"Scrubbing the church floors, on a pilgrimage, I don't know."

"She's been sitting—"

"I don't want to know." The piece of cookie in Jen's fingers disintegrated into crumbs. She held her grandmother's gaze. "I don't want to talk about her."

Dorothy nodded once. She picked up the teapot and poured tea. Jen broke off another bit of biscuit and popped it in her mouth. She chewed, but it tasted like dust and didn't seem to get any smaller. Dorothy offered her a napkin and she spat the chewed biscuit into it screwed it up into a ball.

"You have to make a decision," Dorothy said.

"Why do I? Why can't I just carry on like this?"

"Because you are neither one thing nor the other."

"I want to be both."

Dorothy smiled. "I'm afraid it doesn't work like that."

"But all these people, in this café, in the cathedral, in the streets – they aren't all dead."

"Most of them are. There are a few like you. And there are some amongst the living who can break through, but most of the people here are dead."

Jen looked around. The café was full, people sitting at tables in groups, some couples, a few children and young people, but more older people. Wasn't that normal for tourist places like this?

"Why aren't there more then?" She looked back at Dorothy who was sipping her tea. "People have been dying for thousands of years. Why isn't it more crowded?"

"People only stay as long as they are remembered. Once a person is forgotten, they fade away."

"So remembering someone keeps them alive?"

"Not really, this isn't…"

"I know. But still. Keeps them in existence."

"I suppose."

"And what if someone has been forgotten, then someone remembers them? Can they be brought back?"

"Possibly. I don't know all of the answers."

"So if I go home, as long as I remember you and Danny, then you will still be here?"

"We will always be with you, even though you may not see us. You won't ever be alone."

"And Ethie?"

"Ethie isn't quite what you think she is."

"She's my cousin. She's a princess and the bride of Christ."

Dorothy shrugged and put her cup down in her saucer with a clatter.

"That's what she is to you."

"I need to find her. She's been kidnapped."

"The best thing you can do – for her as well as yourself – is to get better and return to your family. One day you will come to this world, but it doesn't have to be now."

"What about Danny? I can't leave without seeing Danny."

"He's waiting for you. He and that girl – Julie, is it? – they've found a car and they'll drive you home."

"Do you think I should go?"

Dorothy took hold of Jen's hand. "If you ever need me, stretch out your hand and I'll take it." Jen felt tears prick her eyes, and Dorothy swam out of sight until she blinked her back again. "And your mum…"

"What about her?"

"It's been hard for her, since Danny died. She's made mistakes."

"She still had me. And Dad."

"She's been trying to make sense of it. And that Terence, he's very convincing."

"Only if you're an idiot."

Dorothy laughed out loud. "Go on, find Danny and let him take you home."

"But…"

"I'll walk with you."

Danny and Jules were waiting at the front of the cathedral, next to a small red car.

"Where did you get that from?"

"The verger said we could borrow it."

"I promised him all would be well," said Jules.

Jen stared at her. "Are you…?"

"There have been many anchorites."

"Yes, but they're not all remembered."

"Come on," said Danny. "Hop in, it's time to go."

Jen turned to Dorothy who wrapped her in a big hug. She smelled of peppermints, just like she used to.

"Sorry about the bottle," Jen said into the fabric of her gran's cardigan. "Do you want the ship?"

She fished into the pocket of her jeans and pulled it out.

"I'm sorry about the bottle too," said Dorothy, taking the broken ship and balancing it on her hand, "and the damage it caused. Now get going."

"Say hello to Grandad for me."

Dorothy smiled and Jen climbed into the back seat of the car. Danny and Jules got into the front and they set off.

***

The first they heard was that there had been an accident. The school phoned, the school that Danny had left a few weeks before, the school that ran the Duke of Edinburgh scheme that he was still involved in, even though he was off to Cambridge in the autumn. He was set to become a civil engineer. One of the best. He would build bridges one day.

"There's been an accident," the school secretary told Donna. "Two of the boys have been taken to hospital in Scarborough." She didn't have any more details.

"Should we come?" Donna asked. "We can set off straight away."

"I'll phone when there's more news."

So they waited in the hallway, the three of them, for the phone to ring. Donna paced up and down and Jen sat on her Dad's lap. She was fifteen and she hadn't sat on his lap for years.

"We should go," said Donna.

"I'll get the car," said Steve.

"It might not be him. She said two boys. There's ten of them on the trip, it might not be him."

"OK, we'll wait then."

Jen felt as though her bones were made of wood, splintered at the ends, brittle, rotting. She sat as still as she could.

"Should we go?" asked Donna.

"It's up to you, love," said Steve.

"We should go," said Jen.

They set off ten minutes later, Jen in the back and Donna in the passenger seat, phone in her hand, checking for messages every few seconds. It was early evening in July and the sun was still high in the sky. They drove west from Ely, towards Cambridge.

"It might not be him. It could be one of the others. It's probably nothing." Donna's words hung in the air of the car. Steve concentrated on the road and Jen looked out at the sky. She would feel it if Danny were in danger. Danny who had always been there. Danny who took her camping, to London. Danny who taught her to play cricket and let her help him make a suspension bridge out of matches. If there was anything wrong, she would feel it in her heart.

Her heart was beating in her chest like a ball in a tin can. She clenched her fingers. She thought, *if I prayed, I would pray*.

They were on the A1 past Huntingdon when the phone rang. Donna answered it and listened.

She listened for two minutes and didn't speak. Steve kept driving.

Eventually she said, "Thank you for letting me know."

She said, "We're on our way."

She finished the call and she said to Steve, "Pull over."

He couldn't immediately, as it was a busy road, but two miles on there was a layby and he pulled in. Nobody spoke for those two miles. As soon as the car stopped, Donna jumped out and ran. Steve followed her. Jen watched them, her parents. She saw Donna's face distorted in a scream, her arms and legs kicking out as Steve tried to hold her, to contain her. She saw the sobs that broke across her father's face. She sat alone in the car as traffic sped by on the A1 and felt her wooden bones crumble away to dust.

It could have been anyone. A man driving his van through the village of Ravenscar had a heart attack at the wheel. He died instantly and the van hurtled down the road, into a crowd of walkers who had just come out of the visitors' centre. Most of them got out of the way, but two of them weren't quick enough. George Hartnell was clipped by the van and sent spinning to the ground. He had three broken ribs and a fractured arm. Danny Mathers was pinned by the van against an elm tree. His ribs cracked and pierced his heart. His lungs filled and he died by drowning in his own blood. The engine was still running, the dead driver hidden in the airbag.

Chapter Thirty-Three

"I'm taking you as far as The Great Ouse," said Danny. "We're meeting Barbara there."

"Barbara! But she's not—"

"—dead. No, she's not. But there are people who can pass between. I phoned her earlier, and we arranged a meeting place. She'll take you the rest of the way."

"What about you? Will I see you again?"

"Not any time soon, I hope."

"But—"

"Look, I'm fine. Me and Jules are going to Spain. We're going to walk the Camino de Santiago. But I'll keep an ear to the ground for how things are with you. I'll look out for you."

"It's been horrible since you went."

"I know. It's shit what happened. Completely buggered up my plans."

"Mum has been..."

"The good thing is, I might get to meet Isambard Kingdom Brunel one day, if I'm lucky."

"After the walk, we're going to Bristol," said Jules. "We've heard he's sometimes seen round there. Then we're going to Lindisfarne to visit Nadia and Berta."

"You have a lot of plans." Jen sank into her seat. The landscape outside the window was flat as the bottom of a snowdome. It stretched on and on, marked by a windfarm in one place, silos in another. The road passed over a drain, long and straight, slicing through the land.

"You have life," said Danny. "You can make a difference in the world. You aren't just tourists like us."

"You're making a difference to me."

"Yes," Jules turned to look at Danny and Jen could see her eyes were shining, "we are helping your sister. We can do something."

Danny smiled at her, then put his hand on her thigh and squeezed.

"Bloody hell, you two have moved fast. You only just met."

"Some things are just clearer here," said Jules.

The journey took just over an hour, but it seemed like no time at all before Ely Cathedral appeared on the horizon. A few more miles, and they pulled up at the side of the road. It was as familiar to Jen as her gran's face, the back of her brother's head.

"You have to get out and walk here," said Danny. "You're meeting Barbara in the marina."

"What about you?"

"This is where we say goodbye."

Danny and Jules got out of the car as well as Jen. There was a footpath at the side of the road leading down to the river.

"Barbara said she'd meet you at the bridge," said Danny.

Jen didn't want to cry. She swallowed and squared her shoulders.

"Will you look out for Ethie?" she asked. "Make sure she's OK?"

"She'll be fine once you're back," said Danny.

"No, I don't think you realise. She's frightened. She needs help."

"All will be well," said Jules. "All will be well."

She hugged Jen, and then Jen turned to her brother and hugged him.

"I'll still talk to you," she said in his ear. "I'm not going to leave you alone."

He squeezed her tight. "I wouldn't have it any other way," he said. "What would eternity be like without little sis nagging in my ear?"

Then he and Jules got back into the car and drove away, and Jen was alone at the side of the road.

She was tempted, for a moment, to stay there and stick out her thumb. To catch a lift somewhere, anywhere. But after a few minutes she turned and walked down the path into the marina.

Aunt Barbara was standing in the middle of the bridge. There was someone else with her, a man that Jen had never seen before. He was tall with a goatee beard and grey hair. He saw Jen approaching before Barbara did, and nudged her. Barbara turned and saw her niece. She walked towards her, holding out her hands.

Jen stepped forward slowly, one foot, then the other. By the time their fingers touched, she was fully on the bridge.

"Jen," whispered Barbara.

Jen said nothing.

Barbara walked backwards slowly, bringing Jen with her into the middle. "Can I take you home?"

Jen nodded. "That's why I'm here," she said. "Danny and Gran, they persuaded me to come."

They reached the man with the goatee. He was watching them, and as Barbara passed him, he stepped forward.

"Come on Jen," said her aunt. "Keep walking, we're nearly there."

"But who..."

"Keep looking at me." Barbara's tone was sharp. "We need to get over the bridge."

Jen had passed the man now. They were nearly at the other end. She felt his hand on her shoulder and turned to look at him.

"Jen, don't stop!"

"Have you seen my son?" said the man.

"Who is your son?" Jen looked into the man's face. She knew those eyes. She'd seen those eyes in another face. "Finn?"

"Have you seen him? Where is he?"

The man stepped closer, but Barbara pulled her, and his hand slipped from Jen's shoulder. Barbara continued walking backwards, faster now, pulling Jen with her. Jen looked back at the man.

"You're Finn's father?"

"Was he there with you?"

Barbara stepped down from the bridge and Jen fell against her. She kept falling, and put out her hands to catch herself, but there was nothing there. Her hands grasped something soft, and she realised her eyes were closed. There was a strange smell, like disinfectant or blood.

"Jen?"

The voice was close. It sounded the way a voice did in a room, not outside. Jen tried to open her eyes, but her eyelids felt heavy.

"Finn." The name fell from her lips in a sigh that was barely audible.

"Jen, did you say something? Can you hear me?"

The voice was her mother's. Jen felt someone grasping her hand. She managed to lift her eyelids a fraction. There was light, there was a face, there was something stuck in the back of her hand.

"I think you should call the nurse," said another voice. Aunt Barbara.

She could hear something beeping.

"Look at the monitor," said Barbara's voice.

"Nurse, nurse, doctor!" Her mother was further away now, and shouting. "I think she's waking up!"

Then there were more people in the room. Jen could hear them moving about, she could feel someone lift her wrist, and then someone opened her eye with their fingers and bright light flooded in. Jen flinched.

"Did you see? Did you see that?" said Donna.

"Yes, I saw," said Barbara.

"I think you should leave, just for the moment," said another voice. Jen couldn't tell if it was a man or a woman. "We need to check all her signs."

"But she's just woken up! You can't send me away!"

"Donna, she's not really awake yet. Let them look after her, come on."

There was a noise like a sob, then someone was breathing close to her face, and her mother's voice was right up close. "Don't you go away again Jen, stay with us. Don't leave."

Jen let her eyelids relax and darkness enveloped her. She fell into a deep sleep.

She didn't dream, but she was aware of time passing, time spent in the dark. It didn't feel threatening, there wasn't anything lurking. It was more like a huge blanket wrapped around her, covering everything except a small gap so she could breathe. She could peek out, but she didn't want to. Not yet.

She heard voices every now and again. Sometimes they were listing numbers or using words she didn't understand. Her mother's voice came and went.

"How is this different from before? How can you tell she's only sleeping?"

A low, patient voice spoke about vital signs, brain activity and REM. Jen stayed under the blanket, grateful to have somewhere to hide.

Eventually, she opened her eyes. She was in a hospital bed. She was attached to monitors. There was something uncomfortable between her legs. A breathing tube covered her face.

Her dad was sitting on one side of the bed, next to an empty chair. Rebecca was sitting in the chair on the other side. Neither of them were looking at her.

She lifted her left hand, which was less encumbered than her right, and took the tube away from her face. Immediately Steve and Rebecca looked up at her.

"Jen!"

"I'll fetch your mum."

Jen glared at her dad and shook her head. Her mouth was too dry to speak. Moving her head made her feel sick. He stayed put.

She licked her lips and opened her mouth, but there was no sound.

"Here." Rebecca put a bottle of water to Jen's lips, poured a little into her mouth. It tasted wonderful, like the purest, cleanest, sweetest drink on earth.

"More?" asked Rebecca, and Jen nodded. It felt like there was a huge weight in the back of her skull. Rebecca poured more water between Jen's lips, and she swallowed. Swallowing hurt and she closed her eyes for a moment.

"Jen?" She felt her dad take her hand between both of his. His skin was warm and dry. She could smell him, the familiar smell of engine oil and soap.

"I'll fetch the doctor," he said, and hurried away.

"More water?" Rebecca put the bottle to Jen's lips again, and this time the swallowing was less painful.

"Is Finn here?" Jen managed to say.

Rebecca smiled at her, but before she could speak Steve came back in with a doctor. He was softly spoken and Jen recognised his voice from before.

"Hello Jennifer." She looked at him. His eyes were deep brown and his skin was the colour of creosote on wood. "Can you hear me, Jennifer?"

She nodded. The weight in her skull shifted and she winced.

"Just blink," said the doctor. "Blink once to say yes." His hair looked like dark silk. Jen imagined touching it. "Does it hurt when you move?"

She blinked.

"You've been lying still for a long time; your muscles are out of practice. You must take it slowly."

She blinked again.

Just then Donna came into the room. She stopped inside the door and stared at Jen.

"Oh my God, you're awake," she said. "Why didn't someone fetch me?" Her face crumpled. "Jen, are you really back?"

Jen blinked.

"That means yes," said Steve.

Donna sat down hard and covered her face with her fingers. She looked at Jen through the gaps and wailed. "I'm so happy. Oh Jen, I'm so happy." Steve put his arm round her shoulder.

Jen looked back at Rebecca.

"Finn," she whispered.

"What was that? What did she say?" Donna leaned forward. The doctor looked at Rebecca questioningly.

Rebecca shrugged, "It sounds like she's saying Finn."

Jen blinked again and again.

"Who's Finn?" Donna asked "Did he do something to you? Did he hurt you? Was it him that...?"

Jen shook her head. Her mother disappeared like she had been pushed under water, then resurfaced again. Jen's stomach clenched.

"Do you want to see him? This Finn?" asked the doctor.

She blinked at the doctor.

"I've never heard of anyone called Finn. Have you heard her talk about him?" Donna asked Rebecca.

"No, I've never heard of Finn either."

"Could he be someone from university?"

Rebecca shook her head, then stopped. "There was someone," she said.

"A boyfriend?"

Jen blinked.

"How can she have a boyfriend I don't know about? She's been lying here for three months, so where is he? Why hasn't he been looking for her?"

Three months.

"No, it was someone she'd seen that she liked. I never saw him. I thought she might have made him up. She liked his coat."

Jen blinked again.

"Well, how can we find him? Is he something to do with this whole mess? Was it because of him…?"

Her dad must have seen the panic in her eyes, because he said "Shh" to Donna, who was astonished and put her hands in her lap. Steve picked up Jen's hand again. Despite the attachments, his hands still swamped hers. When she was tiny, there were days when Donna was angry. Not necessarily with her. Often she was angry with Danny, or her mother, or with her sister Barbara who she never saw, which made her more angry than anything. She would slam about the kitchen, opening doors, putting things away as loudly as she could, swearing. Jen would creep onto Steve's lap in the living room and together they watched kids' TV until Donna had calmed down. That was before she found God. Recently she had missed out the swearing, most of the time.

"It's OK, love," said Steve. "We'll see what we can do. We'll find Finn."

Sometimes she fell asleep on her dad's lap. He never moved. An hour later when Donna came in to tell them tea was ready and Jen woke up, he'd still be watching *Blue Peter* or *Art Attack*. She remembered the dark blanket. She closed her eyes.

When she woke, it was night. Aunt Barbara was sitting in the chair on the right and Rebecca was in one of the chairs on the left. The other chair was empty.

"Hello, love," said Barbara.

"Hello."

The word slipped out smoothly. Jen moved her arms and used her elbows to shuffle up the bed a bit.

"Want to sit up? You don't need to do it yourself."

Barbara pressed a button on the side of the bed and the top end rose up so that Jen was in a half-seated position.

"I can talk."

"That's brilliant. You're doing really well."

Barbara poured her a glass of water from the jug on the table. She picked it up and moved it to Jen's lips, but Jen took the glass from her. Her hand shook, and she only managed one sip before Barbara had to take it back.

"Have I really been here for three months?"

They both nodded.

"Since June," said Rebecca.

"Do you remember what happened?"

"The ship in the bottle," said Jen.

"What?"

"I kept a piece of the glass."

"Did you know you were...?"

"It was sharper than I realised."

"The vicar found you, in a church. He was locking up for the day. Lucky he saw you, because you'd hidden behind an altar. You'd lost so much blood that your brain wasn't getting enough oxygen."

"Did you find Finn?"

They exchanged a glance, and Jen sat further forward on the bed. "What's happened? Where is he?"

The man on the bridge had been looking for Finn. He must have been his father.

"You need to rest," said Barbara.

"No!"

Her aunt smoothed Jen's hair back from her forehead.

"It's OK, Jen," she said. "We're all here for you."

"Where is Finn?" said Jen.

"We phoned the university," said Rebecca. Barbara glared at her, but Rebecca carried on. "They only had one person enrolled called Finn, but he can't be the person you met."

"Rebecca, Donna doesn't want her getting upset."

"She's already upset."

They stared at each other across the bed, then Barbara got to her feet. "You better be right about this," she said, and walked out of the room.

Jen looked at Rebecca. "Well?"

Now that Barbara had gone, Rebecca looked much less sure of herself. She fiddled with her hands in her lap and didn't meet Jen's gaze.

"What do you mean, he can't be the one I met?" said Jen. "I did meet him. He's studying geology. We're in love."

Rebecca looked up sharply. She shook her head as though to clear it. "There was a Finn, and he did study geology, though I don't know how you knew that. He was in the year above us."

"We went to Whitby together. He loves fossils and dinosaurs."

"No, Jen, you can't have. He wasn't at uni when we were there."

"He bought me a jacket."

Rebecca's eyes had tears in them, but her face was still. "Finn went on a field trip to France the year before we even went to York."

"Yes, to Angeac-Charente, the quarries full of fossils. He should be back now."

"He fell from a ledge. He landed on his head."

"What?"

"He's on a life support machine in Paris. He's been there for over a year. So you can't have met him."

Jen swung her legs across the bed and sat up.

"Lie down Jen, you're not ready to get up yet."

Why hadn't she looked for him at the cathedral? Why hadn't she demanded he come with her to the bridge? If she'd brought him with her in the car, he would have met his dad on the bridge. He'd be waking up right now in a hospital in Paris.

"Can you fetch the doctor?" she said.

Rebecca stood up straight away. "Is something wrong?"

Jen laughed out loud. "Yes, something's wrong. I need to find out how soon I can leave this place and get to Paris."

Act Five

Chapter Thirty-Four

She liked to work out who was visiting before letting on she was awake. This time it was Barbara and her dad.

They weren't talking. She could tell it was her dad from the way he breathed through his moustache, as though filtering the air. She could smell her aunt's perfume, which made her think of the heather on the island where she lived.

"I'm going to get some tea, Babs," he said after a while. "Want some?"

Babs?

"I'm fine, thanks."

Jen made a groaning noise, as though she were just waking up. She heard her dad's footsteps stop halfway across the room, and opened her eyes. He was looking back at her.

"Can I have some tea?" she said, sleepily.

He came back with two mugs and a Twix. He tore open the wrapper and gave one stick to Jen, who pressed the button on the bed so that she was sitting up.

"Where's Mum?"

"She's doing some shopping."

"Not with Terence, then?"

"She told Terence to sod off weeks ago," said Steve.

"She did what?" asked Jen.

"He kept telling her that God would take care of you and not to worry."

"That sounds like Terence."

"In the end she snapped and yelled at him. She said this was one situation where doctors were more useful than a prayer meeting. She slammed the door in his face."

Steve handed her a mug of tea.

"I wish I'd seen it," said Jen quietly.

"She's been out of her mind with worry, pet." Her dad touched her on the shoulder. "We all have."

Jen sipped her tea and smiled at Barbara. She didn't know which was more astonishing, her mum's outburst at Terence or her dad's words. She knew he wouldn't say anything else, and that whatever her mum said, which would probably be a lot, those three words from her dad would be more powerful than all of it.

**

The path led out of the woods onto open grassland. We were at the top of a slope and the world rolled out before us like a carpet, unfurling into a patchwork of wheat, oats, and brown earth.

"This begins to feel like home," I said to Brother Wilfrid, and he nodded.

"We can use the Roman roads to take us most of the way from here. The travelling will be easier from now on."

The ridge was called the Lincoln Cliff. We had passed through the old settlement and were now heading south.

The sky was blue and huge. I felt my ribcage lift as my heart filled. I stretched my arms out to the side, and it seemed my fingers could reach a little further than before. My head felt light and the air we breathed was sweet with the scent of hay and chamomile.

"We are covering more ground each day," said Wilfrid. "You have grown in strength. Sometimes I struggle to keep up with you."

I could feel the new vigour in my limbs as I stretched my toes and brought my hands in to meet at my chest. I thanked the Lord for bringing me safely this far, for this vista, the joy I had begun to find in movement, the peace of a summer's day.

We moved on. The hedge to our left was alive with sparrows that flew up into the air at our approach. Bees buzzed amongst the wildflowers that edged the path, and a dragonfly hovered in the air ahead of us.

"There must be water close by," said Wilfrid.

We stopped at an inn for sustenance. The innkeeper brought us meat and bread and small ale, which we ate outside at a table overlooking the village pond.

I noticed a bird sitting on a pole on the other side of the water. It was a falcon.

"Brother Wilfrid," I turned to him, and for a moment the sun glared in my eyes and it seemed that Wilfrid had changed. He was wearing different clothes, made of black leather, and his hair was long like a woman's. I blinked. A small cloud passed in front of the sun, and Wilfrid was himself again, tonsured, in brown robes, an ornate cross hung about his neck. "Look at that bird," I said.

But when we looked, the bird had gone.

Soon after, we reached the Roman road, Ermine Street. I always marvelled at the skill of those ancient roadbuilders who let nothing get in their way, took their roads over hills and through swamps, opening the world up for the rest of us that we might travel through wild terrains in relative safety.

This road stretched away to the south, straight as a ribbon, cutting a path that would lead me home.

"We can continue to Huntingdon," said Wilfrid, "then head west. It should take less than a week."

A shadow passed over us and I looked up. Again, the sun blinded me for a moment. I saw the falcon flying across the blue of the sky, its wings spread at right angles from its body, its tail fanning out. It swooped down low and I could see the speckled underbody.

"Jennet?" I whispered.

I looked down again and gasped. The road had changed. It had narrowed to a path only wide enough for two to walk abreast, and trees had grown up alongside it, with shrubs beneath crowding the edges. I looked for Wilfrid, but there was no sign of him. I heard someone laugh and swung round.

A man, dressed in strange black garb, was walking towards me.

"At last I find you, *ma chérie*," he said.

I opened my mouth wide.

***

Jen sat up in the bed, swallowing a scream.

Donna was sitting in a chair reading a magazine. There were no other visitors. She smiled at Jen.

"Dreaming again, love?"

Jen nodded and sank back against the pillows.

"The doctor says it's the meds. They're going to do that for a while."

Jen closed her eyes. The back of her eyelids swirled with black and red patterns. No sky, no birds, no men in leather or Victorian suits.

She heard the slap of her mother dropping the magazine on the floor, the scrape of the chair being pulled forward. She felt the weight of Donna leaning her elbows on the bed, and then her hand was lifted and held. There was a time when holding her mother's hand was the most comforting thing she knew. When she could look at her mother's face and know everything would be alright.

Jen opened her eyes. "Do you still love Dad?" she said.

Donna blinked in surprise, then looked down at their two hands clasped on top of the hospital blanket.

"Yes," she said after a while. "We've not been very close these past years, and that's..." She choked for a moment and Jen was alarmed. She hadn't seen her mum cry since Danny died. "It's probably my fault. I know I've been preoccupied with

300

the Church, and Terence, well, he's a very large character. He tends to take over."

There were tears in her eyes, but they didn't fall. Her cheeks were smooth and unblemished.

"I threw him out of the house, you know," said Donna.

"Dad said."

"He said we should pray together. He said that we must accept whatever God sent us, that all suffering was a gift from the Lord. When I said I only wanted to be with family at the moment, he said he was my Brother in Christ. I told him to fuck off."

"Bloody hell!"

"He couldn't believe it. You should have seen his face."

"I wish I had."

"I thought he was going to hang on to the doorpost and I'd have to get your dad to come and punch him."

"Dad would have liked that."

Donna looked at her, surprised, then the laughter took over and the tears began to fall. "He would, wouldn't he?"

Jen laughed too.

"We've talked a lot these past weeks, me and your dad," said Donna.

"Really? Dad talked?"

"You being so ill... all this... it made me see what a crap mum I've been to you... no, I know that I have."

They sat in silence holding hands.

"Your dad told me how he used to bring you food when you weren't eating. How he made you tea in the middle of the night. He's a good man."

Jen nodded, unable to speak.

"Jen, I don't want to rush you, but when you're ready to talk about what happened – you know – before – I know about the... the doctors told us... You can tell me anything."

"Thanks Mum."

"I want to make it up to you," Donna said. "I know I can't give you back your teenage years, can't change what's already

301

happened. But if you ever see me going that way again, so absorbed in something that I can't even find time for my own family, and my own daughter can't tell me she's in trouble... just say, Mum, you're going again, come back."

Jen tried to imagine doing that. Tried to imagine Steve doing that. They had always been the quiet ones, keeping their feelings to themselves in the face of Donna's huge enthusiasm. Could they stop her? Did they really have that power?

"I have to go to France," she said.

Donna frowned and sat back in her chair. "You have a lot of getting better to do."

"I will be better."

"The doctors are talking about physio. You've been lying still for three months; your muscles need to build up."

Jen stretched out her arms and waved them to and fro so that the attached tubes waved violently.

"Jen, careful!"

"I don't have to walk there."

"We'll see. Perhaps in a few weeks."

"Sooner."

"Jen, you have to..."

"I have to see Finn." She lowered her hands. "It will help me get better. Don't you see?"

Donna gave a weak smile and said nothing.

Her mum had gone upstairs with a shiny, red face, and Aunty Barbara was in the kitchen cooking fish fingers and peas for their tea. Lyddie and Grace were still in the garden. Barbara was peeling potatoes and cutting them into long thin pieces.

"Are you making chips?" asked Jen.

"Yes, I'm going to cook them in the oven."

"My mum gets chips in a bag from the shop."

"Well, that's quicker," said her aunt.

"Can I have some milk?"

"Help yourself."

Her mum never said that. She either said no or she poured it for her.

The cupboard where the glasses were kept was too high for Jen to reach, so she stood on a chair. Jen reached gingerly into the cupboard and picked up one of the glasses. The bottom was dusty. When she turned round, Aunty Barbara was looking at her.

"I remember that dress," she said.

"Gran gave it to me."

"It suits you."

"Gran says I remind her of you." She was standing on the chair, holding the glass in both hands. "What's a bortion?"

Her aunt's eyes changed. They had been soft but now they glittered. Jen wondered if she was in trouble, but when her aunt spoke her voice wasn't cross.

"How old are you, Jennie?"

"Nearly seven."

The glitter disappeared. "Here," she said, "give me that glass and I'll give it a rinse."

Jen handed over the glass and climbed down from the chair. Aunty Barbara washed the glass and dried it with a tea towel. Jen got the milk from the fridge and poured some into the glass.

"Do you know what it means to be pregnant?" Aunty Barbara asked.

"Yes, it's when you're going to have a baby and you get really fat."

"Yes, that's right. But at first, before it grows into a baby, it's called an embryo and it's really tiny."

"Like a tadpole."

"Kind of. Smaller even than that at first." Barbara picked up the milk and put it back in the fridge. "Sometimes, when a woman finds out she's pregnant, and it's still tiny like that, the doctor can take it away, if there are reasons she can't have a baby. That's called an abortion."

"Did you have one?"

Aunty Barbara picked up the knife and started cutting the potatoes again. "Yes. I was sixteen. I was too young to have a baby."

"What are they called – ember...?"

"Embryos."

"Do they have a daddy, like babies?"

"Yes, they do." Barbara sprinkled the raw chips with salt, then poured oil on to them from a bottle. She stirred them around so the oil covered the chips. "He was my boyfriend," she said, when Jen didn't say anything else. "But soon after he got a new girlfriend." She looked up sharply, but Jen was drinking, using both hands to hold the glass. "He's married now, and he's got two children of his own."

Jen put the glass on the table. She wondered if she had a milk moustache and wiped her mouth with the back of her hand.

"Like you," she said.

Aunty Barbara smiled. "Yes, like me."

Jen said, "When can I go to France?"

"Jen, I don't think your mum..."

"I need to see Finn."

"You'll have to rest for a while."

"I could take her," said Barbara.

Steve and Jen both turned to look at her.

"Lyddie starts at uni in Paris in a couple of weeks and I'm taking her over. If you're up and about by then, you could come with us."

"Don't you think that's a bit soon, Babs?"

Babs again. She'd never heard Donna call her sister Babs.

Something caught her eye. There was a bird on the windowsill outside, looking into the room. A bird of prey, with a curved beak and speckled front. Its eyes were orange and watchful. It was looking at her.

"Look!" She pointed to the window. Her aunt and her dad both turned to look, but the bird took off and flew up into the sky.

Chapter Thirty-Five

On the island Barbara made blueberry porridge for breakfast. She went for long rambles with her girls and taught them to paint. Grace was good at painting, and then she was good at sculpture. She had already sold stuff to galleries and she was only fifteen. Jen used to wish she was one of Barbara's daughters, living there on the island with the sun and sand and wind in the heather, even though Lyddie told her it was hell in winter, when winds swept across the low land of the island, bending the trees, moving everything moveable in its path. People hunkered down in their houses listening to it roar, feeling the cold gusts down the chimneys, not daring to go out. Jen thought that could be fun too. She imagined dressing in layer upon layer just to walk from the house to the car, or walking with her head down, the wind denting her eyeballs. She imagined log fires and knitted blankets.

They let her out of the hospital five days later. Donna brought a duvet to wrap round her in the car, as well as flasks of soup and tea, and mounds of crisps in case she got car sick.

"It's September, Mum," said Jen. "And it only takes three hours."

The soup was homemade. It would be awful, her mum was a terrible cook.

"Your mum was up making that after midnight," Steve told her.

Donna hadn't cooked much since Danny died. The only soup they normally had was from tins or cartons. Home cooking didn't go beyond a pasta bake or jacket potato.

"Thanks Mum," she said.

The last time she remembered her mum cooking was at Easter, when Lee had been staying. Steve had reassured her that Lee was long gone.

"I think he left Ely. Terence was really disappointed. He came round and sat in the kitchen drinking tea and yakking on about how we hadn't been hospitable enough."

Jen grinned at her dad. She'd not heard him talk so much for years.

Barbara and Rebecca were waiting for them at the house with a slap-up meal. Barbara had made beef stew and the savoury smell greeted them when they came into the hall. Jen wanted to walk from the car by herself, but halfway up the path her legs buckled and Steve took her arm for the rest of the way. Jen was glad Donna was in front and hadn't seen. Steve walked her through to the kitchen, and she sat at the table.

Barbara handed her a cold beer from the fridge.

"Dinner will be ready in half an hour," she said.

Rebecca sat down opposite her. "Welcome home," she said.

Jen looked around, at the shelves where her mum's pots were gathering dust, the window onto the garden where the crocosmia was in flower and the grass needed mowing. Rebecca said, "I've made brownies for pudding, with ice-cream and raspberries."

She'd been just about managing the hospital food – they'd insisted on her being able to keep it down before they let her out. The thought of beef stew and chocolate made her stomach churn a bit.

Her aunt saw her face. "You just eat what you can," said Barbara.

The next day she walked around the garden, and the day after that she walked to the end of the road and back. At the weekend she said she would like to walk into town and visit the cathedral.

"Would you like me to come with you?" asked Barbara. She was going back to Scotland the next day to help Lyddie pack for Paris.

Jen nodded.

They walked slowly. Jen's legs were gaining strength. Yesterday when she was sitting in an armchair with her feet up on a stool, she'd imagined walking, no, striding along a clifftop, the wind in her sleeves and salt in the air. She felt the movement in her muscles. She breathed deep into her lungs. When she opened her eyes her mum and dad were looking at her, concerned.

By the time they reached the cathedral gardens, Jen felt a bit sick and her legs were hot. She stopped under a tree and closed her eyes for a moment.

"Let's go in," said Barbara. "It will be cooler inside."

It wasn't Mrs Shepherd on the till today. Jen sat down on a chair and waited while her aunt paid. There were a few visitors wandering around in ones and twos, and a group was gathering for a tour of the bell tower. Their voices were swallowed up by the space. Jen could feel the air above her, and she wondered what it would feel like to sit on the floor of the ocean with all that water between her and the surface. The water wouldn't allow it; it would carry her up, straighten out her legs, push her up and up until her head broke the surface and she gasped for air. Here, gravity held her down. She tipped her head back and looked at the painted roof. Was that what heaven was, a place you broke through into, gasping, when you couldn't breathe the air anymore?

Barbara sat down beside her and looked up too.

"Can you imagine what it was like painting that?" she said.

"Did he actually go up there? The artist?"

"Yes. I think there was more than one. The first one died."

"Did he fall?"

"No, nothing so dramatic. I remember coming here on school visits and being told that a boy used to go up to mark out the outlines. I wasn't sure if I felt sorry for him or envied him."

"I suppose it depends if he was scared of heights."

Jen's neck began to ache. She stretched it and lowered her head. The return to the ground made her vision swim and she blinked.

"Did something happen at Easter?" said Barbara. She was still looking up at the ceiling and Jen thought for a moment that her aunt was talking about the paintings.

"What do you mean?"

There was a silence, then they turned to look at each other. Jen held her aunt's gaze, then looked away.

"When they found you in the church, the blood... it wasn't just from the glass. You'd lost a baby."

The air of the cathedral was chilly against Jen's skin, and her legs were sticking to the wooden chair. She stood up.

"I want to see Etheldreda," she said.

They walked together through the nave and the octagon, past the back of the choir stalls to where the statue of Saint Etheldreda stood at the far end. Her face was peaceful and the stone she was made of glowed warmly in the light of half a dozen candles. Barbara fished in her bag and found a coin, which she passed to Jen. She dropped it in the honesty box, took a tealight and placed it on the rack, not far from Etheldreda's elbow. She lit it with a match.

"I met her," she said, "when I was away, in the coma. I made friends with her. She was trying to come home, back here to Ely."

"What was she like?"

"Fun, serious, both. She was actually in love with Egfrith, her husband, but she felt guilty about it."

"She was much older than him."

"I know, he was only seventeen or something, and she was definitely older than me."

"At least ten years. When they married, he was fourteen and she was well into her twenties I think."

"Oh."

"His father had sent him away when he was a child, as a hostage in war, to keep the peace. I think he was quite a disturbed individual."

"How do you know?"

"We learned some of it at school. And Dorothy used to tell me all the old stories too. You know she was a history teacher? Well her bones were drenched with it. I used to get Anglo Saxon tales as bedtime stories."

"The red book."

"That's right," Barbara smiled at her. "Did she read it to you as well?"

"I must have remembered Etheldreda's story wrong."

"Egfrith had another woman, a mistress. He married her after Etheldreda returned to Ely with Ovin."

"Ovin?"

"Didn't you learn about him? He was her steward. He travelled with her, protected her."

"I'd forgotten about him. I thought it was Saint Wilfrid that helped her. I must have mixed them up."

The light from the candle flickered with Jen's breath and she took a step back. This wasn't what Etheldreda really looked like, this was just an artist's representation. Even the illustrations from the ancient manuscripts, they were just guesswork too. The real saint was faceless, unknowable.

"Was it that Lee? The one from the Church?"

Somewhere in the cathedral, someone was walking on high heels. The sound bounced off the stone and echoed in the huge space. A couple came out of the chapel and stopped for a moment to look at the statue of Etheldreda before moving on.

"Yes," whispered Jen.

The candle flames broadened and liquefied into streaks of light as her eyes filled with tears, but she blinked and swallowed. She felt her aunt take hold of her hand.

"It wasn't a baby," said Jen.

"Come on," said Barbara gently. "Let's go and sit in the Lady Chapel."

She allowed herself to be led. The chapel was the brightest part of the cathedral. Light poured in through the high clear windows. Today it was empty, the floor gleaming in the sunshine. The statue of the Lady stood with her arms raised, her hair and her belt glittering disco gold, her hips thrust forward like a ballerina's. Her eyes were closed and her mother's figure showed through the folds of her blue dress.

A nun was kneeling before her, head bowed. Barbara and Jen sat on chairs at the back of the chapel. Jen's legs trembled as she took the weight off them.

"You're not on your own, Jen."

"I didn't think Mum would believe me."

The nun dropped her head to her praying hands, then lifted it again and got to her feet. She turned and walked across the middle of the chapel in front of Jen and Barbara. She had a swelling on her neck and wore a gold coloured necklace. She looked across to them, inclined her head and smiled, before sweeping on and out of the chapel.

"Tell her," said Barbara. "She will listen to you now."

Rebecca was back from her Easter break. Jen opened the door and she was standing in the corridor.

"Hey Jen, what's up? I've been texting all morning."

"Sorry, my phone wasn't on."

The phone was on. Jen had seen the texts. She just hadn't answered.

"I just got back. Do you want to go down to the bar?"

Jen shrugged.

"Hey, you're not dressed." Rebecca laughed and looked down at her clothes. Jen was wearing white pyjamas decorated with small purple flowers. Her feet were bare.

"Give me half an hour."

"Sure thing." Rebecca walked into the room and sat down on the bed. "Did you have a good holiday? When did you get back, anyway?"

"I'll just get in the shower," Jen said.

"Great. OK."

Rebecca frowned a little and Jen realised she had been standing there too long. She backed into the bathroom and turned on the water. She hadn't showered for over a week, but at least she'd finally taken all the rubbish out yesterday, the first time in two weeks she had left campus. Her floor had been covered in packaging and leftover food. Sometimes she'd ordered pizzas and asked them to leave them on the step downstairs. She hadn't seen anyone in the past two weeks other than the caretaker. She'd watched his movements carefully, making sure he never saw her. Until she saw his car leaving the campus she didn't leave her room; when he'd gone, she went out and sat in front of the Buddha, sometimes until it got dark, and sometimes much later.

She scrubbed at her hair with shampoo, turned the water up to full heat and let it burn her skin. She ran her fingers up her side from her hip to her armpit. If she closed her eyes, she could see the Buddha's lips, his rounded cheeks, the lashes of his closed eyes lying flat against his cheek. She knew the way his robes fell from his shoulder, the number of folds, the curve of fabric into his lap. She knew the way he held his hands, palm upwards, fingers curled in, thumbs touching. She'd sat that way herself, hands held in the diamond shape made by her crossed legs. Even now with the scalding water cascading down her limbs and back, she could feel the remembered shape, the folded legs, the dropped shoulders, the peace of eyes closed against the world.

When she emerged wrapped in a towel that really could have done with a trip to the launderette, Rebecca was on the phone by the window, her back to Jen. Jen got another towel from the cupboard and rubbed at her hair. She found a pair of white jeans and a broderie anglais top embroidered with a hummingbird.

Rebecca finished her call and turned around.

"That was Craig. He's meeting us at the bar."

The campus was filling like water running into a warren; she couldn't hide any more. She turned her head upside down and blew her hair with the hairdryer.

I could smell water. Salt. I could hear the cries of seagulls circling high in the air. But when I opened my eyes, there was only darkness. I put my hand to my neck. The medallion was still in place.

I felt about me with my hands. The surface I lay on was like rough velvet; it should be soft but actually it made the skin of my face itch. I was lying on my side, and I put my left elbow under my head so I was no longer touching the floor. My hands and legs were free. I tried stretching out, but there wasn't room to straighten. I reached out with my right arm and my fingers grazed the furthest wall, which seemed to be made of metal. Behind me was a wall covered in the same fabric as the floor.

I listened carefully. Occasionally there was another noise, a roaring which approached from far away, got closer, then when it was at its loudest, it went past and the noise receded.

Cars. I must be near a road. A road by the sea. I could be in the boot of a car.

I heard another bird call out, nearer than the seagulls, its scream rougher, vibrating with something that sounded like emotion. A falcon.

I banged on the roof of the boot and shouted. "Let me out!"

A voice called back. "Tais-toi!"

A voice I knew.

Jen switched on the light. Everything was OK. She was in her own room and no one else was there. Her teddies were lined up on top of the bookcase, and her white jacket was hanging on the back of a chair.

She got out of bed and went downstairs to the kitchen, where the light was on even though it was five-thirty in the morning. Barbara was sitting at the table with a cup of tea, wearing one of Donna's dressing gowns.

"I dreamed about her again."

"Tea?"

Jen nodded and her aunt got up, started filling the kettle, finding cups and teabags.

"She was trapped. Captured. In danger."

"I'll put some sugar in it."

"When are you and Lyddie going to France?"

"Next week."

"I'm coming with you."

Barbara stirred the tea. She opened the cupboard and found a packet of gingernuts, brought them to the table and sat down opposite Jen.

"Are you going to tell your mum and dad about Lee?"

Jen looked down. She tore the red plastic stripe off the biscuit packet and the top few gingernuts slid onto the table. She picked one up and dunked it in her tea.

"He should be reported," said Barbara.

Jen bit off the soggy half of the biscuit, and dipped the remaining half back into the drink. She ate that half too and took another from the packet.

"If I tell them, will you take me to France?"

"I'm not making a bargain. You need to report him whatever. And I'll take you to France if you're well enough."

"I will be well enough. I need to see Finn."

"We'll see," said Barbara. "Are you going to eat all of them, or can I have one?"

Chapter Thirty-Six

I still couldn't stretch my legs. I hadn't had any food or water since I'd been in there. I could feel the fabric of the car lining, but now the car was in a different place. We had moved while I slept.

I could smell the sea, but there were other smells too. Hot metal, oil, exhaust fumes. And there was movement now, a gentle rocking which might, in other circumstances, have been pleasant.

The car was on a boat. And the boat was at sea.

Behind my closed eyes I saw rows of cars, nose to bumper like a traffic jam, but quiet and still. Parked. This was the car deck. I was on the car deck of a ferry.

I opened my eyes and stared into the darkness.

"Brother Wilfrid," I said. "Help me, Brother Wilfrid. This is not my place. Help me to get home."

Then I banged on the boot lid again, but this time there was no answer.

I listened for bird calls. I could hear nothing but the thrum of the boat's engine.

I was alone.

Jen sat with her cousin in the ferry cafeteria. Lyddie's blonde hair had been bleached white by a summer outdoors on the island. She wore short denim shorts and a Ramones t-shirt that had been roughly cut with scissors at the neck and hem, its arms cut off completely. Her pierced belly button showed between the shorts and the cropped shirt.

"So, what are you going to do when you get there?" said Lyddie, "Do you think you'll recognise him?"

"I don't know."

"Will you play him some music? Did you have a song? Like, your song?"

"I don't even know what music he likes."

"So you'll just talk to him?"

Jen shrugged.

"I was scared when you were in hospital. I wanted to come down with Mum, but I had a summer job and Mum said there was no point. Not until you woke up."

Jen thought about Lyddie on the island, serving roast dinners to tourists at the hotel. She didn't expect people to think about her when she wasn't there.

"Your mum says she told me stories."

"I wonder what it will be like in Paris," said Lyddie.

"Have you been before?"

Lyddie shook her head. Her hair was in pigtails and she was wearing blue mascara. She looked very young, but also completely at ease, as if that was the look she intended. Jen had always felt like the outsider, the vulnerable one, the person who didn't quite get things right. She wished she was as cool.

Lyddie took Jen's hands and held them in her own on the table, and the two cousins smiled at each other.

Later, Jen, Lyddie and Barbara walked on the deck and looked at the water. They were nearer to France now and the coastline was a thick wedged line between sun and sky.

A man was standing by the railings, looking back towards England. A boy, really. He was tall and skinny and his clothes were odd, as though he were in costume. He had long cloth boots and baggy trousers in a soft fabric which draped, tied at his waist and knees.

Lyddie nudged Jen with her elbow. "Look at that guy!"

He whistled, held out an arm, and a bird flew down from the sky. At first just a dot, it swooped and called out, gliding on air currents, then flapping its curved wings until it was near enough for them to make out its speckled front.

"Jennet," whispered Jen.

"What?"

"Nothing. I was just looking at the falcon."

The boy was wearing a leather glove and the bird landed on it. Jen could see the jesses hanging down behind.

"That's so cool," said Lyddie. "It can just fly through customs, then land on the boat. They can't do anything about it."

She and her mum were both smiling.

The boy looked back in their direction, caught Jen's eye, and nodded. She nodded in reply. The falcon spread its wings, bowed its head and called out to her.

So it wasn't just Finn she had to find in France. If Eg was on his way, then Ethie must be there as well. Maybe she would have to find Ethie in order to bring Finn back.

They saw him again as they were leaving the port in Barbara's van, the back piled up with Lyddie's belongings for her year at uni. He was standing at the side of the road, looking at a smartphone, jabbing at it with his fingers. Jen looked up and saw Jennet hovering high above in the clear grey sky.

The drive to Paris was smooth and fast, but the nearer they got, the more agitated Jen became. She would have liked to go straight to the hospital, but the plan was to go to the university first to find Lyddie's accommodation. That, after all, was the purpose of the trip.

She remembered her mother's words to her sister as they left. "Don't let her out of your sight. Don't let her overdo it. Look after her, Barbara." Donna had gone from one extreme to the other, but Jen found she quite liked this overprotective mother. She was approachable. If Jen wanted a hug, she could snuggle up to her on the sofa. She never had anything more important to do.

Barbara was treating her like a grown up, which was better really. But there was no way she was going to let Jen wander the streets of Paris on her own, so Jen went with them to the university and helped unpack Lyddie's belongings, although they wouldn't let her carry anything heavier than a pot plant.

Then Lyddie was hungry, so they went to find a place to eat. Jen sat in the café staring at her croque monsieur avec frites, occasionally picking up one of the chips and licking the salt from it.

"You not hungry?" asked Barbara.

"Can we to go to the hospital after this?"

"Could it wait until tomorrow? We still have to find the hostel and check in..." Barbara looked at Jen's face and stopped. "OK. We'll go after we've checked in. It will be pretty late by then though. I'm sure they won't allow visitors."

Barbara was right; they didn't allow visitors on the general wards. But Finn was in a room of his own, in a far corner of the hospital. Lyddie was the best French speaker of the three of them, so she spoke to the woman on the reception desk. The woman frowned and shook her head, then shrugged and gestured with her arms, all the time talking nineteen to the dozen.

"What did she say?" asked Jen when Lyddie came back to where they were waiting.

"She told me where he is, but she doesn't think we'll be able to see him tonight. His father is with him. We can go up if we want and talk to him or to the doctors."

"Which way?"

Lyddie started to explain and Jen set off immediately at a fast clip.

They walked along long white corridors, up flights of stairs, through set after set of double doors. Eventually they came to a short quiet corridor with seven doors leading from it. "This is it," said Lyddie, and went to speak to the nurse in charge. Barbara and Jen waited in the staff room for what seemed like an age before Lyddie came back. "She's gone to speak to Finn's dad," she told them.

Then there were footsteps in the corridor and a man walked into the room. Jen knew him immediately. He was the man she'd seen on the bridge in Ely, standing next to her aunt, just before she'd woken from her coma.

She'd asked Barbara about that. "How did you do that? How did you get onto the bridge?" Barbara had looked at her sideways and not replied. But Jen could tell from her aunt's surprised expression that she recognised Finn's father too.

The man was frowning at Jen. "Have we met before?" He couldn't place her.

"I'm Jen," she said, and stepped forward to take his outstretched hand. "Sorry I couldn't come sooner."

"I'm Patrick. You're a friend of my son's?"

"I'm at York University, I met him there. I've been ill myself and only just heard..."

"Perhaps we met there, when we visited. You seem very familiar."

"Could I see Finn?"

"I don't suppose it would hurt. There's no change."

He took them back along the corridor into a room with a bed. There was a small pile of books and an open laptop on it.

"I was working. Me and Celie – my wife – we take it in turns, so one of us is always here."

"Will she...?"

"She's in Australia at the moment, visiting our daughter. She has a child, our grandson..."

"Joe."

Patrick smiled at her. "Yes." He pointed to another door, leading into the next room. "Through here."

The rest of the hospital had moved into sleep mode, monitored only by the soft soles of nurses padding the corridors, the occasional flurry of muffled emergency. It was very quiet. Patrick's room was lit by the soft bulb of a bedside lamp, but the room next door was in semi-darkness. Lyddie and Barbara waited behind whilst Jen went in with Patrick.

Light came through the glass panels of the doors and from the screen at the top of the bed. Finn was lying very still. The wound in his head had healed to a livid scar, but he wasn't breathing on his own. A plastic tube wheezed and sighed oxygen into his body. A monitor showed the green line of his heartbeat, once a second, a jagged peak, then flatness. The sound was small and pitiful compared to the heaving of the breathing apparatus.

Jen and Patrick stood next to each other.

"They say that if things don't improve, we may have to decide if we want the machine turned off." His father's voice was light and dry, like there was no saliva in his mouth. "We're praying for a miracle." His voice snagged, and Jen suddenly heard Finn's voice: *I'd love to find something, something new.*

"Can I stay with him?" she asked. "Can I sit with him tonight?"

There were chairs in the room. Patrick looked at her.

"Your mother..."

"She's my aunt. She won't mind."

He was staring at her again. She could tell he knew her, knew he'd met her somewhere important. He came to a decision.

"I'll go and talk to her."

He left the room, and Jen could hear the murmur of voices through the door. She pulled a chair up next to the bed near Finn's head. His arm lay above the sheet, wrist up, blue veins showing through pale skin. She reached out a finger and ran it along his arm, from his elbow to his wrist.

"Finn," she whispered. "I've come to find you."

His father came back into the room and sat in one of the other chairs.

"I've promised to look after you," he said.

"It's a hospital," said Jen. "If anything happens to me, I'm in the right place."

He nodded and they sat in silence, listening to the machine breathing, the bleep of Finn's heart, the ticking of the clock.

She dozed and woke. Patrick had closed his eyes and his breathing was heavy, though not as loud as the machine that breathed for Finn.

She watched them, father and son, their long dark lashes lying against their cheeks. She recognised the slope of the father's nose. Finn's nose was hidden beneath the plastic tube. Jen's head lolled and her eyes closed again.

She dreamed.

She dreamed that she was in a small dark space, that her body was limp and unresisting. She dreamed that someone lifted her by the waist and flung her over their shoulder. She dreamed the words, *fireman's lift, ragdoll, unconscious, drugged.* She dreamed she could smell something thick and sweet, that beneath her fingers she could feel rough fabric.

She dreamed that someone whispered into her ear, "Sleep well, my pretty."

She woke with a start.

"Are you OK?" asked Patrick. "You were breathing very fast."

She nodded. "Just a dream."

In the morning Barbara and Lyddie returned. They took Jen for breakfast and a walk about the city.

"We should do a Baudelaire trail," said Lyddie.

"I don't think his version of Paris exists anymore," said Jen.

Barbara suggested she return to the hotel for some sleep, but Jen shook her head.

"I'm here to see Finn," she said.

Barbara was planning to spend two nights in Paris before returning to England. "I promised to take you home safely," she said.

"All the more reason for me to stay with him, then."

They took her back to the hospital and went off to do some sightseeing. The doctor was with Finn, and then nurses came to clean him and change the bed. After a while they let Jen and Patrick back into the room where nothing had changed. The breathing tube heaved and wheezed. The monitor blipped, the green arrow of hope flickering on the screen like a candle flame when the wick was nearly gone.

Patrick said, "We can't let them turn it off. We gave him life, we can't take it away."

Jen thought she saw something flap at the window, but when she turned her head to look there was nothing but sky.

Outside, the sun began its descent. The light faded. In the hospital it made little difference. The strip lights glared white right into the evening.

"Are you sure you don't want to sleep?" Patrick asked at ten o'clock when the lights were dimmed.

"I only have tonight. I want to be with him."

"Were the two of you...?"

Jen shrugged. "We didn't have time... maybe..."

Patrick nodded and smiled.

Midnight struck. There was a church not far away and they heard the chimes as another day began.

"Day four hundred and two," said Patrick.

At one o'clock he fell asleep sitting up in his chair, his mouth lolling open.

By two, Jen could feel her own eyes drooping. She forced them open. Finn's hair had fallen away from his forehead. The pale skin had a thin layer of sweat. Jen looked away. To see him like this, so vulnerable, so exposed, seemed wrong – yet also right. There was nowhere else she could be.

"Wake up, Finn," she whispered.

The monitor bleeped on, one, two, three. She didn't mean to count his heartbeats, but it was irresistible; it had the same effect as counting sheep. She had been awake for a long time, and sleep gave a sharp tug at her ankle, bringing her under.

It was dark. Black. She could see nothing. Perhaps there was a red glow at the edges of her vision, like the glow of the sun during an eclipse, except that this was faint, barely there.

"Is that you, Jen?"

She peered into the darkness, willing it to lighten. Gradually the dense blackness dispersed into grains, like the first glimmers of dawn. She could make out a pathway in front of her, and she felt the ground with her foot. It was smooth and hard, like a tarmacked road.

"Jen, are you there?"

Either side of her something was glinting, and she saw it was water, a wide river, reflecting pieces of the weird red light. She was on a bridge, and there was someone standing in the middle of it. She stepped forward, one step, then another.

"Finn?"

It wasn't Finn, it was Patrick. He stood waiting for her, and when she reached him, he took both her hands in his.

"Can you reach him, Jen? Can you find him and bring him back?"

She looked over his shoulder. The road continued over the bridge and on the other side were the dark shapes of buildings. The nearest were in complete darkness, but further away there were lights – streetlamps, a few glowing windows, illuminated street signs.

"Where are we?" she asked.

"Paris," he said, sounding surprised. "Still in Paris."

She nodded. Finn was in Paris. Ethie was also in Paris. And that afternoon she had seen Jennet at the window of Finn's hospital room.

"I'll do my best," she said.

She gave Patrick a quick hug, then walked on, across the bridge into the dark city.

Chapter Thirty-Seven

There was a sweet smell in the room. I felt about me with my fingers. I was in a sitting position, on a chair which had arms and a back and was covered with some sort of fabric, soft and smooth in places, worn in others. A comfortable chair. This wasn't the boot of a car. It was no prison cell. I moved my feet. They were free. There was carpet beneath them.

I ran my fingers up my legs and my body. I was still wearing the same clothes; jeans, shirt, trainers. But when I felt underneath the shirt, the medallion wasn't there. I breathed in sharply. This was nothing to do with Egfrith. He would not have taken the medallion. He may want me to give it up, but he wouldn't take it from me.

I pushed myself to standing and felt about in front of me with my hands. They touched nothing, so I tried some shuffling steps. After a moment I encountered a table. I felt its surface and it was soft, like felt. A card table maybe. In the middle was a large vase with flowers in it, fleshy petals. This was the source of the smell. They were lilies, and although I couldn't see them, I imagined they were white. I touched the stamens and felt powder on my fingers. It would be pollen, red and staining. I wiped it on the table top.

I turned the other way and bumped into a sofa. It was covered in the same fabric as the chair. It had a couple of cushions on it and large rolling arms with studs at the front. I felt my way behind it to the wall.

Now I could explore the dimensions of the room. Keeping my hands on the wall, I felt my way along. I encountered a bookcase full of clothbound books, and past that some sort of desk, made of wood. There were two picture frames leaning against it. I reached a corner and started along the next wall.

I found the door to the room and tried the handle, but the door was locked. I knocked on it loudly and waited, but there was no sound. The smell of the lilies was overpowering, but I thought I could smell something else too, a spicier, musky smell, like incense. If incense was burning in the room, surely I would see some sort of glow. There was nothing. Not even a line of light at the bottom of the door.

I ran my hands over the wall at the sides of the door, and encountered what I had hoped I would find: a light switch. I flicked it and the light came on, dazzling me.

The room was furnished with faded splendour. The carpet was threadbare in places, and the red chairs, which were once luxurious, were now pale and bulging with overuse. The wallpaper was yellow with dirty patches near the door and the light switch. The thick brown curtains were closed.

There was a chaise longue near the window. Beau was lying on it, watching me.

"Well done," he said. "The bringer of light."

"Lucifer."

"No, that is not my name, though I am flattered that you mistake me for such a distinguished gentleman."

"Lucifer is the bringer of light. That's me, not you. You prefer to keep people in the dark."

"Well," he looked me up and down, "I'm not sure that I ever pictured him quite that way. But who knows? The devil has many disguises."

"Where is my medallion?"

"Ah, the medallion. *Ma chérie*, I think you'll find it's actually my medallion. A small matter of a poker game, if you remember, which you lost. You're not a sore loser, are you?"

"I need it back."

"But why should I give it to you my dear? Tell me that."

"I can get you money."

"Yes, I'm sure you can. Egfrith would pay handsomely for the return of his queen, I'm sure. But I quite like the medallion." He took it from his pocket and held it up by the chain, examining the coin as it dangled in front of his face. "It's rather beautiful. And so very, very old. I'm sure its value is much greater than the gold it's made of. If I were to take this to a museum..."

"You can't. It's mine."

"No, it's mine. If you can't stand losing you really shouldn't play games, *ma petite fille.*"

"I'm not a little girl."

"*Peut-être pas,*" he said. He dropped the medallion into his other hand and put it back into his pocket. "We shall see."

"What do you mean? Why have you brought me here?"

He rolled onto his side, bending his left arm to support his head. The smell I'd noticed before wafted more strongly when he moved. I recognised it as sandalwood. He was gazing at me intensely and I wanted to twist myself away.

"Do you have visions, Saint Etheldreda?"

Even when I closed my eyes, I could see him watching me.

"Does the Lord Jesus Christ visit you in the night? Does He show you His body? His wounds?"

I had been so busy recently, rushing about the country with Jen, that I hadn't even thought about visions. I suddenly wondered where Wolf was, if he'd got to Rome.

"I have been visiting your friend, Jules. She has visions. But she is a very stubborn woman and will tell me nothing about them."

"Why should she?" I said.

"Ah, why indeed." Beau smiled at me. "Why don't you sit down, have a drink. There is a carafe of water on my desk, and I have a bottle here if you want something stronger."

My throat was parched. I couldn't remember when I last had water. I went to the desk and poured myself a glass.

"I have been unable to persuade Jules to tell me anything, despite offering many temptations. She has struggled. She is not made of stone, and I flatter myself that I have made it very hard for her to keep her promises to God."

"What temptations?"

"Temptations of the flesh, my child." I snorted. "Ah, I see you don't know your friend as well as you think. Jules has desires that she struggles to keep from her mind. All those lonely hours in her cell, with nothing to distract her. Her thoughts go wayward sometimes."

"Why would she tell you about her visions?"

"I have offered her pleasures which make her eyes shine. She tries to keep her face clean of desire, but she is not the poker player that you are. I can see which things stir her. She found it easy to abandon the plodding folk of her village, the vanilla life she had with her husband. But when I talked to her of darker deeds, of the things a man and woman might do with each other without the grace of God, then she paced her cell, unable to keep her equilibrium."

"She was probably disgusted by you."

"No, she was not troubled by me. It was her own desire which caused her to request sackcloth to wear beneath her clothes. But in the end, I could not break her. Despite my tales of depravity, she would tell me none of her own."

I drank the water from the glass in three gulps and poured another.

"What has this got to do with me?"

"You are going to tell me about your visions. You are going to describe what the Lord our Saviour does that makes young girls so keen to devote themselves to him. You are going to give me all the details."

"No, I'm not."

As I drained the second glass, I detected an aftertaste, something bitter which I'd missed in the haste of the first.

"But you are."

"What was in that water?"

"Before long, you'll be telling me everything I want to know," he said.

The bitter taste was flooding through me. I put my fingers down my throat to make myself sick.

"I wouldn't bother," he said, holding up a small blue bottle. "It's very fast. It will be in your system already." He swung his legs around and stood up, then gestured to the chaise longue. "You might want to lie down."

"What is it?" I asked.

"An opiate. I've been working on it for a while. I wanted something that would bring visions without producing a catatonic state. So that the subject would be able to speak, to describe what they are seeing as it happens. I've tried it out on some of the young girls and boys who tout their wares in the marketplace. It worked very well, although their visions were really quite tame, considering their profession. I'm hoping for something better from you."

"You'll get nothing from me."

"I love your spirit," he said. "Lie on the chaise longue," as I stumbled a little, "you'll find your legs are getting weak."

I wanted to argue, but at that moment my legs gave way beneath me.

"Ah, too late. I will need to assist you I see."

He grabbed me beneath the arms. I wanted to fight him off, but my limbs were now beyond my control, and he dragged me across the carpet and half lifted, half rolled me onto the chaise longue.

"Comfortable?"

I was more comfortable than I had ever been in my life, my body suffused with a delicious languor.

"No," I managed to whisper, but the poison was flooding into my mind as well now and it was hard to focus on my anger.

"Just lie back," he said. "Let it come to you. Invite Him in, your beloved, your Lord Jesus. Let Him come to you as you like Him to, and let the words flow from your lips."

"He's here," I said.

"*Dis-moi.* What does He look like? What is He wearing?"

"He's wearing the clothes of crucifixion."

"Ah, the loin cloth. Is it before or after?"

"They are bloodstained. He has wounds."

"Describe them."

"He has holes in His hands, and His legs are bloody and torn from where He was tied. He has welts on His back from being beaten, raised stripes of red, which leak blood."

"What is He doing?"

"He kneels before me. He offers me His wounds that I may touch them. He offers me His blood that I might drink."

"Ah!"

"He has tears in His eyes."

"Do as He says. Touch. Drink."

"My mouth is in His palm. My tongue is exploring the hole. The blood is sweet and tastes of metal."

"And His side? Does He have a wound in His side?"

"The wound gapes in His side. He is taking my hand and guiding it to the wound."

"Ah, *oui!* Continue."

"He puts my fingers between the lips of His wound. New blood trickles from it. He presses my head to His side that I may drink of it."

"And your hand?"

"My fingers are sliding into His flesh. It is hot. I can no longer see my fingers; my palm disappears into His body."

"And what of Him? Does He feel pain?"

"He groans with ecstasy. I can feel His groans vibrate through His body. My fingers are touching His organs."

"And His other organ? Is He aroused?"

"It is hidden by His loin cloth."

"Remove the loin cloth."

"The loin cloth is on the floor. His organ is proud and ready."

"Is your hand still inside Him?"

"The wound is gone. He has changed."

"What do you mean changed? Healed?"

"He has changed. He is no longer my Lord and Saviour. He is my beloved."

"What do you mean?"

"He is inside me, we are moving together."

"You're fucking Jesus?"

"Egfrith. I am with my beloved."

"Egfrith! You're not meant to be with Egfrith, fucking like humans."

"Oh, this is sweeter than anything I have imagined."

"Fucking hell! I should have broken that wall down and forced the other one from her cell. She'd have given me something better than this."

"Eg!"

"Oh, fucking shut up, I don't want to hear about you and your bloody Egfrith."

"I love him. He is my husband."

A door slammed and he left the room. I was alone with the dream of Egfrith, his body above mine, his dear face looking down at me. Beau had taken the medallion with him, but I didn't care. I no longer had need of it.

Chapter Thirty-Eight

The streets weren't as dark as they'd seemed from the middle of the bridge. There were lights in some of the windows, but they flickered like candles, and sometimes went out altogether. Jen turned down a narrow alleyway, then another and another. She should be lost, but her feet seemed to know where she was going.

The street widened. She turned a corner into a row of tall houses, steps leading up to painted front doors. Some of the windows had the same strange flickering lights. One house in the middle of the row had lights blazing on the middle floor.

Jennet was sitting on the windowsill, cleaning her feathers. The bird lifted her head and looked at Jen, then flew up into the air, calling out. At the same moment, the front door opened to reveal a crack of light and the silhouette of a girl. The falcon called out again, circling above them.

"Ethie," said Jen.

She ran towards her friend, but Ethie was looking further down the street, and when Jen turned she saw Eg standing in the shadows. Ethie ran full pelt down the steps, along the street and threw herself into Eg's arms.

Jennet hovered in the air above the two of them. They were hugging each other as tightly as they could. Ethie lifted her face to Eg's and they kissed, a long kiss as though they were being given water when they had been dying of thirst in the desert.

It happened so quickly that Jen didn't have time to shout before the hand was over her mouth. She'd been looking at Ethie and

Eg and the falcon and hadn't heard anything. Although she struggled, kicked out against his shins, her assailant had the advantage of surprise. He dragged her into the house and the door slammed shut behind them. He released her and she spun round ready to shout, but stopped. She stared at him in wonder. Whatever she'd expected her attacker to look like, it wasn't this. This wasn't a French poet or a man from a poker game. It was Finn.

"Surprised?" he said. The voice wasn't Finn's. "There are two sides to everyone."

"Who are you?"

"Come, don't you recognise me? Do you think you're the only one who can do this? I can play games as well, you know."

"What do you want?"

"*Viens.*"

He held out his hand to her and smiled, the smile she knew so well. His dark eyes had a hint of mischief in them. How could she not take his hand when he looked like Finn? She had crossed the bridge to find him.

He led her up many flights of stairs to the attic. The room at the top of the house was large and mostly bare, with wooden boards on the floor. A window was open to the air, and through it Jen could make out the dark shapes of roofs and turrets. There was a narrow iron frame bed against the back wall, and a wooden table in the middle of the room. On the table were a selection of tools.

"Are you going to torture me?" she asked, her eyes wide.

"*Mon ange*, I would never harm you."

"Then...?"

"Swallow this."

He held out a small blue bottle and she took it. Their eyes were locked, and he was Finn, her rock to lean on. He said he would never harm her.

She tipped the contents of the bottle down her throat. It was bitter as aspirin.

"Come," he said, "look at these."

He led her to the table and she stood looking down at the tools. There were knives in different sizes, some serrated, some not. There were screw drivers, a spanner, a pair of pliers.

"They're all brand new," he said. "Sterilised. Top brands, too. Nothing but the best for you, *ma chérie*."

She turned to look at him, and still he was smiling. But his face had gone hazy at the edges, his features were blurred.

"Would you like me to stay with you, or would you rather be left alone?"

"I don't want this," she said. Her voice sounded strange, and the words felt like pebbles plopping into the cold air.

"You've always wanted this. Don't you remember?"

Of course she remembered. She remembered the knife stolen from the kitchen drawer and kept under her pillow. The excitement of the first incision. The way the blood would spring up so quickly beneath its point. The time she'd woken up in A&E with her dad there, waiting. Worrying. Her mum had been on an all-night prayer vigil that night.

But all that had changed since she met Finn.

"You have to let it out. I know you tried, but you went about it the wrong way. He entered you through the side, so you have to let it out through your side too. Here, how about this one?" He handed her a small sharp knife, the sort you might use for chopping vegetables.

"It's very sharp," he said, and he ran the blade across his thumb, drawing blood. It rose up just as she remembered, flooding into the grooves of his fingerprint. "No nasty snagging, it will cut right through."

She felt dizzy. His eyes had changed, his nose too, he didn't look like Finn anymore.

"I don't want to cut myself," she said. And this time her words were a white ribbon which unreeled from her mouth into the room, wafting and floating in the currents of air. She watched it floating. Saw the words hanging.

I don't want to cut myself.

He grabbed the ribbon and stuffed it into his pocket.

"Jen, we both know that's not true."

"I don't want to cut myself," she said again, and another ribbon floated into the air.

He looked annoyed.

"You had a dream, remember? A dream where you cut yourself, but this time it wasn't your leg. You dreamed about making a wound in your side, where the elephant entered. Let it out again."

"I don't want this." Pebbles. She heard them drop to the floor. One, two, three, four. *I don't want this.* He had to move his feet out of the way.

He frowned and thrust the knife towards her.

"I don't want this. I don't want to cut myself." Pebbles and ribbon. Jen laughed out loud as he kicked at the pebbles. "I don't want this. I don't want this. I don't want to cut myself."

She moved away from him, grabbing at the ribbons, chanting the words over and over until it was hard to see him as the air was filled with dancing strands of white silk.

"Jennifer, don't do this."

"You're not Finn," she said, and this time it was flowers, huge white chrysanthemums which burst from her like explosions.

He grabbed at them and tore them apart, scattering the petals, and the air was filled with their smell.

"You have no power over me," she shouted. The flowers hit him in the face and fell to the ground. "I don't want to cut myself," she repeated until he was surrounded with ribbons, batting at them with his hands, and she turned him, spun him round and round so he was tied, his arms bound to his side, his legs strapped together, and he fell to the ground.

She turned to the table and picked up the knives one by one, stabbing them into the table top until they stood there in a row, their blades quivering.

She laughed, and a spray of diamonds sprang from her mouth, hung sparkling in the air before tinkling to the floor.

Someone was climbing in through the window. She spun round. The room still danced, but the ribbons had changed into shafts of light. Light was coming from the window, and a dark figure was climbing in over the sill.

"Jen?" said a voice she knew.

"Finn!"

It was so bright it was hard to see him. He came to her.

"Are you alright, Jen?"

She looked at the floor, and he followed her gaze. Beau was sleeping, gently breathing, his chest rising and falling. He looked nothing like Finn any more. His high forehead glistened with sweat and his lips were thin and straight.

Finn took a deep intake of breath. "Jen, what's been going on?"

"He gave me something. A drug. But I'm OK."

Finn held her. She could feel his heart beating in his chest. She could feel warmth where their bodies met, a contrast to the freezing air of the room.

"Is it morning?" she asked, her voice muffled by his hair.

Something was happening to him. She could feel movement where her hands touched his back, something creeping over him. It slid across her skin, and the hairs on her hands raised to meet it. It passed on, through Finn's t-shirt, through his skin. His body convulsed as it entered him.

Jen pushed him away and looked into his face. His eyes were darkened and he began to shake. She held on to his shoulders. His face changed shape, his hair receded like the tide to reveal a high domed head and jutting eyebrows. His body shook violently and he pushed her away as he bent double and shouted, "No! Get out of me!" A stream of brown vomit poured from his mouth, but never reached the floor. It kept coming, and Jen put her hand on his back, and rubbed from side to side.

Eventually it stopped. He was hugging his stomach as though in pain, but he looked like himself again, his eyes were the right colour and his hair flopped forward onto his face. She kissed him on the temple. There was a bit of white ribbon caught in his hair, and white petals were scattered across the floor. Amongst them, something was shining.

Beau had disappeared, leaving only a heap of ribbons. A shadow lurked in the corner of the room. It moved back and forth but had no substance.

"Let's go," said Finn, straightening up.

Jen moved her legs and the room tipped alarmingly. Finn held her, and leaning against each other they walked towards the door. He saw the row of knives standing up from the table and gave her a questioning look. She grinned.

Light from the window caught the shining thing on the floor. She bent and picked it up.

It was Ethie's medallion.

Outside, there was no sign of Ethie, nor Eg or the falcon, but the dark was lifting. There was a line of shining white along the horizon as the night came untucked.

"Come on," Jen said. "We need to get to the bridge. There's someone waiting there for you."

Jen opened her eyes. The clock was still ticking. There was the sound of the breathing tube. The monitor was beeping, but sounded different. The green line was following the same pattern, but the peaks were higher, much higher, and slightly closer together.

Then she saw Finn's father had tears in his eyes. He was holding Finn's hand.

He looked at Jen. "The doctor's on her way," he said.

"What happened?"

"His eyes moved. And look – his heart. Something has changed."

At that moment the door burst open and a doctor and two nurses came in.

"Monsieur, Mademoiselle, I must ask you to leave the room."

They surrounded the bed and began to take readings. They lifted Finn's arms, checked the monitors. Patrick took Jen's elbow.

"Come on, Jen."

She let him propel her from the room, but at the door she looked back. Finn's eyelashes were moving, and the skin of his eyelids trembled a little. For a moment she thought he was going to open his eyes. Then she was out of the room and she and Patrick were looking at each other wide-eyed.

"I don't want to speak too soon," said Patrick, "but I think he's waking up."

Chapter Thirty-Nine

Barbara insisted on taking Jen home. She didn't mind too much. The doctors said progress would be slow, and Jen wasn't even sure that Finn would know who she was. She'd never met him in real life.

When they arrived back in Ely there was a pile of cardboard boxes in the living room.

"It's your stuff from uni," said Donna. "They needed to clear out your room for the summer. These have been in the garage."

Rebecca came round and together they opened the boxes. Whoever had packed them had just shoved things in willy-nilly, so there were books packed with toiletries, a dirty towel with her course notes.

"Are you going to see him again?"

"I hope so. We're both still studying at York. If he comes back, that is." Rebecca was taking books from the box and making a neat pile. "I thought I might write to him."

"What, like actual letters? On paper?"

"Yes. We said we'd write to each other before he set off for France."

"You mean – in your coma dream."

Jen shook her head. "Yes, I suppose. It seems so real."

Franny and Zooey was in between some folded clothes. She leaned over and added it to the book pile. "I just feel, if I write, and he hasn't a clue who I am, then he can ignore it if he wants."

Rebecca was pulling handfuls of underwear from the bottom of the box she was unpacking. Something yellow and woolly came with them and landed on her lap.

Rebecca dropped the underwear on the floor and picked up the yellow hat. Something changed in the room. The sun was glaring through the window, highlighting the dust that had gathered over the summer.

"Where did you get this?" asked Rebecca.

"From eBay. You know when I saw those people, at the Angel of the North, well one of them..."

"My mum had this hat."

"I was just sure there was really someone there."

"Two people? You saw two people, didn't you?"

"You never talk about your parents."

Rebecca was scrolling through the photos on her phone. She found the one she wanted and showed Jen.

"This is them."

They were sitting on a bench by the sea. They were both wearing waterproof clothes, and Rebecca's mum was wearing the yellow hat. They were laughing at the camera, and strands of brown hair peeped out from under the yellow wool. Rebecca had her dad's smile.

Jen took her friend's hand. Neither of them said anything for a while. A blackbird sang in the garden and an aeroplane flew overhead.

She wrote to Finn, addressing her letter to the hospital. Then she tried to forget about it. Tried not to watch the post every day. He might not physically be able to write. He would be with his family – his mother and sister would have flown from Australia with baby Joe.

Donna decided to clear out Dorothy's room, and Jen helped. The furniture was old and heavy and they sent most of it to a charity shop. Jen said she'd like the bedside cupboard. She also kept a few of the books. They sorted the clothes into two piles – charity shop and rubbish. They painted the empty room in bright colours, put in a new sofa bed. "In case we have guests," said Donna.

"We'll have to do the same with Danny's room at some point," said Jen. A look of panic flashed in Donna's eyes. Jen was beginning to realise how effective a mask her mother had been wearing, now that she had taken it off. She took her hand.

"Not yet," said Donna. "I'm not ready yet."

"Do you mind if I wear his leather jacket? The one that's hanging on the back of his door?"

Donna walked to the window and looked out into the garden. Jen remembered the day after Aunt Barbara had left, all those years ago, the first visit after the long separation. Her mother had gone into her bedroom, shut the door and cried. Jen hadn't realised grown-ups could cry. She'd sat on the floor on the landing and hugged her knees, her world shaken. When her mother emerged later, there was no sign on her face. Jen had never known her to cry again, except once, until the last few weeks.

"Why not? There's no point in it hanging there gathering dust."

The shingle slid beneath Jen's feet with each footstep. The wind whipped her hair into her eyes and blasted beneath her clothes, making her coat billow out in front of her and her trousers stick to the back of her legs. It had been a lovely day in Ely. It was a lovely day here too, the sky blue and the sun a beacon in the sky, but it was always windy on this stretch of the Essex coast. She remembered visits as a child, and how she had crept close to her dad so he'd put his arm round her, protecting her from the worst of the wind. How she and Danny had leaned into it, seeing how far forward they could go before gravity took over.

Her mum and dad were quite far ahead, walking along hand in hand. She hadn't quite got used to this new thing between her parents, the touching, the affectionate looks across the table, occasional squeals and giggles coming from the kitchen. She'd even heard some noises coming from their bedroom one night and had to put her fingers in her ears.

They'd got here first and decided to go for a walk along the beach before Finn and his parents arrived. They'd booked a table at the pub for lunch. They were meeting on neutral ground, a place that both families knew.

The first letter had arrived a week after she'd sent hers. It had been a cautious letter, thanking her for writing and for her visit to the hospital in Paris, which his parents had told him about. As Jen read it, her heart sank a little. Then, turning the page she saw the postscript – *Have you ever been to Whitby?*

She wrote back immediately and soon their letters were pinging back and forth across the English Channel. They mostly wrote about their lives, what they were doing and what they were reading, but both of them dropped hints, and Jen was sure that he shared at least some of the same memories as her.

Her mum and dad were standing at the edge of the waves. Jen reached the chapel at the end of the beach and went in.

It was fourteen hundred years old, one of the oldest chapels in the country. She sat in a pew and listened to the sea. She loved the bare stone walls, the simplicity of the windows. She imagined people coming here through the ages, on Sundays to hear the word of God, but on their own too, to find peace. To be as still as the stones it was built from, as silent as the grass in the churchyard, to be moved like the shingle on the beach. Here you could imagine you were all these things, that there was no difference, you could feel that breakdown in your bones and body until you were made of cells, of atoms, the same atoms as everything around you. There was a peace in that.

"Hello, Jen."

Jen swivelled in her seat and Ethie was sitting beside her. She looked around the church, through the open door.

"It's just me," said Ethie. "I came to say goodbye."

"I..."

"I'm sorry about Paris, but I had to go. Time was changing too fast, I might have been trapped. And you had your family to get back to."

"I miss you."

Ethie took her hand, and they sat silently for a few moments.

"What do you mean about time changing?"

"There are moments, openings, like doors in time. Mostly we can slip through, but sometimes they close, and once they do that they tend to stay closed, seal up, and if you're on the wrong side you might get stuck in a place you don't want to be."

"What, like a ghost, haunting somewhere?"

"Sometimes. Or you might become part of something else, someone else."

"What, absorbed by them?"

Ethie shrugged. "I don't really know how it works."

Jen remembered that night in the room in Paris. Of the empty space on the floor where a body had been, and the convulsions that racked Finn's body.

"Might it be that the host's body rejects them?"

"Well, it wouldn't be possible to join with someone completely different to yourself. There wouldn't be enough points of entry. I could join with you, but I could never become your mother or your aunt."

"So then the dead person would become a ghost?"

"Maybe."

Jen remembered the shadow in the corner of the room, coiling upon itself like a snake. She shook the image from her head.

"What about you?" she asked. "Are you still with Eg?"

Ethie nodded. "I didn't know I could be so happy," she said. It was true, her skin glowed, her eyes shone and she'd put on a little bit of weight. "Wolf says hello, by the way. I was down at Dissolution the other night and he was there."

"I've been learning poker."

"Well, if you're ever up in Newcastle, pop in."

Jen knew she'd never find it. She had a feeling this was the last time she'd ever see Ethie. Like this, anyway. There might be shadows, glimpses, but for a proper flesh and blood conversation, this was it.

At home in her drawer, underneath her underwear, there was a huge, ancient, gold medallion. She'd found it in her pocket on the way back from France. She knew she ought to take it somewhere – a museum or something – but she didn't know how she would answer their questions. Maybe one day.

She and Ethie hugged each other, and Jen didn't want to let her go.

"You're my sister," Jen whispered.

"I know," said Ethie. Then she was gone.

Someone else was standing in the doorway to the church, silhouetted by the brightness outside.

Jen took a step forward. "Finn?"

He came into the church. He was wearing a t-shirt with the Buddha on it. His hair was cropped short and there was a scar on his temple. Jen thought about the night in the B&B in Filey, his fingers massaging her scalp in the bath, the streetlight falling across his naked back.

"You look just like I remember," he said. "Exactly the same."

"So you do remember?"

"I feel like I know you."

Jen walked up to him. "I'd like to get to know you," she said.

She kissed him on one cheek, and he kissed her on the other. He smelled very faintly of sandalwood.

St Etheldreda: A Timeline

630AD – Etheldreda, daughter of King Anna of Anglia, is born near what is now Newmarket in Suffolk

Etheldreda was the fourth daughter of King Anna of Anglia. Her mother died giving birth to her younger sister. It was the seventh century, the days of early Christianity, and her two eldest sisters travelled to France to become nuns. Her third sister, Sexburga, married Earconbert of Kent; later, she too became a nun and a saint. Etheldreda's aunt was St Hilda, who founded the Synod of Whitby, and she was a contemporary of St Cuthbert, St Aidan and St Wilfrid, who was the Bishop of York.

At an early age Etheldreda decided that she also wanted to become a nun. However, Britain was a land of warring kingdoms and marriage was a way of making friendly alliances. By the time Etheldreda was sixteen, her father had made other plans for her.

652AD – Aged 22, Etheldreda marries Tonberg, Prince of the South Gyrwe of the Fens.

Her first husband, Tonberg, was in his late middle age and agreed that Etheldreda should keep her vow of perpetual virginity. The marriage was a political arrangement and Etheldreda lived mainly in seclusion. This was a happy time for her, and she learned to love Ely – so much so, that when Tonberg died three years later, he left it to her as a gift.

655AD – Tonberg dies and leaves the Isle of Ely to Etheldreda.

Etheldreda established a religious community at Cratendune, near Ely. Four years later, however, she was summoned by her father to be married to 14-year-old Egfrith, heir to the throne of Northumbria, son of King Oswy. Etheldreda travelled north under the protection of her steward, Ovin, probably along the Great North Road (now the A1).

659AD – Aged 29, Etheldreda travels to Northumbria to marry 14-year-old Egfrith, the son of the king.

670AD – Egfrith becomes King of Northumbria.

672AD – Egfrith insists on the marriage being consummated. Etheldreda retires to Coldingham Abbey.

Egfrith, like Tonberg, had agreed that Etheldreda should retain her virginity. However, two years after taking the throne, when he was 27 and Etheldreda 42, he changed his mind. He wanted a legitimate heir and insisted that the marriage be consummated. Wilfrid, Bishop of York, negotiated on Etheldreda's behalf, and it was agreed that she should withdraw from the marriage to reside at Coldingham Abbey under the auspices of St Ebba, Egfrith's aunt. Before long, Egfrith changed his mind again about this arrangement and threatened to take Etheldreda from Coldingham by force.

673AD – Etheldreda flees and returns to Ely.

With the assistance of Wilfrid, Etheldreda ran away with her maids, Sewenna and Sewara. On the early part of the journey, she was pursued by Egfrith and his men. Various miracles happened on the way, giving evidence of Etheldreda's sainthood.

One of these was on the Northumbrian coast. Egfrith and his men were in hot pursuit of Etheldreda, Sewenna and Sewara. The women took refuge on a rock out to sea as the tide changed, and the sea filled the gap between them and their pursuers. Egfrith settled down to wait, but the tide didn't change for two days, by which time he had given up. Not only this, but the rock produced a spring of fresh water to quench the women's thirst and kept an imprint of Etheldreda's footprints after she had gone.

At Stow near Lincoln, Etheldreda stuck her staff in the ground; in the morning it had sprouted leaves and set roots. This is now the site of Stow Minster, where the story is celebrated in stained glass windows.

Eventually, Etheldreda arrived safely back in Ely. Her marriage was subsequently annulled and Egfrith married again, this time to Eormenburg, his mistress.

673AD – Aged 43, Etheldreda founds a double monastery in Ely on the site which is now Ely Cathedral.

23 June 679AD – Aged 49, Etheldreda dies with a large growth on her neck.

Etheldreda developed a large growth on her neck which she believed to be a punishment from God for her attachment to jewellery, particularly in her youth. Ethedreda is also known as St Audrey. There used to be a fair in Ely called St Audrey's Fair, which specialised in cheap lace and decorative goods, perhaps jewellery. The word 'tawdry' comes from a contraction of St Audrey, and refers to these cheap decorations.

695AD – Sexburga, Etheldreda's third sister, supervises the removal of Etheldreda's body to the new church in Ely. When the body is exhumed, it is found to be uncorrupted and the growth on the neck has gone. This is seen as further, conclusive evidence of her sainthood.

A Note on the Text

I first became aware of Etheldreda when I visited Ely Cathedral in 2002. I was working on a novel about a girl from Ely, in which my main character formed a relationship with the saint. Most of that novel was jettisoned and I went on to a new project, but the connection stayed with me and became the backbone of East Coast Road.

When I started writing about Jen and Ethie, I knew some of the places on their journey already, but there were stretches of the journey I was unfamiliar with and I wanted to get a feel of how it actually felt to walk that far. I applied to the Arts Council in 2015 and was delighted that they agreed to fund my walk as research for my novel. I didn't walk the 500 miles in one go, or even quite in the right order – but I did it. I dragged along various family members for company and met some great people along the way. More information about the journey can be found on my website at www.annachilvers.co.uk/eastcoastroad.

Those of you already familiar with Etheldreda's story – or those of you with eagle eyes glancing at her timeline – will realise that I have taken liberties with her story. I have created a love story between Etheldreda and Egfrith, although history suggests that no such thing existed – quite the contrary, in fact. I have also completely erased one of the most important people in her story – her steward, Ovin. This is because East Coast Road isn't a novel about St Etheldreda: it's a novel about Jen, a twenty-first century girl coming to terms with loss, loneliness and growing up. The Ethie in this story is Jen's own invention, made up of fragments of Etheldreda's story that she remembers, or misremembers.

Acknowledgements

I would like to thank all of the team at Bluemoose, in particular my wonderful editor Annie Warren, for her clear eye and spot-on advice; and Kevin and Hetha Duffy for their continued support and dedication. Thank you to Fiachra McCarthy for the beautiful cover design, and to the chapel of St Peter-on-the Wall at Bradwell-on-Sea, Essex, for allowing us to use the photograph.

Thank you all those who read versions of the novel as it progressed – Poppy Turner, Johnny Turner, Sarah Mackey, Alison Taft, Henrietta Bond, SJ Bradley, Helen Mort – your advice and feedback was invaluable. Thank you to Sarah Dunnakey for being a writing buddy, and all of the Northern Women Writers Network for your companionship and support.

Thank you to Barbara Allen for letting me stay in your house in Whitby – much of the editing work was done while I was there. It was fabulous to walk to the sea and the Abbey when I needed a break.

A huge thank you to The Arts Council for funding my walk down the country, in particular to Stephen May for your advice. Thank you to the library staff at Berwick-upon-Tweed Halifax, Scarborough, Scalby, Filey, Lincoln, Oakham, Huntingdon and Ely for welcoming me, Jen and Ethie to your libraries. And of course, to my fellow walkers, Poppy Turner, Izzy Turner, Wilf Turner and Johnny Turner; and to Betty our lovely border collie, who walked nearly all of the way with me, and covered much more than five hundred miles.

Betty, Oct 2008 – July 2020